He Strode
Down the Passageway,
Knocked Twice Loudly,
and Then
Swung Open the Door.

He was stunned to see a beautiful young woman in the act of hurriedly straightening her dress, her hair tumbling in chestnut waves around her face. Looking up, the woman gasped and stood still. Then, realizing that the dark and wild-looking intruder was a pirate, Heather, skirts whirling, grabbed the water pitcher and hurled it at him.

He quickly ducked as the water splashed over him and as shards of pottery fell at his feet. "Well, at last I encounter someone aboard this ship willing to fight," he said and laughed.

"If you're looking for valuables, I haven't any," she said, trying to distract those piercing eyes.

"That, my lady, is false on the face of it," he answered. Hesitating a moment, reluctant to leave, he saluted her. "We'll meet again. A promise."

Dear Reader,

We, the editors of Tapestry Romances, are committed to bringing you two outstanding original romantic historical novels each and every month.

From Kentucky in the 1850s to the court of Louis XIII, from the deck of a pirate ship within sight of Gibraltar to a mining camp high in the Sierra Nevadas, our heroines experience life and love, romance and adventure.

Our aim is to give you the kind of historical romances that you want to read. We would enjoy hearing your thoughts about this book and all future Tapestry Romances. Please write to us at the address below.

The Editors
Tapestry Romances
POCKET BOOKS
1230 Avenue of the Americas
Box TAP
New York, N.Y. 10020

Pirate's Promise

Ann Cockcroft

A TAPESTRY BOOK
PUBLISHED BY POCKET BOOKS NEW YORK

An *Original* publication of TAPESTRY BOOKS

 A Tapestry Book published by
POCKET BOOKS, a division of Simon & Schuster, Inc.
1230 Avenue of the Americas, New York, N.Y. 10020

ISBN: 0-671-53018-6

First Tapestry Books printing August, 1984

10 9 8 7 6 5 4 3 2 1

POCKET and colophon are registered trademarks
of Simon & Schuster, Inc.

Tapestry is a trademark of Simon & Schuster, Inc.

Printed in the U.S.A.

For My Mother

Pirate's Promise

Chapter One

HEATHER WOODE SAT SILENTLY AS SHE WAS BORNE SLOWLY toward a massive black cargo ship looming larger every minute on the Thames. The little skiff heaved and jerked on the rough sea, and salt spray flew into her face however much she tried to bury it in the hood of her long cloak. Her feet were wet and cold from the water sloshing in the boat's fishy smelling bottom, and she noticed with dismay the hems of her petticoats and dress getting damp and soiled.

"It's lucky ye are to be catchin' a Somerset ship, miss," the stout sailor pulling at the oars said, grinning at her as if reading her thoughts. For Heather was feeling she had made the worst possible of bargains in indenturing herself and leaving behind the only place she'd ever known to sail on the *Prospect* to New York.

"Cap'n McFadden runs a tight ship," agreed the bosun, who was listening. "He don't tolerate shirkin' and works 'em hard, but they stays healthy and hale and gets their pay regular, and that's better than the jails that most the

1

poor blokes come from." He closed his thin mouth tight and turned his attention to business as they neared the ship's side.

"I don't think Miss Woode feels very lucky, bosun," said William Barrett, her "agent," as he called himself, "although she might if she knew better."

Heather stole a look at Barrett. His nose and hands were as red as beefsteak in a butcher's shop from the sharp spring gusts and wet spray, and looked, she thought, as if they'd fetch good prices for stew.

"Never saw a ladylike lass indentured afore this," said the bosun, his attention brought back once more to his passengers. His small eyes appraised Heather's green linen frock, dark green cloak, and dignified manner and then looked questioningly back at Barrett.

"I'm an honest man, bosun. I always deliver what I'm given money for and in good shape. I struck a good bargain and so has she." He pointed a rude red finger at Heather and continued. "She lost her father not more 'n a month back. Died in a debtor's prison. And she, having no place to go, sold herself as an indentured servant to me for five years. There's many what find a place for themselves in the Colonies and a chance to come up in the world. An honest bargain that 'n more, by my oath!" Barrett steamed, concluding his speech and sitting as straight as his rotund body would allow while he tugged at the lapels of his greatcoat.

"You promised me a good home, sir!" Heather said with heat, angry at his exposure of her life and its burdens. "I trust you intend to deliver!"

"You've a nasty tongue, Miss Woode." He lowered his voice and rasped at her. "If ye wants to find a good home, ye better watch yer manners."

"Are you threatening me, Mr. Barrett?"

In her excitement, Heather's hood fell back. The two men rowing and the bosun all caught a look as the skiff bobbed and lurched alongside *Prospect*, but, unfortunately, they had the business of handing up the passengers and keeping the skiff steady so they could not sit staring. Yet the picture of the stunning young woman glaring at Barrett told them well why the "agent" had indentured Heather, although the bosun secretly felt sure the young lady might end up in less than the best of circumstances. He had no great respect for London's indenturing agents—a cut above slave traders, as he saw them, trafficking in human flesh and getting fat on it.

"Come, miss, up you go," the bosun said. "And stop your gawking, you lubbers! Hold fast there!" He shouted commands at his crew to get the boarding done.

Heather readjusted her hood over her thick, shining chestnut hair. "How am I to get up?" she asked, surveying the whole precarious scene.

"That, miss, is how ye will board her," said the bosun, and she looked up to see a swaying basket chair being lowered.

Heather was aghast to realize that such a contraption was meant to take her up, but she obediently got into it, seeing no other alternative but to climb the ship's unsteady ladder hand over hand while the big ship rolled in the nasty shorebound sea.

"Hurry there afore we break up beside the ship," muttered the bosun to no one in particular as he watched Heather being lifted up to the ship's deck.

"I trust that conveyance can be lowered for me as well, bosun?" Barrett asked.

"It cannot and will not. Ye get aboard as we—up now, and if ye fall into the sea, it's nothing to me!"

"I knew you for a ship's bastard the moment I laid eyes on you!" the red and portly Barrett blurted as he climbed, exerting most of his strength and courage in the effort.

As he breathlessly clambered over the ship's rail onto the deck, a gust of wind lifted his beaverskin hat and sent it sailing down past the skiff and into the sea.

"My hat! My hat!" Barrett yelled as he leaned over the rail and shook his fist at the bosun, who ignored the man and went about his work. "The captain will hear about this!" the "agent" shouted.

As Heather stood getting her balance, she wrapped herself tightly in her cloak as she awaited the next episode in this journey. Barrett was fumbling with a not-too-white handkerchief, blowing his nose and coughing and trembling slightly, the exertion of climbing having really been too much for him. Over the side came her small trunk and Barrett's other "prize" indentured servant, a strapping blond farmboy named Billy O'Toole, who was about Heather's age of seventeen and slightly green from his very first boating experience. Putting down her trunk, which had been tied to his back, Billy ran to the ship's side to unload his stomach's burden. Feeling her own stomach churn at the sound of him, Heather moved farther away and took several deep breaths. She stared at the English shoreline as if hoping the sight of solid ground would transport her to the nonswaying earth.

That small trick helped calm Heather's queasy stomach, yet seeing the land she was about to leave, perhaps forever, also sent through her a cruel, sad stab. It was gone, her life in those happier days before her mother's untimely death and her father's unfortunate speculations in trade that had left them after one short year living in terror of creditors' demanding knocks on their door. They had sold nearly everything they owned and had watched helplessly while her father's good name had been smeared with accusations of fraud and his business ruined. He had invested heavily in the buying and selling of Spanish wines, but his very first venture, which he had counted on to regain not only his own investment but to pay back substantial loans from several friends, had resulted in the loss of both cargo and ships to piracy and storm. He and his daughter soon found themselves in a debtor's prison, where he had died within a matter of months. Where money is concerned, she thought bitterly, a man and his friends can soon be made mortal enemies.

Heather was pulled back from her unhappy memories by the harsh sounds of Barrett berating the poor lad still hanging over the ship's side. She jumped slightly when a cultured, tenor voice spoke from behind her.

"Not an auspicious beginning for him," the voice said, indicating the retching Billy O'Toole. "But I'd say my lot has vastly improved with your appearance."

Heather turned to see a handsomely dressed man of

4

about thirty-three who doffed his hat and made a pleasing bow as a wide smile spread across his lean features. His dark brown eyes were firmly fixed on hers.

"Duncan Crawley, my lady. At your service." He offered his arm and Heather took it readily, not certain who her escort was but trusting his easy gallantry by assuming he meant simply to show her to her quarters. He was, she noted, only a few inches taller than herself, but broad-shouldered with tapering limbs. She smiled graciously.

"May I ask your name, lovely lady?"

"Heather Woode, sir."

"Ah! The sound of it brings to my mind a picture of distant wild hills with the blooms of your namesake bending in the wind." He smiled as Heather laughed delightedly at his romantic image.

"Heather Woode!" William Barrett came pounding up beside her, giving a short bow to Duncan Crawley. His small eyes were blinking rapidly. "Sir! This girl's no lady but my indentured servant, and she needs be off below decks and not traipsing about and puttin' on airs."

"Your servant?" Crawley looked at Heather as if assessing her. "Surely not." But at seeing Heather's downcast face, he let his arm drop.

"My apologies," he said quickly to Barrett. He then turned to Heather, "A mistake that will be made often, madam, with beauty such as yours."

Heather tilted her chin up and looked Crawley in the eyes.

"I thank you for your attention to me, sir. But I *am* a lady, even so!"

"No doubt," Crawley replied, and when Barrett began to push Heather forward, he put up a restraining hand.

"A moment, Mr. Barrett, if you please," he said and hesitated, his eyes darting about while his mind worked rapidly. "There is a matter I wish to speak to you about."

"Later! Later, Mr. Crawley! I must get this girl below."

"Mr. Barrett," he insisted, "I must first inform you that Miss Southey is far from satisfied with the girl she hired from you as a maid."

"What's this?" Barrett snorted in annoyance. "Miss Southey not satisfied?"

"Regrettably, she finds your Maggie to be rather vulgar and rude," Crawley said, releasing Barrett's arm and staring confidently at Heather. "I suggest that Miss Woode here might be an excellent replacement."

Barrett looked at Crawley and then at Heather, suddenly aware that the gentleman's interest in Heather was far more than in simply assisting Elizabeth Southey. He shifted nervously and manufactured a brief fit of coughing to stall for time.

"That Miss Southey is nothing but complaints," he muttered.

With a tilt to his head and a glance down his aquiline nose, Crawley said, "Miss Southey has connections, Mr. Barrett—a commodity no man can do without, especially in the rough and backward world we shall soon be entering. Indians, my man, and rabble! Think of it! Providing Miss Woode might stand you in quite good stead."

Heather felt a rush of color to her cheeks. "I'm still here, Mr. Crawley, and would prefer to be asked whether I would like to be this lady's maid. There is nothing in our contract, Mr. Barrett, that supposes I have to do anything other than cross the sea on this ship!" Heather drew her cloak around her defiantly and turned aside.

"By God. . . ." Barrett began, but Crawley put up his hand to restrain him.

"Don't get into a disturbed temper, my dear Miss Woode," he said, turning to Heather. "You'll not be ill-used. I assure you that the alternative will not be as pleasant."

"That, sir, is for me to decide!" Heather returned.

"Be still, girl," Barrett said loudly, "and show proper respect! I've gone to a lot of trouble for you!"

"I gather you'll recover your expenses, Mr. Barrett," Crawley said with a sardonic smile.

Heather lifted her chin, her green eyes sparkling. "And are you the same, Mr. Crawley, bartering for people like animals?"

As Barrett reddened and let out a gasp of stung anger, Crawley said, narrowing his eyes, "I doubt that concerns you, Miss Woode. I've nothing to gain. My sole interest is in helping Miss Southey."

"You'll do as you're told!" Barrett exploded. "We accept, Mr. Crawley! And no sulking or words, Heather Woode! Count yourself lucky once more. A lady's cabin is much better than where you were going to be lodged, no mistake."

"I'll see Miss Woode safely to Miss Southey's cabin," Crawley drawled, then with a nod, he turned back to Heather. "If you'll kindly follow me, Miss Woode."

"Go ahead, sir," Barrett barked as they moved away. "But see to it that she knows the rules!"

Heather reluctantly trailed behind this stranger, her thoughts scattered. "What did Mr. Barrett mean by rules, Mr. Crawley?" she asked, steadying herself as they entered the companionway and walked down a passage toward the private cabins.

Duncan Crawley paused and looked at Heather, amused by the question. "There are many rough men aboard ship and few women, but if you don't go below the level of your cabin nor on deck except during those hours permitted, you'll be safe. I'm sure you wouldn't want a man whipped for your honor."

Heather blushed at the implication and looked away. "I'm virtually a prisoner then."

"Hardly, my dear. But you understand that a ship needs strict discipline."

"I always thought kindness and generosity were better disciplinarians than whips," she retorted. "In any event, I can promise you no man shall be whipped on my account."

"It might be worth it," Crawley replied, his mouth stretched in an ironic smile. Then he turned to knock on a cabin door.

"Miss Southey?"

Heather was aware of a change of tone in his voice. It was now softer and more considerate.

A feeble, high-pitched feminine voice inquired who was there.

"It's Duncan Crawley, my lady, and I've found you a suitable maid. A Miss Heather Woode."

"I'm not in a fit state to receive you, Mr. Crawley, but the maid is most welcome."

"I understand, my lady," Duncan replied, "and hope to see you recovered soon." Then he turned to face Heather. "Well, my lovely, I leave you for the moment to your fate. But whenever you need a benefactor, know that you have one in me. Au revoir." He lifted her hand to his lips, held it there a long moment, and then left. Heather felt stunned by his abrupt courtliness, but quickly she gathered her wits and opened the door.

She was struck immediately with the powerful stench of vomit. "Dear heaven," she said softly.

"Heaven," sighed a young lady lying in bed, "is where I'd rather be, God knows. But, oh . . . I'm . . ." She turned to look at Heather, her pale face like a cameo in the dim room, and reached out a thin, small hand. "I'm so glad you've arrived. Oh! I've made a mess of it, this ship. I don't travel well, I'm afraid. The other girl Mr. Barrett sent to me, Maggie, impossible! A street girl! I couldn't abide her, and she smelled so!"

"I'm sorry," Heather said truthfully, but she felt a brief smile tug at her lips when Miss Southey complained about another woman's smell.

"I can't keep anything down, Miss Woode. Is it Heather? We've been lying at anchor three days now. The sea's abated somewhat, but still the ship heaves, and me with it." There were tears of self-pity welling in her eyes.

"Be still now," Heather urged the sick woman, who, though at least four years older, seemed a child by comparison. Heather was tall, richly curved but slender, and vibrant with health and high energy, while Miss Southey was languid and thin, her pale face set in dark brown hair adding to the impression of delicacy. Elizabeth Southey was not a pretty woman, but her even features and small bones lent themselves to a picture of fashionable attractiveness. Heather, in contrast, had slanting green eyes above high cheekbones and a wide, full mouth that produced a dimple in one cheek when she smiled. Her features taken individually might have caused reason for quarrel, but the total effect was one of great beauty.

Looking around, Heather threw off her cloak and set to work. Finding the bosun in the companionway, she asked him for a tub of hot water only to discover that it was an impossible luxury.

"Sorry, miss, but 'tis the only way on a ship. A gallon a day of fresh water per person regardless," the bosun offered.

"Can it be heated, please? And this other girl, Maggie, can she at least clean the floors and do the linen? Please tell the captain it's necessary, for Miss Southey must not suffer anymore like this." As Heather turned away, the bosun muttered his disapproval at being ordered about by a female.

"Women aboard a cargo ship—a nuisance and, more likely, trouble." But he did her bidding.

"Oh, Heather! How much longer like this, do you imagine?" Miss Southey asked as Heather returned to the cabin. "If only the ship were larger and my quarters more accommodating. My trunks take up so much room, but I've need of my clothes and I didn't trust my dowry in the hold. The sea was quite still when I boarded, but a tempest was on the horizon and hit so hard. I am not a sailor, it seems. Nor will I ever set foot on a ship again!" Elizabeth Southey reached for Heather's hand shyly while still babbling. "My personal maid, ungrateful girl, left me! Disappeared just as we were to embark! My relatives send me with the hope that I shall marry my cousin, Bruce Somerset, on Staten Island, a place I've never even heard of. But what a poor show I shall make . . . like this."

"Miss Southey, please," said Heather, who, while she felt no calling to nursing, always sympathized with another's distress. "You must rest or you'll only make yourself worse. I shall be here, I promise. I'm sure this being at anchor and waiting is your trouble." Heather looked out the porthole at the shore to regain her own failing sense of equilibrium and then turned to answer the knock at the cabin door. A small but rounded blond woman pushed her way in from the companionway with mop and pail.

Her hair was disheveled, her grayish dress soiled, and a sleeve torn.

"Me name's Maggie Pipes," she puffed at Heather and, setting her tools down, went rapidly on. "I weren't good enough for her ladyship! Didn't like me smell, says her!" Maggie surveyed the scene. "Ugh! She'll never stop! I'd rather me own job, rough as 'tis, than yours, by me mother's tits, I would!"

"Maggie! Watch your tongue in here!" Heather said. "I don't care what you say anywhere else, but in this room, be as ladylike as you can. And start over there at once." Heather pointed to the worst of the small puddles of vomit.

Maggie looked Heather up and down. "Uppity, ain't ye? You've no cause to be. Ye be indentured, same as me." Her eyes narrowed as she caught Heather's cool stare. "I see the way of it, I do. A virgin as pretty as ye will bring a good price for that pork-barreled rogue."

Heather's eyes widened and she was about to question Maggie when a moan from the bed drew her attention to where her duty lay. She swiftly ordered the slow-moving Maggie back to her task and together they put the room and Miss Southey in a comfortable state. When they had nearly done, Heather said in a determined voice, "I hope we can be friends, Maggie, for I'm sure I shall need your help again."

Maggie grinned. "It's plain as can be you're an innocent. The more's the pity for ye. I'm a friend to none and all at the same time. I've learned survival in me twenty-two or three years." Sucking in her lower lip with a smacking sound, she continued, "I forget which I am now. Ain't it a pip!"

Heather looked at her seriously. She was not used to such plain-spokenness in a serving girl, but her statements were amusingly honest. Heather was considering how to handle Maggie when a small voice piped up from the bed.

"I don't think Mr. Barrett or the captain will tolerate such impertinences, Maggie, and I certainly shan't! Please leave us now! I've heard enough of your woes to last a lifetime!"

10

"Yes, Miss Southey." Maggie made a curtsy bordering on disrespect.

"Maggie," Heather said in a quiet tone as she accompanied her to the door, "launder your own dress as well as these linens, and do change. I may need you tomorrow and, well, your dress. . . . It's not proper."

"Not proper, you say," said Maggie, her blue eyes flashing. "Miss, I've none other but the clothes on me back and a shawl, and that's the truth on it. So help me."

Heather stared at her a moment, trying to decide whether to argue with her or dismiss her, but suddenly took another tack altogether. "Can you sew, Maggie?"

"'ell's bells, yes! It's the one lady skill I've a callin' for! But I ain't got a scrap to sew nor even a needle." Maggie looked down at her torn dress, and her face hardened again.

Heather ran over to her little trunk, and although she had few dresses to her name, she pulled out a worn but serviceable blue dress and a little basket of sewing notions and offered them to Maggie, whose mouth fell open in amazement.

"Why, miss! Ye ain't got no call to do that." She fingered gingerly the beautiful blue material, the color of which almost matched her eyes.

"It will be too long for you," Heather said, "but if you're as clever as you say, you can alter it and at least have something decent to wear. Go now, and do come tomorrow if you can. This cabin could use some polish and I . . . I need your help."

Maggie stood rooted and continued to stare at the dress. "I'm beholdin' to ye." She narrowed her eyes in thought. "When them other hags sees this dress, they'll be greener than grass with envy. I shall 'av to watch it careful. In New York, I will put it on. Til then, this rag is more 'n good enough for my kind o' work." Maggie left then, but with lighter steps than when she had come.

"Heather," came the light soprano voice from the bed. "You shouldn't have. That wretch of a girl will have that blue dress of yours looking like the rag she has on in two days' time. I can't imagine what possessed you."

Heather closed her small trunk, feeling a tightness in her throat and a surge of warmth that so little should be so much to someone else. "For a brief moment, it was so easy for me to feel that I was as destitute as she and as helplessly borne by the sea's tides. Just now, I feel the tide in my own life is very low."

"Times change, Heather, but you must wait for them. I would never have expected a year ago to be sailing to New York with the hope of marrying. Yet here I am, and I'm told my cousin Bruce is a most handsome young man. The Somersets are a very prominent family with many enterprises and properties. A new and promising world awaits me there, and I had been ready for a quiet spinsterhood. So you see . . ." She stopped and turned pale as both women experienced the ship seeming to fall through space.

"Oh, Heather . . ." Miss Southey groaned as another wave of her *mal de mer* returned.

Realizing that the ship was doing a turn, Heather heard from overhead a loud, rhythmic clanking sound and the shouts and tramping of men.

Excitedly, she ran to the porthole to see what was happening. As the ship continued to swing, she suddenly saw the gigantic rings of the ship's anchor chain rising slowly from the sea, trailing a shawl of seaweed behind.

"We sail!" Heather cried. "Miss Southey, we sail!"

Chapter Two

WHENEVER JOHN SOMERSET SAW HIS ELDEST SON AFTER A separation, his heart gave a lurch. Rigo had in him so much of both John and of Contessa Elena, his departed first wife. During this meeting now, as the two smoked and drank, John felt more than ever that at twenty-eight, Rigo was exactly the same sort of handsome, reckless man that he himself had been thirty years ago at the same age—and trying to make the same mistakes, too.

Rigo paced with long, powerful strides back and forth across the beautifully patterned floral rug of the music room, leaving his glass of Madeira untouched on the elegant piano. As John watched, he was reminded of that same fire that had once raged so deeply within himself, and now he found himself playing the role of the conservative, disapproving father—the role that his own father had once played with him.

"This is no time for me to marry," Rigo said firmly, running one of his large hands through his thick, curly, black hair. "A man without a business, with his country in turmoil," he emphasized, "hardly has much to offer a wife!"

"Perhaps so," John replied, lifting his leonine head and leaning forward from the blue cushioned wing chair near the fireplace. "But from my point of view, that is precisely why you should marry Arabella now. Her fortune is solid, even if ours is not."

"I'm not a man to marry for money," Rigo replied, stopping at the window to stare out over the lawns toward the waters of New York Bay. Staring out to sea was as characteristic of John's elder son as was his younger son Bruce's habit of staring at his account books.

"My dear Richard," John Somerset went on, using Rigo's formal name rather than the intimate one only he and Rigo's half sister, Amy, ever used. "Bruce is willing to contemplate marrying a woman he has never met, whom I remember as a quite unpromising stick, and one whose fortune, while quite large, is no greater than Arabella's, while you, quite familiar with Arabella's beauty, hesitate. There are many men, and I thought you were one of them, who would be happy to marry Arabella even if she were a pauper!"

Rigo turned to his father and smiled that vibrant, dazzling smile that so warmed John's heart—and women's, too, he guessed. Standing erect and broad-shouldered while dressed in the height of fashion in white silk shirt, gray dress coat and breeches, and black leather boots, Rigo always looked the cynical dandy—until he smiled.

"If Arabella weren't so rich, I might have bedded her and then eloped with her months ago, but as it is, courting her is like courting all of Staten Island. That lady has more rich relatives than we have ships!"

"Those rich relatives could help us hold on to our ships if you would just act with reason."

"Ah, yes. Reason," Rigo replied with a sigh. "The Parliament passes so many oppressive tax and trading laws that Somerset Shipping is practically bankrupt, the Colonies are driven toward declaring a new nation, and I am left with nothing to do but manage a fleet of empty, anchored ships."

John pulled himself more upright in his chair and took a cheroot from the gleaming fruitwood table beside him. His every movement was regal and dignified, his full dark hair peppered with gray. Rigo was right about Parliament, he thought, right about the rebellion, and right about their frozen business. However, siding with the rebels was hardly the answer. Marrying well was.

"We survive," he said, leaning forward to the elaborately carved silver candelabra. "The *Glasgow* sails. The *Prospect* sails."

"With both of them reduced to carrying rum, timber, and indentured servants," Rigo countered, grimacing. "There's as much profit in anchoring."

"Ah," John said, "but one of them will be bringing Elizabeth Southey and her dowry. There'll be more profit in that than anchoring, I assure you." Holding the cheroot to the candelabra, John inhaled deeply as Rigo picked up his glass of wine and strode to the window, where he again stood with his back to his father.

"If I were to marry," Rigo said softly, "then I suppose Arabella would be as good a choice as any, but I just don't think it would be fair to her."

"Fair!" John said, exploding a small cloud of smoke out into the room toward Rigo. "My dear boy, fairness has nothing to do with it. Arabella wants to marry you, and your mother and I wish it so."

"My stepmother," Rigo corrected quietly, his back still to John.

"Yes. Margaret," John continued, aware of a pang at the allusion to Rigo's natural mother, Elena, of so long ago. "Margaret and I . . ." When Rigo turned from the window to face him, John was aware of the tension in his son's handsome features, the furrow in his brow and the sparkle missing from his clear blue eyes. He had sensed for weeks that something was bothering Rigo, something clearly to do with the war that seemed to have started with the battles at Concord and Lexington a half year earlier.

Was Rigo thinking of fighting King George the Third? It hardly seemed possible.

"My son," he finally went on, "you might as well marry. Until this impasse between the Colonies and Parliament is resolved, you've nothing else to do."

Rigo's tense face fragmented into a smile, his eyes again filling with light.

"Sir, only you could have marshaled such a reason for marriage," he said, smiling.

"It keeps a man out of mischief," John Somerset answered gravely. "Before I married Margaret, I was a rakehell rapidly dissipating my inheritance. A snobbish good-for-nothing."

"You sired me," Rigo replied.

"Aye, that I did. The one great act of my wild youth. But the Contessa was Catholic and . . ."

"And you let her get away . . ."

John didn't answer but instead found himself groping for his own glass filled with brandy.

"I married her," he said defensively, clasping his brandy. But even as he did, he felt that stab of sadness at having first let the Spanish Catholic church annul their marriage and then having let his father talk him into not remarrying her in the Anglican church. Following Elena's tragic death giving birth to their son—his Rigo—he'd had to kidnap the infant to get him back from the Contessa's family: almost the last reckless act of his life. Two years later, John had married the wealthy Margaret Morgan and settled into developing a shipping business between the West Indies, England, and New York.

"Father," Rigo began, making John aware that he'd been staring into his brandy while immersed in memories. "We have only two ships in New York ready to sail, the *Yorkshire* and the *Contessa*. Neither has cargo. I'd like to take the *Contessa* to Puerto Rico and take on a full shipment of rum, sugar, molasses, and whatever else is available."

"The *Contessa* . . ." John echoed vaguely, sipping his brandy. The schooner was the Somerset's fastest, most beautiful ship.

16

"She's small," Rigo went on, "but she's the best we have for outrunning the British blockade and smuggling the cargo back to New York."

"Yes . . ." John agreed, but then with sudden vigor added, "But *you* don't have to go! Have William Hatch take her. Or Ben Simpson. I don't want you involved."

"No matter who tries to run the blockade, I'm involved. We're both involved. It's our ship."

"But you don't have to be its captain."

"On this trip, I do."

"But why?"

John again saw that unfamiliar cloud cross Rigo's face, as if he were hiding some problem.

"Because if Hatch or Simpson failed, I wouldn't be certain if it were bad luck, bad seamanship, or because the task was impossible. If I go, I'll know."

Listening, John knew that Rigo was right. Since Rigo had run away to sea at the age of fourteen—partly to escape Margaret, John knew—he had been one of the best natural sailors John had ever known. A natural leader, too, as judged by the fact that he was the captain of a brigantine at eighteen and manager of the Somerset fleet at twenty-two. Standing by the window, dressed in that lace-trimmed, brocaded long coat, Rigo looked like a London dandy, but John had seen him outfight the biggest men in any ship's crew and outsail captains twice his age. Now with this foolish rebellion, he sensed Rigo would be tempted to pit his skills against the English fleet, an act of revolution against both his father's country and his own social class. An act of tragic madness. Better even marriage than that. John smiled at his own cynicism.

"Well, I'll let you decide," he said. "Before this mess, you'd managed to triple our profits. It would be foolish of me to overrule you now."

"Thank you, sir."

"But don't forget your Arabella," John added as he stood, leaving his cheroot unfinished on the table. "She's a prize well worth fighting for."

Rigo finished the last of his wine. "She's a prize I believe

17

I've already won," he said, smiling. "The question is whether I'll bring her into port."

"Aye, and you'd better. Prizes will be getting harder and harder to bring home."

Rigo shot his father a glance, as if the talk of prizes were a strange one. Then, putting his wineglass on the deep sill of the window, he came over to the older man.

"In any case, I must go, sir," he said gently, and John became aware of Rigo's love for him and of his own love for his firstborn son. He could no better control Rigo than could a sailor control the wind, but John knew that he now depended on him. Somerset Shipping was being ground down into bankruptcy, first by the tax and trade laws and now the rebellion. If anyone could somehow save it all, it was Rigo.

"Well, son, if you must, you must," John said with a sigh. The two men held each other by the elbows, too formal for an embrace, too bound to each other not to touch. "But be careful. Your life is worth more than all the rum in the world."

Rigo smiled, squeezed his father's arms once, and released him.

"Perhaps not *that* valuable," he said, turning to go.

"To me, Rigo, to me. . . ."

And Rigo was gone.

In the small sailboat taking him from Staten Island to the Somerset docks on the Hudson River in New York City, Rigo felt that peculiar heaviness and tension in his gut that seemed to afflict him these days after he'd been with his family. The gracious and elegant Somerset world was breaking up. During this brief stay, he had found time to make only the most perfunctory of visits to his stepmother and to his half brother, Bruce. Their disapproval of him and his rebel sympathies made their relations difficult.

Bruce—charming, outwardly polite and, as always, distant—had dominated the conversation. He was in charge of all the Somerset estates: the land, buildings, and tenancies mostly owned by Margaret Somerset who, at the

18

time of her marriage, had retained independent wealth.
Bruce had expressed his fears that the Somerset tenant
farmers might use the rebellion as an excuse to revolt
against the landlords, and he had asked Rigo if he thought
General Howe would soon be coming with his British and
Hessian troops to protect New York and New Jersey. Rigo
had shrugged his lack of knowledge and generally remained silent, but Bruce and Margaret had rightly interpreted his silence as sympathy for the tenant farmers. The
tension had been painful. Amy had looked from one
brother to another with affection and fear. She would do
anything to avoid an open breach in the family.

Rigo realized that he was depressed about having to
deceive his father even a little about the extent of his
commitment to the rebellion. Yet he felt that only by
acting independently of his father could he keep the older
man clear of blame should the Colonies' cause fail. Rigo
had been offered a commission in the new Navy being
formed but had instead asked for and been given a letter of
marque. This gave him the right to seize English cargoes
not headed to or from the Colonies, which meant almost
all English shipping. These prizes—Rigo had wondered at
his father's use of the word—would be split between the
crew and the Continental Congress. Rigo was indeed, as
he'd told his father, going after rum and molasses, but not
by buying it in Puerto Rico. He would be pirating it in the
Atlantic only a few hundred miles from New York—if he
could.

So as to implicate the Somersets as little as possible in
his piracy, Rigo had gathered a special crew that included
only five trusted sailors from his own Somerset ships. He
was known to all as Captain Rigo, since Rigo was a name
that only his father and Amy ever used and was known
only to his immediate family and Arabella. Most of his
secret crew was a ragbag collection of seamen thrown out
of work by the British tariffs and blockade. Although all
were committed rebels, few, if any, had ever been in
battle. Their skill with the five cannons Rigo had installed
aboard the *Contessa* was ludicrously inadequate, and he'd
have to train them further as they sailed out to seek their

prey. The *Contessa,* too, would have to be disguised and renamed—the *Conte* would be simplest, he guessed—to avoid implicating his father. But Rigo had to use the schooner. She was the only ship he knew that would consistently outsail the British frigates that would be after him. Outnumbered ten to one and outgunned sixty to one, he knew he had damn well better be able to dodge well and run fast. That the *Contessa* could do.

In Manhattan, Rigo went to the Somerset townhouse on the west side and changed from his formal clothing into the high boots, woolen pants, and long, deerskin cape he wore at sea. When he arrived at the schooner on the Hudson in the early evening, he was no longer the London dandy but a seaman. Noah Wiggens, his short, thickset, energetic first mate, greeted him at the gangplank. Noah, like most of his crew, was wearing an almost comic selection of woolens and animal skins to keep off the anticipated cold wetness of the North Atlantic.

"She's ready, Captain Rigo," Noah said proudly. "Got the last of the supplies on board not an hour ago."

"All the men aboard?" Rigo asked, noticing that his crew was forward, laying out the anchor lines.

"All but Watson," Noah replied.

"If he's not here by eight, we sail without him."

"Wind's barely fair."

"That's why we go. Are the decks cleared for sea?"

"They will be by nine."

"Good."

The two men looked lovingly at the long curve of the schooner's deck, the sweep of her two masts high up into the purplish sky of the sunset, then they looked out at New York harbor stretching south to the ocean, where a dozen or so sails could be seen taking on a pinkish glow in the fading light.

"Interesting, this pirate business," Noah said tentatively, glancing up at Rigo.

"They stole our right to sail and trade, so we'll steal their cargoes," Rigo replied after a pause. "And it will be hard, dangerous, bloody, and sad. We'll kill men we've

20

sailed with, and some of us will be killed—and I damn well wish we didn't have to do it."

"Aye, sir."

Rigo moved past Noah up the plank and set foot on the *Contessa's* deck. "Loose all but the fore and aft mooring lines," Rigo added coolly. "We sail in forty minutes."

"Aye, sir."

"And Noah?"

"Cap'n?"

Rigo smiled.

"It *will* be interesting."

Chapter Three

THE *PROSPECT* SAILED DOWN THE THAMES, OUT THE ENGLISH Channel, and into the Atlantic. Heather was confined below helping Elizabeth Southey and each night fell asleep exhausted. After an initial queasiness, she found herself well attuned to the roll of the ship, and only occasionally would she be surprised by a sudden pitch throwing her into a chair or against the ship's side. Other than an occasional bruised shin or arm, her only real discomfort came from being confined below since she and the other indentured servants were allowed up on deck only once a day, and then only in nice weather. Heather noticed that the other women looked very pale and were all suffering coughs from, she assumed, being below decks too much. She was only just able to convince Miss Southey of the need for sun, but when she bundled her up as if for winter and led her to a chair, the other woman complained of the bracing air rather than reveling in it, as did Heather.

On those rare occasions that Miss Southey went on deck, Duncan Crawley hovered near them, courting the frail lady with anecdotes of people they both knew in

London, bringing some color into her cheeks. It was clear from his conversation that he was from a wealthy family whose export business had been badly hurt by the rebellion of the Colonies. Crawley himself, Heather gathered by reading between the lines, had had some severe financial reversals in the last year and hoped, with some sort of commission he had from King George, to recoup his fortunes in the New World. He rarely directed a word to Heather, although she caught him more than once looking at her with a sly smile or an expression that caused her to feel uncomfortable and turn away. It was a look that he never directed at Miss Southey, and Heather decided she wouldn't like to know what the expression meant.

Miss Southey, when her health permitted, dined at the captain's table and announced that she liked the old whiskered Scottish seaman, who told wonderful tales of his childhood in Glasgow. She also confided in Heather that Duncan Crawley was a witty and considerate gentleman who was showering her with his attentions.

"I do believe that he would propose were I to give him any encouragement, but I feel my obligation to Bruce Somerset and so must resist his charms," she told Heather. "Still, it is an honor to be courted by such a worthy man."

Miss Southey's occasional dining at the captain's table seemed the one cheerful aspect of her otherwise miserable trip. Heather felt acutely her own exclusion from the dining privilege and the few other social occasions at which the gentlefolk gathered. She felt that she belonged there had not fate dealt her so unkind a blow. Duncan Crawley's occasional attentions to Heather were pleasant enough, but she sensed that he now treated her quite differently from the way he courted Miss Southey. In particular, she remembered the last occasion when he had come upon her outside Miss Southey's cabin as she was about to deliver linens for Maggie to wash.

Crawley had stopped in front of her and had put his hands on her waist.

"Ah, Miss Woode," he said. "What a pity that you must sully your hands with such tasks."

"Yes, sir," she answered carefully. "I certainly hope

one day to do easier work, but for now, I am happy to help Miss Southey."

"You belong on the arm of a gentleman," he said smiling. "Or better yet, in them." His smile broadened.

Heather, resenting his hands on her waist, was aware that his breath smelled of wine.

"When I find a gentleman," she said, "that may well be true." She freed herself and began to move by him, but Crawley put out a hand to detain her.

"I must deliver these linens, sir," she said coldly. "Let me pass."

"Ah, but to pass, you must first pay a toll," Crawley replied and, to Heather's astonishment, quickly leaned forward and pressed his lips on hers. She turned her face and shoved at him, the linen spilling in a heap on the floor. Her hands now free, Heather let one fly in a stinging slap to his cheek, her eyes glittering with anger.

"I may not have Miss Southey's charms, Mr. Crawley," she snapped, "but I have an equal amount of pride, and I will not be treated like a . . . barmaid!"

Rigid at first and ready to retaliate, Duncan Crawley suddenly seemed to change his mind and backed off with a short laugh.

"You have spirit," he said, bringing a tentative hand to his cheek. "I won't apologize for my stolen kiss, but I do for not seeing your more tender feelings."

"Your courting Miss Southey and dallying with me shows disrespect for us both." Heather leaned down to gather up the spilled linen. When she straightened and turned to leave, Crawley grasped her arm.

"Your destiny is in a man's arms, Heather," he said in a low, harsh voice. "I can assure you that the day will come when you will be very glad of my attentions. I suggest you think about it." And he had turned and left.

Heather watched him retreat, not failing to notice the anger in his stride. He doesn't like being crossed, she realized, and wondered if she had made an enemy.

In order to be alone and not bothered by anyone, Heather began to sneak out on deck after midnight, careful that no one should see her. Watching the stars and feeling the night wind on her body gave her a feeling of power, a feeling of getting away with a special treasure. Such moments compensated for her otherwise uncertain future and the small day-to-day indignities she was made to suffer as Miss Southey's personal maid.

In the evenings, she began reading aloud to Miss Southey from a small store of the lady's books. A good dramatic reader, Heather confided that at home her parents had put on little playlets and entertainments for their guests. "My mother," she said, "read well and knew how to costume, and my father had such a magnificent voice. . . ." Heather trailed off, pained at the memory of her happier times.

"'Tis a pity," Miss Southey said. "I know well how you feel. I, too, am orphaned, but it was so long ago that I have few memories to keep. I think that is why I've undertaken this journey—to be with a loving family. I've missed so much, and the Somersets' letters to me have been so welcoming, especially Bruce's. He seems such a courtly man. I treasure each one." Elizabeth suddenly pulled herself into a sitting position on her bed, adjusting the covers modestly. "If you'll fetch them for me now, there's something I want to show you."

Heather put the book on the shelf at the head of Miss Southey's berth and stood.

"They're in the largest of my three trunks," Miss Southey went on.

Heather went over and began to undo its fastening. She was already familiar with the vast array of expensive dresses, gowns, footwear, silks, and linens in the other two trunks, but she was unprepared for what she now found. The trunk open, Heather stood amazed. Gleaming silver winked at her beneath thin, soft coverings, heavy packets of sterling coins seemed to fill one whole side of the chest, and several caskets of jewelry were carefully packed on the other. She turned to Miss Southey, completely taken aback at the great wealth displayed.

"That is my dowry," Miss Southey said to Heather's silently questioning face. "I didn't trust it to be laid in the ship's hold and had it brought with me in here. Do you see the little pink silk box in the left corner? Fetch it here to me." She gestured with a small, pale finger.

Heather brought the box to her and watched as Elizabeth opened it tenderly. After a few seconds, she brought forth from atop a small bundle of letters a bit of lace and unwrapped it. She held up for Heather an exquisite heart-shaped locket of gold and amethyst.

Heather drew in her breath. "It's beautiful!" she sighed.

"A gift from Bruce Somerset," Miss Southey said softly. "It is true we have never met, but I feel I know his heart already. Years ago, at the age of ten, I met his father in London, and he made a fine impression on me—a handsome man with great dignity and lively manners. I can only assume his son is the same. There is another son and a daughter, but I fear the other son is not all he should be. In one of these letters, Bruce refers to 'my disreputable half brother, Richard'—I believe that was the phrase he used. Yes, that's it! But every family has its black sheep. Bruce's sister, Amy, however, is a dear. She has sent me a tender letter of welcome." Miss Southey's hand trembled and fell as she sighed, "I do prattle on so, and now I'm afraid I'm very weary."

When Heather moved to replace the letters and locket in the dowry trunk, Miss Southey asked her not to lock them away but to place them instead in her large reticule on the fixed desk, where they would be within easier reach. As Heather then moved to retire to her tiny berth in the corner of the cabin behind a curtain, Miss Southey called out in a shaky voice.

"Heather, dear, I know it's late, but could you just go below and get me one of Maggie's sleeping remedies." She coughed lightly, and Heather could see dampness on her forehead again. "Maggie knows a thing or two about herbs, I must say," Elizabeth continued, rubbing her temples with her fingers. "I shall toss all night without it."

"Yes, of course, Miss Southey." Even as she spoke, Heather remembered the warnings against going below without an escort but brushed them away. She went first to the pitcher of water, wrung out a cool cloth, and placed it on Miss Southey's hot brow. "I shall be right back with the tea," she whispered.

Quietly opening the door to the darkened passageway and seeing no one about, Heather grabbed a candle from a sconce on the wall and set out on her errand. She could hear more sharply now the familiar sounds of the ship plowing forward, its pitch and roll more animated than usual. From somewhere below, she heard voices talking and a chantey being sung, followed by low laughter. Feeling along the sides of the ship, Heather eased her way down to the lower deck toward Maggie's cabin. The ship's cat jumped away with a yowl when she accidentally kicked it, setting her heart thudding, and a few steps farther, she sensed movement off to the side that wasn't the cat. She stopped uncertainly.

"Who's there?" she asked. Whispers, one of them from a woman, came from the floor to her right.

"Heather? Be ye there?"

"Maggie?" Heather asked, surprised to recognize that voice from the darkness. Maggie came out of the dark shadows, buttoning her front and twisting her petticoat into place.

"So this is the beauty ye girls be talking about," came a husky voice from behind Maggie, and a powerfully built sailor emerged to look Heather blatantly up and down, slowly buttoning up the front of his trousers.

"Be away with you, matey," Maggie said sharply. "You've got what you come for, and Miss Woode is none of your business."

"Aye, I got it," he replied with a sneer. "But if I hadn't, I might teach your snooty friend here a thing or two about rocking in a boat."

"Shoo!" Maggie snapped, and with a laugh, the sailor marched off into the darkness. "Be ye shocked?" Maggie asked Heather when the man was gone. "Aye, I see your look of disgust." Maggie spat out the words in a low voice. "Well, yer not far from it yourself, believe me."

"Maggie . . . I . . . I'm sorry," Heather blurted.

"Nay, don't be sorry. I'm not carin', neither should

27

you." Maggie tossed her blond curls saucily, her eyes boldly questioning Heather. The candle flickered uncertainly between them.

"Miss Southey can't sleep and asked me to get your tea remedy."

"That be it?" Maggie's small mouth pursed. "She's sickly, that one. Well, let's fetch the brew. I'll get the hot water and meet you in my cabin." She hurried off into the darkness, leaving Heather leaning against the rough wood of the darkened passageway as she listened to the moans of the straining, plunging ship. Why had Maggie given herself to that sailor? And what had she meant by "not far from it yourself"? When Heather heard someone descending the companionway off to the right, she pulled her shawl closer and hurried off toward Maggie's cabin and knocked.

A sick-looking girl opened the door into a small, dark room containing a row of wooden bunks tightly packed in tiers of two against the wall and small heaps of what must have been the occupants' meager possessions on the floor. There was no other furniture. The room stank of unwashed women and clothes and a foul slop pot. Three women were lying like prisoners in their own filth. Heather realized with horror that, except for Miss Southey, this is where she, too, would have been lodged. The girl at the door staggered back into the cabin and fell on her bunk, groaning softly. Ignoring Heather, she blew her nose and, pulling a coarse blanket around her shoulders, turned her face to the wall. Heather took two tentative steps into the room and then stopped.

"Come in, come in, Miss Woode," said a tiny woman, rolling over in the bunk above the first woman. "How honored we be by your visit." Propping herself up on one elbow, she examined Heather with large dark eyes. "Meet the girls you take the air with on the ship's deck," she snickered. "We seem never to be introduced, but then you and Miss Southey is always puttin' on such airs. But you'll change your tune when we're in New York, you'll see. You'll be servin' some gent right quick!" When she laughed a short, throaty, sarcastic series of notes, Heather felt as if she had been struck.

"Take no offense, Heather," put in Maggie, who appeared behind her with the hot water from the galley. "This here's Jane, and she's cuttin' tongue what never shuts up day nor night. That below her is Pauline. She's got the flu. Same as the cabin boy Tim's got, and your Miss Southey, and half the crew of this poor ship. That other lady there is Beth."

Jane sniggered again, her hand flicking her lank brown hair off her shoulder. "And we're ladies, too, Miss Woode. Miss Jane Tilser to you," she said emphatically, lifting her eyebrows for punctuation. "Indentured, just like you. Well, except for Pauline here, she's . . ."

"Shut up, you spittoon!" Maggie hissed at her.

"No, Maggie," Heather said, "don't stop her." She looked directly at Jane. "I realize only too well I'm in the same circumstances as yourself, but it isn't fair to blame me for being chosen as Miss Southey's maid instead of you."

"Who's blamin' you?" Jane asked. "The only complaint I have is the food you get. You don't eat beans and hard biscuits and weak tea day after day." She fell back and sighed disgustedly. "Lordie, what a bloomin' princess you are."

"I've just been luckier than you," Heather said, her voice soft and low as she watched Maggie prepare the special strong tea for Miss Southey. "But what did you mean when you said that in New York I'd be serving some . . . gentleman?" Heather's voice wavered at the end.

Maggie sniffed at the tea and then looked up at Heather. "You ain't got no idea, have ye?" she asked.

"I thought I would be apprenticed as a lady's maid or a governess or something similar in a good home. That's what Mr. Barrett led me to think. How would I . . . serve a gentleman?"

Jane broke out into a high cackle of laughter, and even Maggie grinned.

"Why, on your back, dearie, how else?" said Jane, smiling. "Lordie, but you are a cluck! Barrett's been bringing girls over and auctionin' 'em in the New World for years, and if the girl's got a good arse or a pretty face, then that's what the buyers will buy. He said he found 'the prettiest of all' this time and is lookin' for top price. Highest bidder. And when the men see you, they won't be thinkin' of no governesses, that's for sure." She laughed again.

Heather gasped. "Then he lied to me!" She clenched her fists. "Maggie, is it true?" she asked despairingly. "Have I given myself into the hands of so unscrupulous a man?"

Maggie set down the large teapot and made a face at the smirking Jane. "Oh, Barrett ain't so bad as the mouth says, but he will sell your contract to the highest bidder and 'e'll get a fancy price for ye."

"I won't be a gentleman's . . . doxy!" Heather exclaimed and stamped a foot. "I won't! I'll run away!"

"You'll be lucky it's a gentleman," Maggie said quietly. "Some of us will be soldier's doxies and some of us will be serving girls working sixteen hours a day without pay for five years."

"It's little better than slavery, Maggie!" Heather felt tears in her eyes.

Jane laughed. "Welcome to the lower decks."

"Come along now," Maggie said to Heather. "The air in here is foul enough without Jane's tongue swillin' it round, and Miss Southey didn't send you down here to play society with us."

As Heather left and trudged through the dark passageways and up the ladders toward Miss Southey's cabin, she felt a heaviness as if something were trying to drag her back down to the lower deck. It was her fate, and she felt the weight of it as hard and immovable as she'd once felt the walls and bars of the debtor's prison. Heather vowed now, as she had vowed then, one thing—to resist and to escape.

Chapter Four

"THERE SHE IS, CAPTAIN," NOAH WIGGENS SAID PROUDLY AS Rigo emerged on deck a little after dawn. "Right where you said she'd be."

To the east, where Noah was pointing, Rigo could see the merchant ship under full sail still laboring to the north toward Boston. When they'd spotted her at dusk the night before and made certain it wasn't a British man-of-war hunting them, Rigo had purposely begun sailing away from his prey, feigning indifference, hoping that the merchantman's captain wouldn't take evasive action during the night. He'd bet Noah their first captured keg of rum that this captain, lulled by the dominance of the British fleet off Cape Cod, would continue north. Rigo had directed the course and speed of his *Contessa* so as to be slightly to windward of the merchant's calculated position at dawn. And there she was.

"Aye," he said, pulling his jacket closer and adjusting the scarf to his neck against the cold spring wind. "There she is. And you may close on her now, Mr. Wiggens." He then glanced aloft and saw his lookout with a spyglass searching the horizon to make certain there were no other ships about.

"Two points to starboard, helmsman," the mate said eagerly, and Rigo wondered just how much fear was embedded in Noah's excitement.

"She's flying the Union Jack, Cap'n," Noah added. "I'll wager he thinks that makes him safe."

"Yes," Rigo said, "I imagine it does." He felt the cool wind ruffle his thick dark hair, and he nervously ran his hand through it as he examined the merchantman. Then he added softly, "Man the guns."

"Phelps and Riggens!" Noah shouted. "Man the guns!"

At the mate's command, half a dozen seamen ran forward to the six cannons lined up port and starboard amidships, and two other men ran forward to man the single cannon on the foredeck. Rigo was aware that his entire crew, even the cook, was now on deck staring at their prey. In three weeks of sailing under their letter of marque, they had seen only four ships: two fishing boats and two British frigates—not exactly the stuff from which fortunes were made. They had ignored the fishing boats and had fled in unseemly haste from the slower frigates. Now his twenty-six men went about their tasks knowing that within a few hours, they might be giving and receiving cannon shot and musket balls. Rigo moved over beside the helmsman to check the compass and their course.

"We're gaining on her, Cap'n, we are," the helmsman said with a grin. "Closed most of a mile since first light."

"Good," said Rigo, smiling at Peters and noting again the excitement he'd sensed in the others. The seas were running four or five feet high in the fifteen knot wind, and the *Contessa* was beginning to slam into them as she tacked after the merchantman, the spray flying back over the ship and falling on Rigo and the helmsman like periodic bursts of rain. When Noah Wiggens returned aft, he was again smiling. "Shall I distribute weapons to the men, Cap'n?" he asked Rigo.

"Not yet, Noah," he said. "Have the men all had breakfast?"

"I'm not sure, sir," Noah said, frowning. "Seems to me maybe they haven't. Hooks is so excited. . . ."

"Order the first watch below to breakfast and the second watch in twenty minutes."

"Aye, sir."

"Helmsman, head her up a point. I want to draw abeam of the merchantman a quarter mile to windward," Rigo said, squinting into the early morning light at the white bloom of sail on the horizon to the north. "Adjust your course as necessary."

"Aye, sir."

With the mate seeing to it that the men were fed, Rigo strode away from the helmsman to stand at the starboard rail and stare out at the rising sun. The die was cast. In an hour, he would fire on a British ship and have cast his lot with America and the rebellion—he, Richard Somerset, son of Staten Island's leading Tory family. Well, so be it. Only Noah and four of the seamen knew that Captain Rigo was actually Richard Somerset, and they were all trusted accomplices. He would hide his piracy and rebel activities from his father and family as long as he could, but sooner or later . . . if there was a later. . . .

The ship they were chasing was an old four-masted, square-rigged barkentine, larger by half than the *Contessa*, but a slow ship except in a full gale. She was armed, Rigo was sure, probably with three or four cannons, like the *Contessa*.

"She's changing course, sir!" the helmsman called out.

The merchantman was now within cannon range, less than a half mile away, and as the *Contessa* drew abeam, the British ship turned away to avoid Rigo's first broadside. It had earlier signaled the *Contessa* to identify herself and her business, and Rigo's failure to reply obviously had her crew worried.

"Fire across his bow, Mr. Wiggens!"

Each cannon was run by a gun crew of two, and of the five cannons that Rigo had prepared for action, only the one on the foredeck could now bear on the target. On Wiggens' command, the cannon exploded with a roar and a clatter. As all watched, a spume of water burst up a hundred feet in front of the merchantman, which quickly began a slow turn to port so as to bring her cannon to bear on the *Contessa*.

"Hard to starboard!" Rigo directly instructed the helmsman. "Prepare to jibe!" he shouted forward.

Instead of turning to the left so that the two ships could blast away at each other side to side, Rigo was swinging his ship to the right, bringing his broadside into play against the merchantman's defenseless stern. A puff of smoke from the side of the merchantman and a splash off their port side showed that the battle was on.

"Guns two and three, prepare to fire!" Rigo shouted forward, and as his boat swung across the merchantman's stern and out of range of its guns, added, "Fire when ready!"

In a few seconds, the two guns seemed to explode simultaneously, one of them knocking one of the gunmen flat on his back. Rigo couldn't see any effects from the two shots, but the merchantman was surging back downwind again.

"Steady as she goes," Rigo ordered, waiting to give his gunners a second shot on this tack, and in a few seconds, a boom from amidships and another from the gun forward sounded. When his third cannon had fired, Rigo ordered his ship swung back downwind to continue the chase.

"We scored a hit, Cap'n!" Noah reported with a grin. "Pretty near tore off the captain's breeches."

"The men are aiming at the spars as ordered?" Rigo asked sharply.

"Aye, sir. Fact is, we holed the two mainsails."

"Good. Tell the bow gunner to fire at will."

As the slow-motion race continued, Rigo found himself smiling with the same excitement he'd seen on the faces of his crew. As they drew nearer, though, his smile faded as he noted that after six shots, the enemy had barely been touched. He'd have to get closer before his inexperienced gun crews could begin to zero in on the masts and rigging to disable the enemy.

Another cannon blast from the forward gun elicited cheers from some of the crew, but the prey still seemed to sail on intact. As the men watched, the merchantman swung again to port to bring its own guns into play.

"Steady as she goes," Rigo said grimly, and the *Contessa* began rapidly to close the distance between herself and her prey.

"A point to port," he added quietly.

Whatever his men had expected, Rigo could see by the horrified expressions on the helmsman's and Wiggens' faces that sailing full-speed directly at the merchantman's impending cannon blasts was not what they had in mind. Yet Rigo knew he had to get close and that his ship made a poor target for the enemy's hopefully equally inexperienced gunners.

"Prepare to haul in the starboard sheets!" Rigo shouted. "Gunners ready?" As Rigo stared forward, he could clearly see the other captain, his mates, and helmsman staring back at him, then the British captain's shouting was followed by twin puffs of smoke from the merchantman's side. Rigo flinched at the fearful rush of a cannonball only a few feet off to the right and at the awful crash of splintering wood as the other ball crashed somewhere forward.

"Hard to port!" Rigo ordered instantly. "Haul in the starboard sheets."

The *Contessa* began to swing to the left to sail parallel to and abeam of the merchantman, which Rigo knew would need a minute to reload her cannons. He watched intently the swing of his ship until it was exactly parallel to the merchantman.

"Keep her steady!" he hissed at the helmsman. They were less than two hundred feet from the enemy, whose crew could be seen scrambling to various tasks or staring fearfully at the onrushing *Contessa*.

"Gunners, fire!" Rigo screamed.

The consecutive booms of the *Contessa's* cannons were followed by a loud crashing from the merchantman's midship. Rigo heard screams and saw the sails beginning to luff, out of control.

Before the merchantman could reload her cannons, Rigo swung the *Contessa* toward her, his schooner moving so fast it seemed that Rigo must be planning to ram the enemy. With the two ships less than fifty feet apart, the *Contessa's* bow cannon boomed. There was another shattering crash, and as the *Contessa* continued to swing, it sailed with a hissing rush past the stern of the merchantman, whose mainmast aft toppled over, followed by a tumult of shouting and screams.

Cheers erupted from the *Contessa's* crew, but Rigo shouted at Wiggens to bring their schooner up into the wind. It would leave her momentarily dead in the water, but the shift would also leave his loaded starboard guns trained on the almost helpless merchantman, since part of its rigging had fallen on the ship's wheel. The *Contessa's* forward cannon boomed again and blasted into the stricken merchantman.

"Hold your fire!" Rigo ordered and waited, watching the crippled merchantman wallowing in the water less than two hundred feet away. If its captain wanted to fight to the last man, Rigo would hate what he would have to do. The price would be awful for both sides. Even as he held his breath, the flutter of white from the stern indicated that the battle was over.

"You may arm the men now for boarding, Mr. Wiggens," he announced formally and felt the tension begin to drain from him.

An hour later, while his men were busy transferring the *Mandrake's* cargo to the *Contessa,* Rigo sat relaxed in the stern cabin of Captain Philip Lofton. The *Mandrake's* captain was a dour man with a pale, lined face. His arm had been badly bruised by a falling spar, and he had greeted Rigo with understandable chilliness.

"I see you get started in piracy rather young on this side of the ocean," Lofton said as he collapsed back into the only other chair in his small cabin. Rigo's dark features were hardly boyish, but to the fortyish Lofton, it was clearly distressing to be bested by a man young enough to be his son.

"I have a letter of marque from the Continental Congress . . ." Rigo began.

36

"I dunnough care about your piece of paper, Captain," Lofton said. "Theft is theft no matter what lies are written."

Rigo smiled, partially agreeing. "And war is war," he countered quietly.

"Aye, it is that," Lofton agreed with a sigh.

"Do you need anything we might have to re-rig your mast?" Rigo asked, rising to take a look out one of the aft windows. He could just make out the *Contessa's* stern sticking out aft from the two boats being lashed together.

"Nay, I can splice a mast as well as the next fellow," Lofton replied. "Just because my gunners can't hit a thing unless it accidentally sails into one of the cannonballs doesn't mean we're not seamen." He paused and sighed again. "Will you have a drink with me?"

"I'd be pleased." Rigo realized Lofton was caught between his depression at losing his cargo and an instinctive elation at having survived and not having had his ship taken, too. He watched as Lofton moved gingerly to his desk and took out a flask of brandy.

"When I cleared the Straits of Florida, I thought my troubles were over," Lofton said as he poured from his flask into a small tin cup. "It's getting so a man isn't safe 'til he's fast in the mud of the Thames."

"Tell that to Parliament," Rigo said, coming forward to accept his drink.

"Aye, I will," Lofton said, frowning. "What were you doing before you became a thief?"

"Just what you're doing, Captain," Rigo replied. He resumed his seat on the hard wooden chair and took a good swig of the brandy.

Lofton nodded. "Aye, I thought your gunners shot not one whit better 'n mine."

"I always say a little prayer that they don't put a shot through my own aft cabin," Rigo countered. The two men smiled at each other.

"Cap'n Rigo!" came Noah's shout as his fists pounded on the cabin door. Rigo leapt up and swung open the door. "Big ship approaching from the northeast!" Noah got out as he stood panting in the entranceway.

Rigo swung around to Captain Lofton.

"I don't think we'll stay to meet your friends," he said.

"It may be another merchant ship," Noah said excitedly.

"Get our men off this ship and raise all sail," Rigo said to Noah and then added to Captain Lofton, "Good-bye, Captain. Sorry for the inconvenience." Without waiting for an answer, he left the cabin and began running up the ladder.

Chapter Five

THE *PROSPECT* WAS NOW A DEEPLY TROUBLED SHIP. DOZENS of the ship's passengers and crew were ill with the flu epidemic, and Captain McFadden was so sick he could no longer appear on deck. Maggie and her roommates were afflicted, and Heather found herself not only nurse to Miss Southey but also to the women below deck plus several additional passengers and crew, including the captain.

As the weather turned foul, the ship's heaving and crashing in heavy seas made Heather's nursing chores even more difficult. With water jugs crashing to the floor and seasickness further weakening the ill, Heather's arms and shoulders began to bruise from her frequent falls against passageways or bed beams.

Miss Southey was among those the most seriously ill. Heather heaped blankets on the woman's feverish body to reduce the chills, and she kept the brazier burning even though it made the room hot and stuffy. She diluted the water and tea with wine to cut its stale, almost foul taste and odor, as Miss Southey had been refusing almost all food for days. Heather had begun to fear for her.

Duncan Crawley visited just once and seemed over-whelmed and frightened by Miss Southey's sickness and frailty. Pale and shaken, he offered only the most perfunc-tory of sympathies and then fled. For a day or two, he sent down brief notes to Miss Southey through his valet, but then even they stopped. When he would meet Heather in a passageway or on one of her brief sojourns on deck, he asked only briefly about Miss Southey but at length about herself. Crawley offered the services of his valet to help with her nursing chores but explained that his own delicate health forbade his exposing himself to those already ill.

The wind relentlessly whistled in the rigging, and the sea pounded the ship's sides with such explosive force that Heather wondered from moment to moment how long they could last. Fear and doubt for their safety grew as she braced herself near Miss Southey's bunk and hung onto the wall to prevent further bumps or falls.

"Heather . . ." came the rasping, high voice of Miss Southey. "Pray for me." Her fever-glazed eyes stared imploringly at Heather, and her bony fingers scratched compulsively atop the blankets.

Heather had been praying for her friends and for the ship, but now she began reciting in a low singsong voice several psalms that she knew by heart. Miss Southey's drawn face took on a trace of a smile, and she slowly sank into a light and uneven sleep. Heather also dozed, resting her head on the lady's bunk, until she was knocked to the floor by a violent pitch. She lay still, her heart beating faster, until she felt the ship resume its more normal rhythm. Then she slowly rose. It was time to visit the others.

Wrapping a shawl around her shoulders, Heather made a last check on Miss Southey and then went to the table where uneaten food had been left. For more than a week now, she had been taking extra tidbits down to the lower deck to the four women in that stifling, stinking cabin. Maggie benefited the most because, although she was ill, she had the spirit to force herself to eat. Heather remem-bered with gratitude the many times before that Maggie had run errands for her and had come daily to help clean Miss Southey's cabin and wash out their personal things. Maggie had even laundered her own tattered dress and had been careful with her language to lessen Miss Southey's objections to her. Once her loyalty had been given to Heather, Maggie didn't shirk hard work and seemed ready to do almost anything for someone she trusted.

But the extra food had been of no help to Pauline, who had died the day before, the third member of the ship's company to die from the epidemic. The body had been immediately wrapped in a sheet by two crewmen and taken topside to be thrown into the sea. Heather had been horrified at the seeming indifference of everyone, though Maggie had been harsh and bitter.

"If they'd given us better food and clean water, she'd still be livin', she would, but they care more for the condition of their tea than us bodies. Pauline's better off feedin' the fish below than she would be lettin' the sharks up here be always at her."

When Heather finally arrived below, she found Maggie flushed and restlessly tossing in her bunk. The seemingly irrepressible Jane was now lying still and pale, her lips parted and her breathing slow and gurgling. Unable to rouse her, Heather proceeded to wash her unmoving, fevered face and strangely chilled hands.

"Jane ain't gettin' no better," the shivering Maggie told her. "I been nursin' her and cleanin' up and doin' the chores, such as they be, but I ain't feelin' perfect yet meself."

"You should stay in bed, Maggie," Heather said, going to her. "I'll come down twice a day now, and I'm afraid rest is the only treatment for both of you."

After she'd changed Maggie's sweaty bedclothes, Heather fed her soup through reluctant lips.

"Eat, Maggie," she encouraged her. "You must keep up your strength."

"Aye, I'll eat," Maggie said with a sigh, letting her head collapse back on the hard mattress. "I'm not in the mood

41

for dyin', leastways until we get to the New World and I find out what happens to you. Lord knows, you need someone to look after you."

"Oh, I do," said Heather, smiling despite the situation. "And just who is nursing whom?"

"Whom!" Maggie exclaimed with a groan. "Oh, you bloody princess! You'll eat the bastards up."

"I think it's your anger that keeps you so lively, Maggie," Heather returned.

"Aye, and me own good luck, not withstandin' all the blokes and dames and gov'ners that try'n walk over me bones!" Maggie turned her face away from the last of the soup, pursing her lips petulantly.

"You make your own good luck, Maggie," Heather said somberly. "Just as I'm determined to make my own."

Maggie raised her head briefly to look at her and then let it fall back.

"Be off with ye," she said and then groaned. "I ain't the only one needin' you."

Indeed, Maggie wasn't. When Heather arrived at the cabin housing the ship's petty officers, she was aghast at their condition. Unwashed and lying in their own filth, they stank and were wet with sweat and urine. Young Billy O'Toole usually accompanied her on this visit, but today he, too, was bedridden. The ship was pitching and rolling so much that Heather felt her stomach was not ready for this further assault, but she steeled herself. After chiding the hapless, wizened cook who arrived with a weak tea, she made him help her bathe, change and feed the men. They were all wasted and thin, but three of the four were no longer feverish and, although weak, seemed actually to be getting better.

"If they get food and attention, they'll do fine, I'm sure," Heather said, throwing the cook a look of reproach.

"Nay, don't ye be pointin' yer finger at meself, fer as I'm standing here, they might all be dead sure now, lass, if'n I didna look after 'em. I may not have the soft hands of a bit of woman like yerself, but I done what I could." He scratched his chest with a rough hand and looked as tired as Heather.

"Cookie, I'm sorry. I believe you," Heather said. "Let's look in on the captain."

As they made their way through the darkened passageways, Heather became aware of how much her skin itched with the cold, dried sweat of her long day's exertions. Her hair fell down her back in a tangled mass of burnished curls, and her dress was wretchedly crumpled and sagging. When she ran into Duncan Crawley outside the captain's cabin, she resented his immaculate dress and the strong smell of his cologne.

"Good afternoon, Miss Woode," Crawley said with the slightest of bows. "I see you also are about to pay Captain McFadden a visit."

"It is hardly a social occasion, Mr. Crawley," Heather replied stiffly, and without further conversation followed the cook into the cabin.

Captain McFadden lay on a large bunk in his relatively luxurious cabin, his thin, deeply lined face unshaven and filmed with sweat. Through glazed eyes, he acknowledged Heather's ministrations with a husky "Thanks."

"How are you feeling today, Captain?" Crawley asked from behind Heather.

Captain McFadden turned his head to look and managed a small smile. "Not well," he uttered in a weak voice.

"I'm sorry to hear it, sir," Crawley replied. "The ship needs your strong hand." He then walked away from the bed to stand near the large windows.

As Heather finished washing the captain's face, he muttered something to her that sounded like "Bonnie lass you are," which made her smile for the first time in days. Although on deck he had always seemed stern and remote, since she had been nursing him, the captain had often had a kind word for her. When the ship lurched down a huge swell and then stopped abruptly with a shuddering crash, the sick man groaned and clutched Heather's arm.

"Sorry, lass," he said, moaning. "Must be hard on you."

"It's a cruel business for us all, Captain, this flu," she said, lifting a cup of water to his parched lips.

43

He nodded weakly, sipped only once, and then rolled away from Heather with another groan.

In the next few days, Miss Southey's condition worsened, and she grew weaker despite all Heather's efforts. On the very morning when they expected to be nearing the New England coast, her fever raged at its highest. As Heather sat at the bedside, Miss Southey's fingers clawed at her hand.

"Heather," she whispered haltingly. "I'm dying . . . !"

"Miss Southey, you aren't! Don't say it!" She pressed Elizabeth's hand to her cheek to reassure her with her own health and strength.

"No, Heather . . ." Miss Southey slowly drew a rasping breath. "While I can, listen. Take my letters with Bruce's locket in my reticule to the Somersets." She coughed and winced with pain. "Tell them it was my wish to have you taken in. My wish . . ." She trailed off, her breath coming slowly in a gasp.

"Don't say such things!" Heather cried, frightened. "You'll live. Everything is before you."

"Heather . . ." she gasped out, but was unable to go on, a gurgling sound welling up from her chest.

"Elizabeth!" Heather whispered urgently. She watched with horror as Miss Southey lapsed into unconsciousness, her body shuddering. Heather smoothed the coverlets gently, her hands caressing them as if she could rub life back into Elizabeth. Finally aware that there was no sound, no movement, she got up slowly and stared unblinkingly out the porthole at the gray sea. The frozen part inside her gave way as a loud wail escaped her lips. Whirling, Heather fell on her bunk to cry out for Elizabeth, for her father and mother, for the Maggies of the world, and for herself, until all her tears were shed and nothing more would come.

The same two crewmen who had taken away Pauline took away Miss Southey. Heather had washed her body and dressed her in the frock she had once worn to impress Duncan Crawley, but the sailors who were on burial duty

44

indifferently wrapped the body in a sheet and hauled it away. One of them said there would be a service, but he didn't know when.

That afternoon, Crawley's valet appeared with two different crewmen and announced that they were to remove Miss Southey's belongings because the cabin was to be used now for someone else. It seemed strange to Heather that the valet would have anything to do with the removal of Miss Southey's trunks, and as the three men struggled with the heaviest of the trunks—the one containing the silver and jewelry—Heather instinctively slid the reticule with the locket and letters behind the soiled bedclothes.

Later, after making her rounds to visit the sick, she returned dispirited to Miss Southey's cabin. The life she had vaguely hoped to find in the New World seemed instead to be filled with death. Her hopes of finding a cultured family that she could serve seemed crushed by the things she was hearing from Maggie and Jane. The kind Miss Southey, who might have bought her contract or taken her to the Somersets, was now dead. Her only friend, Maggie, was sick and, in any case, powerless. Heather knew, as she sat on her own bunk in the darkened room, that now she was totally dependent on the likes of William Barrett and Duncan Crawley, whose offer of help was not to be trusted.

As she sat there, Billy O'Toole arrived and, shamefaced, explained that he had been ordered to tell her that she would have to move down with the other indentured women. She would have Pauline's berth. Heather merely nodded and began packing her meager goods and straightening up the room.

She was ready to leave when Duncan Crawley entered. Since he hadn't knocked and Heather had just finished changing her clothes, she reddened at his appearance.

"My apologies, Heather," he said, "I . . . ah . . . had been told that you had . . . ah, moved."

"That is my intention, sir," she replied. "But I was only told a few minutes ago."

"It's a shame," Crawley said, looking around the room

45

that, having only one porthole, was dark even though it was still afternoon. "I urged Mr. Barrett to let you stay, but he insisted they needed the room for the ship's business."

"I'm sure he did," Heather said. "I'm afraid I'm coming to know my place in the world."

"No, Heather!" Crawley said with sudden energy. "Your place is not below with the likes of Maggie. It is up here with people like Miss Southey and . . . myself."

"I thank you, but my fortunes seem to dictate otherwise," Heather said, feeling grateful to Mr. Crawley for saying what he did yet also suspicious of the man, despite the fact that he was dressed, as always, with care and elegance.

"Yes," he said with a sigh, "fate has been unkind to you. But in your meeting me, I'm sure it is trying to change your course." He came up to her and took one of her hands in his. "You are a lovely woman, Heather, and I want to help you."

As Mr. Crawley looked at her warmly, Heather felt tears welling into her eyes. It had been so long since anyone had taken care of *her,* and now her only benefactor was this untrustworthy man.

"I don't need your help," she said, feeling herself stiffen, "but your sympathies are much appreciated."

"It is possible that I can get Mr. Barrett to change his mind about making you move down below."

"Don't trouble yourself," Heather said. "I'll take care of myself, and I am needed down there."

Ignoring her comment, Crawley took the distressed young woman's other hand in his and moved closer. "I can do more than simply see to it that you have a nice stateroom," he said. "It is within my power to alter your whole life. If you befriend me, I think I can promise that you will never again have to fear the likes of Mr. Barrett."

"Perhaps so," Heather replied, finding his closeness oppressive, "but I'd still have to fear the likes of you."

Duncan Crawley laughed nervously, baring his slightly crooked teeth. "My intentions are simply to help you," he insisted. "It must seem to you that I've been forward, but you are a lovely woman, Heather. . . ."

Still uncertain how to handle the situation, Heather made the mistake of hesitating, and Crawley put his arms around her and brought her close. "With me, you will always have the best." Abruptly, he lowered his mouth to hers and kissed her.

Startled, Heather pushed the man away.

"I feared your intentions were the same!" she exclaimed angrily.

"I have so much to give you, Heather," Crawley went on without pause, recapturing her hands, "and I ask for so little in return."

"I know what you ask for!" Heather countered, trying to pull away.

"I ask only that you return the genuine affection I feel for you. If you give me that, I assure you, I can vastly improve your lot."

"Let me go!" Heather cried.

"You are young and innocent," Crawley persisted, hurting her with the tightness of his grip. Lowering his voice in what he must have presumed to be a seductive tone, he added, "I've been told I am quite a good lover."

"No!" Heather said sharply. "Can't you see I won't be that sort of woman!" She at last pulled her hands free and began to run to the door, but Crawley grabbed her roughly and swung her back into his arms.

"You are doomed to be that sort of woman, my dear girl," he said. He twisted one of Heather's hands behind her back and pressed her against him, his face only inches away. When he again brought his lips down on hers and pulled her to him, Heather bit him.

In a rage, Crawley pushed her backward onto her bunk and threw himself on top of her, pinning her beneath him. When she scratched at his face with a free hand, he struck a vicious blow across her cheek. Dizzy, she felt his mouth again on hers and, resuming her struggle, began kicking at him with both legs.

Crawley raised himself again and struck her a second time.

"You bitch!" he rasped.

"Let me go!" Heather hissed.

"Not until I've gotten what I want!" His mouth came down a third time on Heather's bruised lips.

Heather was heaving from her struggles to be free, and Crawley was himself breathless from the effort to control her when he suddenly lifted himself up.

Raising herself up while trying to pull herself out from under him, Heather stopped when she saw Crawley's tense expression.

From the deck above came the clamor of rushing feet and shouting and, for a dim moment, Heather thought it might be someone rushing to her aid. Then a male voice came clearly down to them in an anguished shout.

"Pirates!"

Duncan Crawley's handsome features paled.

"My God," he said in a low voice. He got up from the bunk, glanced back once at Heather in a distracted way, and then rushed from the room.

Rigo watched with Noah as the *Prospect* luffed up into the wind a hundred feet away. He shook his head at the irony of the situation. He'd sailed eight hundred miles in nineteen days without sighting a prize, and today, within four hours, he had two—one of them his own Somerset ship carrying, he knew, so little of value as to preclude his bothering to take her. Besides, if her destination was New York and not the British forces in Halifax, then he would have no right to take her anyway. Yet Rigo had had to go through the motions of attacking her since only a Somerset would recognize the *Prospect* and know its plans, and he didn't want his crew to know he was Richard Somerset. Fortunately, Captain McFadden had had the good sense to surrender without bothering to fire back, probably because he, in turn, recognized the *Contessa* beneath her thin disguise and altered name of the *Conte*. Or perhaps he knew he was being stopped by a Colonial privateer who would set him free.

Rigo knew he would have to board this ship as he had

the *Mandrake* and warn McFadden not to betray who Rigo was to anyone else. The old captain had strong rebel sympathies and would protect him, but Rigo would have to disguise himself to avoid recognition by some of the *Prospect*'s crew who might have sailed with him.

"What are we going to do, Captain?" Noah asked from his side as they both stared down at the pinnace being prepared to transport Rigo for boarding.

"We'll have to treat her as any prize," he answered. "Although more gently, perhaps," he added, smiling at Noah, who, like him, knew the *Prospect*.

"What does she carry?"

"Nothing of value. Even if she were a legitimate prize, we'd be robbing the poor."

A shout from below indicated that the pinnace was in the water and ready, and Noah and Rigo went down to it. The two officers and five armed crewmen were then rowed across the short stretch of water to the *Prospect*. As they approached, Rigo pulled his scarf up over his mouth. Since he was already wearing a borrowed beaverskin, foul-weather hood, all but his eyes were masked. As he climbed up the rope ladder to board, he decided to alter even his accustomed walk and posture, as well, at least until alone with McFadden.

On deck, he was surprised to be greeted by the first mate, a man named Clubb whom Rigo had never met.

"What's your destination?" Rigo asked loudly.

"New York," the mate answered. "What's this all about?"

"I'd like to speak to your captain," Rigo commanded.

"He's down sick," the mate replied. "The whole ship is infected. The only thing you'll get from us is disease."

"I want your captain!" Rigo persisted, concerned with the news of McFadden's illness and the distress of the ship.

"Bosun!" the mate barked. "Take this man below to Captain McFadden."

After ordering Noah and his five men to search the ship and make certain it was carrying nothing intended for the British army, Rigo followed the bosun below. He had once captained the *Prospect* on a trans-Atlantic voyage and was depressed to see that the ship was now dirty, that lines were loose and uncoiled, and that the few crewmen topside seemed thin and weak. As they were nearing the captain's cabin, he noticed a well-dressed man scurrying into one of the passenger cabins.

"A moment," Rigo said to the bosun and, without knocking, swung open the cabin door.

"I've nothing of worth! Nothing!" the man said when confronted by the towering Rigo. He was dressed in the height of fashion, and the smell of his cologne was overwhelming. Rigo disliked the man on sight.

"Empty your pockets," he demanded, drawing his sword.

Duncan Crawley produced a snuff box and a few coins and looked up expectantly. "I fear you are wasting your time," he said, trying a smile that looked more like a grimace.

"The rest!" Rigo snapped. "Hurry! I'm not a patient man!" Rigo stuck the point of his sword out toward Crawley's shirt, his legs in a stance of readiness to lunge.

Crawley tremblingly produced a watch that was clearly of considerable value. He put it next to the snuff box on the little table.

Rigo swept the entire hoard off onto the floor with the blade of his sword.

"Next time," he said, "I suggest you value your life more than those trinkets." He made a quick cut on Crawley's ruffled shirt, the frothy white ruffling falling to the floor.

A look of terror crept across Crawley's face as he looked down to see if he had been slashed. Then he flushed.

"When the British fleet catches up with you," he said, his face red with anger, "I trust they will make you pay for this insolence."

"Sir," Rigo said, "the English can do nothing worse to me than they've already done."

"They can kill you!" Crawley countered, his face contorted with hatred.

"True. But it will take more than a London dandy with

50

empty pockets and an overflowing mouth to do it." He turned and went out.

Captain McFadden was somewhat delirious and barely able to recognize Rigo, who dismissed the bosun and applied wet towels to the captain's feverish brow. He tried explaining the situation as best he could, but when Captain McFadden tried to talk, all Rigo could grasp was something that sounded like "bonnie lass," and he wondered whether any of his instructions had gotten through. Nevertheless, if McFadden recovered, Rigo knew he could count on him to act in Rigo's interests. After ten minutes, he arose to leave.

There was only one other cabin assigned for use by the gentry and he decided to check it. He strode down the passageway, knocked twice loudly, and then swung open the door. He was stunned to see a beautiful young woman in the act of hurriedly straightening her dress with her hair tumbling in chestnut waves around her face. Looking up, the woman gasped and stood still. For a long moment, the two of them simply stood staring at each other.

Then realizing that the dark and wild-looking intruder was a pirate, Heather grabbed the water pitcher and, with skirts whirling, hurled it at him.

Rigo quickly ducked as the water splashed over him and shards of pottery fell at his feet. Leaping forward, he easily grasped her slender wrists in an iron grip.

"Well, at least I encounter someone aboard this ship willing to fight," he said and laughed. "But I haven't sailed the seas to lose my head to a water jug." His blue eyes sparkled. "And who are you?"

"Heather Woode!" she blurted without thinking, all the while trying to pull her wrists free. "You're hurting me!" She stopped a moment to look up at him and felt the rush of blood to her cheeks as she saw his eyes sweep over her appraisingly.

"I'll let you go if you promise not to attack me again." There was amusement in his voice.

"Do I have yours not to attack me?" she retorted.

He raised a black eyebrow and chuckled. "You have my promise." He released her wrists, and she stood rubbing them tenderly. His closeness had sent her pulses running, and Heather felt captured by this pirate, by the strength he exuded just standing so solidly before her.

"If you're looking for valuables, I haven't any," she said, trying to distract those piercing eyes.

"That, my lady, is false on the face of it," he answered.

Heather flushed. "I'm not your lady and I wouldn't give you a penny if I had it!"

"So the last hapless victim told me," Rigo said, looking around the cabin. "A ship of paupers, it would seem."

Heather blanched. She knew that up to now he had been playing with her and enjoying it, but now it returned to her that he might have killed and could be a dangerous man. Would he hesitate to harm a woman? He had one hand casually at rest on his sword, the other on his hip. Heather caught sight of a curved knife handle protruding from the topside of his boot. If he attacked, she might be able to reach it.

Rigo laughed heartily when he saw the direction her eyes took. "Have no fear. Your life is safe, and I've not enough time for taking anything else," he said wickedly, his eyes alight.

"Believe me, had you anything else in mind, *your* life wouldn't be safe!" she tossed back at him. Even as she spoke, she was aware that her momentary fear of him had disappeared.

"Well said," Rigo replied. "I almost wish I had time to test the theory." He reached out a hand and flicked one of her long, silken curls, his hand brushing against her soft, creamy neck.

Heather stepped back, feeling a tingling heat where his skin touched hers. Her hand went to the spot and her eyes widened.

"Don't be alarmed," Rigo said softly. "It's natural for fire to leap where it meets tinder."

"Apparently, I didn't douse you quite enough!"

He laughed. "Lady, I've got to rush off. My men will wonder what treasure I've found and why I'm not sharing it." He moved toward the door. "Is there another like you aboard?" he asked. "More like a kitten than a lioness?" His lips curved in a smile.

Heather flashed him a defiant look and was about to retort but was suddenly sobered by the memory of Miss Southey's death. "No," she said quietly.

Rigo hesitated a moment, reluctant to leave. He saluted her. "We'll meet again. Another promise." He stood in the door frame, his tall, dark figure filling it as his eyes met hers.

Heather felt unwillingly caressed by the look and a wave of warmth rushed through her.

"I've no fear of that. I'm sure New York is free of men like yourself," she said, trying to shake off the strange and unwanted feelings he aroused in her.

"Oh, you'd be surprised," Rigo concluded with a smile and then left.

In another fifteen minutes, he and his crew had left the *Prospect* and were back aboard the *Contessa*. The men of the privateer were a little disappointed that the ship was headed for the Colonies and, thus, couldn't be sacked but soon were too busy raising sail to complain.

The two ships' sails began to fill, and as the vessels glided in opposite directions in the soft twilight air, Noah Wiggens came up beside Rigo at the rail. For a moment, the two men watched the receding blossom of white that was the *Prospect* on the horizon.

"No treasure there," Noah finally said with a sigh. For a while, Rigo said nothing, his mind strangely filled with the image of chestnut hair and sparkling green eyes.

"Only one," he finally said with an enigmatic smile. "Only one."

Chapter Six

As the *Prospect* sailed past the last western islets of Long Island before entering New York harbor two days later, she was intercepted at dawn by the British squadron blockading the harbor. When the investigating British frigate had determined that the *Prospect* was American-owned, it commandeered the ship and its crew to sail to Halifax to help transport General Howe's men and supplies to their next destination in the Colonies. Only the passengers and their belongings were permitted to transfer to land.

The four-hour trip from the *Prospect*, anchored off Sandy Hook, to New York City was accomplished by putting the passengers aboard a small fishing sloop that the British fleet was permitting to return to port. Heather found herself ordered, along with Maggie, who was thin but perky after the flu, and the still sniffling Jane, to gather her belongings and climb down into the *Marybelle*, where the smell and scales of fish seemed to permeate everything. William Barrett, Duncan Crawley, six more indentured servants, and almost a dozen assorted commoners were crowded in. They were now, all of them, a huddling, sneezing, coughing, exasperated mass sitting atop their trunks as the sloop crept through the early morning chill and dampness toward shore.

Shivering, Heather noticed but ignored a rawness in her throat. She couldn't get the flu now! She concentrated on what would happen next on this incredible journey as Barrett and Crawley talked about the colonial uprising and its effect upon their business interests. Crawley seemed more knowledgeable and had a commission from King George to purchase ships for the British Navy. There was no doubt in his mind that England would quell the rebellious elements quickly. He sneered at the idea of freedom as little more than anarchy and likened it to taking a sword to one's own mother. For a moment Crawley relived his anger over the pirate who had slashed his shirt, and hoped the man hung soon. Barrett only wanted to conclude his auctioning of the indentured servants and be on his way back to home and civilization.

Listening, Heather was amazed that the two of them could talk as if no one else existed. She supposed that, for them, they did not. She also found it interesting that Duncan Crawley, who was usually condescending to Barrett, seemed now to bend his ear to that fat toad as they conferred with rapt attention on some matter of importance to them both.

The information she was gathering willy-nilly about the colonial rebellion had a chilling effect on Heather. Her concern was not for her life but that in some way, the abnormal events in wartime might mean more difficulties for herself. There was no doubt in her mind that she had to escape from Barrett and make another path for herself. She had been thinking of little else since Miss Southey's death. If Duncan Crawley was livid over his encounter with the pirate, Heather was furious at Barrett for his perfidy. It was almost beyond her comprehension that the others would accept being auctioned off, except that they had never known anything but poverty and servitude and scrounging for twopence just to eat. A promise of regular meals, a steady roof, and eventual freedom in a new land was simply more than they had ever been offered in their lives. An auction of their services was their ticket to opportunity—what matter that the work was dirty, hard, or demeaning, or that they would be abused. Thus, she sympathized with Maggie and Jane for taking such a path even as she rebelled at it for herself. She wished she could do more for them than just sympathize.

In a moment of anxiety aboard the *Prospect*, Heather had confided to Maggie her vague plan to escape the machinations of Barrett. Maggie had at first scoffed, calling her a "bloody idiot"—for what did Heather know about what lay in store for her without a shilling to her name nor a door to knock upon for help. It was then that Heather told Maggie how she hoped to find the Somersets, give them Miss Southey's letters and locket, tell them the sad story of Elizabeth's untimely death, and throw herself on their mercy. Maggie had pursed her lips in thought, decided the plan was a bold one, and had agreed to aid her if she could.

There was yet another fact in favor of her plan. Maggie had overheard Crawley promise the first mate to see that the Somersets received Miss Southey's trunks, and that man had given his consent for Crawley to take them. Maggie had next startled Heather with the idea that Crawley and Barrett were in cahoots and never intended to let the contents of the trunks go anywhere but into their pockets. Knowing the two of them, Heather thought that Maggie just might be right. Surely the Somersets would find this information valuable. Remembering all this, Heather tightly clutched her reticule that now contained Miss Southey's letters and locket as the plodding, overladen fishing sloop transported her to her fate.

When they were finally able to disembark, Barrett marched his charges toward a small waterfront tavern called The King's Arms. As they walked along, Heather looked all around, trying to take everything in at once. The scene was unexpectedly bucolic but new and different. It didn't seem to have the varied layers of London, whose surface was like a dowager queen—opulent, resplendent in lace and diadems; whose next layer, the petticoats—bankers and merchants like her father, industrious and shrewd—provided the warmth and props for the dowager's gowns; and then beneath all, in voluminous bloomers, the teeming populace that supported the outer layers.

Heather hadn't known what to expect but was happily surprised with the richness she saw. The wharf was bustling and energetic. Carts and wagons were being loaded and unloaded with barrels, sacks, and baskets of goods and materials. The men were dressed in practical leather jerkins, comfortable breeches, and rolled-up shirts of homespun cloth. Women and men were vending their goods and wares from carts parked along the streets, calling out their specialties from time to time. Carriages jogged along, and she caught a glimpse of an elegantly dressed couple that reminded her of her present rumpled shabbiness. Heather looked down the broad streets to see neat wooden and brick houses and solid-looking public buildings. If there were layers of society, such as London's, they were not much in evidence. The people had an air of health and vigor about them. Here, all seemed in flux, undecided, with lots of margin for change. Heather couldn't help feeling excited, and, she thought, the island was small. If she were lucky, it might not be too hard to find the Somersets.

Barrett locked the ladies into two adjoining rooms of The King's Arms inn after a lengthy bargaining scene that Heather had found embarrassing. The tavernkeeper didn't want ladies "of that sort" in his establishment, but Barrett paraded Heather and stated she was "a lady of quality and not a frippet, either, nor were any of the other girls!" Jane had roared with laughter, and Maggie had joined in the snickering. Heather, seeing the situation through their eyes, finally saw it as amusing, too.

No sooner was the door to their room locked than Heather began to pace back and forth impatiently.

"Ye'll wear out that floor, Heather," Maggie said to her, plumping herself down on the big bed while admiring the feather pillows, smelling the fresh, clean linen, and exclaiming over the worn but beautiful patchwork quilt.

"The women 'ere do fine needlework," she said, tracing the pattern. "Lookee 'ere, it's stars, big stars made o' worn-out frocks and stuff," she exclaimed wonderingly. "I never in me life was in a bed this big and soft."

"Maggie, you won't let me down, will you?" Heather stopped her pacing and looked out the window at the busy waterfront and then back at Maggie, who was sprawled in satisfaction on the bed.

"Nay, don't you be frettin'. I spoke to Billy and he's as good as got the key, but I regret involvin' 'im. He's a heart o' gold." She sighed, flipped onto her stomach, and propped her chin in both hands. "Barrett'd have 'im whipped for aidin' ye, Heather." Maggie eyed her seriously.

"I'll repay him someday, somehow, and you, too. I will, Maggie, even if," Heather's voice lowered to a whisper, "I don't get to the Somersets or they won't have me." She ran to the window and stared out. "They must! I won't be sold like a cow in heat." She turned around. "Are you sure you don't want to come with me?"

"Aye, I'm sure. I ain't afraid as you o' losin' me maidenhead," she laughed, "'n I never heard o' no colonist bein' so cruel to an indentured lass what a little female coaxin' can't fix. Mayhap the tavernkeeper can be persuaded to buy me papers. Tavern work's a sight better'n scrubbin' a bleedin' scullery or milkin' a cow fer some ploddin' farmer. I'll find me way. Yer the one that's in fer it and takin' yer chances." Maggie sat up and kicked off her dirty, worn-out shoes.

"I'll take those risks, Maggie. I will not be used unless I choose."

"Tsk!" said Maggie, clucking her tongue and getting up. She went over to the tall dresser and peered into the small looking glass nailed above it.

"If I had the looks o' ye, I'd be the belle of New York in two months' time!" Maggie pinched her cheeks for color. "More's the pity! Ye've got it all and don't know how to use it!" Maggie cocked her head and giggled, looking at Heather mischievously. "Leastways, not yet!"

Heather smiled. "You're a tease, Maggie, but I never intend letting myself be a victim again. I made a mistake in London with Barrett, a rash and foolish one, but I'm not going to let it destroy my life." She was feeling very tired—almost feverish—and her throat was hurting, but her anxiety made her push herself, and she paced restlessly as if every step she took would take her farther away from her present predicament and into a future where all was perfect.

"Did ye never think, Heather, that ye was brought here on purpose? That this is yer fate? An' ye'll be lucky?"

"Maggie, that's ridiculous! How can you, of all people, think that? Pooh! Fate? And *damn* such resignation. I know this, that even in the best of worlds, with my parents alive and in money, I would be a commodity of sorts. I've learned! And I'm going to make my own way, you'll see."

"Gawd! But ye takes it all so serious." Maggie smiled. "Yer escape's as good as done, I tell ye, as soon as darkness comes."

Heather finally relaxed, pacified, and set about getting herself washed and dressed.

With Maggie's help, she swept up her hair, letting four fat curls drape elegantly down her neck. Her wheat-colored traveling dress, with its tucks at the waist and lace at the cuffs and bosom, fit her ripening shape perfectly, enhancing her tall, slender figure. Maggie, too, had finally divested herself of her rags, washing and scrubbing herself until she shone like a painted china doll. The blue dress Heather had given her was exactly the color of Maggie's eyes—eyes that were sparkling with the delight of her new gown.

Heather slipped into the fitted short jacket that matched her dress then stood before the looking glass and pinned a large black ribbon low to the back of her head with two black hat pins. Standing back, she saw that Maggie was looking at her. "You look better'n the Queen's rose!" Maggie exclaimed.

Heather worried. "Perhaps it's a mistake to turn myself out so. I should have thought . . . but no. Even the colonists must have fashionably dressed women. The Somersets will surely recognize that I am more than . . ." She halted, looking at Maggie apologetically.

"Nay, Heather. I am used to bawdy tales, a heap o' swearin' such as would scald yer ears, and I've been called more'n Maggie by more'n one lady. Don't ye fear sayin' what's on yer tongue." She shrugged. "Whore is the best of 'em." She giggled.

"My quick tongue will be my ruin. Maggie, you look like a pretty girl fresh from the country and about to go to a dance. You look lovely."

Maggie grinned, chortling merrily as she bent down to straighten the folds of Heather's dress.

"Ye has hours to go," she whispered, "afore evenin' and Barrett be well into his cups so ye can slip out." She lowered her voice even more, as if someone might hear. "It'll be done, Heather, and ye'll have yer chance. Rest yer bones now and gather yer strength, for I don't like the sound of yer voice. It's raspy." She turned to go into the adjoining room. "I'm goin' in to talk a bit with Jane. She's less a madwoman than ye be. Leastways, this day." Then she left and Heather carefully lay down on the bed. Her nerves were wound tight as a spring and a million questions went round in her head, but she was soon asleep.

The next thing she knew, Maggie was shaking her.

"Heather, ye sleep like the dead! Wake up! Supper's been brought up long ago and yer tea is cold."

Heather sat up shocked. It was dark and her heart pounded. Had she missed her opportunity?

"Maggie, what's happening?"

"Nay, don't get yerself worked up. Eat. Ye'll be on yer way soon. Barrett's doin' well and primed as a greased goose. He's struttin' down in the hall like a peacock sayin' as how he'd made a good penny this time." She sat down to Heather's food herself since Heather pushed it away. "Ain' ye goin' to eat none?" she asked Heather between mouthfuls of cold meat.

"No, I couldn't, Maggie. Not a bite." Heather got up

and began straightening her dress and fixing her hair, her eyes bright with more than increasing excitement. She was about to ask Maggie about her escape plan again when there was a knock at the door.

"Come!" Maggie shouted.

The door opened and Billy O'Toole hesitantly entered.

"Ye be early," Maggie said to him. "Our plan ain't to begin 'til ten."

Billy's eyes were on the floor. "I don't be coming for that," he almost whispered.

"Well, speak up, ye dummy," Maggie said, reaching for a crust of bread. "We can't read yer mind."

"Mr. Barrett sent me to fetch Miss Woode," he said, his eyes still on the floor. "He . . . he sold her contract to . . . Mr. Crawley."

Heather paled and murmured, "No." She swung about as if looking for a way to escape. "Maggie, what shall I do?"

With unaccustomed deliberation, Maggie put down the bread she was chewing on. "If it were me," she said, "I'd jump at the chance, him bein' rich an' all." She had stopped eating and now wiped her mouth with the back of her hand.

"Maggie, don't do that!" Heather admonished in her agitation. She sat on the edge of the bed, too weak to stand. "He wouldn't dare! I won't suffer the humiliation of it!"

"He's a devil, he is, but a sight better than a lot o' others not half as set up as 'e is. He'd be easy twistin' on yer finger, Heather. I'm sure o' it!" Maggie got up to help Heather with her boots.

"Maggie, can't you understand? I won't be his mistress. Oh, what's the use!"

"Then ye'll be someone else's, less I miss my guess," Maggie said with a shrug, then added, "Maybe he'll marry ye."

Heather could feel tears of frustration beading in the corners of her eyes. "After all he's done? I'd rather bed with an eel!" She stood up defiantly.

"He's not to yer taste then." Maggie also stood. "Well, there ye be. Billy, ye think we might sneak Heather down the stairs now?"

Billy, still standing where he had entered as if rooted to the spot, simply shook his head. "Mr. Barrett and Mr. Crawley are at the bottom of the stairs waitin' on us."

"The window," Heather suddenly said, turning and running to the one window in the room. "If we can fashion a rope. . . ."

A violent knocking on the door stopped her. Billy, with a fearful glance at Heather, slowly moved back to the door and opened it. Standing there were Duncan Crawley and William Barrett.

"Heather, where are you going?" Crawley said, taking in her outfit, a bare smile on his lips. "Did you think the auction was today? Surely you weren't planning to go to it unescorted." His eyes narrowed knowingly.

"Heather Woode, I'm rid of you at last," said Barrett, stepping over to her and clearing his beefy throat. "I see you got yerself up right well, 'n it's a boon," he added, rubbing his fat red hands together, "for I've found a good place for you with Mr. Crawley."

Heather let out one long wail and then went stony silent. As she stood in a daze, Crawley took her arm and, ordering Billy O'Toole and Maggie to make certain all her things were in her trunk, escorted a stunned Heather outside the tavern and into a waiting carriage. After he had given a certain address and instructions to his driver to head into Manhattan, they waited until Heather's trunk was added to the carriage.

With barely a tearful wave at Maggie, who hung out of the window blowing her kisses, Heather found herself jouncing along into the dark streets of Manhattan. She turned with fury to Duncan Crawley.

"Damn you!" she cried hoarsely. "I will not be yours!"

Duncan Crawley merely smiled. "You already are, my dear," he said.

Chapter Seven

HEATHER FELT A WAVE OF FATIGUE AND LEANED AGAINST THE corner of the carriage as far from Duncan Crawley as she could. She feigned sleep, needing time to think. Fortunately, Crawley and his valet were distracted by their search for the correct address and ignored her as she stared disconsolately into the dark streets as the carriage swayed and bounced over the rough, bumpy surface.

"I won't go mad," Heather vowed to herself. "The thing to fear most is losing heart, giving up and becoming what the Crawleys and the Barretts of the world wish me to be—servant or whore!" When two hot tears ran down her cheek, she let them course their way without check.

They were not far from the wharf in a section of town that was full of townhouses and public buildings and even a park. Occasionally, another carriage would pass, and a man with a lighted torch walked by. Heather supposed he was checking and lighting the street lamps, which were few and far between. The man's actions drew an exclamation of disgust from Duncan Crawley regarding the rudimentary town lighting and speculations on his part about a curfew.

Suddenly, the carriage lurched to a stop, and the valet got out. Heather heard Crawley call her name but still pretended sleep. There was a ruckus outside, with someone loudly arguing with the valet, and then Crawley, too, alighted. Heather sat up, her heart beating quickly. The house to which the valet and Crawley had gone lay some distance from the darkened street, and it seemed the man in charge was not about to let two strangers enter, whereupon Crawley had to produce papers to prove he had rented quarters there.

Without hesitation, Heather reached for her reticule, forced open the carriage door, and stepped down into the street unnoticed by either the valet or Crawley, who were barely visible in the darkness thirty feet away. Keeping to the dark shadows and moving as swiftly as her tired legs would carry her, Heather ran, cutting and bending into alleys and down narrow streets. Only when forced to rest a moment or else collapse did she stop to get her bearings. She had no idea where she was going nor did she know the way back to the wharf. Her only thought was to escape and then get directions to the Somersets. She had no time yet to rejoice at her deliverance from her tormentor, for even as she was catching her breath, she could hear distant shouts and a carriage rumbling along a nearby street. A feeling of terror ran through her, and she flew forward again.

There were few street lights, and most houses were either dark or shuttered. Here and there, cats yowled and packs of stray dogs yipped and fought as they roamed the streets. Across the way, a muttering drunk was weaving his way home. Heather picked up her skirts and ran headlong in the direction where she saw the most light, but when a carriage or horseman would come into view, she'd pin herself to the shadows until it had passed by.

She lost track of time as she ran and hid, trying to put distance between her and possible discovery. Then she spied a more open broadway and a well-lit building from which people were emerging to enter waiting carriages. A meeting of some kind had taken place, Heather thought, and gave a sigh of relief. Surely good citizens would be there in numbers. She aimed herself toward the group, her heart in her throat, and forced herself to walk more deliberately and sedately.

"Ho, pretty lady. A night out on the town, heh?" a well-dressed man called to her as he mounted his horse and ran the animal up next to her. He smiled and tipped his tricorn. Heather was bewildered but pretended not to hear his coarse statements, and the man finally veered away laughing. She began to be aware of the stares of a handful of men who seemed to have come out of the building, and none of the faces were friendly. A few made unkind references to street women. Heather stiffened. She then saw two gaily dressed women hovering nearby, obviously not minding being stared at—in fact, they were openly encouraging the attentions of the men. Heather suddenly knew they were plying their trade, and the men thought she was doing the same.

Stumbling, Heather knew she had to get away from there. She must find shelter, a place to stay until morning, when it would be safe to travel. But dare she wait? Crawley would surely waste no time trying to find her. She heard a loud conversation behind her and then shouts. Casting a glance behind her, Heather saw two men running toward her. She gasped, "They're coming for me!" and ran as if her life depended upon it.

"Stop! Stop!" a deep and harsh voice called out.

She turned down a dark side street and slammed against a tall figure. Off balance, she sprawled painfully in the dirt. The man, recovering his balance, growled, "What the . . . !" and then, seeing Heather, stooped hurriedly to help her up.

"Oh, please! I've got to go!" She twisted free of his grasp and, hiking up her skirts, began her flight once more. She heard the angry shouts of her pursuers coming closer, but she hadn't taken three steps when the man she had run into grabbed her wrist, pulled her into his arms, and lowered his mouth to hers in a fierce kiss.

Heather was too shocked to do anything but yield to his

hard masculinity. Slowly, the man's kiss softened, and he pressed her tightly to him. When he finally released her, though still holding her close against his warm body, she realized that her pursuers had passed by within yards of them and she hadn't even noticed.

"Come with me," the man whispered.

"No," Heather responded instinctively, aware of a strange tingling of her lips and a rush of warmth inside her. When she trembled in his arms and took a shaky breath, he added, "You have two choices before you. You can come with me now to an inn where I know you'll be safe, or," he paused, "you can take your chances on the street."

As Heather raised her eyes to the stranger's face, trying in the dark to read his expression, she was still disturbed by the unaccustomed sensations apparently caused by their long kiss. Would she be safe in a public house with this man? She wondered whether she should now fear this stranger more than those she fled. His voice had the tone of a gentleman, but . . .

"Who are you?" she whispered hoarsely. As she tried to free herself, she realized that she half wished she could simply give up and lean on his strength.

"Captain Rigo," he answered in a low voice. "And you'll either have to trust me or go your own way. Which is it to be?" When Heather still seemed to be frozen with indecision, he took her arm firmly and guided her hurriedly along until he reached a small courtyard and a darkened back door. He yanked down on a chain that rang a bell inside. While Heather was catching her breath, he banged impatiently until, finally, a light came on and the door opened.

"Yes? What is it?" a stoop-shouldered man asked, holding a lantern aloft.

"Let us in and shut the door," Rigo ordered. "The lady and I would like to discuss some private business in a quiet place. Tell Daniel I need him."

The man hesitated and then motioned them forward into the hallway, quickly closing the door behind them.

"Will you require food and drink, sir?"

"Have you had supper?" Rigo asked Heather, looking down at her.

"No," she said uncertainly. Something about his manner and voice echoed within her, but she couldn't pin down what it was that was so familiar about this man.

"We'll have a light supper and ale," he ordered easily, and the other man left.

A short, chubby man with a puffy face and receding hairline came forward quickly.

"Ahh, Captain Rigo," he said, clasping the tall man's arm with a smile. "Always good to see you. My man said you wanted something private. I've just the room down the hallway, second door on the right. Please seat yourself. We'll be serving straight away."

"Thanks, Daniel," Rigo said, ushering Heather through the door. "I count on your discretion." Rigo winked at Daniel and guided Heather to a small, homey room. A clean, white cloth was on the table and a small fire burned in a blackened hearth. There were two other small tables, highly polished, and several long benches, all unoccupied at present. Heather heard the noise of several men drinking coming from another room. She looked up at Rigo, a dart of fear in her eyes.

"Trust me. You're safe here," he said, reading her mind. After closing the door of the room, he pulled out a chair for her.

Heather hadn't yet had the chance to look closely at the man called Captain Rigo, but as he seated himself opposite her, she took him all in. He was tall, darkly handsome, and dressed as a gentleman, all of which gave her confidence, but not enough to stem entirely the fear of him or the memory of his kiss.

"Now, why don't you begin by telling me what this is all about?"

"Captain Rigo," she began, looking into his startling blue eyes. She hesitated as something jolted her memory back to the *Prospect*.

"The pirate! You're the pirate!" she blurted out in surprise.

"No one's perfect," Rigo replied, his teeth flashing as he smiled, his eyes alive as they searched hers.

Heather moved back, ready to make a dash, but his hand reached out and grasped her wrist.

"Sit down. You're not going anywhere until I get an explanation of this race you were running and who those men were." His tone brooked no refusal, and Heather sat tensely for a moment after he released her wrist but kept his hand on the table.

"How is it that you roam free while I'm pursued?" she asked in a rush, disbelieving the whole topsy-turvy order of the world she found herself in.

"The Colonies are at war with England," Rigo said with sudden seriousness. "My attacking English ships is in accordance with the law. I'm an American. And why are *you* being pursued, I'd like to know."

"But to the English, you are a pirate!"

"True, but that doesn't explain why you're running like a thief in the night, hm?"

Heather blushed. "I'm not a thief!" she exclaimed.

"You don't look like a thief," Rigo teased, "except of hearts, maybe." As he regarded her steadily, waiting for her to explain, there was a knock at the door. The tavernkeeper came in with dishes of cold meats, hot baked potatoes, and steaming greens. Placing the food and tankards of ale before them with a lighted candle, he smiled at Rigo and left.

As Rigo cut the meat and began to serve them both, Heather took a closer look at him and was taken aback. He was disturbingly handsome. Barely tamed curling black hair framed his head. He had fine, even features, a strong jawline, and a full, sensuous mouth. His well-fitting gray breeches, dark blue frock coat with silver buttons, and white shirt ruffled at the neck all manifested both taste and wealth. Pirating, she surmised, must yield a good earning.

"Do I meet your approval?" he questioned with a grin, catching her guileless perusal. When Heather blushed and looked away, Rigo picked up his fork. "I know you must be hungry," he said to ease her embarrassment, "and the chase has given me an appetite. Please. Join me." With a smile and a nod, he began eating heartily.

Looking down at the food, Heather realized she hadn't eaten since morning. When her stomach gave a small growl, she flushed again and then took up her fork. The two ate in silence. For the first time since meeting him, Heather was barely aware of Rigo, so ravenous and thirsty was she. As she was mopping up the last of her supper with a crusty piece of bread, she looked up to see Rigo watching her, the corners of his mouth turned up in a smile. Heather smiled back.

"I haven't eaten since . . . breakfast," she explained. "Thank you . . . and thank you for rescuing me."

"You're welcome," he answered easily, lighting up a cheroot. "Now tell me, what did I rescue you from?"

Heather let a finger trail down the cool pewter tankard of ale as she tried to decide what she could tell this disturbing man.

"You have a bruise on your cheek," Rigo added quietly when she failed to answer his question. "What happened?"

Heather touched her cheek lightly, startled by his observation. The memory of Crawley's striking her aboard the *Prospect* still aroused anger. She sat up straighter and glared at Rigo, having lost her fear of him.

"The man who struck me had previously offered me his protection," she began with a toss of her head that sent her curls cascading down her shoulders. "I wasn't deceived by him, and what he wanted of me was very clear, but when he first met me, he, too, had seemed a . . . gentleman." Heather paused to meet Rigo's unblinking gaze. "Although you've rescued me from humiliation at the hands of those men, I am not as foolish as I was a month ago. You want the truth? The truth is I'm alone and penniless, but not so stupid as to trust a pirate, and especially not one who takes liberties even before he knows my name!" Heather's cheeks were heightened with color, her green eyes sparkling. She wasn't aware how pretty a picture she presented to the intent and admiring Rigo.

"I don't recall offering you my protection," he said

lazily, raising a brow. Calmly exhaling the cheroot smoke and hooking a hand on a pants pocket, he regarded her closely.

Heather sat back in her chair, suddenly deflated. She smoothed her skirts with a trembling hand. "But . . . I thought . . ." Her eyes were troubled as she glanced up at him.

"I do so now," Rigo said, smiling, "*if* you'll tell me who those men were and why they were chasing you."

Before she could decide how to reply, a knock came at the door, and Daniel abruptly came in unannounced.

"I beg your pardon, Captain Rigo."

"It's quite all right, Daniel," Rigo said. "The lady and I have just finished our dinner."

"Yes," Daniel said diffidently. "I'll clear these things away, but . . ."

"What's the trouble, Daniel?"

"A gentleman was just here," Daniel began nervously, "looking for a runaway indentured girl. I told him I didn't know of any here, but . . . I thought you should know." He cleared his throat and avoided looking at Heather, who began examining the empty tankard in front of her with lowered eyes and a stiffened back.

"Interesting," Rigo said. "You didn't happen to catch the name of the gentleman, did you?"

"Sorry, Captain. I didn't."

"No matter," Rigo said. "Let us hope the girl is soon taken into the appropriate hands." He smiled at Heather.

"Yes, sir. It's not safe for a girl alone, not at night. I've heard of indentured lads running off, but a girl! Why, she must be a desperate one. What's to become of her?"

"What, indeed?" Rigo echoed, smiling, and pressed a coin into Daniel's hand. "Take care that we're not disturbed again, will you?"

Daniel nodded and, after refilling their glasses and clearing away the dishes, left. Rigo hoisted the tankard of ale and drank from it, then returned it slowly to the table.

"Well?" he asked calmly, raising an eyebrow.

Heather lowered her eyes for a moment and then looked

up at him defiantly. "The man is Duncan Crawley," she announced. "He was a passenger on the *Prospect* and I was . . . running from him. He's . . . a thief and . . . a spider!"

"With many arms and legs, it seems. Is he the same man who struck you?" Rigo asked.

"Yes," Heather answered quietly.

Rigo took another long drink of his ale. "A man who strikes a woman should be hoisted in a halyard by the thumbs," he said sharply, his mind flashing to the dandy he had confronted on the *Prospect*. "If I had known a few days ago who your abuser was, I might have put my sword in a few inches deeper."

Heather looked up, startled, and didn't doubt him. He was powerfully built, and she thought he would be a formidable enemy to those who chose to align themselves against him, but there was also something about his bearing, a sureness of purpose and a confidence of his own abilities, that gave her a measure of confidence in him. Then there was the light of humor and aliveness in his eyes when he was amused or delighted. A man who could play joyfully and without malice could not be altogether untrustworthy. Perhaps he *could* help her.

"Was he legally your master?" Rigo asked.

Heather let out a shuddering breath, her eyes darting to the door as if Crawley might come through it at any moment.

"He bought my contract from William Barrett, that toad!" she burst out. "He knew full well that Mr. Crawley wanted more of me than—keeping house." Heather blushed, and her eyes suddenly misted with threatening tears.

"And Crawley struck you to get it!" Rigo said, his face fierce with an anger she'd never seen before.

"He tried, but with no success!" she exclaimed, horrified that this man might think otherwise. "That was when we heard the cry of pirates and you arrived." Heather watched as Rigo's face slowly lost its ferocity and the beginnings of a smile appeared.

71

"And then you nearly decapitated me with the water pitcher," he said.

"A warning."

"An attack!" he corrected and laughed. "You're quite a woman, Heather, and unusual, as I'm sure you've guessed by now. Tell me, how did you come to be indentured? You're beautiful, with gracious speech and manners, and you have obviously known better times."

Heather raised her eyes to his and felt a stirring inside her. She found she wanted to unburden herself to this Captain Rigo, and she didn't question why. She only knew that somehow she had traveled the path from not trusting to feeling at home with him. In a low voice, she began telling him of her father's misfortune, of the terrors of being in a debtor's prison, and of how all their friends had abandoned them. Then she told of her meeting Barrett after her father's death in the prison and of her impulsive decision to come to the Colonies to escape the unhappy past and her humiliation. She had known nothing of indentured servants, but now that she knew something firsthand, she had sympathy for their plight.

"And now, here I am, and while I think I've good reason to be wary of you, I am truly grateful." She gave him a beautiful smile.

Rigo's eyes lit with blue fire and the distance between them seemed to evaporate. Heather felt invaded by his look and a warmth flooded through her.

"How easily the truth can change us," he said, his voice low. "Now I'll tell you something, with no apologies—just an explanation. When you ran into me, I might have fought with your pursuers, but I recognized you, even in the dark. I didn't know what was going on, but since I had wanted to kiss you from the moment I first saw you on that ship, I used that little ruse to throw them off. You'll have to admit it worked." Rigo stood up and went over to the hearth. He kicked at a log with a booted toe before turning to face her.

Heather shifted uneasily in her chair, unused to such declarations from a man. Again, she felt like running away, but now for an entirely different reason. She didn't know how she should behave while enjoying a man's attentions and, aware of his eyes flowing over her, she stood up, her skirts swaying around her.

"You have me confused," Heather whispered.

"So you should be," Rigo said softly. "Forgive me." He was watching her, fascinated. "You've caught me, my lady. I'm disarmed, so don't run away. We've just begun." He crossed the few steps to stand towering in front of Heather and took her chin in his warm hand, tilting her face up to his.

"Please . . ." she said.

"Please what? Please don't look at you? When I love everything I see? Please don't help you? When it gives me so much pleasure?"

As Heather reached out to dislodge his hand, her eyes widened when a jolt of passion passed along her hand to her body, completely unnerving her. She felt an opening of all her senses to his nearness.

Rigo lowered his mouth to hers, at first gently, just teasing her lips with his. She leaned into him, unable to pull away. He enveloped her in his strong arms, tightening his hold, deepening his kiss. Heather felt a headiness that was both exhilarating and frightening. She wanted to resist but couldn't as he lifted his lips from hers and trailed feathery kisses across her cheek to her ear, which he nibbled, sending shivers of delight down to her fingertips. Heather breathlessly stirred against him.

"I must go," she whispered shakily.

"Go?" Rigo stopped his slow descent to her soft, creamy neck. "Where?"

"I don't know. I'm not sure what you expect. . . ." She swallowed. "I'm not a . . . lady of the night." Heather pulled back from his embrace, leaning her forehead on his shoulder. She could feel his warm breath caressing her face as he laughed softly.

"I know you're not. I'm also aware that you need me." He withdrew one arm and flicked her nose with a finger. "I've no intention of taking advantage of that need." He smiled. "Certainly not tonight. You need rest and I need to do some thinking. Do I guess rightly that you've no place to go?"

Heather avoided his eyes. "But . . . don't suppose I'll come with you!"

"Lady, you've no compassion." Rigo laughed lightly. "I suggest, then, you stay here tonight, and tomorrow we'll plan what to do next."

"Here?" she hesitated.

"The tavernkeeper and I are old friends. I promise you'll sleep soundly."

While she was considering, Rigo guided her toward the door. He left her alone for a few moments to arrange for the room and Heather, after catching her breath, retrieved her reticule with Miss Southey's letters and locket, wondering if she should tell him of her hope to be taken in by the Somersets. She decided to tell him in the morning, when she was less tired and could think straight.

When Rigo came back with Daniel, she was shown to a small, simply furnished room. Rigo assured the tavernkeeper the room would do well, and Daniel took his leave after bidding Heather a good night. When Rigo didn't follow, Heather turned to him, her green eyes slanting him a wary look.

"I said you were safe, and you are—from me, as well, Heather," he said quietly.

Heather moved away from him and put her reticule on the nightstand next to the small bed. Every nerve in her body was aware of the dark man behind her.

Rigo crossed to where she stood and turned her to face him. "Nothing to say?" he teased. He reached up a hand and twined a finger around a thick, chestnut curl. Heather took in her breath.

"If you don't leave, Daniel will have the wrong idea of us."

"No better idea than I have, I'm sure."

Reaching up a hand to free her hair, Heather's fingers brushed his, and her startled senses were awakened once more. She quickly pulled her hand back, but Rigo caught it and laced it with his. Cupping her head with his free hand, he lowered his lips to hers. Heather felt herself opening like a rose to the sun. "Rigo . . ." she tried to protest, a last sound of defense, but it seemed to her the tones came out like a song. She felt her body falling away, and she leaned into him, into the low fire he was building with his mouth. Reaching up to curve her hand around his neck, she let her fingers curl in his black hair. She didn't know when it had happened, but she was surrendering her mouth to his intimate searching. She didn't want the piercing sweetness to end.

His breath ragged, Rigo pulled away to stare down at Heather, his eyes glowing. A smile lit his face.

"You would tempt a saint," he said softly. "I'd better take my leave while I still can." He leaned forward to just brush his lips against her forehead and then released her to walk slowly away.

Heather stood rooted to the spot, wondering over the sudden blossoming of feeling between them and what it might mean, aware that she had made a leap into womanhood. Her lips parted and she trembled with the knowledge that she wanted to reach out and touch him. She didn't want him to leave.

Before going to the door, Rigo put a small leather purse on the nightstand. "For breakfast," he said. "Have it brought up. Don't go down until I return. Promise?"

Heather thought she saw the look of a conqueror on his face, and when she looked down at the nightstand and realized he was leaving her coins, she felt her cheeks heat.

"Are you paying me for my kisses?" she asked, her eyes flashing.

Rigo chuckled. "No, you changeling. I'm not rich enough to pay their worth." He stepped to the door. "Dream of me," he said, his eyes drinking in her deliciously disheveled hair and sweet, swollen lips.

"I shall have nightmares of pirates chasing me!" Heather said, smiling.

"And I shall have dreams of your capture." His eyes caught hers, giving her an unspoken promise. Then he was gone.

Heather bolted the door and leaned against it. Was he

now her lover? She didn't know. She traced a finger over her lips, still tasting him. She made a little dance of joy to the washstand, and as she made a hasty toilet, she shivered in the chill of her unheated room.

She got into the cold bed and, as if the cold and chill were harbingers of doubt, she wondered if she was being foolish to trust such a worldly man. Heather felt dizzy. But the day's adventures had taken their toll, and with Rigo's glowing eyes dancing before her, she fell into a fitful sleep.

Chapter Eight

STRIDING THROUGH THE WET AND MUDDY STREETS OF MAN-
hattan toward The Harbor Inn the next morning, Rigo felt
torn between his powerful desire to be with Heather again
and his thoughts about the meeting he had just attended.
He had known his share of lovely women, and Arabella
was an acknowledged beauty, but this green-eyed English
girl had him hurrying toward her as if he'd just discovered
that women differed from men.

As he hurried, his mind kept returning to his morning
meeting with General George Washington, Esek Hopkins,
the head of the new navy, and half a dozen leaders.
During the discussion of where British General Howe was
most likely to next move his forces, General Washington
had first struck Rigo as a cold, rigid man, but he'd soon
come to appreciate the general's occasional grimace at
someone's patent nonsense or his small smile at a piece of
wit. After an hour, during which Rigo's mind frequently
wandered to some of the delightful details of his chance
meeting with Heather, Washington had abruptly asked

everyone to leave except for Hopkins and Rigo, who hadn't said a word during the talk and had been wondering why he'd been invited in the first place.

Washington, a man as tall as Rigo and dressed in a formal waistcoat but without a wig, stood up when the others had left and paced across the ornate rug to the windows. He then turned back to the short, bald-headed Hopkins.

"Whether Howe lands in Brooklyn, Staten Island, or New Jersey," he said to Hopkins, "our primary task is to defend New York and the Hudson, but we need to know as soon as possible if and when Howe's ships arrive in our area. Do you have the boats to establish a patrol?"

"No, sir," Hopkins answered in a shrill voice. "The navy's ships are all being built, but Captain Rigo here has one we can use."

Washington turned to Rigo, who stood with his back to the fireplace. "Captain Rigo?" he asked with a frown. "That's an unusual name."

"It's a pseudonym, General," Rigo replied.

"Captain Rigo is from a prominent Tory family," Hopkins explained, "and doesn't wish to compromise his parents."

"I see." Washington examined Rigo. "And what guarantee do we have that your loyalties are with us, Captain?"

"None, General," Rigo answered promptly. "In these days, a man's loyalty is only as reliable as his face."

Washington scrutinized Rigo a moment more, then nodded. Hopkins stepped in.

"Captain Rigo has already brought in one prize under his letter of marque," he said with a scowl. "Less than a week ago, he took a well-armed ship twice his size." When Washington remained silent, Hopkins went on. "His commitment to the Colonies has meant forfeiting his claim on a successful shipping business."

For a moment more, Washington's granite face remained stern, but then it relaxed into a slight smile.

"And you're willing to risk the British fleet to try to give us advance warning of Howe's arrival?" he asked.

"Certainly, General," Rigo replied. "I'm here to serve you."

Washington smiled and came forward to Rigo. "I'm happy you're with us, Captain," he said, offering his large hand. "Some men are patriots because it serves their fortunes. It's good to meet a man who's a patriot for other reasons."

The meeting ended not long after, with Rigo and Hopkins working out the details of his patrolling with the *Contessa* off Long Island to intercept Howe's convoy, if it came. After he'd left, Rigo had wondered about Washington's last words. He knew he had become a rebel as much out of a personal dislike for many of his pigheaded Tory acquaintances as for any other reason. Although Hopkins had been right in saying that his rebel acts would eventually mean forfeiture of any claim in Somerset Shipping, it was also true that the acts of the English Parliament had severely hurt that business. His father was loyal to England more out of loyalty to class than to country, but Rigo had a disdain for his class that made rebellion easy. A woman like Heather was proof to Rigo that personal worth could not be reliably estimated by social position. His mother would reject Heather because she was nothing but an indentured servant. Worse—a runaway indentured servant. But Rigo knew her for more than he dared admit.

Knowing that her trunk had been lost when the *Prospect* had been commandeered by the British, Rigo stopped at a dress shop. He planned to bring Heather there later in the day for a fitting, but first he wanted to buy her a gift. Walking out of the shop with a package containing a lovely white, woolen shawl under his arm, Rigo felt like a country beau about to call on his new fiancée, but when he entered The Harbor Inn at noon, Daniel met him with a frightened look.

"I've bad news, Captain Rigo," he said, looking nervously over his shoulder. "She's gone! Your lady's gone!"

"What are you saying?" Rigo snapped. "What happened here?"

"A Mr. Crawley and a constable arrived early this morning looking for a runaway indentured girl fitting your lady's description. I insisted we had no such girl here, but, well, they made a search. My wife was just able to warn her in time, and she made good her escape."

Rigo expelled a breath heavily through his nose, his lips compressed tightly. Daniel's wife came bustling into the room, her round face creased in concern.

"Annie, what did you tell her?" Rigo asked. "Where did she go?"

"I told her there was trouble," Annie answered. "That she was in danger. She looked peaky, Captain, but there was no stalling the constable, and she seemed to know it. She asked where you lived, but I didn't know."

"Didn't you tell her to come back here later?" Rigo asked, still shocked by this sudden turn of events.

"Annie was afraid," Daniel replied. "If she was caught here after the search, we—you, too—would be guilty of harboring a fugitive."

"Damn it, Daniel!" Rigo said, banging his fist on the counter. "Annie, you didn't tell her that, did you?"

"No, Captain. She was frightened enough."

"What did she say?"

"She just took flight."

Rigo raked a hand through his hair.

"All right," he said. "Daniel, do me a favor and have your boy check at the other inns and see if she's gone to one. I'll be on the *Contessa* at Tudor Wharf this evening if she returns or if you find her."

"I'm sorry, Rigo . . ." Daniel began.

"It's not your fault," Rigo interrupted. "I'm just upset that I didn't anticipate this and tell her where to find me. But she'll come back here, I'm sure. She has no other place to go."

After leaving the inn, Rigo spent two hours wandering the streets of lower Manhattan, even sending the *Contessa*'s bosun to make discreet inquiries at the dockside taverns. He then went to the constabulary to ascertain whether Heather had, in fact, been located, but they had no information, not even an address for Duncan Crawley.

Returning to The Harbor Inn late in the afternoon,

Rigo learned that Daniel still had heard nothing, and by evening, as he sat in the stern of the *Contessa* with Noah Wiggens, Rigo was baffled.

Heather had simply vanished. She had come into his life like the sudden appearance of a comet across the night sky at sea, and now she had disappeared as abruptly. It was as if her light had been snuffed out by an immense swallow of the ocean, and his life was the darker for it.

Heather shivered as she lay huddled under the hay. Drawing up her knees to escape the clamminess of her still-damp skirts, she listened, bewildered by the strange sounds penetrating her feverish consciousness. Low voices filtered above the light staccato sound of rain on the barn's roof, mixed with the stamping feet of cows and their melodic lowing. Slowly, she pushed the hay back and sat up, trying to remember where she was.

When her foot knocked over an object, Heather reached for it, her head swimming, until she finally focused on the reticule holding Miss Southey's letters from Bruce Somerset. Her memory jogged, Heather clutched the bag in one hand and tremblingly touched the heart-shaped locket she had fastened around her neck last night. When she had handed the coins from Captain Rigo as payment to the man who had ferried her across the bay to Staten Island, she saw his ferret-like eyes on her reticule. Frightened that he might try to take it from her and, thus, steal her entrée to the Somersets, she had decided to hide the locket and a few of the letters on her person.

When they finally landed in Staten Island, she had hurried from the ferryman like the fugitive she'd become and had hidden herself in a stand of trees until he and the two other passengers had gone. By then, darkness had approached, and a cold, needle-like rain had driven her into a nearby barn, too weak to continue her search for the Somerset home. There she had bedded for the night in the soft hay—wet, miserable and fervently wishing she had tried to return to The Harbor Inn. Yet the one time she had tried to return after her early morning flight, she had seen Crawley's valet lounging outside. So, she had fled again. It was later, as she was wandering around the docks looking for Captain Rigo or his ship, that Heather had learned she could take a ferry to Staten Island and, when she was frightened by too many suspicious looks being directed her way, she had decided her only hope lay in finding the Somersets.

Remembering Captain Rigo, Heather was overcome with a feeling of hopelessness about ever finding him again, and she felt tears welling. In an effort to fight them back, she coughed. Her chest hurt with the effort and, steadying herself with a hand on the rough brace of a stall, she levered herself upright. And froze. Watching her through the gloom was a stout, roughly dressed, whiskered man, his great hands hanging loosely at his sides. Heather returned his look, too ill to be frightened.

"I'm . . . I'm lost, sir. Sorry if I frightened you. Perhaps you can direct me?" she whispered, her voice raw and throaty.

"Depends," the man's low, quiet voice answered. Appearing suddenly like a shadow beside him was a young girl, her long red braids hanging over thin and plainly dressed shoulders.

Heather forced herself to stand still, her eyes glassily surveying the staring duo.

"I'm trying to find the Somerset family," she said. "Are they near here?"

The man nodded. "Ye've found them. This is Somerset land."

"Thank heaven." Heather sighed with relief and swayed unsteadily.

"English," the farmer said without feeling. "Expecting you, miss?"

"No." She hesitated a moment. "But I'm sure they'll help me when they hear my story. They are gentry, after all, and have it in their power." Heather passed a hand over her hot, damp brow.

The farmer and girl looked at each other meaningfully.

"True enough those words be, but I wouldn't be expecting help if I were you," the farmer said. "They have no fondness for strangers, nor the poor either, and more so in these times." He examined Heather with a critical eye.

"But I'm desperate! Surely they wouldn't turn me away when . . . when I have news for them."

"She would, too. She'd turn away her own sister if it didn't suit her ladyship," piped the young girl, her face screwed up in dislike.

"Molly! That's no way to speak of Mrs. Somerset, not in front of a stranger. Go tend the milkin' now. Be off!"

"Yes, papa." The little girl hung her head and retreated.

"Milk?" Heather said weakly. "Please, may I have a small cup? I'd be grateful to you."

The farmer moved away and let the fevered young woman have a cup of rich, warm milk, mumbling to her not to say a word to Mrs. Somerset about being in the barn nor about the cup of milk. It wouldn't go well with him if she did, he warned her.

Amazed at these revelations, Heather privately wondered if the farmer was not just a grumbling sort. She was not yet ready to have her hopes dashed.

The farmer, whose name she learned was Isaiah, told her the Somerset manor was about a mile off, but first she'd have to cross the field to the dirt road before the great house would come into view. With a final gesture of pity for Heather, he gave her a dusty grain sack to protect her from the rain, apologizing for being unable to do more.

"You have one thing in your favor, and that's your being English. For pity's sake, don't be using my name, or my tenancy be worth dung," Isaiah warned again.

Heather thanked him weakly and began plodding across the wet fields in a daze, mud sucking at her soaked shoes. Her mind began to wander and at one point, she found herself leaning against a tree, not remembering where she was going. Her cold hands clutched the reticule and her sodden feet stumbled forward with a will of their own. She saw the graceful stone manor dimly through the mist as a beacon in an unfriendly world.

When she finally arrived, Heather was amazed at the immensity of the mansion, which seemed, in her feverish state, to rise among the elms and maple trees like a giant fairy-tale palace. Fearfully, she raised a trembling hand and lifted the lion's head knocker. As it dropped, she leaned against the large, white door, drawing in a shaky breath.

When the door opened, Heather fell forward, nearly toppling over the frightened serving girl who, when she saw Heather's condition, let out a shriek.

"Please . . ." said Heather, her voice slurred, "Mrs. Somerset . . ." She then began crying uncontrollably, her cracking and hoarse sobs intermixed with a fit of coughing. Hands helped her into the warmth of the kitchen, where she was shoved into a chair before a fire in the hearth. Hands held her head as others gave her a drink of tea, which half spilled down the front of her dress. Hands dabbed at the soaked lace.

Babbling between sobs, Heather tried to get out her story. "Miss Southey . . . Crawley . . ." She heard whisperings around her.

"My lady will be livid. See here, girl! We don't take in beggars. She'll see you in jail, she will. You're a fool to come here! Who are you?"

"Elizabeth . . ." Heather whispered and then stopped, trying to focus on a young girl's pretty face that had suddenly appeared to float before her.

"What are we to do, Amy?" the first voice asked. "Your mother will be in a fine state to know we allowed her in the kitchen!"

When the young girl reached tenderly down to straighten Heather's dress, she touched the heart-shaped locket and then let out a startled gasp.

"Please . . ." Heather clutched the young girl's hand in desperation. "Elizabeth Southey . . . said . . ." She coughed again and then knew no more as the room turned and went black.

When she finally awoke, it seemed to Heather that a long time had passed. She tentatively touched the bedding and realized she was covered with dry, clean sheets and was in a soft bed. When she opened her eyes, she found herself in a large, beautiful room. A pretty pattern floated on the walls and lacy curtains hung at the windows.

"It's so bright," she whispered.

"Yes, of course, Miss Southey . . ." a voice said and, mercifully, the room was darkened by rose-colored draperies. A middle-aged woman with a lace cap and a kindly face emerged from the shadows to stand at Heather's bedside.

"Miss Southey . . ." Heather murmured.

"Yes, dear. We know," the woman said. "Amy discovered Bruce's locket around your neck, and then we found the letters. You gave us a fright, fainting like that." She reached down to adjust the rose-patterned spread. "You've been . . . asleep for a day. You're safe now, my dear Miss Southey, though you've been through a terrible ordeal." The woman's hand patted Heather's shoulder reassuringly.

"But . . . you found the letters?"

"Yes, dear, and it's a good thing, too. That wretched scullery girl was ready to turn you out. Ignorant, they are. Don't know who their betters are. Why, anyone could tell you was well born by the look of your sweet face." She stopped chattering and raised Heather's head to plump up the pillows. "Here, dear. A little broth will do you good," the woman said, bringing a cup to Heather's lips.

"But what would have happened to me if the letters had not been discovered?" Heather asked weakly.

"Why, Mrs. Somerset would have called the magistrate. Heavens, Miss Southey, you don't know what it's like here in the Colonies. Why, there are beggars and such about.

The Somersets have a position to maintain. You don't know how glad Bruce was when he heard you'd been found."

"Magistrate . . . ?" Heather whispered, grasping the fact with fear.

"The law, dear."

Heather listened to the woman's chatter, absorbing more than the words while silently weighing her new identity.

Chapter Nine

HEATHER HAD BEEN TAKING A LATE AFTERNOON NAP WHEN she stirred, feeling a presence in the room unlike the ones she had been accustomed to. There was no sound, no bustling tread of a servant, or the quiet step of Amy Somerset, the pretty, dark-haired girl of eighteen who daily came to sit and talk to her in a quiet, soothing voice. Nó, this was more like she was being critically examined by someone in minute detail, and the feeling was not comfortable.

Opening her eyes, Heather saw a small woman with graying reddish blond hair tucked neatly into a lace cap looking at her from a straight-back chair near the bed. The woman's regal bearing gave the lie to the simple cut of her dark blue dress with its stark white cuffs and collar. Heather focused on the lightly lined face that had a stern mouth and brown eyes, eyes that seemed to watch her every move, and realized she had seen the woman before when she had been feverish.

"Well, my dear Elizabeth, it's good to see you looking

so much better," the woman said in a crisp and haughty voice. "We were quite concerned about you. I'm Amy and Bruce's mother. You may call me Aunt Margaret, if you wish. All of our cousins do."

Heather was startled at first but recovered quickly. "Aunt Margaret," she said quietly, testing the sound. So be it, she mused. One must take one's aunt as she comes and not hope for fairy godmothers. "Yes, I am better, thank you. I've been up and about already." Heather paused and then added, "Thank you for all your kindnesses to me."

"It's no more than your due." Mrs. Somerset leaned forward. "You are much prettier than your letters to Amy and Bruce let on. I'm quite glad to know you are modest about the gifts God has given you. It's the mark of a well-brought-up young lady and one that I heartily approve."

Heather shrank under the quilt at the iron in the woman's voice. "Yes, Aunt," she said dutifully but feeling the opposite.

"We received quite a garbled report of the fate of your ship," Mrs. Somerset continued. "But pirates! My word! There was even a rumor that you had died. I would say you had a very narrow escape. You must tell me the whole story when you are not so haunted by the memories." She paused. "And what a pity it is to have lost your trunks. Your clothes and your dowry both missing. It's a tragedy."

"It's very upsetting, Mrs. . . . Aunt."

"Surely you remember if they were taken off the ship?"

"I'm not sure. . . ." Heather said, wondering if this was the moment to tell the truth. What if she were to say that she thought a certain Duncan Crawley would know of their whereabouts? She stopped herself, thinking better of it while wishing Mrs. Somerset were a more sympathetic lady. She let out a soft sigh.

"Don't fret, Elizabeth. Rest assured, I have asked your uncle to do all he can to recover your belongings. I'm sure you know how important it is . . . a dowry, in these difficult times."

"I well know the value of a dowry, Aunt," Heather said, pink staining her cheeks.

Mrs. Somerset sat up even straighter and pursed her lips before regaining her poise. "Well, we will have the matter cleared up shortly." She went on in a more pleasant tone. "Amy tells me you will join us for dinner tonight."

"I have said I will try."

"Please do. Your uncle and cousin Bruce are waiting to meet you and have daily asked after you. I promise you won't be expected to linger or entertain. It's quite enough to have you with us and well again."

When Margaret Somerset had taken her leave, Heather had a moment of panic over the lost trunks. If they were recovered, it would mean Duncan Crawley would be known and he would be told Elizabeth Southey was alive. Heather had no doubt he would expose her as an impostor and, somehow, excuse himself of theft. Then she would have to flee again, if she could. She looked around the lovely room as if she might never see its likes again. Well, it couldn't be helped, and Heather wondered if it was sinful to pray the trunks were permanently lost.

Throwing back the coverlets, she slowly sat up, testing her strength. Feeling a little dizzy at first, she pinched her cheeks and shook her feet to get her blood flowing. Then she focused on her immediate worry—meeting Bruce Somerset at dinner. Heather had to try and remember all that Elizabeth had said to her about him. For her first big test in her new identity, she decided her best course would be to smile and let him do the talking. It might be best to avoid saying too much before she had a better sense of what was expected of her.

Sighing, Heather surprised herself by whispering aloud, "Oh, Rigo! Why couldn't you have been Bruce?" Then she shook her head. There was no sense getting into a state about the man she had lost when she had to face the one Elizabeth Southey had hoped to marry.

Heather threw her legs off the bed and slowly stood up, fighting off a brief wave of dizziness. Then she took a few tentative steps, glad to find her limbs less shaky than the previous day. A light tapping at the door was followed by the appearance of the smiling round face of Amy.

"Elizabeth. Mama said you were awake," Amy said in her light voice, whose gentle tones had so soothed her during the fever.

"I'm afraid my time as an invalid is finished," Heather said spontaneously as she slowly circled the room.

"Afraid!" Amy exclaimed. "Oh, Elizabeth! I'm looking forward to showing you the house and gardens. We'll have such a good time. Your coming here has been the best thing to happen. Though I suppose Bruce will want to keep you for himself."

"Oh, no," Heather burst out, then stopped. "I mean, I hope you will be with us at all times. It wouldn't be proper . . ." She trailed off, startled at the idea of having to contend with Bruce alone. The thought that he might ask questions she couldn't answer was frightening, let alone the thought that he might mention marriage.

"You're right," said Amy, going to the bed and straightening the bedclothes. "Mama would agree with you. But Bruce . . ." She hesitated and turned with a shy smile to face Heather. "Bruce is quite used to getting his own way. Mama thinks he can do no wrong, but, in this instance, she will agree with you." Giving a last pat to the bedspread, Amy crossed to the wardrobe and opened it.

"My dress!" Heather exclaimed, seeing her wheat frock hanging, freshly laundered and ironed. "It looks wonderful! And my shoes. . . . They're shining!"

Amy smiled. "I've also loaned you a thing or two of mine," she said. "But we're arranging to have you fitted for your own new dresses. Otherwise, you would be quite tired of what I found for you. I can't imagine what I would do if I lost everything."

"It wouldn't happen to you because you have parents," Heather said, fingering her dress and noticing two additional dresses that must be Amy's. She wondered how so sweet a young woman as Amy could be the daughter of the very proper and very cold lady she had just met. "And you are sure to marry well," she added.

"I'm afraid I shall be an old maid," Amy said softly.

"Of course you won't," Heather replied quickly.

"I haven't a suitable caller," Amy said shyly. "Mama tries, but she says I'm always tongue-tied and that I lack the social graces."

"That's ridiculous," Heather returned, flushing with anger. "You are the best person in this world, and some lucky man will see it soon, I'm sure of it!" Heather smiled warmly at the young woman, already feeling a great affection for her.

"You are kind, Elizabeth," Amy said. "My half brother, Richard, tries to reassure me, too." She smiled suddenly. "He says he'd marry me himself if it weren't considered so improper." She flushed shyly.

"There, you see! Never doubt your worth," Heather said, taking out a simple green muslin gown Amy was loaning her and holding it against her figure. Someone had thoughtfully lengthened it to fit her taller frame and had also tucked it in at the waist to suit her relative slenderness. "Amy! This is beautiful! But I can't. It isn't right," Heather said, upset by Amy's generosity.

"But it would please me, and Bruce suggested it. He said it would go well with your coloring."

"But he's not seen me!" Heather said, turning in surprise to face Amy.

"It was he who carried you upstairs the day you collapsed," Amy explained with her shy smile. "He was quite taken," she added, blushing. "I mean . . . we thought from your letters that you would be plain and retiring, just what Mama wants for Bruce but not, I think, what he would prefer." Amy stopped and blushed in embarrassment. "Oh, dear. I shouldn't be saying these things! Forgive me!"

Heather, a little stunned and intrigued by all Amy was saying, went up to her and gave her a brief hug. "Don't be silly, Amy. It will show me the way I can please your mother, and Bruce," she added, though she had no intention of getting close enough to Bruce for him to be pleased. The whole charade was a dangerous course, and it didn't sit well with Heather to deceive anyone. She felt a heaviness of heart and passed a hand over her brow.

"You're tired," Amy said, concern in her large brown eyes. "I'll send Mary in to help you dress and do your hair."

"Oh, thank you, Amy. I suppose I must get ready."

After Amy had left, Heather quickly seated herself on the bed and wondered what would happen if the Somersets knew the whole story. Perhaps they would let her stay on as Amy's companion. The memory of Margaret Somerset's fierce eyes chilled that hope, though, and a fine perspiration broke out on her brow. Until she could think of a way out, Heather seemed doomed to be Elizabeth Southey.

The arrival of Mary interrupted her worrying. Mary was, thankfully, a very docile girl of about sixteen who needed no instruction in helping Heather don her dress and arrange her hair. It was clear that Mrs. Somerset ran her household meticulously, supervising her servants closely. Mary gossiped freely as she helped Heather fit the dress, and soon Heather found herself hearing many new things about the Somersets, including the recent dismissal of a kitchen girl who had gotten herself pregnant. Mrs. Somerset blamed her pregnancy on the absent stepson, Richard, who spent most of his time in Manhattan. While cautioning that the whole affair was to be kept secret, Mary hinted that it was not Richard who was to blame but another on the estate whom she would not name.

Heather was sorry for the girl in the scandalous story, especially as it seemed to reflect badly on Amy's favorite, Richard. When Mary finally left, Heather knew her real ordeal was about to begin. She took a last look at herself in the mirror and saw that her high cheekbones were too prominent with her recent loss of weight. She patted her cheeks vigorously and took a few last strokes with the brush to her hair. Dissatisfied, she stood up and walked to the door to go find Amy. She didn't realize that in her excitement, her green eyes with their dark lashes were like jewels in her face and that her beauty was enhanced by an inner radiance shining forth in spite of her delicate and temporary paleness.

When, fifteen minutes later, she and Amy descended

the stairs and then entered the huge main drawing room, they were like two glowing flowers. Heather was astounded by the size and elegance of the room, larger by half than any she had ever been in. Its very immensity increased her fears, but they were calmed somewhat by the warm greeting she received from the calm and dignified John Somerset.

"Welcome to Somerset Manor," he said, taking her hand in his and smiling warmly. "We've long looked forward to having you with us."

"Thank you, sir," Heather replied, curtsying as she nervously wondered where her intended was. "I'm sorry to have put your household to such trouble with my illness. In England, I was never sick." As soon as she had uttered the words, Heather knew, from the expression on John Somerset's face, that she had blundered. "I . . . had some difficult times, to be sure, but I actually was rarely ill . . ." she tried desperately to correct.

"Miss Southey? At last!" a deep voice from behind her intoned.

Heather turned, thankful of the unintended rescue, and saw a boyishly handsome man of about twenty-five dressed with cool formality in black coat and fawn-colored trousers. He took her hand and raised it smoothly to his lips.

"Bruce Somerset, at your service, dear cousin," he said smiling, his brown eyes shining with admiration. "May I say that if you are this lovely when ill, I tremble to look upon you when healthy."

Heather flushed, not sure whether from pleasure or from concern that he was still holding her hand.

"I thank you, sir," she replied, determined to try to hold her tongue after her last blunder.

"Your recovery pleases us all," Bruce went on. "Especially me," he added in a lower tone, giving her hand a gentle squeeze.

Heather flushed at the implied intimacy of his tone and pulled her hand free.

"We mustn't tire Elizabeth, dear," Margaret Somerset said, appearing at her son's side with a frown on her face. "We can't linger here talking, and dinner is served." With a brief artificial smile at Heather, she took Bruce's arm and swept them both away toward the dining room. Gallantly, John Somerset appeared at Heather's side and, smiling down at her, offered his arm.

As they entered the dining room and John seated her, Heather found John's deeper tones had a quieting effect on her. She also noticed that there was something about him that seemed familiar, although she couldn't account for it.

John Somerset said a simple grace, and the family began eating with a certain reserve that Heather attributed to her presence. It was served with stiff formality by several servants who arrived and departed like mechanical dolls. Heather accepted a glass of a fine claret that was served immediately, and then there was a clear broth, roast duck, a squash baked with orange and honey sauce, creamed onions, preserved crab apples, several loaves of freshly baked bread, and more wine. Through all of the first part of the dinner, Bruce sat opposite with his gaze fixed on her, his face alternately registering admiration, serious dignity, and occasionally, curiosity.

Meanwhile, Heather was having to struggle with the most vacuous of generalities about the friends and relatives she was supposed to have in London. John Somerset, although his face and voice always expressed warmth, asked a few brief questions at the very beginning of the meal that unsettled Heather, and then he spent the remainder of the dinner in equally unsettling silence. Bruce seemed relatively oblivious to her total lack of interest in and knowledge of her own supposed aunts and uncles back in London, and as he began to dominate the talk, the subject, to Heather's relief, was finally dropped.

Except that Bruce now turned the conversation to one that Heather found equally difficult.

"Do you think you'll be well enough to go on an outing tomorrow?" he asked easily, a smile of encouragement on his lips.

Heather hesitated a moment, then plunged into her first speech of more than a few words.

"Amy and I have discussed touring the estate with some

pleasure, if it could be arranged. But not for too long, as I'm still a little shaky."

Bruce looked askance at his sister. "So, my little sister is planning to break out of her homey cocoon. That is good news!"

"Bruce!" his mother admonished.

"But it is wonderful, Mother. Elizabeth seems to have brought out the best in Amy. Why, soon she'll be dancing every dance at our next ball," Bruce teased his red-faced sister.

"Amy has been very sweet to me and has hastened my return to health with her fine spirits, for which I will always remember her," Heather interjected in Amy's defense, surprising herself by her own boldness with this imposing family.

"What ball? Mama! Have you planned a ball?" Amy asked, distressed by her brother's taunts.

"Yes, it's just been decided. In fact, it was Bruce's suggestion, and we've been planning the details of the event these past two days," Margaret Somerset said with some satisfaction.

"Mother, you didn't tell me!"

"There hasn't been time," Margaret said, touching her lace cap, "and the decision wasn't made until today. It will be the occasion of the year, I can promise you." She turned to her son, "You're not to tease your sister, Bruce."

"Mama, you haven't . . ." Amy started, her hands clasped in her lap, a pained expression on her face.

"Now, dear, leave everything to me. I haven't arranged, ah, for an escort, but I do expect you will receive several invitations. The choice will be yours."

Amy lapsed into silence, her cheeks rosy, while the serving girl cleared the table for a dessert of pound cake and preserved peaches.

"It appears you have an ally in Elizabeth, Amy, and a good one," Bruce said smoothly to his sister. "When you've decided on your escort, we can all have the best of times together. Elizabeth, I assume, of course, that I have your permission to escort you?"

Heather had become increasing uncomfortable over the talk of the ball and was vaguely plotting an indisposition of some kind. Now she paled. The last thing she wanted was a public appearance as Miss Southey, yet she saw no way out at this juncture and so hedged.

"I don't know. I fear I'm not up to a night of dancing."

"In three weeks time, I'm sure you will be restored to perfect health, and we will all see that you have the best of care," Bruce said smiling. "You'll be the belle, I've no doubt."

"But . . . I haven't a gown," Heather protested weakly.

"That will be arranged," Mrs. Somerset interjected. "We have the best of seamstresses here. Perhaps we are not as fashionable as in London, but we've managed. A trip to Manhattan with Amy and Bruce will take care of your needs . . . until your trunks have arrived." She turned to her husband and added, "John, you must write at once to your cousin, Alfred Southey, apprising him of our dear Elizabeth's plight."

Heather's hand trembled slightly as she put down her water glass and clutched her napkin.

"Do I have your permission, Elizabeth?" John asked Heather in a quiet voice.

"You must do what is best," Heather answered, looking at him directly. She still found it difficult to address him as uncle and simply avoided naming the man at all. He seemed, she thought, to be assessing her, but not in the same way as Margaret, who was concerned only with her suitability as Bruce's fiancée. John Somerset, instead, was quietly considering her other qualities, and she was a little in awe of him.

"Well spoken," John said to her in his rich baritone.

"She is rather perfect, isn't she?" Bruce said, his expression flattering to Heather. "I congratulate myself on my own good sense in having corresponded with you and on persuading you to come."

"Bruce, you are far too forward and are embarrassing your cousin," Mrs. Somerset said, with emphasis on the word forward.

"I should hope Richard won't make one of his appearances on this occasion," Bruce said, changing the subject. "Though I suppose he will. I should warn you, Elizabeth, of my older brother's reputation. Some of his exploits would burn your ears."

"That will be enough, Bruce," John said firmly.

"You must admit, Father, it would be most inopportune. I've heard a rumor of his actually meeting with Washington."

"We'll not mention that name in this household at my table!" Margaret said heatedly.

"Sorry, Mother," Bruce said quickly, then turned to Heather, who had recovered her senses and applied herself, without appetite, to her dessert. "You've no idea, Elizabeth, what times these are here. We've a rebellious element that threatens, but we'll rout them soon enough." Then he raised his glass and said, "I propose a toast, to King George the Third and his valiant soldiers who will make this colony safe for all Englishmen!" Bruce looked at each one of his family, in turn, until all glasses were raised.

"And that is well spoken, too," Margaret said, beaming, her ill humor of a moment ago forgotten.

Heather drank a sip of her wine, somewhat confused by all she had heard, yet knew she was, after all, English and a subject of George the Third.

John drank the toast but cautioned his son, "Remember that should the rebels achieve any of their goals—and I've no doubt they will try, even though they seem undisciplined—our fortunes would be in some jeopardy. Our good friends the Moncriefs, as well as the Allendales, have discussed with me their plans to leave for England should we fail. I would hope that will not be our fate."

"I, for one, would not regret leaving should your fears come to pass, John," Margaret said with asperity.

"Papa, we can't!" Amy said, at last rejoining the family conversation, her anxieties over the coming ball buried for awhile.

"I hope not, Amy. I'm too old for a change like that," John said.

"Another toast. This one to victory and happier times,"

97

said Bruce, who seemed to want to end the discussion of war. "We mustn't air our troubles on this occasion, with Elizabeth brightening our table. She brings the spirit of England to us, and that's bound to be our good fortune." Bruce smiled at Heather, his eyes fastening on hers.

"Thank you for your faith in me and all your kindnesses, each. You can't know how very grateful I am to have arrived here safely," Heather said in response. She felt very sincere in her words, and very troubled.

Chapter Ten

Rigo's week had been hectic and unsatisfactory. First, he had had no success at all in relocating Heather. Despite inquiries made by himself, his two Manhattan servants, and several of his crew, no trace of her had turned up in any of the taverns, livery stables, carriage services, and even a brothel that they had checked. She seemed to have left the city as totally and as quickly as she'd left Daniel's inn.

When not involved in the search for Heather, the rest of Rigo's time was spent preparing the *Contessa* for sea again. Although the ship itself was ready, fresh supplies had to be gotten aboard and, most frustrating, the crew had to be pulled back together from their various homes scattered about the New York–New Jersey area. Spies in General Howe's Halifax camp were supposed to race south the moment the Englishman's troops began to exit Canada, but Rigo had no confidence that such a message would reach New York much before General Howe's fleet might reach Long Island. He wanted to begin his patrol immediately; however, his crew had just been paid for delivering a prize and was showing a natural lethargy in returning for another, much less promising voyage. The little money Esek Hopkins had been able to offer Rigo and his crew from the coffers of the Continental Congress was so ridiculously meager that it barely paid for a week's supply of food, much less for the ship or the crew's wages. That would have to come from Rigo's own pocket.

Then to top off his frustrating week, the man named Duncan Crawley had unexpectedly written him to announce he was prepared to make a generous offer for all of the Somerset ships—both those in England and those in the Colonies. Through their servants, a meeting had been arranged for noon at Rigo's small townhouse.

Rigo awaited the meeting with both interest and anger. After receiving the letter two days before, he had made inquiries and had discovered that Crawley was contacting local shipowners and making disgustingly low offers for their idle ships. When Rigo added this information to the fact that this Crawley was the primary cause of Heather's precipitous flight and disappearance, he was rather tempted to hold their conference in a small dinghy in rough seas—and hope that Crawley couldn't swim.

But when Crawley arrived punctually at noon, it was at Rigo's townhouse near South Street on the East River. Aware that there was a slim possibility that Crawley might recognize him as the pirate who had manhandled him on the *Prospect,* Rigo nevertheless felt confident that the shrouded face of the rough pirate would not be remembered in the elegant drawing room of the son of John Somerset. To further the contrast, he made sure he was dressed in the height of fashion, with one of his father's best wigs and even an old monocle. Crawley's class bias made it doubtful he would think of Richard Somerset as a pirate.

"Good day, sir," Rigo said, rising from an elegant chair when his manservant showed Crawley into the small drawing room. "I doubt we can do business, but still, I would be happy to listen to your offer."

"Ah, Mr. Somerset. A pleasure to meet you, sir," said

Crawley, shaking hands and looking around the room with studied coolness. "I had the honor of meeting your father two years ago in London."

"I'm sure," said Rigo, returning to his chair and casually motioning to Crawley to be seated on the small couch opposite. "Although he failed to mention the event."

Crawley started at the tiny barb and, with a forced smile, sat down on the settee.

"Of course, those were flush days for shipping," Crawley said. "Not the way things are now, I fear."

"We make do in good times and bad," Rigo said lazily. "There are always uses for fine ships."

"Oh, really?" said Crawley, his eyebrow arching in exaggerated doubt. "Then there can't be many fine ships in New York. All I see are rotting at the docks."

"Not Somerset ships."

"Perhaps not," said Crawley, at last narrowing his eyes on Rigo as if examining someone vaguely familiar or scrutinizing an insect about to be squashed. "But I had the misfortune to sail in your *Prospect,* and I don't see much profit in a ship's being commandeered by the English fleet."

Rigo frowned.

"No, not much," he said, standing up irritably and walking to the bookshelves, where he kept a bottle of cognac. "But then, I'm sure His Majesty will compensate us royally for the inconvenience." He turned to smile at the small man seated on the settee. They both knew the Somersets would never receive fair value for the seizure, but Crawley would be too strong a Tory to speak ill of the Crown.

"Ah, yes. No doubt," Crawley agreed, flushing as he tapped his walking cane nervously between his knees. "But I have been led to believe that you also have two ships stuck idle here in New York. I am prepared to make a generous offer to take their burden from you."

"How sweet!" Rigo said with such an exaggerated smile that Crawley flinched. "But if the ships are useless to me, how, might I ask, can they have any value to you?"

"Oh, I dare say, I'll make do. I'll offer you, sight

unseen, fourteen hundred pounds for your *Contessa* and *Yorkshire* together."

"Fourteen hundred pounds . . ." Rigo said, raising an eyebrow with a glint in his eyes. It was, at best, a fifth the ships' value in normal times. "That *is* generous," he said. "So generous, I fear that you may not know the business. Are you sure you are willing to pay that much?"

Crawley, though meeting Rigo's smiling gaze, was obviously discomfitted by Rigo's unexpected response. "Of course, only half would be down and the balance a note for two years," he countered.

"Of course," Rigo agreed amiably. "Tell me, sir," he went on, taking the cognac bottle from the bookshelf. "Do your contracts for ships turn out as well as your contracts for female indentured servants?"

"I beg your pardon," said Crawley, his face pinched with sudden annoyance.

With the cognac in hand, Rigo strode to the little table where several glasses stood. He filled a small one and turned to face Crawley.

"I had the pleasure of meeting a lovely young woman who said she had the misfortune to be owned by you," he said, after taking a sip of his drink. "It appears she had left your employ after only a few hours and, unless you have reclaimed her, she would seem to be a dead loss. I simply wondered if ships you bought sank as rapidly from view as did Miss Woode."

Duncan Crawley stood up.

"I have not come here to discuss a whore of an indentured servant," he said sharply. "I have made you an offer for two ships. If . . ."

"Miss Woode called you a thief and a spider," Rigo interrupted placidly. "I tried to defend your honor, but her facts were simply too overwhelming."

"If you have knowledge of that vixen's whereabouts," Crawley snapped, "it is your legal obligation to turn her over to me."

"Alas, sir, I confess I don't," said Rigo, draining his cognac. "But if I did, I assure you, you would be the last person to know."

"It seems, sir," said Crawley, tapping his cane impatiently on the floor, "that we are not to do business together."

"Very observant, Mr. Crawley. But perhaps not true. Although I have no ships to sell, it is possible I might be in the market to *buy*."

"Of what are you talking?"

"Although you do not own Miss Woode," Rigo said, "since she had the good sense to disappear, you do own her contract. Like an empty ship, however, its value is somewhat reduced. Still, I am prepared to pay the price you paid for her—so that you can be more generous in your offers to us American shipowners."

Crawley's small eyes narrowed as if examining an opportunity he hadn't seen before. "You will buy the contract of this girl even though she has fled and you say you don't know where?"

"I will. I assume you paid no more than sixteen guinea for her contract."

"I paid twenty," Crawley said angrily.

"Ah, well, she *was* attractive, wasn't she? And a good cook, I'm sure."

"I'll sell you her contract for a hundred guinea."

"Will you now?"

"Or for twenty guinea, with one condition."

"Ah, yes, a condition," Rigo said. "And what may that be?"

"That when she is recovered, I have the . . . shall we say 'use,' of her for one week. Then she is yours."

Rigo hurled his cognac glass across the room, where it shattered against the mantlepiece.

"Go to hell!" he said.

"I thought so," said Crawley, sneering. "You have been ensnared by that damn bitch." Then he frowned. "No, sir," he finally went on, stiffening and moving to the door. "I shall not sell her contract—to you or anyone else. And I shall continue my efforts to find her. And when I do . . ." He hesitated, nodding his head to himself and smirking. "When I find her, I shall not sell her until I am tired of pleasuring myself and punishing her."

Rigo crossed the room and planted himself at the door, barring Crawley's exit.

"You do that, Mr. Crawley," Rigo said evenly, "and you will be lucky to have an unbroken bone left in your body."

Crawley cringed slightly as Rigo towered over him, but he met Rigo's gaze. "I would like to leave, sir."

"It is not our custom here, as it may be in London, to abuse our servants," Rigo continued coldly. "I suggest you abandon your lust for Miss Woode and sell her contract while it still has value."

Crawley hesitated, obviously tempted. "If she is worth twenty guineas to you lost, then I assume," he said with a smile, "that she will be worth even more when I have found her."

"Perhaps," Rigo said. "And I suggest you remember that your life will be worth more if Miss Woode is not abused, and very little indeed if she is. You may leave."

Without a backward glance, Rigo returned to the table with the cognac, and Crawley, pale and shaken, opened the door to make his way out.

Chapter Eleven

As Heather sat in front of her mirror brushing out her long hair, she thought of how relentlessly she was being drawn into the life of Somerset Manor since her recovery. She had quickly regained her original vibrant health, with her cheeks blooming, eyes sparkling, and figure full again. However, her recovered health and beauty increasingly brought Bruce swooping to her side with his ardent attentions. Although he devoted about four hours of each day to the management of the estate by collecting rents from and overseeing the disputes of the tenant farmers, selling produce, and keeping the books, the rest of his time he spent pursuing Heather. Walks in the gardens, tours of the estate, regular afternoon teas, social visits with neighbors, games of whist or a musical hour in the evenings, always, it seemed, found Bruce there, smiling, flirting, and charming.

If she were walking in the garden with Amy, he would often take her arm with a distinct soft pressure. His hand occasionally touched her when he made some flattering comment on her dress or her hair. He would pick a perfect rose and offer it to her with a flourish. More than once, Heather asked him to desist and pulled away, and Bruce would always give her a hurt expression followed by one of puzzlement over her behavior. When he managed to kiss her and wanted to persist, Heather pointed out that such forward behavior might be *de rigueur* in the Colonies but was considered a *faux pas* in England. Lie or not, he seemed to respect her opinion on current manners, but each time, it would only stop him for a day or two. Soon she was again fending him off.

Little notes began appearing in the morning, delivered by Mary, who usually came in to help her dress. One such came this morning. "How lovely you looked yesterday, as pretty as a tea rose in that yellow dress—and as sweet. A token of my esteem is enclosed. Can you arrange for us to have a moment alone today? I must speak with you. Yours devotedly, Bruce." A small china box, suitable for holding rings, had accompanied the note.

Although she admitted to herself that she enjoyed his flattering attentions, Heather found herself sometimes comparing him to Rigo. Bruce, like Rigo, was confident, sure of his place in the world. But Bruce, she decided, was more set in his ways, more conventional, while Rigo was independent and unpredictable. These musings gave over to wondering if he was off pirating somewhere and whether he remembered the woman he had rescued. This life was much like the life Heather had been used to in the days when her parents had been alive, and a pirate's life was not likely to yield a home, was it? Where would she be now if, instead of running to the Somersets, she had tried to hide and return to him? Perhaps he would have deserted her? Heather blushed. Was she, after all, any better than Rigo? Here she was assuming the role of Elizabeth Southey and accepting the love and shelter meant for that woman. Wasn't that a kind of piracy?

Heather hadn't found a moment yet when it was appropriate to reveal herself, and it was increasingly difficult to remember what she had said from one time to another about her past life in England or about those whom she was supposed to have known. Perhaps today she would grant Bruce a moment alone and then tell him she was not Elizabeth Southey. She would conceal who she truly was until she discovered first what Bruce would do with the idea that she was an impostor. It was not totally honest, Heather conceded, but it was prudent. Bruce was his mother's child and had many of her traits, at least regarding social distinctions, and Heather was wary of it. She suspected Mrs. Somerset wanted to guard Bruce from any precipitous actions regarding marriage—the dowry seeming to be an important consideration—and would do all in her power to make certain that any woman he married was rich and suitable in every way. She also felt Mrs. Somerset wanted a lady willing to submit to her rule. Heather smiled to herself. The present Elizabeth Southey didn't add up too well to all those requirements.

Today Bruce was escorting her to Manhattan for a trip to a dressmaker on Crown Street. She was to have a gown made for the ball the Somersets were planning for July eighth. Although a midsummer ball was an annual event, Bruce made it seem the affair was dedicated almost solely to honoring Heather's arrival. He had even begun hinting that "an announcement of great personal significance might be in order." Heather feared he meant to propose even without the recovery of the trunks since he seemed certain of a matching dowry by Miss Southey's remaining uncle in England.

Heather knew she would say "no" to any serious proposal of marriage, but she also knew that her refusal would be baffling and, thus, she had to delay the question being asked. Her charade could not last much longer, but the desire to confess the truth was frozen by the chill she felt when she contemplated Margaret Somerset's reaction to learning of her deceit and her indentured state. There were times when Heather desperately wanted to unburden herself to someone, and she caught herself more than once near John Somerset's study, her hand raised to tap on the closed door. But she never did. Either there were interruptions or else she lost courage, especially when she'd overhear Mrs. Somerset unmercifully upbraid a serving girl, since Heather could feel herself in the girl's place, reduced to tears or red-faced in humiliation.

Once at breakfast, Mrs. Somerset had asked her to send back an omelet not done to her taste, even though it looked perfectly all right to Heather. Impulsively, Heather had said as much as Amy froze in her seat.

"My dear, you must keep these people in line," Mrs. Somerset had said firmly, sitting erect in the high-backed chair. "It keeps them on their toes. I won't allow one ounce of disobedience or slackness. Ever. Nor should you. I notice you are tenderhearted, but I will tell you now, keep them in their place or your household will fall into disorder. Class is class, and the boundaries must always be maintained. Servants are like children and cannot be trusted to know right from wrong without our telling them. Now, send it back," she demanded, giving a vigorous shake of the bell on the table.

Heather looked down at the defenseless omelet, now getting cold. When the hapless girl who had been summoned arrived, silent as a shadow, Heather smiled up at her and said she wasn't hungry and would she remove the omelet? She would just take toast this morning.

Mrs. Somerset went rigid with anger but contained herself until the girl had left.

"I couldn't," Heather interjected quickly. "She did nothing wrong, and it seemed cruel to hurt her and make her day miserable. She has feelings, too!" she added with more heat.

Mrs. Somerset took in her breath. "Young woman, is that a criticism of my household?"

"You have a beautiful home and I cannot fault it. I simply feel since we depend on the services of so many to make life so pleasant for us that they should receive thanks and praise and not be condemned unfairly. We shouldn't take it all for granted, surely!" Heather tried her best to restrain her anger and find the right words to express her feelings without causing a severe rift. Increasing tension was already straining this relationship.

"Those are not the words of a proper English lady," Mrs. Somerset said coldly. "I can't say I've ever heard a properly brought up Colonist uttering such nonsense. Why, you'd have them eating with us next! Unheard of! I would expect such a speech from Richard!" She rang imperiously again, and a girl quickly appeared.

"I'll have morning tea in my room, at once!" When the girl swiftly left to do her bidding, Margaret got up, straightened herself, held her head high, and said, "I suggest you think on what has transpired, Elizabeth. It won't do. I won't have you coddling these wretched girls and not, most certainly, in my household. Good morning, Elizabeth."

When Mrs. Somerset had left, Heather leaned over to the silently stricken Amy and asked, "What should I do, Amy? I hate to be the cause of so much dissension."

Amy let out a long sigh. "I would ask Bruce to pick her some of her favorite roses. That always sweetens Mama," Amy whispered. "And then you must apologize for having disturbed the peace. Mama won't ask you to upbraid Polly again. She'll do it herself. She considers she is teaching us anyway with her example."

"Do you think I'll be forgiven?" Heather asked.

Amy looked at her as if she had taken leave of her senses. "Everyone has at least one black mark in Mama's book."

It was the only time Heather had ever heard Amy say anything remotely like a word of criticism against a member of her family.

Descending the stairs to the sitting room, where she knew Amy awaited her, Heather entered to find the young woman working quietly on a lovely embroidery of a covering for a pillow that would be presented to her father on his birthday. As she embellished his name on the covering, Amy looked up happily at Heather's approach.

"It's coming out beautifully," Heather said as she watched Amy deftly finish a row of tiny stitches.

"I hope Papa likes it," Amy said softly.

"I'm sure he will," Heather returned, then added, "Where is Bruce? He said he would take us to the stables before we left for Manhattan. I must confess to a weakness for horses."

"He should be here shortly. He always keeps his word where you're concerned, Elizabeth."

Heather blushed. "He is attentive," she said, looking away.

"I, for one, will be very happy to have you as my sister-in-law."

Heather moved restlessly. "You are like a sister to me already, but I think you should not count on too much, Amy. There is the matter of the dowry . . . and other things."

"Our lot is not an easy one—being so dependent—is it?" Amy mused aloud. She's thinking of herself, Heather knew.

"At best!" Heather said, then changed the subject. "Do we have to take the carriage to the shore, Amy? Would there be suitable mounts for us to take instead?"

The doorway filled at that moment with a flushed-faced Bruce, who had just returned from being out-of-doors and who had obviously hurried to be in their company. He was wearing a fawn-colored suit, the one he usually wore when making his rounds of the tenant farmers.

"Did I hear mention of horseback riding? Not you, Amy! What is this? Another new side of you?" Bruce smilingly teased his sister as he came to Heather's side to take her hand and raise it to his lips. She retracted it when he seemed to linger too long.

"I do ride!" Amy said, her cheeks flushing. "Richard gave me a mount that suits me well!"

"Ah, your champion again. I must admit, Richard did a credible turn in ridding you of your fear of horseflesh."

"And Elizabeth is ready to accompany us to the boat on horses!"

Bruce looked startled. "I thought . . . but Elizabeth, you led me to believe that you found such pursuits tiring and that you never went on the hunt. I'm sure I remember such a letter."

Heather turned away but quickly recovered. "I don't hunt, but I've since changed my mind about horses. Country living is conducive to riding, isn't it?" Heather

110

smiled at him almost impishly and then blushed at her dissembling.

But Bruce accepted her explanation without a qualm. "That's marvelous! We can go riding in the mornings then. You might even enjoy coming with me on my rounds. But now we must be off to Manhattan."

"That's what I was asking Amy before you came in. Can we ride to the shore?"

"Of course. Ladies, shall we proceed to the stables?" Bruce offered his arm to Heather, who took it with a light laugh, and they were off.

The stable was a long, low barn of substantial proportions with a good choice of mounts. Heather immediately admired a powerful black stallion named Triumph and stroked his soft muzzle, crooning to him. He nickered his approval as his ears pricked up.

"That's Richard's mount," Bruce said, his face expressing displeasure. "He can be a handful, Elizabeth, as Richard is not often here, and only the handler rides him. I thought you might like Beauty. I ride her myself and know her habits." Bruce led her to a sleek chestnut mare who docilely let her muzzle fall toward Heather.

"She's lovely," Heather said, though she looked back wistfully at Triumph, who followed her with his dark eyes. Heather vowed one morning soon to ride Triumph when she and Amy went riding alone, but she maintained her silence as she sensed Bruce's disapproval.

The three were soon mounted and riding gently over the fields, then onto the hard-packed road to the shore. At the private dock of the Somersets', a small but fast sloop waited to take them to Manhattan. Amy, sitting a very correct sidesaddle, rode stiffly, keeping her attention on the steady gait of her slow mount. Heather was riding easily, exhilarated just being mounted and exercising again. With Bruce keeping close beside Heather, Amy was left to follow at her more cautious pace.

"Elizabeth, this is the first time I've had a moment, without someone hovering near, to say what I've wanted to from the moment of your arrival," Bruce began, a flush

111

on his face. His eyes sought hers as he pressed his horse closer.

Heather felt gooseflesh crawl up and down her spine and wanted to stall his saying anything more. Ignoring his personal tone, she smiled brightly and called attention to the bucolic scenery full of the splendors of summer—green woods nearby, wild flowers along the road, cows and sheep in the fields, and a soft breeze blowing gently at their backs. Bruce, however, was not to be put off by her admiration of a flock of quail or fat ewes, and his brown eyes flashed a look of temper though he at first said nothing to stop her chatter.

"Don't make light of my words, Elizabeth," he finally broke in, "when I'm sure you must know how I feel about you. Look at me! You know I spend every moment I can with you. Why do you torture me this way? Is it because you don't care for me?"

Bruce, caught up in his own feelings, was unable to see Heather's swift intake of breath and the flush on her own cheeks as she tried to think of a way to ward off his headlong rush into a declaration.

"Bruce, please! Amy will hear!" she whispered to stall him.

"Let her! I don't care! Besides, I'm sure she guesses. I've hardly tried to deceive anyone in my family about my feelings. They all know how fond I am of you . . . as you do. Don't deny it!"

". . . I . . . Yes, I don't deny I've been more than just a friend to you. You've been very . . . charming, and I will admit to enjoying your company, but there are things I haven't told you that you should know. Were you to know me, your eyes would see me differently."

"What are you saying?" Bruce asked in an irritated tone. "I thought it was agreed between us that we would, if we both desired it, have a future together. I've seen all I need to about you since your arrival. I know you are a beautiful woman, and you have the power to make me happy. That's all I need to know." Bruce's voice lowered and became melodious as his excitement increased.

"But you don't know what you're saying. I . . ." In her

distress over Bruce's continuing declaration, Heather impulsively kicked her mount, spurring him into a canter. She headed toward a shady tree, where she meant to stop and ride back to Amy. She didn't want to have to say no to Bruce, but she also had no plan in mind except to tell him who she was, frightening as that idea was.

Bruce had to pay attention to his own riding and was not about to shout over the beating hooves of the horses, but looking back, Heather could see his expression was taut and that he had a determined look to his jaw. She was breathless by the time she arrived at the tree, where Beauty restively refused to turn, fired up by the exercise she had just received. Amy was plodding toward them at a great distance while Bruce swiftly drew in his horse and grabbed her reins, forcing Heather to a standstill next to him.

"Elizabeth . . ." Bruce knotted his tanned brow. "I know you are young, but you're not shy, like Amy, and you have allowed me liberties that a woman who hated my touch wouldn't, not a woman of your breeding. Then why this coy denial?" He had brought his face close to hers. "Give me an explanation! I deserve that much, don't you agree? And don't fob me off with that nonsense that I don't know you. I live with you! I see you daily!" Bruce's tone was one of frustration and his eyes flashed with an anger she hadn't seen in him before.

Heather squared her shoulders with her own temper. "You want to know why I keep you at a distance? Very well, because you don't know me as you think. I'm not your cousin . . . and I have no money. I'm an orphan!" Heather's eyes were sparkling, and her face flushed with the enormity of her confession.

"What difference if we are first or third cousins twice removed," Bruce said, brushing off her objections with a shrug. "I like it better that we have fewer blood ties. It suits me. As for the dowry, if that is truly your concern, I know my father has written to your uncle and I've no doubt another is on its way. Did you think your uncle would deny you or refuse to believe your loss? I know he will believe Father. And I've always known you were an orphan. None of it matters. The bloodlines are there, and that is all that counts . . . except your acceptance of my courtship . . ."

Heather's eyes opened wide with incredulity. Bruce didn't understand. He had misinterpreted her words. "Would you still care for me if I were a penniless orphan with questionable family ties?" Heather asked him, her cheeks stained with red.

Bruce continued to hold their two horses close together, and she was aware that his thigh was pressed hard against hers. He glanced back irritably at the slow approach of Amy.

"Elizabeth, you haven't given me much opportunity to show you how I care for you," he said in a low, intense voice, lowering his face closer to hers. "I am tired of waiting and always having to restrain myself, playing the courtier. Love needs more than words and looks to grow." As if the saying of it gave him his clue, he reached over with his arm and encircled her small waist, bending his lips to hers in a long, warm kiss. Unable to loose her reins to push him away, Heather accepted the kiss, feeling a bewildering array of emotions at Bruce's failure to comprehend her confession. He didn't press her for more intimacy at the moment, but Heather was again aware that there was nothing tentative or unpracticed in his kiss, and there was a promise in his eyes of more to come when the right moment arrived.

Heather finally put up her hand to his cheek to restrain him and looked seriously into his eyes, reading there his victory that he had achieved part of his objective. His arm was still around her waist and his leg pressing against hers. "But I am dowerless," she repeated. "Don't you understand? Would you want me still?" Heather was unaware how her green eyes took on a depth with her question, and the pretty flush that colored her clear complexion heightened her beauty.

"But it's foolishness to throw such a cruel gauntlet," Bruce said lightly. "We have everything in our favor, and I'm glad. Why even consider the trouble of being penniless when it's not so?"

Heather tossed her chestnut curls, tied neatly back and pinned on top by one of Amy's small, peacock blue riding hats. "Oh, but I am!" Heather let out a deep sigh of exasperation and then let a small peal of laughter escape her full lips. She looked up at him, arching a curved brow and slanting him a mischievous look. "You still refuse to answer me, cousin Bruce. Tell me you'll marry me penniless or not."

Bruce smiled down at Heather and released her waist as he heard his sister's mount arriving. "You tease me, Elizabeth, but I will repay you soon, and no bargaining allowed!"

Heather moved her horse away and straightened her skirt, realizing that not only had she failed to convince him but that her coquettish manner had challenged him to increase his attentions rather than cease them. But she felt, from his hedging, that he would not propose to a Heather Woode that he *knew* was, indeed, penniless, though he might be willing to dally. Bruce would give the lady of his choice an interesting time, but he might also be faithless.

Amy now drew alongside them. If she had seen Bruce's kiss, she made no show of it and merely smiled at the two of them.

Bruce remained in great spirits all the way to the docks, even though Heather insisted on keeping Amy close by, chatting with her exclusively. Bruce interjected his willingness to give her horseback tours of the estate, and there was a gleam in his eyes whenever he glanced Heather's way. She had tried to confess, but she knew the masquerade was not yet ended.

Chapter Twelve

HEATHER PUT HER FEET DOWN AGAIN ON MANHATTAN'S SOIL
with great reluctance. Worms of doubt wiggled in the pit of
her stomach. If Mrs. Somerset hadn't insisted on her
having a suitable gown, she would not have come unless
disguised so no one could possibly recognize her. Then she
might have enjoyed exploring the flourishing new city, but
with just a bonnet and parasol to hide her face, she felt
vulnerable to discovery. Her suspicions were further enhanced when they docked, and she vaguely recognized the
landing place. When she saw The King's Arms, Heather
knew her doubts were not misplaced. She began averting
her face to any man who represented Duncan Crawley and
wondered if his Royal Pork Barrel, William Barrett, might
possibly pop out at her from around the corner. She even
had a fear she might run into Rigo, half hoping and half
fearing how she might explain why she had run away.
Heather shrugged and kept her parasol opened at an
angle, just in case.

When Amy, who felt queasy from the boat crossing,
begged Bruce to let her rest an hour in The King's Arms,

Heather blanched and even began to look around for a possible avenue of escape. Finally, she resigned herself to playing her role to the hilt but keeping her face hidden, just for good measure. Bruce had obviously had to deal with Amy's seasickness before and, taking the two women by the arms, led them to the inn. There he ordered a private room and tea, then took his leave to fetch a carriage for their trip into town.

By keeping her face averted and staying close to the shadows, Heather felt she did a credible job of protecting her identity for the tavernkeeper was the same man she had been paraded before by William Barrett as "a lady of quality and not a frippet, either." Since she saw neither of her two arch-enemies, she relaxed but was still grateful for the room's privacy. Finally, a tapping at the door brought her from her musings.

"That will be tea," she said to Amy, who was reclining on the small bed with a wet cloth over her eyes, recovering. Heather took off her bonnet and cautiously opened the door only a crack. Her eyes widened as she saw the small blond woman in front of her.

"Maggie!" she gasped and then quickly put a hand over the startled Maggie's gaping mouth before her friend could utter Heather's name. Heather opened the door only enough to squeeze herself out and then rapidly closed it behind her.

"Yes, it's me, Maggie," she said, smiling broadly. "Oh, it's so good to see you!" Heather nearly giggled in her glee to see the familiar face before her. For the first time in too long, she felt a relaxing of tension within her, not because all was well but simply because she wouldn't have to pretend for a brief time that she was someone else.

"I never thought to see ye again, Heather," Maggie said, looking stunned. "Where've ye been? All kinds of rogues came in here alookin' for ye, includin' that devil Dunc'n Crawl."

"He isn't here, is he?" Heather asked, stiffening slightly.

"No, an' hasn't come round in a while. Don't you fear 'im. But yer still in trouble?" Maggie sucked in her breath and shook her head, her blond curls tucked into a large, floppy white cap.

"Elizabeth?" The soft voice of Amy called, and Heather remembered Maggie was still holding the tray of tea. She immediately took it and whispered to Maggie to wait a moment.

Amy was too tired to even be curious about who was at the door, so when Heather rejoined Maggie, she asked for someplace to talk without being overheard. Maggie took them into the darkened linen closet, saying she couldn't stay long or she'd be beaten within an inch of her life. At first surprised, Heather decided it was just a figure of speech—one of Maggie's many.

Heather quickly proceeded to tell Maggie what had happened to her, a lot of which she had to omit though all she told of it was the truth. "And so I'm now Elizabeth Southey and about to be either discovered or betrothed," Heather concluded. As she related her story, she was oddly detached, although she knew only too well that once back with the actual Somersets, it was no matter to make light of it.

"And so that lady in there is the sister of Elizabeth's intended?" Maggie asked, almost to herself, as she grasped the situation.

Heather nodded. "And I expect her brother to appear soon with a carriage for us."

"I told ye, Heather, ye be lucky. By the stars, ye be!"

"You may yet see me in irons!" Heather said. "Never let on you've seen me, or I'm done."

Maggie tossed her head sideways back and forth. "Now why should I do that an' cast a blot on me good name?"

Then Heather asked Maggie about herself and soon had her eyes opened about the life of being a barmaid. Maggie wasn't lying about being beaten and bore several bruises from having been knocked about, once by a customer in his cups wanting favors she wasn't willing to give and once by a swat from the tavernkeeper himself who, when he'd had a drink, was abusive.

"He's a slaver," Maggie concluded, "night and day. And when he sees fit, he keeps me pittance of an allowance—for slackin', or so he says. Before long, I'll leave, papers or no, and he can empty his own slop pots."

"You haven't changed a bit!" Heather said, smiling. "But I'm sorry to hear of your misery. I once promised you that I'd try to help and now . . ."

Just then, they heard heavy footfalls on the stairs and Maggie clapped a hand to her head. "He's comin' for me! I'm off."

"Maggie!" a harsh man's voice called gruffly.

"I'll be back to see you," Heather told her hurriedly as Maggie backed out of the linen closet, her finger to her lips.

When Heather, deep in thought, returned to the recovered Amy, the young woman was up and ready to leave, her eyes full of concern.

"Bruce is waiting in the carriage. Where did you get to?" Amy asked.

"I? Oh, I was talking to one of the servants," Heather said distractedly, not seeing the look of wonder on Amy's face.

Bruce helped the women into the carriage, placing Heather beside him, his own body close to hers. His hand occasionally touched some part of her when he moved or when pointing out an interesting landmark, and once, with a cross expression, Heather gave him a light tap on the knuckles as a reprimand. Bruce obeyed, but with a roguish grin that made it appear he thought she was just flirting.

Amy was now feeling very fit and chattered happily about her coming visit to the Somerset townhouse, where she hoped her brother Richard would be at home.

"Though I don't suppose he is this time of day, I do hope so," Amy went on. "He has such lively friends, and I think it's time he met you."

"I doubt that will be possible this trip," Bruce countered swiftly, with a tight expression. "We haven't much time before we leave, and we can't wait for him to put in an appearance." Heather had been searching for an excuse to avoid meeting yet another member of the Somerset clan, let alone one who lived in Manhattan where, in her naive fear, Heather believed her story was widely known.

Now she saw with relief that Bruce had taken the trouble off her hands.

Amy pursed her lips but still seemed to be looking forward to being at the townhouse, so Bruce suggested he leave Heather at the dressmaker's and retrieve her in an hour's time, which suited Heather. He took the liberty of brushing his lips against her cheek before alighting from the carriage and assisting her down, and as the carriage moved off with Bruce and Amy, Heather found herself in a very fashionable shopping district. Carriages and men on horseback rode up and down, and the streets were surprisingly crowded with pedestrians.

The dressmaker, a widow by the name of Mrs. Osborne, was a very capable though somewhat talkative lady who seemed happy enough to fit Heather into an exquisite creation of lime green batiste of many layers with tiny satin bows stitched around the full skirt. The bodice was low but had a little lace inset that just peeked above the swelling of her breasts. When the fitting was over, Heather chose a piece of brilliant blue cloth for Amy and prepared to leave, promising to herself to return in half an hour's time for Bruce's arrival. Then she took to the street, parasol in hand, looking forward to doing some window-shopping alone.

It was reckless of her, she thought, as she indulged a fancy for a white lace fan and a small velvet purse to be carried on the wrist. She told herself it would be Amy's in the event she had to leave precipitously. Coming out of the shop with purchases in hand, Heather was about to cross the street when she saw a horseman approaching whose bearing captured her eye. She stopped in her path at the curb to discreetly watch the man from beneath her lowered parasol. Her heart started beating faster and her mouth parted as he approached. Heather stood frozen, unable to move. Her breathing constricted as she recognized the black hair and broad shoulders of Rigo, who was about to pass within a few yards of her.

His eyes, though shaded by a black hat, were suddenly trained on her. As he drew up closer, holding the reins tightly, his handsome face took on a look of disbelief. The power he exuded finally struck Heather, and she panicked as she saw his expression changing to anger: this Rigo was not in a rescuing mood. She pivoted and began to hurry in the other direction but hadn't taken more than three strides when she felt a strong hand on her arm—it spun her around. She stared up at him.

Caught in a web of tangled feelings, Heather drowned in his fierce eyes as a wild fluttering raced through her stomach. Crushed was her brief longing to be in his arms as those intense eyes thoroughly ran over her body and then came back to her face.

"I wasn't sure," his low voice said slowly. Still holding her arm in a vise of iron, Rigo inclined his head toward her, a sardonic twist to his lips. "You're looking well."

"I am . . . well," Heather said, blushing.

Rigo released her arm and stood, reins in hand, as his horse obediently waited. Looking down at her, his eyes took on the cool of ice chips.

"Do I get to hear the history of your remarkable climb in the world," he said smiling, though his eyes remained frosted. "Or will you simply tell me another story?"

"I never thought I'd see you again," Heather whispered.

"I said I'd return. Didn't you trust me to keep my word?"

"I was too frightened," Heather said, her breath coming fast, "and I needed a safe place to go." She could see the anger and contempt in his eyes but still couldn't seem to say the right thing.

"And you weren't sure I would provide that," Rigo stated flatly, finishing her thought. A bare smile creased the corners of his mouth but didn't reach his eyes. "Have you found a safe place?"

"I've been taken in by a family on Staten Island."

"By a family?" Rigo asked, raising a black eyebrow. "Then I must know of them."

Heather flushed and murmured, "I hope you do not."

Rigo stood very still while he interpreted her refusal to name the family. Then he said, "Let me congratulate you on your swift rise in the world. You had me fooled, but

121

then I always did like a pretty face." He smiled sardonical-ly and added, "I could have taken care of you well enough, but I gather you've found another man to do that for you."

Heather's blush took on a deeper hue, and her eyes flashed angrily. "If that's what you think, then you don't need an explanation. I did what I had to do."

Rigo bowed. "Obviously, lady. The choice was yours." He leapt on his horse, gave him a quick kick, and left without looking back.

Heather was stunned and then distraught by his sudden departure. She hadn't expected he would leave and chided herself for handling the meeting badly, realizing she might never see him again. Heather wondered if she should go to the inn where he had taken her and speak to Daniel—if she could find it again. Rigo might have helped her, but the story of her impersonating Miss Southey seemed too farfetched even to begin.

Turning back toward the dressmaker's, tears threaten-ing in her eyes, Heather discovered Bruce and Amy were waiting for her, with Bruce impatient to be going.

When he finally registered that Heather was distracted, both he and Amy tried to find the cause. Heather found herself telling them Maggie's story, wanting to give them good reason for her distress by adding that Maggie had taken care of her aboard the ship and that she felt she owed her a debt. Amy suggested they find Maggie and take her away from the tavernkeeper, perhaps hiring her as Heather's personal maid. Heather was amazed that her story had brought about a solution for Maggie and asked Bruce his opinion.

"Of course, Elizabeth, if it pleases you," Bruce re-joined.

And so they traveled to The King's Arms once again and, for a sum, secured Maggie's contract and services. When an overwhelmed Maggie saw Heather waiting in the carriage, she flew to her side and whispered for her ears alone, "You've done it now! You're in water hotter than a pig's scalding."

Heather shushed her. "No sass, Maggie," she said, "or I'll ask to have you peeling potatoes instead of mending clothes." Then she smiled teasingly at Maggie, who rolled her eyes heavenward.

The journey back to Staten Island began, but for Heather, her pleasure in the presence of Maggie was not enough to overcome the feelings of gloom caused by her unhappy encounter with Rigo. She had lost her pirate again. This time, she feared, it was forever.

Chapter Thirteen

RIGO HAD BEEN AT SEA ALMOST TWO WEEKS, PATROLLING twenty to fifty miles off the south shore of Long Island, when his lookout spotted the first ships of what soon emerged as a vast fleet. Uncertain at first whether it was a naval armada or General Howe's troop convoy, Rigo directed the *Contessa* southeast toward the very heart of the armada and, as he feared, discovered two British frigates leaving the convoy to challenge him. He sailed as close as he dared and was able to see that the two huge ships were obviously troop carriers. Mission accomplished, he ordered his ship swung about to escape the closing frigates.

He was barely in time. A wind shift permitted one of the British warships to gain on him while the fading afternoon light made the *Contessa* still visible, and cannonballs hissed past them into the sea. As the *Contessa* raced north toward the shoals off Jones inlet, darkness finally lowered its protective cape and the *Contessa* escaped.

At midnight, Rigo anchored off the inlet and sent two of

his men ashore in a ship's boat with both oral and written versions of what he had seen. By dawn at the latest, they would be able to locate the posted courier, who would hurry with the messages to General Washington in Manhattan. Without waiting for his men to return, Rigo put to sea again, sailing south without running lights. He had decided on the bold plan of sailing into the middle of the convoy under the cover of darkness to sail with the fleet wherever it might be going while flying the English flag. He felt that in the huge ragtag convoy, another cargo ship would go undetected—unless the same frigate that had chased him the previous evening chanced to fall back to where the *Contessa* would be and recognize her.

In any case, Rigo felt it was worth the risk. His task was to let General Washington know where General Howe's fleet was going, and by insinuating himself into its very midst, he would be the first to know. If the fleet passed New York harbor and began sailing south down the New Jersey coast, he would leave the convoy and sail to Manhattan to inform General Washington that New York appeared safe.

But Rigo doubted it. The direction of the convoy strongly suggested that it was headed for New York harbor. If so, then the only questions remaining would be where Howe would disembark his troops and how many he had brought with him.

In the early light of dawn, the *Contessa* found herself sailing along in the middle of almost a dozen ships, several of which took long looks at her through the glasses. But none signaled her, and the single British man-of-war in the vicinity seemed indifferent.

As the hours passed and they drew nearer to the mouth of New York harbor, Rigo felt a rising excitement. He had felt dejected since his upsetting encounter with Heather two weeks earlier, and the boredom of patrolling the empty sea hadn't helped any. He had gone over and over Heather's evasive replies to his questions, but he still found it hard to believe that the fresh, vibrant, innocent girl he had met had already become some man's mistress. Yet how else could he explain her obvious rise in station and her refusal to reveal the reasons for her finery?

Such brooding had kept Rigo low, but now the prospect of sailing into New York harbor with General Howe's fleet and then proceeding on to Manhattan to warn General Washington had him and Noah smiling. Of course, others would rush to tell the authorities of the massive arrival, but none would be able to provide the details that Rigo now could.

He was glad, too, that the military confrontation was going to take place where General Washington had predicted—on Rigo's own home ground. It would mean, he supposed, a formal and total break with his family—except for Amy and, perhaps, even his father—but the invasion would force people to decide where their loyalties lay. Rigo would have to see his father as soon as possible and reveal to him all his recent activities. While on Staten Island, he would certainly also see if anyone knew of a chestnut-haired beauty who had recently arrived in the area. His stepmother, who made it a point to know of every lady and gentleman within twenty miles, would certainly have information—unless Heather were being "kept" hidden. The thought of Heather in the arms of another man sent Rigo's blood racing in anger, and he had to shout out a meaningless order to restore his balance.

That night, the whole convoy hove to less than ten miles, by Rigo's reckoning, from Sandy Hook and the entrance to New York. He guessed that while the first part of the convoy had already entered, perhaps even begun disembarking, the rest would wait for daylight. Rigo's message would be old news by the time he got into New York the next day. He considered sailing the *Contessa* through the fleet at night but knew that the chance both of an accident or of being challenged by an English man-of-war was too great to risk it. He could make a greater contribution by staying with the convoy and trying to make an estimate of General Howe's troop strength. It began to look like he might have several reasons now for wanting to visit Staten Island. With a sigh, Rigo left Noah in command and went below to sleep.

Heather and Amy waited on the porch while Arabella Moncrief descended from the open carriage, gathering the folds of her pale blue dress and holding her parasol over her head to shield her fine, creamy complexion from the summer sun.

"She's exquisite," Heather whispered to Amy as she watched the elegantly beautiful woman with carefully curled dark blond hair coming slowly toward them.

Introductions were made and Arabella's large, gray eyes glanced at Heather in a very quick appraisal.

She was taller than Amy but two inches shorter than Heather and very slender, with small, high breasts, the slight rise of which just peeked above the molded perfection of her gown. She folded her parasol and gave Heather a small smile.

"Bruce has told me so much about you," Arabella said coolly to Heather. "It's a pleasure to meet you at last."

"I am pleased to meet you as well," Heather returned. "I have yet to meet your betrothed who, as I understand it, is away at sea this summer, but Amy says he is wonderful. You must be very happy." Then she added spontaneously, "You are every bit as lovely as Bruce and Amy have said."

Arabella seemed pleased with Heather's response, and her smile became more cordial and her tone more relaxed.

"Richard is quite terrible to leave me so much on my own, but I was able to dine with him several times in Manhattan before he sailed for the West Indies."

The women swept into the sitting room, where tea was waiting to be poured, with Margaret Somerset doing the honors. After tea and cakes were served, they began discussing the upcoming ball, with the talk centering on gowns and who was coming and how they were hoping for relief from the uncommonly hot spell, especially for the ball, now only a day away. Finally, Arabella wanted to hear from Heather of London society and what was in fashion there.

Heather smiled graciously, now quite used to her role, and answered, using her own knowledge with considerable expansion and imagination about places and people she didn't know. Like a storyteller, she was enjoying embellishing a good tale.

She ended by turning the talk back to the ball, since she knew the women would easily pick up the topic. "I haven't done much dancing in some time, and I'm looking forward to it."

"You are so different from my expectations," Arabella said, her fan waving to and fro in a graceful arc. "We had all expected a near invalid. Of course, Bruce has been over to see us since you've arrived and mentioned the country air seems to have done wonders for your health. Living in the Colonies agrees with you, then?"

"Very much," Heather returned easily. "My London life was wearying."

"And I'm told you found your own maid again in Manhattan after a separation and that she's quite . . . entertaining!"

Heather blushed, wondering who could have told Arabella that piece of her story, concluding it must have been Bruce, who was finding Maggie an aggravating obstacle when it came to seeing Heather alone.

"Maggie does need polish yet, but I'm pleased to have her with me again."

The women all stopped, teacups in hand, at a commotion in the hall. They heard Bruce's voice rising above the excited talk.

He burst into the drawing room with long strides and with an exultant expression on his face. To the astonishment of all, at his side was a resplendent English officer.

"Excuse the interruption, ladies, but I'd like you to meet Captain Robert Blair of His Majesty's Third Regiment of Hussars, newly arrived on Staten Island."

The women stared, their eyes widening. Margaret Somerset exclaimed with pleasure and rose to welcome the young officer.

Bruce proceeded to introduce each of the younger women as Captain Blair bowed formally and smiled, offering his apologies for having interrupted their tea and adding a simple pleasantry, by rote, to each.

Then he said stiffly, still a little ill at ease in the company of the three young, attractive women, "This is, indeed, a fortunate day for me."

"I've just invited Captain Blair and a number of his officers to join in tomorrow night's festivities," Bruce said smiling, "and he's accepted on his and their behalf. But there's more good news," Bruce went on. "The troops have landed here in force and are setting up camp. We'll soon see the colonists' rebellion routed once and for all!"

Bruce went over to the liquor cabinet and, opening a bottle of a fine port wine, said, "I think a small celebration is called for. So, ladies, join us in a glass and we'll toast to the arrival of His Majesty's army." Bruce distributed the wine and raised his glass in salute. "To King George!"

Captain Blair drank soberly and thanked all for their gracious welcome. "And now, I must return to my men. We have much to do before nightfall." With more good-byes and a promise to return for dinner, he left, Bruce with him.

"What a fine young man!" Margaret said when he'd disappeared, directing her description in Amy's direction. Amy visibly squirmed.

Arabella chose this time to take her leave, having declined to stay for dinner, stating she had much to do before the ball.

"If Richard were here for dinner, I'd drop everything—gown, bath, and all," she said with a sigh.

"I do hope he'll return soon from his silly sailing errands, for your sake," Margaret said.

"If only . . ." Arabella began, then changed her mind. She turned at the door. "I'm sure Richard would wish to be here now that the army has arrived. He's so interested in things to do with government."

"Far too interested, if you ask me," Margaret shot back in her fierce voice. "He'll get us all in trouble with his so-called interest. I feel far safer with him out at sea."

"Oh, Mother!" said Amy with a look of distress.

"No, Mrs. Somerset," Arabella said quietly. "You

really shouldn't worry about Richard. He talks sometimes like a fierce tiger, but at bottom, I assure you, he's the gentlest pussycat." She held her head high and Heather could see by the glint in her eye that she thought she had this Richard wound around her little finger. For some reason, this self-confidence annoyed Heather. Then, with a graceful, all-encompassing curtsy, Arabella departed.

After Mrs. Somerset went off to the kitchen to give orders for the evening meal, Heather and Amy spent a few minutes talking of the surprising arrival of the English troops. They looked up as Bruce hurried into the room a second time.

"Elizabeth," he said breathlessly. "You must come and see! It's an incredible sight! Please, come. You, too, Amy."

The two young women followed Bruce out the door and through the garden to climb the small knoll to the right of the house. When she arrived, what Heather saw took her breath away.

Below her, the narrows that separated Staten Island from Brooklyn was filled seemingly from horizon to horizon with ships. Never had she seen so many. And on the land below Somerset Manor—less than a quarter mile away—were hundreds, no, thousands of red-coated men. It was as if Heather had been sleeping and were now awakened to a new and totally different world.

"What is it?" Amy asked from beside her in an awed voice.

"That, my dear sister," Bruce answered proudly, "is our English navy and our English army. That is our salvation."

"There are so many . . ." Amy said softly.

"But why are they landing here?" Heather asked.

"The rebels have a large number of men in New York. I imagine these men have come to rout them."

"Where will they live?" Amy asked.

"They'll set up tents," Bruce answered, squinting as he stared off to his right toward the open sea. "We may invite a few of the senior officers to billet with us."

"It's beautiful," Heather said, feeling a pleasant excitement at the vast array of ships and men. "I've never seen so many ships."

"And you never will again," Bruce agreed, his eyes bright with excitement, too. "Oh, Elizabeth! It's as if the whole English navy had arrived just for our ball and to celebrate with us our . . ." He stopped himself and glanced at Amy.

"Amy," he said, going to her quickly. "Tell Mother what you've seen. She won't want to miss this sight."

"Oh, yes," said Amy, smiling. "I will." She pulled up her skirts and hurried down the path back toward the house.

With Amy gone, Bruce seemed to lapse into quiet for a moment, crossing his arms over his chest, his feet apart, while he viewed the scene. Heather began to wish she'd gone with Amy—not because Bruce made her uncomfortable but because she sensed something in him tightly strung.

"Shall we go?" she asked.

Bruce turned his head and looked down at her. Smiling, he held out his hand.

"Come for a walk with me," he said, his voice soft and enticing.

"But I have things to do, and . . ."

"Don't," Bruce interrupted. "Please don't find excuses not to be with me." He put out his other hand to take hers and playfully pull her along while Heather smiled and only partly resisted his effort. Then he smiled fully and threw his head back to laugh.

"How I adore you!" Bruce said, when he stopped and slipped his arm around her waist, directing her feet over the fields toward a lovely shelter of trees.

"You have a look in your eyes that gives me a shiver," Heather said playfully as she followed his lead.

"My intentions are honorable," Bruce returned lightly. "But barely."

The air was soft and filled with the wild, sweet smell of honeysuckle. A gentle wind stirred the grasses and the long skirt of her dress. Below them, the vast armada of ships still floated serenely in the narrows. Bruce talked quietly of what he had seen and heard of the British forces, distracting Heather while he led her into a quiet copse of trees.

"Events are moving rapidly," Bruce said as he stopped their forward movement and slipped his arm around her waist. Heather took hold of his hand to keep it from slipping too high and near her breast, as he had done on several other occasions when he thought they weren't observed.

"It's so hot," Heather said, trying to find another safe topic.

"You'll not get me to talk of the weather or anything else your devious feminine mind can think of to keep me away, not this time, my sweet." Bruce's voice had dropped a note, becoming huskier. He turned Heather into his arms. She resisted the movement, which only made his hold harder.

"Elizabeth," he said softly, looking down into her eyes, "I want you to marry me."

Heather took in a deep breath, surprised by the suddenness of his asking. She stood still, braced against his warmth, then lifted her head to look at him directly.

"A pretty speech. Not even the question, will you, but only, I want you to," she said, teasing him lightly, while trying to pull away.

Bruce's eyes darkened. "You're mocking me." He tightened his arm, refusing to let her slip out by pressing her against his length.

"Do you think I don't mean what I say?"

Heather put her hands on his chest and looked away, uncertain of how she should respond this time. He was serious, and her former reasons for refusing him were confusing her, since Rigo now seemed to be a part of her past. Perhaps she would marry him, Heather thought. And then again, she knew she couldn't, not as things stood.

Bruce watched her indecision and then simply brought his head down and claimed her lips, this time with the force of passion. His arms went around Heather like a vise, pressing the breath from her while his hands roved freely over her back and down to her hips, where he held on tight.

When Bruce released her, she gasped for air while he still held her tightly, his warm breath fanning her face.

"I mean to have you, Elizabeth," he said thickly. "Do you want me to look foolish and go down on one knee? Is that it?" Bruce rained soft kisses on her face. "Say yes! Make me a happy man," he whispered against her cheek and lips. "Allow me to announce our engagement at the ball."

Heather pulled away, putting up a finger to cover his lips, which he then kissed and licked tenderly with his tongue.

"Bruce," she started, her voice slightly shaky from the force of his kisses and the surprise of his passion.

"We must wait . . ." she finally finished.

"I can't wait any longer," he said, his eyes half closed, and, taking her hand in his, he kissed it on the back and on the palm.

"You take my breath away," Heather said softly, "but you must stop. I don't think your parents would approve."

Bruce stopped kissing her hand and laughed lightly.

"No, they won't approve, but I'm beyond caring who approves. I adore you."

"I can't . . . say yes . . . and not just because of your parents. I mean, yes, because of them. Oh, Bruce, you have me confused." Heather rubbed her hands against the thin cloth of his shirt with her hands, feeling the beat of his heart with her palms.

"Say yes to me and be damned with the rest. We'll keep it our secret, but say yes to me," Bruce whispered, his voice thick with the intensity of his passion.

Heather sucked in her breath, aware of his arousal and a little under the spell of his ardor.

"Yes," she said softly, looking up at him with a sweet smile, "but with a condition."

"Anything . . ."

"Promise to tell no one. Promise me. It's our secret."

"Done!" Bruce said, his voice rich with joy before he swooped down on her mouth with a feverish kiss, his hands beginning an exploration of her body that made her wish she hadn't been so impetuous. He pushed the low-cut neckline of her gown aside to hold the fullness of her breast in his hand.

"Bruce . . . !" Heather gasped, but he continued his caress and went on whispering tenderly against her throat.

"Oh, my beautiful one . . . no more 'no's' . . . not now . . . not ever . . . I adore you so . . ."

"Bruce . . . please . . ."

He scooped her up in his arms and lay her gently down on the soft grasses. Bruce covered her body with his, pinning her beneath him as his mouth again sought and found hers in a probing kiss.

"No! Stop!" Heather said as she managed to pull her mouth away from his, surprised to realize that her hands were pinned above her head by one of his hands.

"Oh, my beautiful one, my betrothed," he murmured softly, holding his head just above hers. "We are soon to be wed and I only ask for what soon will always be mine. . . ." As she tried to twist away and out from under him, Bruce pressed himself down with a strength that frightened and angered Heather. Pinching her captive hands and forcing his mouth again down upon hers, his free hand pulled at her undergarment. When she again managed to twist her mouth away, he lowered his mouth to kiss her neck, then her collarbone, then he lowered himself toward her exposed breast.

"Bruce!" a shocked feminine voice suddenly called from a few yards away.

Bruce raised himself off Heather slightly at the sound and turned, a low growl of disgust in his throat. Heather recognized Amy's voice.

"What are you doing here?" Bruce rasped. "Go back to the house!"

"Mama sent me!" Amy replied in a high, hysterical voice. "And she'll come herself if you don't return. The captain and a major and some other men are all here and waiting for you. It's time for dinner."

With a violent shove, Heather at last got herself free from Bruce's weight and scrambled a few feet away, angrily pulling up her bodice and adjusting her skirts. She noted that Amy, looking stricken, didn't look at her. Bruce, also not looking at her, sprawled a moment more and then slowly stood up.

"Hell!" he announced softly.

"I shall tell!" Amy said warningly, whether of the swear word or the kissing Heather couldn't tell.

"Grow up, prissy," Bruce said in a low hiss and then turned to offer a hand to Heather.

"Oh!" Amy gasped.

Heather ignored Bruce's outstretched hand and got to her feet with her back to him. She began marching determinedly toward the house, brushing at her hair as she went. Bruce and Amy hurried to catch up with her.

"I rushed things. . . ." Bruce said in a low tone when he arrived at her side.

"Don't tussle me in the bushes again!" Heather said sharply.

"You won't change your mind about our . . . secret?" he asked urgently as they neared the side entrance of the manor.

"Do I have your word that you won't try to take such liberties again?" Heather countered, stopping at the entrance with her head tilted stiffly to one side.

Bruce made a grimace and shrugged.

"It must be dull in London these days with the women making all the rules," he said.

Heather gave one last brush to her skirts and to her hair before entering.

"Oh, we have our share of pirates, too!" she said and sailed into the house, Bruce and Amy following.

Chapter Fourteen

THE JULY DAY WAS GLORIOUS, AND RIGO FELT EXHILARATED as his *Contessa* sailed along in a file of cargo ships past Sandy Hook and into the narrows that separated Brooklyn and Staten Island. There was something grand about being part of such a large fleet sailing in close order in a restricted body of water, even if he alone didn't belong there and might at any moment be discovered for the spy he was. Ahead and behind, as far as his eye could see, stretched an incredible fleet of English ships with flags flying and decks crowded with sailors and, in some cases, troops. All were drinking in the splendid parade of ships and the exciting unfolding spectacle of the two shorelines as were Rigo and his mates.

Standing aft with Noah and two other mates, Rigo was trying to pick out the familiar shape of Somerset Manor on the hilltop five miles ahead when the lookout posted in the crow's nest shouted down and began pointing—almost, it seemed to Rigo, at Somerset Manor itself. Lowering the angle of his glass, Rigo soon saw what had so excited the lookout. The shore of Staten Island seemed to be teeming

136

with tiny insects and waterbugs scampering between anchored cargo ships and the shore, but it was really General Howe landing his troops on Staten Island.

Rigo felt a peculiar sinking of the heart at the sight of his own home being invaded. In fact, he knew—although he could not yet see—that General Howe would be bivouacking some of his men on part of the five hundred acres of the Somerset estate.

Even as he strained to see through the glass exactly where the tents were being set up, Rigo knew immediately that his task had changed. Now he had to get himself ashore, change back to Richard Somerset, and spy on the newly arrived English forces. Dozens of rebel colonists would already be telling those in New York of the arrival of General Howe, and Noah could be depended on to sail the *Contessa* back to Manhattan. Now, only Richard Somerset would make an effective spy.

As they continued sailing northward into the narrows toward New York harbor, Rigo began to see more clearly the long line of ships anchored close to the Staten Island side of the narrows, each with long boats loaded with troops or supplies pulling to land. Along the shore itself, an incredible lawn of tents had sprouted up several hillsides, and everywhere there were men moving, marching, and building. Further up the narrows, just before New York harbor, Rigo could make out two or three English warships patrolling. Still further, in the harbor itself, were a few more. The sea belonged to the English and the land—well, that's what this whole invasion was all about, Rigo thought. In any case, Staten Island now belonged, once again, to England.

"They're signaling us, Cap'n," Noah said from beside him, and when Rigo lowered his glass, he saw Noah pointing dead ahead. A large, two-decked galleon was hove to in the middle of the channel and was directing the cargo ships in the file to the left or right. It was ordering the *Contessa* to turn to port toward the Staten Island shore to anchor there.

Rigo ordered his own signalman to acknowledge the directions and gave the appropriate commands to his crew to begin turning the boat to port. He told his third mate, Mr. Maitland, to go forward and prepare to anchor. Then he took Noah aside to explain the plans that were even now still unfolding in his own mind.

"I want to get myself ashore," Rigo said in a rapid whisper, away from the helmsman and the other mate. "But we've also got to get the *Contessa* out of this crowd before she's discovered to be what she is."

"I was wondering what the redcoats were going to think when we didn't begin sending ashore any of their troops," Noah said with a smile.

"They'd send a longboat to investigate, and we'd be in trouble," Rigo replied quickly. "Look, here's what I want you to do. Go forward and tell Maitland that after I give the command to drop anchor, he's to lower it only three fathoms and then to pretend it's jammed. Order the men to run to the capstan and make a lot of motion and noise. The tide and wind are both taking us toward New York, so if we pretend we're out of control and can't anchor, we'll be able to drift and sail past this line of anchored ships into New York harbor. Then you should be free to outrun any frigates into Manhattan."

"What if they're blocking our way?" asked Noah with a frown.

"Nothing can block the *Contessa* with the wind behind her," said Rigo, watching as his ship made its slow turn to port and began to crawl toward the shore a half mile away. The ship just ahead of him was already heaving to and dropping her anchor. "You're still flying the English flag," he continued to Noah, "and keep flying it until our rebel batteries on lower Manhattan start firing at you. The British will signal you about your intentions, but by the time you send them some confused answer, you'll easily be able to outrun them up the Hudson to Tudor Wharf. Lower the topsails!" he suddenly shouted forward and then commanded the helmsman to point her up higher.

For a moment, both Rigo and Noah watched as the *Contessa* nosed up into the wind, now only a few hundred yards from shore. Rigo noticed that there would be plenty of room between the ships at anchor and the land for the *Contessa* to "drift" with the tide toward New York.

"How will you get ashore?" Noah asked.

Rigo glanced swiftly aft once to gauge his position in relation to the other boats and then forward again.

"I'm swimming," he suddenly decided. "Hard to port! Lower all sails!" he shouted to the helmsman and then to the crew. "Noah! Go warn Maitland! Quick!"

The mainsail was fluttering and snapping in the wind as his crew aloft grappled to bring it down and lash it to the spar. The *Contessa* was dead in the water as Noah raced down the ladder from the poop, where Rigo still stood, to go forward to give Maitland his orders. When Noah arrived, Rigo could see—even at sixty feet—the perplexed expression on Maitland's face as he tried to absorb Rigo's plan. As Rigo checked his position a last time to make certain he would drift clear of the ship downwind from him that was already at anchor, he knew there was no time for further explanations. Maitland had it or he didn't.

"Anchors away forward!" he shouted, and then, "Get that sail in!" to the crew still battling with the flapping mainsail. There was an unusual delay forward at obeying his command, but Rigo assumed it was because Noah and Maitland had to organize the crew to stop the fall of the anchor after twenty feet—a job not in the crew's usual repertoire. Finally, there was the shattering clatter of the heavy anchor chain running out through the anchor block and the creaking of the capstan. Then an abrupt and unexpected silence. Two crewmen aft turned to stare forward, knowing something was wrong.

"Anchor jammed!" Noah shouted, and Rigo watched as the charade began around the capstan with men wrestling with the huge chain as if to free it.

"Raise the jib again!" Rigo shouted forward, and Noah repeated the command to the sailors there who had just managed to get the foresail tied down. The *Contessa*'s bow swung slowly toward land as the whole ship began to drift sideways parallel to the shore. The line of ships anchored along Staten Island's shore stretched almost a mile, and

Rigo would have to guide the *Contessa* between them and the land the whole way. The only real danger was the busy traffic in ships' longboats ferrying troops and supplies ashore.

Rigo shouted a few colorful obscenities forward for the benefit of the officers of the cargo ship they were drifting past and then gave a few more moderate and accurate instructions to the helmsman to keep the *Contessa* from getting too close to land. The jib finally exploded out into the air and filled with wind, and Rigo had his ship turned to begin sailing slowly down the longboat-filled lane toward New York harbor.

"Signal 'anchor jammed,' " Rigo said quietly to the signalman on the poop beside him. As they drifted and sailed past the next ship, Rigo screamed a series of foul-mouthed commands to his anchor crew, who promptly redoubled their efforts at doing nothing. Rigo smiled to see Noah jumping up and down as if in uncontrolled fury. The ship's officer of a longboat shouted obscenely at them for sailing in restricted waters, and Rigo gaily shouted back, implying the man was a numbskull of doubtful parentage.

They had passed a dozen anchored ships and were halfway through the narrows when Noah returned aft.

"When we reach Bitter Point, it'll be time for you to fish or cut bait," he said quietly to Rigo. "Out in New York harbor dodging the frigates will be too late for an afternoon swim."

"You think you can get the *Contessa* back to Tudor Wharf without too many holes in her?" Rigo asked, frowning down at his mate.

"I'd rather be doing that," Noah answered promptly, "than swimming into the biggest nest of unfriendlies I ever saw. You got a lady friend you planning to see ashore?" Noah asked with a wink.

"I wish I did," Rigo answered, noting with a rueful smile that the mention of a lady friend had immediately brought the heart-thumping image of Heather to his mind and not that of his betrothed, Arabella, of whom he hadn't had a thought in days. "If the other mates ask about me, tell them I got frightened and abandoned ship."

"They won't believe me," Noah said, frowning up at Rigo.

"I hope not, but if anyone ever gets captured, that's the story I want told, understand?"

"Aye, sir," Noah said with a sigh. "It makes more sense, I'm sure, than whatever the real reason may be."

The *Contessa* was now nearing the end of the line, and so, too, was Rigo. The Staten Island shore was a quarter mile off and crowded with English troops. He would be swimming into a viper's nest, indeed. Beyond the troops high on the hill stood his home, Somerset Manor. Unfortunately, he couldn't don the protective identity of Richard Somerset until he was through that line of troops. After all, there could be no explanation for Richard Somerset's swimming ashore from a spy ship except that Richard Somerset was a spy—and Rigo could not have that.

"Report everything you've seen to General Washington's headquarters," Rigo said as he removed his seaboots and his heavy cape. "Except about me. Officially, for the time being, Captain Rigo was lost at sea, understand?"

"You sure you can make it all the way to shore?" Noah asked as he took Rigo's cape and sword.

"I once swam across to Brooklyn," Rigo replied, gauging the slow pace of his ship past the last anchored cargo vessel. "I become a very good swimmer when the alternative is drowning." He strode forward to the rail. "Prepare to raise the mainsail!" he shouted, and then more quietly to Noah, "Just let her drift up the harbor toward the Hudson until someone starts firing at you. Then get your sails up and run like hell."

"Maybe I'll go for a swim after all," said Noah with a big grin.

"You've always wanted to be captain," Rigo said, smiling back. "Here's your chance."

"Somehow, I didn't think it would be when we were surrounded by enemy ships," Noah countered.

"I'll stay if you'd like," Rigo said to reassure the man. "I don't want . . ."

"I'm joshing," Noah interrupted. "And you'd better go."

For another few seconds, Rigo hesitated, wondering whether the ship and his crew would be all right with Noah in command, but he was certain there was no serious danger in the confusion of the day.

Barefoot and wearing only a single shirt and pantaloons, Rigo walked aft to the rail, turned to nod once to Noah, and then swung himself up over the rail and down into the water.

The cold water of the incoming tide was a shock, and for a while, Rigo floundered in the *Contessa*'s wake, getting used to the heavy pull of his clothing. In the summer, he usually swam naked and, thus felt hampered by the clinging of his cotton pants and shirt. Shaking his head, Rigo finally set out for the Staten Island shore. He had considered who he was going to be when he reached land and knew that his claim to be a loyalist gentleman who happened to be swimming ashore from a troop carrier rang spectacularly false. A sailor fallen overboard—that would have to do.

Although he was fully capable of swimming to land on his own, when a longboat began to approach him, Rigo felt he'd better wave to it as if in distress. As it neared, he saw the boat was filled mostly with redcoats. There were also four blue-suited sailors and a ship's officer. Two heavyset soldiers leaned over the side offering their hands to help pull Rigo up. To his amazement, they shouted something at him that sounded like a foreign language—Dutch or German.

With a mighty heave, they pulled him into the longboat where, exaggeratedly gasping for breath, Rigo sat on the floorboards in between the boots of two soldiers. When one of them spoke in what Rigo now recognized as gutteral German, a few of the soldiers laughed.

"Where's your ship?" a voice cut through from aft.

Rigo slowly raised his head, mouth stupidly open, to look back bleary-eyed at the ensign who was in command of the longboat, a young man with a wisp of a blond mustache.

"Off the *Prospect*, sir," Rigo answered after a brief pause. "Fell overboard, I did, and no one saw me."

"Jumped overboard more likely," the ensign shot back. "You don't swim like any sailor I ever saw."

Rigo had to smile to himself. Most of his own crew couldn't swim a stroke, and those that did looked like broken windmills gone amok. Only gentlemen sometimes learned to become good swimmers.

"My master taught me, he did," Rigo said. "Afore I got shanghaied."

"What's this *Prospect?*" the ensign asked next. He was seated at the stern of the longboat and controlled the tiller. The four sailors did all the rowing while the German troops sat stolidly along the seats looking uncomfortable.

"A colonial merchant ship the navy took over a month ago," Rigo answered.

"And ye be of America?" the ensign asked.

"Aye, but true to King George."

"Aye, I'll bet ye are. Pull there, Clark, or you'll have us going in circles!"

Rigo remained seated uncomfortably on the bottom of the boat and began to worry that the ensign would insist that Rigo go back with him to the ensign's own ship. They were less than a minute away now from shore.

"I say, sir," he piped up to the ensign, "ain't this here Staten Island we be rowing to?"

"It is, sailor. What be it to you?"

"It's me home," Rigo replied. "I was born and bred on a wee farm not twenty leagues from here."

"Well, ye'll not be jumping ship here, if that's what you have in mind."

"No, sir. But I'd make a good guide to the soldiers, I would."

"You'll make a good guide to the ship's irons if I have my way," the ensign returned sharply. "Easy, lads. We're about to take the ground."

"You live here?" a redcoat in officer's brocade asked Rigo in heavily accented English.

"Aye, sir. I do."

"Goot," the officer said, nodding emphatically. These were Hessian mercenaries, Rigo knew, come to help put down the rebellion because King George couldn't always trust his English troops to kill his English rebels.

The boat crunched into the stony shingle of the beach and the four sailors quickly locked their oars in place and leaped into the water to drag the boat further in. Then, amidst confused bursts of commands in German and a lot of grumbling, the Hessian troops climbed over the coaming into the water and waded ashore, some of them looking at their soaked pantaloons like children who'd accidentally wet their pants. Rigo jumped out, too.

The ensign immediately ordered one of the sailors to take hold of Rigo, but the German officer began making loud noises in his broken English. He and the ensign then began a long, inarticulate debate about what should be done with Rigo when another English officer, an elegantly turned out major, made an appearance. As Rigo stood there in the loose clutch of a small sailor whom Rigo could have pitched into the sea with ease, the discussion continued until the new officer, a Major Keilly, strode up.

"You are familiar with these environs?" Major Keilly asked, looking Rigo fiercely in the eye.

"Aye, sir! Like the back of me hand," Rigo replied, smiling.

"I see. Then you will begin temporary duty as my regimental guide," the major said. "And if you desert, you will be shot." Major Keilly turned away with disdain, informed the ensign of his decision, and strode off up the hill. A tough-looking sergeant who had accompanied him came up to Rigo and took him by the arm.

"All right, laddie," he said gruffly. "Ye be a soldier, now, so look lively and come with me."

Over the next four hours and on into the early evening, Rigo had the tense task of pretending to be a country bumpkin giving the aristocratic Major Keilly geographic and social information about Staten Island. Major Keilly wanted to know who the leading landowners were, which were reliable loyalists, where he could feed his horses, bivouac his men, buy grain and vegetables for his men. The situation was filled with ironies, and as he accompanied Major Keilly and two junior officers on their rounds and answered their questions, Rigo was, of course, busy estimating the number of troops in each area, the nature of their artillery, and asking innocently straightforward questions about where they were planning to invade and how many more troops they were expecting. To his questions, Major Keilly never condescended to reply, but Rigo's eyes picked up a great deal of information, and one item, of doubtful military significance, particularly interested Rigo—a visiting officer announced that all senior officers were invited to a grand ball being held this very night at Somerset Manor.

At dusk, Rigo was turned back to the gruff sergeant and led away to be fed and bivouacked for the night. After picking at a meal that Rigo felt closely resembled what he usually fed his golden retriever, he was led to a small tent, given a single light blanket, and told that he was to sleep there for the night with three other soldiers. The sergeant ordered the others to make certain that their strangely dressed and barefooted guide didn't run away.

As he lay back on his blanket in the darkness of early evening listening to the disjointed conversations of the three soldiers, to a harmonica playing softly in the tent across the lane, and to drunken laughter coming from further away, Rigo decided it would take more than three inattentive and indifferent soldiers to keep him here. He had realized as he accompanied the English officers that he was in real danger of accidentally being recognized as Richard Somerset by some of the locals mingling with or serving the English army. Were Major Keilly to force Rigo to lead him to Somerset Manor, there was no way he would be able to avoid catastrophic explanations. His life as a country bumpkin spy would have to end as quickly as it had begun. It was time for Richard Somerset to return from the West Indies—and attend the Somersets' annual summer ball.

As soon as the sun had fully set, Rigo sat up and stretched, yawning. Then he stood up.

"Got to take a piss," he announced.

As he ambled casually from the tent, the three soldiers began arguing about which of them should accompany him. One finally scurried out of the tent after Rigo. The two strolled off into a small copse of poplar and each relieved himself. As they turned to go, Rigo remarked, "Here comes the major." When the soldier looked away, Rigo struck the man hard in the side of his head, sending him sprawling onto the grass. He then leaped on the soldier and hit him again, leaving the man limp and unconscious.

Then he strolled along the line of tents climbing the hill. A half a mile away loomed Somerset Manor, lit majestically against the night sky, aglow with preparations for the ball. With rising excitement, Rigo directed his steps that way.

Chapter Fifteen

HEATHER SMOOTHED HER PALE LIME-GREEN GOWN AND AD-
justed the sash around her slim waist while Maggie
fluttered around her, as excited as a butterfly.

For many hours the day before, the two of them along
with Amy had helped with preparations for the ball by
arranging bouquets of flowers and helping to unpack the
china and stemware used only on special occasions—Mrs.
Somerset didn't trust the servants to handle her most
precious heirlooms. Today Heather and Amy had taken a
nap to gather their energies for the evening's festivities.
The whole house was abuzz with excitement. The musi-
cians could be heard warming up in the great hall downstairs, and the servants were dressed in clean blue dresses
with white pinafores and caps for the women and the men
in deeper blue.

Heather's stomach was doing flip-flops in anticipation of
the evening. She felt she was preparing herself for her
formal entrance into Staten Island society. Although she
had already met many of the expected guests at church or

147

at home for tea, this occasion was still something of a debut, and Heather found herself having to take deep breaths to quiet her nerves. With the evening still hot and sultry, she continually had to fan herself to keep cool.

Maggie placed a black bow in the back of Heather's hair, which was fashioned to let ringlets of chestnut curls bounce around her shoulders. Heather had added a narrow black velvet ribbon around her pale honey-colored neck in lieu of jewelry. The whole costume was romantically feminine, yet the cut of her gown revealed just enough of the creamy perfection of her womanly curves to tantalize.

A light knock at the door brought Amy and Arabella into the room. Amy's dark coloring was set off by the pink lace gown she wore. Her hair was piled high, adding inches to her height and a touch of glamour to her pretty girlishness. Arabella was resplendent in a silver and white striped gown, her dusky blond hair pinned back in a fashionable twist of curls.

"Captain Blair has arrived with five officers," Arabella announced as she walked to the tall standing mirror and surveyed herself. "I only hope they can dance."

"Papa invited them into his study for a smoke and wine to await the other guests," Amy added with excitement in her eyes.

Maggie ran to the window to check the drive. "I see two carriages coming now," she reported, pushing the white curtain aside further so the women could peek discreetly.

After watching briefly with the others at the window, Heather whirled away and picked up her black lace fan. Her cheeks were flushed with pleasure as she stepped toward the door.

"Well, then, let's not keep them waiting," Heather said, a devilish smile curving her full, rosy lips. "This is going to be an occasion to remember. I noticed Captain Blair has an eye for you, Amy, and Arabella will have her choice of officers, so it's to the ramparts! Let's dance till our shoes fall off!"

Amy laughed gaily and Arabella smiled as they gathered themselves to descend to the ballroom.

The rustle of their skirts and gay chatter was noted by Bruce and several officers, all of whom gathered admiringly at the bottom of the stairs. Bruce was smiling broadly, and Heather noticed that his dark gray coat and white breeches fit his trim figure neatly.

She took his proffered arm, a lace fan spread in front of her. He bowed elegantly to Arabella and Amy before his eyes once more came back to Heather.

"I see the three of you are set to turn all heads this evening," he said gallantly before introducing first Heather, then Arabella and Amy to several officers, all handsome in their red coats, white breeches, and polished black boots.

Heather and Bruce went to stand in line at the door to receive the arriving guests, joining Margaret Somerset, who was first in line. John and Amy made further introductions inside and saw their guests made at home.

Bruce bent and whispered, "I've seen more than one man wish he were in my shoes this evening. You look splendid." His glance strayed from Heather's vibrantly beautiful face to the low cut of her gown. Heather tucked him lightly under the chin with the edge of her closed fan to turn his eyes in the direction of the guests.

"I warn you now, I never tire of dancing," Heather said lightly as she smiled politely at a new arrival.

"As long as you save most for me, I won't be jealous," Bruce said quickly, then turned to bow to an elderly lady and her married daughter, who seemed flustered as Bruce took her hand and lightly brought it up to his lips.

"I see you've plucked many a rose in this country garden," Heather whispered, fanning herself gracefully and slanting Bruce a teasing look.

"None as sweet as you," Bruce returned.

Heather gave a small, low, throaty laugh. "This rose will draw blood if she has any more thorny garden problems, sir." She raised a beautifully arched eyebrow and tilted her chin to show him she meant what she said, in spite of the banter.

"At least today I'm not getting haughty looks," Bruce said smiling. "You've forgiven me, then?"

"For tonight," Heather said as they walked into the ballroom to begin dancing.

Heather danced continuously, first with Bruce and then with a series of officers who cut in with the regularity of clockwork. She saw Bruce dance with Arabella and then lost track of him for a time, enjoying the dancing and the compliments and light flirting too much to notice where he'd gotten to. In between dances, the young gathered around a punch bowl in the dining room to cool off and refresh themselves. All the windows were opened to the night air, which now was bringing a much needed breeze, though it was still warm with the day's heat.

Amy confided once as they sipped wine near a window that she had invited Captain Blair to tea tomorrow and that he had accepted, providing he could get away. Her face was flushed and her eyes shone. "And Richard's here. I haven't yet had a chance to be alone with him, but Bruce has and Arabella immediately raced to be with him. I swear, this is the best night of my life!"

Heather didn't have a chance to respond to Amy's confidences as Bruce came to claim her for a dance, but she was very happy for Amy.

The dance floor and the rooms were filled to capacity now, and Heather could feel the trickle of perspiration between her breasts as the heat in the room increased with the feverish dancing of the dozens of local belles and their swains and the newly arrived officers. As Bruce led her in long graceful arcs to the measure of a minuet, Heather became vaguely aware of a stir at the edge of the dance floor near the dining room door. She felt a peculiar prickling on her skin, as if she were being watched, but as Bruce was blocking her view, she couldn't see who might be causing the commotion.

"Richard just came in with Arabella," Bruce announced as he whirled Heather on the dance floor. "Poor mother. She thinks Arabella will reform him once they're married, but I know my stepbrother too well. He'll never submit to a woman's domination."

Heather got a brief glimpse of a group of people

clustered near the door with John and Margaret. A very tall, black-haired man dressed formally in black stood beside Arabella, who was glowing. This time Heather caught a very brief look at his bent profile before she was swirled again in a new direction. Another little shiver went down her spine that she couldn't account for and thought perhaps she'd been dancing too long in the hot room.

"Perhaps Arabella likes your brother the way he is," Heather said, and then asked Bruce to slow his dancing.

"Possibly. But I think she likes the challenge. With all the men at her command, she prefers the most difficult. It's an amusing match."

Just then Heather caught a glimpse of Richard Somerset and, had she not been clinging to Bruce, the shock of it might have made her fall. As it was, she missed a step and tripped, bringing them to a halt.

"What is it?" Bruce asked, his eyes full of concern. "You look pale."

"It's nothing . . . just the heat," Heather got out. Her breathing seemed constricted. "Did you say that man is your brother?" Heather asked with disbelief, gesturing toward Richard but not daring to again look. She opened her fan and moved it rapidly in agitation while clinging to Bruce for support.

"My stepbrother," Bruce corrected, and he began to guide her toward the family group.

As she found herself being relentlessly propelled toward the man who so unsettled her, Heather felt her eyes widen and stare. She whispered to herself, "My Lord!"

Brought to the group, which parted to receive them, she found herself being introduced to Richard Somerset, the man whose striking good looks and blue eyes she would recognize anywhere, in any guise, as Rigo.

Heather was struck dumb before his brazen look and collected poise. He took her hand, raised it to his lips, and coolly bowed before her.

"Miss Southey," he said in a low voice, his eyes intense, "an unexpected pleasure . . ." Rigo continued to hold her eyes with his, the curve of a smile appearing, and when she didn't respond but merely blushed deeply under his gaze, he released her hand and, to end the embarrassment, began to talk.

"You've already made a great impression on my family," he said in a deep, formal voice but with his eyes a brilliant blue. "As I'm the only member left to meet you, I suggest we begin our acquaintance by dancing." He then turned to Bruce for permission and murmured something quickly to Arabella. Bruce complied, though stiffly, and went to Arabella, whose face looked unaccustomedly tense.

Still not recovered from the shock of the meeting, Heather found herself now swept away into Rigo's arms, away from his family and onto the dance floor. For a seemingly endless moment, Rigo swept her gracefully around the room, his eyes never leaving hers. Nor hers his. Then, too overcome with the power of her confused feelings, Heather tried to break free of his arms to flee, but Rigo effortlessly held her firm, finally guiding them toward the garden door, which opened onto a porch.

Heather's senses had reawakened from the moment Rigo's hand took hers and the flash of body knowledge that was theirs struck her. She knew that the bolt that had gone through her had nothing to do with fear but with desire.

"I don't believe it!" Heather finally whispered once they were out on the porch and he had released her sufficiently so that, breathless, she stood next to him in his loose embrace.

"*You* don't believe it!" Rigo said. "I almost choked on my wine when I first saw you. And then I had to restrain myself from carrying you bodily out of the room and paddling your sweet, lying bottom!"

"Oh!" She took a wild swing at his face with her fan, but Rigo easily caught her wrist. Heather blushed when she realized there were two other couples taking air on the porch. "You're a bounder!" she hissed.

Rigo kept hold of her wrist and half dragged Heather down some stone steps and deeper into the garden, away from sight or sound of others.

"How dare you!" Heather said, stumbling behind him. He stopped short, and she fell against him before quickly righting herself. The contact with him again jolted her senses.

"I dare, lady, as you've dared insinuate yourself into my family!" he said, his eyes flashing a warning. "And you'd better have some answers ready."

Heather could feel tears whelming in her eyes but fought them back.

"I am ashamed of my imposture," she finally said softly, "and though I felt I had no choice and tried several times to tell your father or Bruce the truth, I . . . I was too frightened of the consequences to do so."

Rigo studied her a long moment, his eyes narrowing.

"But *why?*" he asked in a fierce voice. "And *how?* I am still too amazed at your reincarnation as Elizabeth Southey to begin to comprehend."

Heather seated herself on a stone bench near a small reflecting pool and, in a low voice, told Rigo of what had happened to her after her flight from Daniel's inn. She mentioned the chilling reports of Margaret Somerset's treatment of servants and runaways but did not emphasize it. She mentioned her confession to Bruce and his failure to understand, but admitted she might have been more completely forthright. All the time, Rigo stood over her staring down, his face—the one time she dared look up at him—now devoid of either the cool intensity or the anger she had seen there earlier.

"I thank you, Heather," he said when she was finished.

"I promise to tell your parents. Tonight, if you wish," she said, looking up at him steadily, feeling tremendous relief at having at last unburdened herself. "It hasn't been an easy secret. I did care for Elizabeth. She was a friend to me."

Rigo nodded. "That's the one crime you've committed —not telling them of her loss. The rest . . . is forgivable."

"Why, thank you, noble pirate!" Heather said with heat, disliking his condescension and wanting to remind him of his own duplicities. "Do any of your family know what you do for a living?"

Rigo's eyes glinted dangerously. "I am in shipping, as is my father," he said, lowering his voice. "No one is to know otherwise."

Heather was confused. "But . . . you were about to rob us!"

"As far as my family is concerned, I have been on a long and unsuccessful cruise to the West Indies," he countered. "I would appreciate it if you told them nothing of my appearance aboard the *Prospect*."

Heather stared at him. "I don't understand."

"Then I'm not going to enlighten you. It's best you don't."

Heather looked down at the grass around the reflecting pool deep in shadows, so that its color appeared a purple black. The toe of her shoe played with the tufts while she thought. Then her head came up, and she saw Rigo watching her intently. There was a coolness on his face and she found the look hurtful.

"I'm ready to confess," she said. "I'm glad it's come to an end at last. Will you be there to listen?" Heather's voice had lost its anger and was merely soft and young.

Rigo was silent a moment, then he spoke in a low, even tone. "Has Bruce been courting you?"

Heather looked at him, but his face was impassive and she couldn't tell what he was thinking. "Yes . . ." she answered tentatively.

"And do you enjoy it?"

"You have a way of twisting things to make them seem wrong. I enjoy Bruce's attentions as you enjoy Arabella's!"

Rigo came up to the bench and, reaching out, grabbed her wrist, bringing her to her feet close to him. "I think we'll leave it for the time being."

"Do you mean I found a weakness? Your love for Arabella?"

"I said we'll leave it!" Rigo's hand increased its viselike hold. "And I want you to continue playing Miss Southey until I've had time to think about it. Were you aware Duncan Crawley is looking for you and has been in touch with me?"

Heather took in her breath. "When? I had hoped . . ."

"Don't bother your pretty head about it. I won't let him take you. But for the time being, you'd best remain as Elizabeth Southey."

Heather could see the slight flaring of his nostrils as Rigo looked down at her. She felt the warm caress of his breath across her face. His nearness had the effect of making her knees feel weak, and Heather reached out her other hand to steady herself on his arm. As she touched him, she heard him take in his breath.

"You still have the power to stir me," he said hoarsely, "but I wonder if I was so wrong about *your* response to me."

Rigo's voice was seductively low, and Heather felt her pulse speed up in anticipation as he brought his mouth down to cover hers in a kiss that had nothing tentative or indecisive about it. It was an onslaught by a master, and Heather was swept away. Her hand that was now curled on his chest opened and crept around his neck to lace through his thick, black hair, urging him against her. She felt herself drowning in the sensual tide that Rigo alone could make happen.

When he finally stopped the deep, sensual probing, he was still languorously teasing her lips with his, his eyes half closed. Heather melted into him, little sighs escaping her involuntarily. Rigo pressed her body into his, where it fit perfectly.

"I don't want to stop," Rigo whispered huskily between heated kisses, "but I'd better get you back in before I'm accused of the act I want to commit."

Heather drew in a shaky breath and pushed away from him. "Whatever gave you the feeling I would consent?"

"I know you would, at the right moment." Rigo let out a small laugh, his eyes gleaming with certainty.

"Then you mistake me for someone else," Heather said sharply. "I wouldn't!" She was breathing rapidly, her hands on his arms to push him off.

"No mistake, Heather," he laughed, his eyes mocking her. He drew her tightly against him, pressing his hips tightly against hers. "Don't fight. I'm not going to do

anything. I just want to hold you and inhale your perfume
. . . and prove something to you." His eyes looked into
hers.

He let his arm muscles relax, yet he still held her in the
same position, his hips tight against hers as she tried to
fight the tide pulling her into the vortex of him. She could
feel the heat between their loins rising and fought their
connection.

"You weren't listening to me," she whispered unevenly.

"I heard you. Morality doesn't interest me."

"What does?"

"You."

"Rigo, let me go, please. You said they would be
waiting for us . . ."

"When you admit there's something between us . . .
that you feel it, too."

"Because you need to be victorious?"

"No. Because just once, I'd like to get an absolutely
honest statement out of you."

"Let me go!" Heather said, twisting to free herself.
"You wouldn't know an honest woman if she had sworn
documents all over her and had been in the cloisters for
twelve of her fifteen years!" Rigo chuckled and let her go,
steadying her so she wouldn't fall. Then he held out his
hand formally.

"Now, take my hand and we'll go back inside," he
commanded, no longer playful.

Heather's face was flushed with her confused feelings of
anger and hurt and her own fight not to give in to her
attraction to Rigo. Seeing the look on his face, she decided
to obey and placed her hand in his, feeling the current
between them as a degrading fact coming from her.

"Then let's go! Why must we stand here!" she said
hotly. "I suppose being a pirate has its advantages. You
can steal and ruin helpless women, and there's no punishment. Except inside you, Rigo! You'll be black! Rotten!"

"You blow hot and cold so fast, Heather. You're quite
amazing. Just let me advise you of two things before we go
in. There's no one here you can depend on except me.
You'd better accept that. But when you do wake up and

156

decide you want me, there are complications, and I warn you that I haven't decided what I will do yet. For the moment, I depend on your discretion, as you do on mine. And lastly, don't call me Rigo in public. It's an intimate childhood name that my stepmother hates." He guided Heather up the porch steps, then stopped just before they reached the door. He caught her eyes a moment with his, then he gave her a cool smile and withdrew his arm as he opened the door and followed her inside. Heather went straight to Bruce, feeling Rigo's eyes on her.

Bruce greeted her with anger. "It looked bad, your going off with my stepbrother. What did the two of you talk about all this time?"

"Much the same as you and I talk about, Bruce," Heather stated, having regained her poise. "He wanted to know all about my past!"

"And did he find it so interesting? You are never so liberal with me!" Bruce was almost petulant.

"But I am kinder to you," Heather said, smiling up at him, and then suggested they dance.

Heather found the room seemed to have shrunk with the presence of Rigo, as if he dominated it just by being there. He spent his time attending to the regal Arabella, who now gave Heather cool looks. Still, a twinge of jealousy caught her by surprise when she saw Rigo's dark head bending to listen to something Arabella was saying. Then he laughed as if he were thoroughly enjoying himself. Angrily, Heather turned to Bruce, determined that she would do the same.

Chapter Sixteen

AFTER THE BALL, HEATHER TOSSED AND TURNED IN HER BED while trying to sort out the incredible events of the day. Rigo had not approached her again but had remained at Arabella's side, and Heather had managed to make it through the rest of the evening without running into him. Her sensitivity to the man was potent. Heather had been aware when he was dancing, aware when he left the ballroom, aware when he bent to the hand of a local lady whose presence demanded his attention. He had bedeviled her, indeed. Gone was the simplicity of that first flush of interest in Manhattan. In its place was an all-consuming consciousness of Rigo and the contest of wills complicated by the web of their mutual and seemingly necessary deceptions. Near dawn, she at last fell asleep and, thankfully, no one roused her until late the next morning.

A routine developed over the next few days that set a pattern for her existence with Rigo in the Somerset household. Mornings she and Amy went riding, most always accompanied by Bruce and sometimes by Rigo on Triumph. Heather didn't know where Rigo spent the rest of the day, but she usually wouldn't see him again until supper. The suppers were becoming increasingly difficult with Bruce continuing his courtship as discreetly as he was capable. Heather was acutely aware that Rigo was watching their moves, occasionally arching an eyebrow or giving one of his sardonic smiles. Usually he would seem to be indifferent, yet on occasion, he would seat her at the table and lightly brush her arm or touch her shoulder, sending a shock throughout her body. Then he would sit opposite her and send a look that would speak volumes of his knowledge of how she had reacted. To her great annoyance, Rigo appeared to enjoy discomforting her by flaunting his effect on her senses. It was a power game, and one time Heather gave him a sharp kick under the table when she was sure no one was looking. Rigo had only laughed.

As with Bruce, she conscientiously avoided being alone with Rigo. It was simple enough, what with servants or other family members in constant attendance. Heather also dreaded another private interview, fearing both his disapproval of her role as Miss Southey and, even more, the powerful effect he had on her—an effect she still couldn't quite decide how she should handle. Unable to reconcile all these warring feelings, she finally decided simply to shrug them off. Brooding never helped, and the helplessness she sometimes felt was only self-defeating.

Heather was disturbed, too, by the family's responses to Rigo. Margaret Somerset more than just disapproved of her stepson, she seemed barely able to tolerate his presence. She ignored him whenever possible. Margaret performed well enough when her husband was there and in society, but on other occasions, Rigo was not addressed at all if it could be helped.

Bruce treated Rigo with a kind of fearfulness mixed with an unacknowledged attachment. There was a sibling rivalry that seemed to Heather to have burned out long ago in Rigo but that still flamed in Bruce, who would challenge Rigo in discussions, especially of colonial politics. On one occasion, it seemed to Heather that Bruce was ready for swords while Rigo remained controlled, ironic, and even cruelly cool—which only angered Bruce more. At tea,

Bruce would flirt with Arabella just to pique Rigo, who usually refused to be drawn. Once they did run a race, which Rigo won on his spirited Triumph, much to the chagrin of Bruce, who then became irritable for the rest of the day.

These tense and tangled family conflicts reached a climax six days after the ball. Heather awakened early to a fog-shrouded dawn and made ready for her morning ride, pulling on her light riding habit of blue linen and tying her hair back. She knew that Bruce had to attend to a tenant who was refusing to work, so he wouldn't be joining Amy and herself as usual. Since Rigo had disappeared the previous evening and wasn't expected back, Heather looked forward to a relaxing ride free of complications. She even planned a brief ride before Amy's usual arrival. After eagerly rushing to the dining hall and grabbing a biscuit, she made her way to the stables, humming to herself. Then she stopped. At the end stall, stroking his magnificent black stallion, was Rigo. He seemed to be holding a silent conversation with the animal, trying to calm him. He turned as Heather, who had regained her equilibrium, approached.

"I thought you had left us for a few days," Heather said, noticing that Triumph was lathered and had obviously been ridden hard for several hours.

Rigo, his broad shoulders free in a loose, white tunic that was shoved into tight, black breeches and belted at the waist, looked down at her as Triumph nuzzled his shoulder.

"I had some business to attend to," he said harshly, looking away.

"I'm sure you did," Heather said, surprised to feel a pang of jealousy at his nocturnal jaunt. "And this morning I had looked forward to riding alone."

He smiled, but it didn't reach his eyes. "Had you hoped this might perhaps be the morning to ride Triumph?"

Heather looked away, realizing he had been told of her attempt. "I was already denied that privilege."

"Quite so. He's not trained to ride sidesaddle nor to tolerate a woman's gentler hand. Don't ever try."

"He likes me!"

"That's not the same as your knowing how to handle him nor his being trained to take you," Rigo said sharply.

"I'm sure I could handle him, but you needn't worry. As he's yours, and your groom is vigilant, it won't happen!" Heather felt exasperated. "Do you think I just look for opportunities to defy you?"

Triumph stamped restlessly at their noisy interchange, and Rigo turned to soothe him. The groom appeared quietly and, noticing Heather, went immediately to begin saddling Beauty.

"You seem to find ways without even looking," Rigo said when he turned once more to her. "Heaven help the man who's around when you start scheming!"

Heather frowned and pursed her lips. "Why are you so harsh with me? I've done nothing to deserve your anger. Or are you always this bad tempered in the early morning?"

For a long moment Rigo ignored her, taking a bucket of water and pouring it into Triumph's trough. When he finally turned to her, she was shocked at the anger in his face.

"I learned last night of an impending marriage—in my own family!" he said, his eyes fierce. "A marriage that will never take place!"

"Oh," Heather said weakly, realizing that Bruce must have told his half brother about their secret betrothal. "It's not meant to," she added, her shoulders squared.

"My brother thinks otherwise!" Rigo threw at her, putting his hands on her exposed and creamy throat, forcing her face up to his. Her eyes met his fiery ones.

"But I only agreed to it because the dowry is lost, and I'll never marry without it. I mean, it's stolen and won't be recovered. It simply doesn't matter!"

"Stolen? What do you mean stolen?" Rigo asked with a frown, his hands sliding to her shoulders but his fingers still gripping her hard.

"Duncan Crawley took it from Elizabeth's stateroom aboard the ship," Heather said. "I can't prove it nor do I know where it is, but he has it or has disposed of it, I'm sure." Under the pressure of Rigo's punishing hands, she got this out and then tried to move.

"Why didn't you tell me this before?" Rigo said, releasing the pressure of his grip.

"I would have if I'd thought it was of use to you," Heather said, confused by Rigo's need to know and uneasy with the glitter of anger still in his eyes. "You're hurting me!" she said and put her hands on his chest. A flicker of some emotion that Heather couldn't define ran briefly across his taut features. Then his eyes narrowed.

Rigo released Heather and leaned one arm on the stall with one booted foot up on a barrel of grain. He seemed to be in thought as Heather rubbed her arms.

"Why is it always like this with you?" she asked, her voice almost trembling. "You bully or yell like a madman!"

"Were you a more ordinary woman, I'd have less trouble," he said, his sensuous mouth at last curving in a smile.

"I know I've been wrong, but why can't you try to understand?"

"I think I've good reason not to trust you, don't you?"

The groom brought forth her saddled mount and Amy's, who could now be seen hurrying toward the stables. Rigo gave Heather a hand up, his touch warm and firm.

"You'll never marry Bruce," he stated in a low, sure voice.

"He might forgive me!" Heather tossed down at him.

Rigo's head came up from checking the strap round Beauty's belly.

"He'd never forgive your being penniless *and* unfaithful. And you are the one and will be the other." He looked at Heather meaningfully, holding her eyes with his own, then he let his hand fall on her thigh and withdrew.

Heather flushed and bent to hit him with her quirt but it merely bounced off his shoulder. Then she hit her horse and let it take her free of his mocking yet amused eyes.

Chapter Seventeen

RIGO WAS BEGINNING TO FEEL THE PRESSURE OF LEADING NOT one but two secret lives. For almost two weeks now, he had been spying on the English forces encamped on Staten Island, forces that he now estimated numbered almost twenty thousand. This was far greater, he knew, than the forces General Washington could muster, and even today, a new fleet of transports had arrived in the narrows. Twice he had ridden twelve miles to the house of Peter Mitchell, a tenant farmer on the Moncrief estate, to give him a sealed report to be taken to General Washington's headquarters in New York City.

This first secret life as a spy forced him to dissemble not only to the English officers he had befriended but also to his own family. His delight in going riding with Heather, Bruce, and Amy was usually directly related to their destination. If they were planning to ride through the camps to the narrows, he would be "in the mood." If their destination was someplace militarily useless, he would "have business to attend to." His occasional overnight jaunts, which he knew Bruce liked to hint to Heather were sexual escapades, were necessary to meet Peter Mitchell undetected.

His other secret life was his role with the damnable "Miss Southey." Although Rigo certainly had no intention of letting her be retaken by Duncan Crawley, he knew that sooner or later Heather's masquerade had to end. Or did it? There were moments when, in bitterness, he tried grinning at the idea of Bruce's marrying Heather for her social position and dowry only later to discover the inconvenient truth. But the grin didn't last. Somehow, the thought of Heather in Bruce's bed was not at all pleasing.

Could he himself marry her as "Miss Southey"? Lord knew he was powerfully attracted to Heather by whatever name she went. If his spying weren't so important, he would like nothing better than to woo the cool "Miss Southey" away from the ardent Bruce. Cool? Heather was about as cool as a branding iron, he thought. He'd never known a woman whose simple presence could so arouse him. Yet he still wasn't sure if her reincarnation as Miss Southey was the luck of a lovely innocent or the shrewdness of a charming schemer.

With a rueful smile, he had to admit that Heather was as unsure of him as he was of her. Still, she so stirred him that he was willing to do for her what he had never considered doing for another woman—he would invite her to Manhattan and install her in his home, offering his protection until such time as they found a suitable position for her or it was safe for her to leave on her own. If he could let her go. For Rigo had further admitted to himself that he wasn't yet ready to let Heather out in the world unless he had the right to see her and court her.

He felt a tightness in his chest as he decided to go to her. Rigo had waited until the whole Somerset household was asleep, with the exception of Bruce, who had not yet returned home from his exploits with either the soldiers or some farm wench he'd taken to relieve his lust. There was only a half-moon for light, so her room was in semidarkness. It smelled of a spicy floral scent he now associated with Heather and that, combined with the indescribable scent that was her own, now sent his pulse racing. Rigo softly approached her bed, where he could barely see the soft curve of her hip and the swell of one firm breast beneath the light coverlet. Her long hair spread out over the pillow in inviting splendor as he stood over her, lightly tracing a hand over one softly rising, delicious mound. Heather stirred and shifted her position onto her back, undulating her body in a small movement that had roused more heat in Rigo. Another movement like that and he would forget his purpose.

"Heather," he whispered close to her face, having seated himself on her bed with one arm straddling her.

She fluttered her eyes and slowly opened them as Rigo brought his lips down over hers in what had begun as a tender exploration but had proceeded to awaken a deeper hunger in both of them. Rigo's tongue tasted the sleep-heated recesses of her mouth while his hands slid over her light chemise and lightly caress the rising nipples. He teased them to a tautness that had Heather thrusting up into his hands as she opened her mouth even more to receive him. When he released her mouth to trail heated kisses from her neck up to her ear, and began to nibble on its soft edge, Heather groaned softly and sleepily reached toward his shoulders to touch him.

"Rigo . . ." she murmured.

She was warm and only half awake, as if in a dream. The room was dark; her dream lover made her feel sleekly sensuous. The man whose hands glided over her body excited her and she wanted him there beside her, his head on her pillow. She wanted him to do delicious, unknown things to her.

She put her hands on his arms and felt the muscles move beneath her fingers, thrilling her. She moved sinuously, artlessly, writhing into his hand, the one stroking, teasing her nipples until they stood hard against his palm. She could hear his breathing and knew that he wanted her. It surprised her, then delighted her, making her want to please him more. Stirrings began in her body that she had never felt before, a heated throbbing between her hips. She opened her lips to his hot probing tongue which plunged deeper, bringing a low moan from her lover.

She arched toward him, her chemise being pushed up high. His hand rested on her thigh, then slid upward in possessive strokes. Then his fingers plunged lower, stroking between her legs, sending sparks jolting through her. She whispered his name hoarsely, pressing her legs together over his hand, half frightened but unable to move away, her breathing constricted. Without understanding why, Heather arched her body to meet his.

Rigo trembled with need, knowing she was innocent but unable to restrain himself. He wanted to taste her, to make her his. Rigo removed his trousers, and kneeled on the bed above her, talking hoarsely of his need, of his desire to know all of her. Asking for her hands on him and guiding her to his throbbing manhood, then nearly exploding with the pleasure of her touch.

He lifted her hips, grasping them tightly.

"Heather". . . he whispered huskily.

Heather was suddenly now fully awake, her heart beating madly. She was aware of Rigo as alive and not as a dream lover. He was here, demanding her body, wanting to touch her as no one had ever done, wanting her surrender. How had it gone from a lovely, tender dream to this real image?

"Oh no . . ." she groaned, "oh, Rigo . . . no . . . ," her voice trembled on a note of panic.

Rigo stopped, moaning as he fought for control. "Beloved girl . . ." he rasped.

"No! Please . . . leave me . . . if you care for me . . . leave me now."

"Heather . . . don't do this to us," he whispered to her urgently." He stroked her cheek with his thumb.

"If you don't go, I will call out . . . and someone will come . . ." She turned away from him, trying to escape his arms.

Rigo slid from her reluctantly. His hand cupped her cheek and he turned her to face him.

"Do you believe me when I say I'm sorry . . . in spite of my pleasure and what I hope you will acknowledge as yours? I would not have hurt you."

She had her eyes closed and refused to look at him.

"You would have ruined me . . ." she whispered, agonizing over what had almost happened. "And then no man would have me."

"You would have ruined me . . ."

"Heather, *I* will have you. I want you and you aren't *ruined!*" he said, impatient with her turning from him and frustrated with her naive thinking. "What gibberish you women are fed! You have nothing to fear—from me. I'll take care of you, I promise," he finished flatly.

Rigo sat up on the edge of the bed. He wanted her again, but knew he needed her consent first. She had to come to him. He knew he could arouse her, but feared she might be filled with remorse. He couldn't see her face but he knew it was tense, strained by the set of her shoulders and the pulling of her body from him. She hastily yanked her chemise down and tried to draw up the sheets, but Rigo's weight held them down. So she scrambled off the bed and into the dark room.

"I want you to leave now," she said, her voice low and shaky, sobs threatening.

"Heather . . . please, listen to me, and try to whisper—unless you want us discovered." He got up and quickly pulled on his trousers and shirt. He could hear her breathing in the room before she said, "Whatever it is you came to say, say it fast and be gone. Or I don't care who finds us together. You're a rake and a bounder who deceives one woman while pursuing boldly another, and I . . . know I can't trust you!"

Rigo rose from the bed, watching her retreat. He advanced slowly but steadily until he had captured her with one arm against the wall. They were near an open window, and her face shone in the moonlight.

"I've found a place for you to go in Manhattan where you'll be safe and cared for until such time as I can purchase the contract from Crawley. In my home there . . ." he whispered, looking down into that angry, flushed face. Her green eyes flashed him a warning.

"You are joking, sir, if you think I'd allow myself to be

at your mercy in your home while every day you promise I'll be free! Do you think I'm such a dolt!" Her chest heaved with agitation.

"Madam, I can't say I'm sorry I didn't resist you a moment ago, but I . . ."

"You almost took from me what I can give no other."

"I apologize and promise that you will be safe from my more ardent advances. . . ."

"I'm safer here masquerading as your poor cousin than my honor would be in your household. Who would there be to protect me, pray tell?"

"I have a manservant and a housekeeper who take care of me well and can be completely trusted. Moreover, I swear I'd not abuse your trust were you to extend it. You sorely try my patience, Heather. I'm giving you a way out of this sticky situation. I know there are certain actions of mine unexplained, but tonight changes everything. You must know that."

"I know you can't be trusted, and that you took advantage of me. It won't happen again. I don't know how I could have . . ." she trailed off, distracted by the memory of what had happened, her cheeks burning.

"Heather, that's nonsense. What happened between us was natural and good. I've asked you to forgive me for being . . . precipitate and I offer you my self, my protection . . ." he would have gone on trying to convince her, but she interrupted him.

"Now who speaks nonsense!" Heather tried to slip past him, but Rigo put his other arm around her waist to stop her. They both stiffened as they heard movement downstairs. A door closed.

"Bruce . . ." Rigo identified for her.

"Oh, no . . . What if he finds us?"

Rigo felt himself stiffen at her choice of words. "Just be still until we hear him enter his room, then I'll leave." Heather moved to disengage herself, but Rigo pulled her tighter against him and once more invaded the reluctant mouth with his tongue and lips, pressing her body close against him. Heather shuddered and tried to pull away, but before long, she let herself melt against his taut body until she became aware of his aroused state. As she pushed him away, Rigo let her go. Heather raced, distracted, to the door, as if to flee, but then turned to him.

"Please, if you have any decency . . ."

"Just barely, my lady, where you're concerned, especially when I'm beset with your tantalizing person every day but still denied the right to court you."

For answer, Heather opened the door and listened for sounds in the hallway. Hearing none, she urged him with a gesture to exit.

Rigo stealthily crept back to his room, but as he crossed the head of the staircase he glanced down and saw Bruce standing at the bottom. The two half brothers stared at each other a moment, both without expression, and then Rigo moved on to his own room.

Heather was left in a state of shock. She had almost given Rigo the only real gift she had left to bring any man, herself, and all he offered was more of the same. Her heart was sore, for she felt he would soon tire of her inexperienced passion. She was left in a state of emotional turmoil over a man who could make her quiver with his touch, who made her want to fly into his arms and fly from them just as fast in fear. Worse, she thought it was just a matter of time before she became his mistress. Then she would never know the joy of a home and children, never have his heart. He would give it to a lady unlike herself—more like Arabella. She couldn't bear it.

He must never know she was in love with him.

She touched all the parts of her he had touched, almost disbelieving what had happened to her even while her body vibrated as she remembered. She caught her breath and moved to the washstand to cleanse herself wonderingly.

What happened to women like herself? What would become of her once she did become his mistress? No respectable woman would receive her in her parlor. Was she now wanton?

She became angry with Rigo, and with herself, for their

shared passion and finally she railed against fate for being so unkind to her.

"Oh Rigo! What should I do?" She didn't quite have the courage yet to consent to become his mistress. She didn't think she could live without honor.

He didn't know what he asked of her. She could not live isolated in society like a leper, voices whispering behind her back, her reputation ruined. It would box her into a position where she could only be unhappy. She had to be free in spirit, know she could go anywhere and be welcomed.

Why didn't he know that?

Her bed would never be the same again. She felt she would never be the same, and she promised herself to avoid Rigo at all costs.

But in the next few days, when she thought he wasn't watching, her eyes would sweep his tall form, caught by his muscled thighs, his lean flat stomach, his manly bulge, and, blushing, she would look away, frightened by her own desire.

He didn't try to corner her, but seemed to be waiting for her to beckon. And he teased her less. He would offer her a seat with grace, almost tenderly. If he touched her, she would flinch, and once she thought she saw a look of pain on his face.

Her distress increased whenever he came near. Rigo seemed to sense this, and thoughtfully kept some distance between them. Once when she saw a look of great hunger in his eyes, she ran from his presence as from a beast.

All this she was aware of, and yet she was afraid of his gentle courtesies, afraid of his power over her, and of her own weakness in his arms.

If he would come to her and offer his love as well as his temporary protection, she knew she would relent. In fact, she longed to have him take her in his arms and tell her he would wed her, that he wanted their children, and a home for them. But he did neither.

If only he wasn't promised to another there might be a chance. If only he would declare he couldn't live without her.

She would shake her head and groan with the endless milling of her mind and the useless "ifs."

Over the next week, Rigo was torn between wanting to shake sense into Heather and giving her time to come to terms having surrendering herself.

There were times when Rigo could see the bewildered, shy questions in her eyes and he wanted nothing more than to answer them, but she shied from his company as if from the plague. And from that night onward the tension between Bruce and him increased tenfold. Rigo's secret life with Miss Southey was thus forced to become even more secret.

He felt badly about keeping all his secrets from his father. When the British forces finally made their move, Rigo had intended to tell John Somerset of his real allegiance and leave Somerset Manor forever—or until the rebels triumphed. In which case, Somerset Manor might well be confiscated by the rebels.

So it was with a sense of a world crumbling apart that Rigo rode over the fields of the Somerset estate on a late July day with Arabella, Heather, and Bruce. There on the hill gently sloping to the narrows were hundreds of English tents. On the shore where, as a boy, he had loved to walk alone and skip stones across the water were a dozen boats loading and unloading supplies and men delivered from the newly arrived ships offshore. This invasion of his property was, for Rigo, a literal invasion. There were now enemy soldiers on his home land and in his homeland.

Seeing his brother and the two beautiful women riding ahead of him, Rigo realized the social part of his life was crumbling, too. Arabella rode with her customary dignity and beauty, seeming to glide gracefully over the ground, belying the fact that she was actually riding a sweaty horse. But Rigo's eyes were constantly drawn to the other woman, the one who rode her horse with the rough, uninhibited mastery of a man. She'd gallop spontaneously off to look at some cows, or rein in sharply to exchange a word with Bruce while almost sliding off her horse at the sudden stop. Laughing, her eyes were always bright with the joy of riding, of summer, of youth. Of being with Bruce?

Aye, there was the rub. Rigo was enraged at the thought that there might be something between his half brother and Heather, but he was confused as to which of the two was more deceiving the other. Their engagement was meaningless, he knew. The eventual exposure of Heather would undoubtedly dampen Bruce's enthusiasm for any more of her than he normally wanted—and got—from a pretty woman. But his own engagement to Arabella was meaningless, too. The outcome of the rebellion would ruin either Rigo or the Moncriefs and make their match as inappropriate socially as it now was emotionally.

His eyes had locked with Heather's more than once, and he was sure she could read his desire in them. His need for Heather was like the flick of a whip, a shock that reverberated through him as he remembered their night together. He could see she wanted him and fought it. Knowing that, he would stand outside her bedroom door at night, longing to enter.

But he needed her to come to him, needed her to acknowledge to herself and him her need and desire. She needed to be treated gently; he could see she was fearful and shy, and that she didn't trust him.

As he rode up now to Bruce and the ladies, who were resting near an old oak tree a hundred feet from the beach and at the edge of the main English encampment, Rigo sighed. His country was divided, his family divided, and his heart was in danger of being given to a suspect lady. Life might have managed to be simpler.

Heather looked up as Rigo approached, then she turned with a smile to Bruce astride his horse beside her.

"One day I'm going to ride as men do," she announced, pushing her blue-brimmed hat back off her head to hang loosely down her back.

"But my dear," Arabella said, irritated. "No woman of

good breeding rides astride. It's not done. Can you imagine throwing your leg over the horse's back?"

"But think how much easier it must be to control the horse," Heather insisted blithely. "Don't you envy the men?"

"I do not," Arabella said. "Nor will I envy your complexion if you continue to expose yourself to this sun without a hat."

"Why is it men don't have that concern? Anyway, it's too hot."

"You look lovely with your hair flying," Bruce interjected. "But Arabella is right about your riding astride. The peasant girls sometimes do it bareback and Indian women do, of course, but Mother would have a fainting fit if someone from our family did it."

"Well, then, I guess I must disguise myself as a peasant girl," Heather said and, shooting a glance at Rigo, added, "I love disguises."

"Shall we ride down to Bitter Point?" Bruce asked the ladies.

"Oh, let's!" said Heather, wheeling her horse. "And even sidesaddle I'll beat you all!" She struck Beauty once and spurred him off to the spit of land half a mile away. After a moment's hesitation, Bruce spurred his horse off after her.

Triumph reared up impatiently, expecting to join the race as he usually did, but Rigo held him back to remain with Arabella.

"Elizabeth is impetuous, which she'll live to regret. I pity Bruce his task. Someone has spoiled her!" Arabella said, glancing at Rigo as they started after the others at a slow trot.

"She's a handful," Rigo agreed, smiling to himself.

"I find some of her behavior quite indecorous," Arabella went on, looking stiffly forward.

"She's young," Rigo said, aware that Arabella must have noticed during their group rides that there was something more than a casual neutrality between Heather and himself.

"Yes, and some of her actions are even more unforgivable for that reason. She flirts at times like a woman of the world."

Rigo laughed. "No, Arabella. She flirts like a young girl. A woman of the world is, I assure you, much more subtle."

"I find nothing amusing," Arabella said sharply, reining in her horse. "Do you enjoy the prospect of having such a creature marrying your brother?"

Rigo stopped beside her.

"As a matter of fact, no," he replied, smiling to himself.

"You are smiling again!" Arabella burst out. "Has that girl bewitched you, too?"

Stunned, Rigo turned in his saddle to face Arabella.

"My apologies, Arabella. My mind was elsewhere," he said.

"It often appears to be elsewhere these days," said Arabella, pouting. "As does the rest of you. Would it be impertinent to ask whom you are visiting on your nocturnal jaunts through our estate?"

Surprised by the direct question, Rigo hesitated. "I have an officer friend I visit at the post at Wembly Creek," he finally answered.

"All night?" Arabella asked archly.

Rigo sensed the distress behind the haughty manner and realized that she suspected an indiscretion rather than spying. Sadly, it seemed the least dangerous of the two suspicions. Rigo held Triumph steady, still fifty yards away from Bruce and Heather, who were laughing together.

"Yes," he finally said with a scowl. "I was away all night, but I fear it's rather personal. I'm sorry I can't explain more."

Arabella held herself erect and expressionless, her horse twisting its neck restlessly.

"I'm sorry, too," she said.

Rigo knew that unless he said more, she would assume he was casually betraying her and not bothering to hide it.

It pained him to hurt her, but for him to indicate some other business might lead her—and others—to suspect the truth.

"May I ask . . ." Arabella began, now biting her lower lip in obvious pain. ". . . if it is still your intention . . . that we be wed?"

"I fear the war has upset everything," Rigo replied, feeling guilt at how much he had ignored this woman over the past four weeks.

"It has not upset my intentions," Arabella countered with dignity.

"Perhaps because you are still ignorant of how it must change things," Rigo replied firmly.

"But that is no longer true," Arabella said, appealing to his reason. "Until General Howe and his gallant soldiers arrived, Father was fearful that we would have to return to England. Even now, he has plans in place to move us and all our valuables to Plymouth should the rebels actually gain the upper hand. But, certainly, that is no longer possible?"

Rigo shook his head. "I'm afraid it is. Although most of the families here on Staten Island are loyalists, you should know that elsewhere, most of the country is ready for independence. I have read the Declaration of Independence drafted on July fourth by the Continental Congress. It is a powerful document and bodes no good for the chances of reconciliation." He paused and watched as Heather and Bruce turned their horses back toward them. "Arabella," Rigo went on quietly and hesitated, wanting to find the right words, "I have to tell you that this conflict has diminished my . . . resources, and, if the war continues, as I believe it will, I will not be a wealthy man."

Arabella paled.

"That can't be possible," she said.

"It is." Rigo frowned. "No matter which side ultimately wins, my personal business is not likely to prosper. I'm telling you so you won't feel obligated to continue an engagement made when my prospects were far different."

Rigo studied Arabella's tense face a moment, shamed by the look of hurt he saw there.

"These are mere words," Arabella broke in angrily, "and not spoken by the man I once knew."

"Nevertheless, they're true."

"You were simply playing with my affections," she cried, "and are too cowardly to admit it."

"I was not playing with . . ."

"How many nights have you spent with that slut of a Wilson woman—a girl not fit for any society? Dare you deny it?" Arabella's face was now flushed, her eyes glowing with anger.

Rigo stared back at her, stunned at her certainty that he was involved with Sandra Wilson, a rather notorious belle from the down-and-out gentry who lived less than half a mile past Peter Mitchell's farm. "I do deny it," Rigo said, unable to lie to her, although he knew it would simplify things if he could.

"You hesitate! You grow pale! I don't believe you! You are as false as Bruce warned me you are, your head turned by any flirtatious woman." Arabella abruptly spurred her horse forward to trot up to Heather and Bruce, who had just arrived.

"Slowpokes!" Heather said, her face still flushed from her race with Bruce. "Triumph will get fat and lazy if he's ridden only by you," she said, forgetting herself and the wisdom of directing her conversation to Richard.

"It's no challenge to race a girl," Rigo responded after a moment's hesitation, unable to resist Heather even with a distressed woman beside him, "especially if she only rides sidesaddle."

"Oh!" Heather exclaimed in exasperation and looked as if she would say more, but when she saw Arabella's tight expression, she stopped and suddenly turned to Bruce, expressing an interest in picking a few wild flowers for Amy. She directed Bruce away, waving a good-bye and telling the other two not to wait for them as they would follow shortly.

"I hate her!" Arabella said unexpectedly and, giving her horse a quick flick of her quirt, raced away.

Rigo followed, wanting to stay with Heather but knowing his obligations dictated he finish with this meeting more delicately than he had. Was there any way to tell a woman she's free of you and do it gracefully? Not likely— but it had to be done.

Chapter Eighteen

DUNCAN CRAWLEY ARRIVED UNEXPECTEDLY AT SOMERSET Manor in the early afternoon, just in time for tea. Since his business was with John Somerset about buying ships, and his social position, while respectable, was not of the highest, Mrs. Somerset declined to bother to be hostess. She asked Amy to take her place. Amy promptly went into the library and asked Heather to assist her.

Heather had been warned by Rigo that Crawley might someday make an appearance. Although the prospect of meeting him as Elizabeth Southey was not high on her list of desires, she knew that now, at last, she would have to. Crawley probably wasn't aware of the resurrection of Miss Southey or of Heather's impersonation, so she decided it would be better to confront him before he was alone with John Somerset, when the surprise would all be his. Heather asked Amy to receive Mr. Crawley, telling her that she herself would see to the bringing in of the cookies and pastries.

So that afternoon, Heather peeked through the door as Amy graciously served tea to a stiff Duncan Crawley and a relaxed John Somerset. Rigo, unfortunately, had ridden away that morning to visit his "officer friends" in the English encampments. Taking a deep breath and checking that the servant carrying the tray had arranged the pastries properly, Heather pushed open the door and, with bright eyes and a brazen smile, marched into the room.

John Somerset arose from his chair with a warm smile, but Crawley remained frozen in his seat, staring at her in disbelief.

"Ah, Elizabeth," John Somerset said, stroking his graying sideburns. "How nice of you to join us. I would like you to meet Mr. Duncan Crawley, fresh arrived from England to buy ships for His Majesty's fleet. Sir, my niece, Elizabeth Southey."

"Oh, Mr. Crawley," Heather said gaily, walking straight up to his chair. "What a delightful surprise to see you again!" As Crawley staggered uncertainly to his feet, Heather turned to John. "Mr. Crawley and I met on our journey over on the *Prospect*," she explained. "He was quite the gallant."

Crawley, still in a state of shock and trying quickly to assess the situation, bowed awkwardly, his mouth open and eyes wide with wonder.

"Would you prefer the trifle or the apple tart?" Heather asked as the serving girl held the tray before them.

Duncan Crawley stared down at the tray as if he had never seen such a strange object in his life.

"Or perhaps you're not hungry," Heather suggested.

Crawley looked up at Heather, seeming at last to have regained his composure.

"I'd like the tart," he said to her with a sardonic smile, "although it seems covered with far too much sugar."

"Oh, no," Amy said. "Mrs. Hendriks makes them perfectly. Do try one."

"Thank you, my dear. I will," he said, taking one from the serving girl and turning to Amy.

"You two knew each other on the *Prospect*?" John Somerset asked as he held a chair for Heather, who had chosen the seat closest to Duncan Crawley.

179

"Oh, yes," Heather said. "Mr. Crawley was quite kind to me during my indisposition."

"We appreciate that, sir," John said.

"It was nothing," Crawley said. "I would have done the same for the lowliest indentured servant."

"Indeed, that's most admirable," John said with a gentle smile. "But you will admit that it is particularly pleasant to be of service to a woman as lovely as our Elizabeth."

"Oh, yes," said Crawley, shooting Heather a sarcastic glance, "I must confess, I find 'Miss Southey' a wondrously various person, always filling life with surprises."

"Yes," said John, now smiling fully, "she is that, too, I must agree."

"I was very sorry I lost contact with 'Miss Southey' after we landed in New York," Crawley went on, sitting again. "Did you meet her in Manhattan?" he asked John.

"No," John replied, accepting a cookie and straightening himself in the high-backed chair. "The arrival of the *Prospect* passengers on a fishing boat was unexpected and unannounced, and poor Elizabeth had to make her way here on her own."

"Indeed," Crawley said. "How plucky of her."

"She almost died," Amy said.

"Yes," said Crawley, his eyes again glittering briefly at Heather. "There was a moment aboard ship when we thought she had."

"But since she's been here," Amy continued, "she's recovered completely."

"How wonderful!" Crawley exclaimed, and with a scowl turned back to John Somerset.

The conversation continued light and inconsequential for another ten minutes, and Heather breathed a sigh of relief at Crawley's apparent decision not to expose her—at least, not for the moment. Then a servant came in and announced that a Major Keilly was here to speak to Mr. Somerset. Excusing himself and assuring them he would return as soon as he could, John left the room.

After a brief and awkward silence, Crawley turned to Heather with a smile and asked her if she would be so kind as to give him a tour of the gardens. Heather hesitated only briefly and then, realizing that sooner or later she would have to face this man alone, decided that now was better than later.

"I'd be delighted," she replied, standing.

"Please don't disturb yourself, Miss Somerset," Crawley said to Amy with a false smile, effectively telling her she was not invited. As Amy flushed with embarrassment at the slight, Crawley made her a bow and then took Heather by the arm to lead her out through the huge drawing room doors onto the porch.

Heather could feel herself on the verge of trembling and recoiled from Crawley's touch. As they took a few steps off to the edge of the garden, she pulled her arm free.

"I do hope you're enjoying your visit, Mr. Crawley," she said in a firm voice, her head held high.

"You can drop the act, you bitch!" he returned angrily.

"Sir!" Heather exclaimed as a hand flew to her mouth. With a look of disgust, Crawley scowled at her.

"What makes you think I won't expose you?" he asked as they stood facing each other a dozen yards from the house. Only a few feet separated them.

"Because you stole Miss Southey's trunks and dowry," Heather replied with a flash of anger. "And the Somersets would go harder on a thief than on a mere impostor."

Crawley flushed.

"I don't know what you're talking about."

"No? Then what happened to my dowry?"

"The English frigate took it," Crawley replied, coming forward and grasping Heather's arm. "And you'd better have more than that if you think I'll let you keep up this act."

Maggie suddenly appeared on the porch carrying a cook's rolling pin. She hurried down into the garden.

"Let 'er alone, you badger," she said, coming up to them, "or you'll be flatter than any pie!"

"And who might this be?" Crawley asked, glaring at Maggie, whom he knew well from the *Prospect*. "Lady Somerset?" Still not releasing his grip on Heather, he grimaced a bitter grin.

"I heard you and that toad Barrett planning to steal

Miss Southey's trunks," Maggie shot back at him. "And I saw the trunks at that fishing boat, I did, and I'd swear to it on a stack of Bibles ten feet high!"

"Your word against mine, my dear?" said Crawley, standing his ground. "I fear you'd need more Bibles than that."

"Let me go, Mr. Crawley," Heather said evenly, "or I shall scream."

"Oh, you will, will you?" Crawley said, squinting at her, his hate-filled face only a foot from hers. "I doubt it. You know I can tell these people who you really are."

"You seem to forget," Heather said coldly, seeking desperately for some leverage against him, "that Richard Somerset will testify that I am who I claim to be." She could sense a tremor of doubt in the man gripping her wrists. He still stared at her, but now with his mind working rapidly on this new consideration.

"Ah, yes. Mr. Richard Somerset," he said slowly. "A man apparently with a fatal attraction to the lower order of women," he added. "And what, may I ask, do you do for him at night in return for his letting you play the lady during the day?"

With a fierce jerk, Heather broke free of Crawley's grasp and would have swung at him had he not hopped quickly back away from her.

"He does it to protect me from you!" she snapped back at the man.

"And you'd need more Bibles than there are in the world to have your word accepted before his," Maggie broke in.

Crawley, red-faced, stood with his back to the manor, eying Heather with unalloyed hatred. Then he turned and paced away from the two women.

"It *is* a complicated situation," he finally said in a low voice, as if to himself. "One that perhaps I shall have to study a bit more before I act." He turned back to Heather and straightened his suit coat. "But you may rest assured, I *shall* act."

Heather, breathing rapidly, glared back at him.

"It has been a pleasure meeting you again, Mr. Crawley," she said, trying to control her trembling. "I trust you will have a good visit with Mr. Somerset."

"I shall," he replied. "But the pleasure I've had in seeing you this time is nothing compared to what I will have the next time we meet." He turned to go. "Sleep well," Crawley concluded, "while you still can."

And he strode off to return to Amy and the tea.

Chapter Nineteen

By THE NEXT MORNING, HEATHER KNEW SHE COULDN'T GO
on. After Crawley had left the evening before, Bruce had
given her a priceless family heirloom, a necklace, arguing
that there was no conceivable reason for her to refuse it.
When she reluctantly accepted the gift, he insisted on
placing it around her neck and, when he was behind her
closing the clasp, suddenly brought both his arms around
her in a tight embrace, his hands rising to cup her breasts.
At the same time, Bruce buried his mouth in her neck in a
wet, passionate kiss. Heather had struggled and tried to
pull away, but, like a practiced wrestler, he had apparently
planned his hold well. Before she broke free, he had
slipped one hand under the top of her gown to fondle a
bare breast. Heather's anger had only seemed to amuse
him this time, as if her rejection were merely a temporary
ploy in a game they both knew he was destined soon to
win.

She had felt very lonely after that meeting and had
wanted to speak to Rigo—to a man who knew her as her

true self—but he was off again on one of his mysterious missions. Bruce had joked that you couldn't keep a tomcat at home on a warm summer night, but the gossipy Mary had uttered several baffling sentences that implied his disappearances had nothing to do with a woman but with something far more dangerous. What the girl had in mind, Heather couldn't guess. Was he pirating again? But could you do any pirating in just one night? It didn't seem possible. And Heather had felt a sinking feeling when Bruce had pointed out that he had ridden off in the direction of the Moncrief estate.

The visit of Duncan Crawley, rather than liberating her from fear of him, had ended in making her realize how hopeless her situation was. Crawley would be back—on that she could count. And even if Rigo lied for her, Crawley could bring too much evidence for them to hope to overcome the questions and doubts that Crawley would raise. They would have to turn her over to that man.

So as she sat in her dressing room the next morning, staring unhappily at herself in the mirror, Heather tried to stiffen her resolution. She knew John Somerset would be in his study at this hour, that Rigo had not yet returned, and that Bruce was out on his morning rounds of the estate. Now! No turning back! She had to go and tell John Somerset all.

She became aware of Maggie standing behind her, staring at Heather's reflection in the mirror.

"Something's amiss this morning," Maggie said, tilting her head with curiosity while stuffing a pillow into a clean pillowcase. "You been twisting that same hank 'o hair 'til I'm surprised it don't come off. What's it for now?"

Heather glanced back at Maggie in the mirror and self-consciously lowered her hand from her hair. She had lain awake earlier that morning wondering what effect her confession might have on Maggie's status. She turned in her chair to face her.

"I . . . I've decided I can't continue the . . . masquerade," she announced quietly. "I'm going to tell them who I really am."

"Aghhh!" Maggie made a strangled sound as if she were suppressing a scream. "And go back to Crawley? Just when we had him stymied?"

"I'm sorry, Maggie," Heather went on, smoothing the folds of the simple white muslin frock she was wearing. "I can't keep the secret any longer. Richard already knows, and it's unfair to mislead Bruce. I was hoping Richard could find some convenient escape for me, but he seems . . . distracted by other duties."

"But you didn't give a body warnin'," Maggie complained. "Her Ladyship will have me hide stretched."

"Don't fret so," Heather said, disturbed by the look of fear on Maggie's face. "They can't blame you for my lies. I hope you can stay on here, perhaps as a maid for Amy."

Maggie hurled the pillow onto the distant bed with a disgusted grunt. "With you gone, I'm as likely to stay on here as a sow in a dining room."

"Then perhaps you can work on one of the tenant farms."

"Me!" Maggie exclaimed, bustling over to stand near Heather and straighten the toilet articles on the vanity. "I tole you once, I'll not be a milkmaid stinkin' of pig slop and dung. Not Maggie Pipes. I'm a house servant, I am."

"Well, then, go back to your tavern!" Heather said sharply, picking up her brush to give her hair a final stroke. "Because that's what'll happen to you if you don't accept what they offer you here."

"They won't offer me nothing here. Her Ladyship thinks I'm the devil's handmaiden and Bruce already pinches me ass, not because he gives a farthing for me ass but to bruise it proper. He don't like my being your watchdog."

"But they must see that you're loyal and hardworking and . . ."

"For *you!*" Maggie interrupted. "They know I wouldn't be loyal or hardworking for the likes of them."

Heather stood up and sat with a bounce on her bed.

"I have to tell, Maggie, whatever falls," she said . sighing.

"I got no way to stop you," Maggie said with a rueful

smile. "I knew it was all too good to last. But you won't be telling Her Ladyship first?" she asked with sudden alertness. "She'll raise a ruckus such as a flock of chickens 'ud envy."

"No, I'm going first to tell John Somerset."

"Well, that's something. Gives me a peck of time before the roof blows."

Heather got up and looked a last time in the mirror, noticing her green eyes seemed larger and knew it was coinciding with the faint fluttering she was feeling in her stomach.

"If you're thinking of packing a satchel of clothes to fly, pack one for me, too. It may be that I'll be leaving just as quickly," Heather told Maggie.

"Now, that's what I call makin' sense," Maggie agreed, going to Heather's armoire and throwing it open.

"Only my own dress, Maggie. I'll not take any others."

"But . . ." Maggie started and then went on, "'Tis foolishness, that's what 'tis. I'm for tellin' Richard. He might set you up in his house cross the bay. He's sweet on you."

Heather blushed deeply and wondered how much Maggie guessed of her relationship with Rigo. Her feelings warred within painfully and she fought to bring them under control.

"Maggie, say no more. I won't be Rigo's . . . mistress, just as you don't want to be a milkmaid!"

"'Tis yer pride and not your insides yer listening to," Maggie grumbled.

"Maybe so, but my pride is a tattered thing right now, and I've no desire to end up hating myself, too." With that, Heather swept across the room and left Maggie to galvanize whatever plans they'd heedlessly tossed out together.

"Come in." Heather heard the low voice of John Somerset through the door.

With his peppered head bent over his accounts and the dark blue frock coat over his wide shoulders, he looked so much like an older version of Rigo that Heather took in her breath for a moment. Even the quick glance looking at her reminded her of his son.

"Why, Elizabeth," John said, rising from his chair. "This is an unexpected pleasure. How are you this morning?" he went on politely to put the distracted Heather at ease. The older man gestured toward a chair, which Heather took, but she sat on its edge with her back ramrod straight.

"I have something to confess," Heather said, letting out a long breath. Two bright patches of color stained her cheeks.

John, who had again seated himself at his desk, brought his head up slowly.

"Confess?" John said. "That sounds forbidding."

"I'm . . . not Elizabeth Southey. My name is Heather Woode. Elizabeth died during a bout of the flu while still on the *Prospect*." Having gotten out the three crucial sentences quickly, Heather now took a shaky breath and looked at the frozen face of John Somerset. She plunged ahead. "Sir, I didn't plan it and would never have done so had it not been the mistaken impression of your servants and family that I was Elizabeth. I was too ill to care or to argue . . . and then, afterwards, I didn't know what else to do or where to go." The continued cold look on John's face made Heather go on in a stream of words. "Before I left England, I had indentured myself to an unscrupulous man. He sold my contract to Duncan Crawley, who wanted to abuse me. He cared not one fig for my life or my honor. I could no more think of returning to him than I would send an innocent man to jail, where he's beaten and starved. I don't want you to think I'm begging your forgiveness. I just needed to unburden myself, and to . . . set things right."

Heather felt her shoulders sag, and she bent her head forward.

"I had wondered . . ." John said finally, his voice restrained. Heather looked up, startled. "You were so different from the child I remembered meeting years ago, and you seemed not to know the people and places I assumed you had intimate knowledge of. But I wasn't

188

sure. I have been making inquiries about what happened aboard the *Prospect*. I suppose the truth would have been unearthed in the long run. It is to your credit that you've taken it upon yourself to confess." He paused and got up, walking slowly to the window to look out at the lawn. "So, Elizabeth is dead," he stated as if to clarify the event.

"Yes, of flu, as I've told you," Heather answered in a low voice. "I had nursed her aboard the ship. Near the end of the voyage, she wanted to help me, and that's how I came in possession of her letters and knew of your family."

There was a long silence, during which John seemed to think deeply as Heather sat tensely waiting.

"And why have you decided to confess at last. A stricken conscience?" John said, looking at her, half turned in the light, so that Heather could see his tired, stern features.

She blushed deeply. "I know I don't deserve your sympathy. I simply came to tell you what happened to Elizabeth and, I . . . needed to halt your son's plans. Bruce, he . . . Thinking me Elizabeth, he has proposed."

John ran a hand over his brow with his handkerchief. Then he sat down in the wing chair in front of Heather. "What is your name again? I've forgotten."

"Heather Woode," Heather repeated for him, noticing he looked more worn than she'd seen him since coming to the Somersets. She hoped she was not the cause.

Relating a few more details of her story, she told him of events both on the ship and in Manhattan, leaving out Rigo's part in her story. Why, she wasn't sure, but Heather felt it would distress the older man further to be reminded of his son's pirating, for she felt sure he must know. He and Rigo seemed to be close as partners and as family. Her final thought was that she hoped Maggie would be spared jail.

"Great thundering heavens, girl! I hadn't planned to call the magistrate and plunge you in irons, if that's what you thought!" He looked at her sharply.

"I did fear it."

John walked to the windows with measured steps and

stood in thought. Then he turned to a tense but slightly relieved Heather.

"I want you to say nothing to the rest of my family," he finally said. "I'll handle that when the time comes."

"Richard knows," Heather said without thinking.

John looked startled and stood still, his hands clasped behind his back.

"You understand Miss Moncrief expects to marry him, and that scandal is the last thing we need on top of this."

A fleeting feeling of grief swept through her, sharp and painful, grabbing her in her middle. Heather stiffened her back, her pretty eyes sparkling.

"I'm sure she shall. I wish them well." She looked away a moment to collect herself.

"Then how is it you came to tell Richard of your story, unless you've been . . . indiscreet?"

Heather felt her face flush, and she felt thoroughly miserable. If he but knew he would surely heap disdain on her head and she would never lift it again. She checked the rise of tears welling up and said, "We met by chance in Manhattan when I had no idea who he was except . . . It was the very day we landed. I was desperate and left him hurriedly. It was a coincidence, sir!"

"This subterfuge of yours, my girl, will cause much embarrassment to my family here, not to mention the pain of writing the Southeys in England and telling them their dear relative not only doesn't need a dowry but is dead! You can see why I've cause to be angry. Had you given a thought to the hurt you will cause Amy and Bruce when they learn of your game? And Margaret will have to suffer the gossip and ridicule of society—while you have enjoyed yourself at our expense!"

"I have been truly wrong and I . . . I'm very sorry!" Heather could no longer sit in the chair and got up in quick agitation. The tears that had threatened while she listened to this man, whom she admired and respected, chastise her now began to flow down her cheeks unchecked, though she put up the back of her hand to wipe them. She turned away. "Please . . ." she said haltingly, "believe me, I'm truly sorry." With her chest heaving and her face reddened and wet with tears, Heather added, "If society thinks any less of Mrs. Somerset for something not her fault, then society isn't worth the bother!'"

"I think I should be spared your truths, Miss Woode . . . Liars shouldn't call others false."

Heather moved with quick steps, her skirt whirling around her legs and one hand clasped to her chest. "Sir! Someday I would like to repay you the trouble you've been to and the expense. I will gladly work . . . on one of your farms . . . if that suits your purposes, until I've repaid my debt to you."

John raised an arm, his hand open to stop her. "Please. Making amends may be an honest feeling on your part, but I doubt it will be possible for you to stay here once your story has been told. You can, however, begin to make amends by being silent for the moment. I'd like to recover the dowry and let the Southeys know of their loss. I can't find it in my heart to turn you into the cold until I've found a way to do so that will not trouble my conscience." John looked directly at Heather. "I have liked you, young woman, and have treated you like one of my own. It troubles me deeply to be so harsh, but I feel ill-used." John stopped a moment to cough and then continued. "One last word. You must dissuade Bruce from any matrimonial inclinations." He looked at her with intense seriousness and then added unexpectedly. "And my other son, as well."

Heather gasped.

"I am not blind to the movements of the heart," John added with a small smile. "And even if Richard already knows the truth about you, I expect you to discourage any noble impulses he may express toward you."

Heather was confused by the contradictory feelings created by John's allusion to something between herself and Rigo. She started toward John, but the man turned his back and stood facing the outdoors, rejecting her. Heather stopped indecisively for a moment, and then moved to go.

"I hope you will one day find it in your heart to forgive me," she said. "I have dearly loved being here with you. You have been my family that I lost in London, and I shall miss you all. Good day, sir." Heather barely got the last words out before she hastily opened the door and fled. In her room, she buried her face in her pillow and sobbed as if her heart would break. Later she hid her puffy face as best she could with powder, and claimed a touch of summer grippe as the cause for her reddened nose.

Chapter Twenty

THE ENGLISH FORCES WERE AT LAST PREPARING TO MOVE. The first great battle of the revolutionary war was soon to begin. One of the advantages of Rigo's being so familiar with the English troops and officers since their arrival was that he became aware of small changes in their daily routines, changes that would have meant nothing to a recent observer but which told Rigo that General Howe was preparing to leave Staten Island.

The most ostensible evidence was the movement of two battalions—about eight hundred men—in a slow and noisy procession out from the beach, up the gentle slope, and across the fields heading westward. They camped the first night less than three miles from the beach and the next only six miles out. Contradicting this move were several small things that, in Rigo's mind, had much more weight. First, there were the longboat forays across the narrows to Brooklyn, three made in the last four days. Secondly, several full regiments were in the process of packing up. Stores were being moved to the beach. The cavalry patrols to the south and west into New Jersey had been reduced.

Some of the artillery that had been positioned fifteen miles to the west of the narrows after the English had first arrived was being brought back—at night—to the narrows. Cargo ships and longboats were gathering there again and in New York harbor.

A month earlier, Rigo had guessed that landing all these men and material on Staten Island meant that eventually General Howe would march inland west and north through the little towns of Elizabeth and Hoboken to attack Manhattan from New Jersey across the Hudson River. But it seemed clear that whether that had once been General Howe's plan or not—perhaps he'd been discouraged by the extensive marshland that lay in his path—that he planned now to take to his boats again and land his men on Brooklyn, across the narrows or perhaps even in Manhattan itself, although that was where General Washington had concentrated his defenses.

In any case, since the move couldn't be more than a few days off, the previous night Rigo had ridden out to Peter Mitchell's farm with a long letter detailing his observations and conclusions. He also gave Peter a complete oral report and underlined the importance of his getting to New York immediately. Peter, a slender, thin-faced man with a fierce hatred of the Moncriefs and their social class and, thus, a lingering suspicion of Richard Somerset, nodded grimly, asked one or two laconic questions and then returned to his wife and bed. He would go the next day. Then Rigo made a check on the defense positions in the area before riding back to Somerset Manor.

Several hours later, as he was striding heavily toward his bedroom, a servant politely intercepted him and stated that his father wished to see him in the library—immediately.

When Rigo entered, John Somerset was standing with his hands clasped behind his back at the long vertical window. He turned to his son with a scowl.

"I believe it's time we talk," he said without expression.

Rigo came forward and threw himself wearily into the big, soft wing chair next to the desk.

"Yes, I think you're right," he said, glad he was at last

going to get things straight with his father but wishing he had a drink first.

"I believe you know that our 'Miss Southey' is actually an indentured servant? A Heather Woode?" John asked, coming forward to stand beside the desk just opposite Rigo.

"Yes, sir. I do," Rigo answered. "How did you find out?"

"She, unlike you, had the decency to tell me this morning."

Rigo nodded, admiring Heather's courage but wondering what had precipitated her confession. His father continued to stare at him sternly.

"You encouraged her in this . . . enterprise?" John asked next.

"Hardly. But I told her to maintain the charade until I could . . ."

"For a *month!*" his father exploded.

Rigo wearily looked away. "I had wanted to find a suitable place for her," he finally said. He looked up. "But I've failed, probably because there is none."

"*Is* none?"

"Heather is an extraordinary young woman, as I think you know," Rigo began.

"I should say so!"

"Although born in the gentry, she's now without family or means but remains—in every other way—a lady."

"Perhaps," John Somerset said and moved with careful steps behind the desk. With an audible groan, he sat down. Rigo was surprised at how drawn his father's face looked and wondered if this mere business of Heather was the sole explanation. "But right now, she's simply the chattel of Duncan Crawley," John concluded.

"You would permit that?" Rigo asked, straightening in his chair.

"No. I but state the facts, something you appear to have trouble doing lately."

"You are right, sir," Rigo said, leaning toward his father. "And there are other facts that I wish now to make known to you."

"This seems to be a day for confessions."

Rigo pulled himself up out of the deep wing chair and went to the store of liquor in the corner of the room.

"May I?" he asked his father.

"Yes. And fix me my usual, too."

Rigo prepared brandy and, after taking the drink to his father, remained standing near the desk, staring out the window. He felt his usual annoyance at seeing the smoke from the English campfires rising lazily into the sky. He took a quick swallow of the brandy, which burned pleasantly.

"You are aware that my sympathies are with the rebels?" he asked after the pause.

"I suspected as much," John answered with a sigh, having also taken a swig. "But you seem discreet enough about it."

"Discreet, yes," Rigo continued, "but not restrained. I was deeply moved by the Declaration of July fourth. I am fully committed to the independence of the Colonies." When Rigo paused, he saw his father, head down, nodding minutely, his eyes bloodshot. "You wondered at my quick return from the West Indies. I never went. I have a letter of marque to attack English shipping and was sailing off New England as a privateer."

John Somerset, slumped in his desk chair, turned his head to look up at Rigo. "With *my* ship?" he asked quietly.

"With our ship, yes," Rigo replied. "But the ship sailed, like me, under a different name. I have tried to keep the Somerset name totally free from all my activities, but I fear that's no longer possible."

"But *why*, Rigo? *Why?* No matter how difficult the times or unfair the taxes, we would have survived. But by your actions, you are giving up everything!"

"The King and Parliament will never understand America," Rigo shot back with sudden energy. "This land is creating a new people, and it demands a new government free of the autocratic traditions that you and so many others happily fled England to escape. We'll never be free to develop our own ways and traditions until and unless

196

we're free, totally independent of a distant government that doesn't understand us in the least."

It was the first time Rigo had been able to express his true beliefs, and he felt his spirit quicken at the chance. But his father stared up at him with a look of distress.

"So you're giving up all to betray your country?" he asked.

"I'm giving up all to help create a country," Rigo countered. "I've never been happy with the absurdities of the King or his government. Anything new we do here will be an improvement. And I must add, sir, that a change in the injustices of the laws regarding tenants and indentured servants is one of the things I expect to come from our independence."

"You are preaching revolution, my son," John Somerset said, now looking away and slumping further in his chair, his brandy glass cupped in his two slender hands.

"I know that," Rigo said, turning to his father and wanting to comfort him. "I realize all this distresses you, Father, but believe me, I feel far worse about the pain of my disloyalty to you than my disloyalty to England. I want you to formally disown me. I don't want my rebel activities to hurt you any more than they already have."

John Somerset took another sip from his drink. "And what will *you* do, my son?" he asked, looking up at Rigo mournfully, the anger apparently gone.

"I will leave," Rigo said, grimacing. "Immediately, if you wish. In any case, within a few days."

"And then?"

"I serve the rebel forces in any way I can."

"Have you been serving them here at Somerset Manor?"

Rigo felt himself stiffen and lifted the brandy glass to his lips for another deep swallow. When he answered, he spoke softly. "When you think about it, you will surely guess. But I'd rather not compromise you further by answering."

Gray-faced, John Somerset struggled to sit up straighter in his chair. He was blankly staring at the scattered papers on his desk.

"Yes . . ." he said slowly. "I had already guessed as much." He finally got himself back to an erect, dignified position. "Well, you wouldn't be Rigo if you didn't choose the hard path. I can't say I sympathize much with your politics, but I admire your courage." Then he frowned again. "And where does Heather Woode fit in all this?"

"Heather?" Rigo said, surprised that in the enormity of his confession about his disloyalty to the Crown, his father should think of Heather. "How do you mean?"

"You have never been blind to the allure of pretty women, and when the girl has spirit, too, you are rarely indifferent."

Rigo was surprised by his anger at his father's putting Heather in the same class as the other women he'd known. "Heather is a separate problem," he said. "If we can find . . ."

"You're not answering my question."

Rigo strode irritably away from his father and drained the last of his brandy. "I don't know where Heather fits in," he said. "I feel she's my responsibility and . . ."

"Do you love her?" John asked quietly.

"I hesitate to tell you . . ." Rigo said, stopping with his back to John, realizing his heart was pounding with more emotion than the whole previous conversation had produced. "I am . . . committed to caring for her," he finally answered. "I, uh, am involved . . . the truth is . . ."

"Never mind," said John Somerset, interrupting quietly. "You obviously know much more about your feelings about independence than you do about your feeling for our pretty impostor."

Rigo smiled.

"But a place must be found for her," John Somerset continued. "In New York, I suspect. Could you do that?"

"Yes, I will. I'm sorry I haven't done it earlier."

"I am, too." John rolled the brandy glass between his two hands. "We'll let her remain Elizabeth Southey to the very end. To our gossipy neighbors, Miss Southey will simply return to England, her possible ties with our family never fulfilled. I see no sense in humiliating Margaret and Bruce by exposing them to ridicule."

"I agree."

John smiled softly.

"I confess I shall miss her," he said.

Rigo put his empty brandy glass down on the bookshelf and returned to his father, who looked up at him with a sad smile.

"But not as much as I shall miss you, my son," he added, tears glistening in his tired eyes.

"And I you, sir," Rigo said quietly, going to him and resting his hand on his shoulder. John reached up a trembling hand and placed it over his.

"Come back, Rigo," he said in a whisper. "No matter what may happen, come back."

"I will," Rigo said, a stab of guilt chilling him as he felt his father's aged fingers clutching his hand. He prayed he could.

Chapter Twenty-one

LATE THAT NIGHT AS HE WAS READY TO RETIRE, JOHN Somerset collapsed and was carried to his bed.

For several days, the whole household was hushed in concentration on the task of caring for him. Curtains were drawn, visitors refused, a physician called, and teas and potions were specially brewed. The elderly physician, long used to the Somerset family's health—or lack of it—at first seemed inclined to call the illness apoplexy, but as John seemed to be capable of moving his limbs and remembering everyone, the physician finally termed it a swoon brought about by too much work. His efforts to bleed the gentleman resulted in his being firmly escorted to the door by Rigo, who refused that form of treatment for his father.

Margaret was at her best organizing the household for the emergency, and she reigned supreme over all matters —save the physician's desire to let blood. She set her daughter and Heather to the job of gathering and drying herbs while storing in tin containers those already prepared. They also brewed all the necessary teas.

Heather would have enjoyed these tasks on other days, but she was now filled with remorse about her confession to John Somerset, certain it had helped to bring on his collapse. Having no one to confess her fear to, she bore it like a permanent cloud until she was told by a tearful Amy that Rigo had locked himself in John's study, drinking rum and asking not to be disturbed. Amy felt he blamed himself for his father's illness and when Heather asked why, Amy said they'd had a lengthy conversation in the study that had upset her father, but she wasn't certain what it was about. Amy guessed it might have something to do with shipping and Rigo's possible departure. Heather felt her heart plummet at the thought of Rigo's leaving but pushed the thought aside. She had no right to be pained. Amy explained that she had tried to talk to Rigo, but he had shooed her away. Now she asked Heather to intervene.

"If Papa knew Richard was locked in the study drinking rum, it would make him worse," Amy said to her as the two of them were putting dried peppermint, spearmint, and comfrey in tins and labeling them by drawing pictures of the leaves and flowers in ink. "Won't you please talk to him? Bruce will not, and Mama says, 'Tis his way.' But it isn't! Only once before have I seen him like this, and it was over the loss of a ship."

Heather asked Amy a question or two and then agreed to try, but it bothered her to be going to see Rigo alone. She was disturbed that Bruce seemed to be becoming suspicious of her every move. In moments alone with her, he hinted that Rigo was not the perfect gentleman that he might seem and told her little snippets of Rigo's life as a free sailor roving the seas, gaming and carousing. He also told her about a certain gay widow on Staten Island and implied that Rigo disappeared in order to "visit her." Heather usually made no comments on Bruce's spicy innuendos, but she did brood silently on Rigo's supposed affair with the bountiful widow. His drinking now made her wonder if these stories about him just might be true.

Heather walked slowly to the study door, smoothing the

simple pink cotton frock, glad her chestnut hair was swept back and tied off her face. She hoped to appear stern. She knocked quickly.

"Get away from the door," a low growl on the other side demanded. "I want nothing except peace for a few hours!"

Heather hesitated and then tried the door. Finding it unlocked, she took a deep breath and entered on tiptoe. She closed the door gently but when she saw Rigo, she caught her breath. He was lying barefoot on the settee in the darkened room, one arm thrown over his brow and the other draped carelessly over the back of the settee, his long legs bent askew. His white shirt was open to the waist, rumpled and half out of his black breeches. His black boots, suit coat, and silk scarf were scattered about the floor.

"I said I wanted to be alone," he repeated from deep within his throat.

Heather jumped, her heart thumping a moment before she calmed herself and boldly swept forward into his view. She was frightened of him in this mood. The thought suddenly occurred to her that John might have told him of her confession so that Rigo was angry with her as well as upset over his father's sudden illness. Rigo had his eyes closed, so, taking heart, she crossed to a chair opposite him and sat down. When she saw his unshaven face with its dark growth, it seemed even more forbidding than his low growls.

"You look terrible. . . ." she said softly, and saw him clench the hand over his brow. A heave in his abdomen was accompanied by a guttural sound, which she soon realized was a grim laugh. Slowly, Rigo turned his dark head and looked at her.

"I feel terrible," he said with emphasis, then added, "You're probably the only one I wouldn't toss out for disturbing me." Although his voice was low and raspy—as if he hadn't gotten enough sleep or had smoked too much—there was a brief spark in his blue eyes that reassured Heather he was not still in a violent mood.

Heather leaned back in her chair and pushed her long legs out in front of her, as if digging in for a battle.

"I'm not going until I've said what I came to say," she said. When he didn't respond but let his eyes run slowly over her, making her feel his presence keenly, she tossed her head and continued. "Your father is recovering. He's eating and has even been sitting up in bed."

"So I've been told, but it was I who sent him there!" Rigo paused. "My father's illness was not the only reason I came in here to think. Think, not drink, as Amy believes. Several glasses of rum do not make a rummy." Heather blinked at the harshness in his voice.

"You shouldn't blame yourself," Heather countered. "I did my share to add to your father's burdens. But you must consider as well the war and the soldiers who daily beset him with their needs. It was not your fault alone."

Rigo raised his head a moment to stare at her.

"We both of us have done our part," he said gruffly. "But I've more reason to be concerned for the welfare of my family, believe me." He propped himself up on an elbow and then said, "Tell me, Heather, do you still think me a man not to be trusted, a man to despise?"

"I have never despised you," she said, surprised at the question and remembering with a flush the rumors of the merry widow. "As to trust, I have already answered that I cannot. I saw how you distressed Arabella a few days ago. I consider myself fortunate not to be in her shoes."

There was a long silence as Rigo ran his hand through his hair, which was wildly unkempt. "Arabella was distressed because I had to tell her that this war has made it impossible for me to marry," he said, staring at the mess of his clothing on the floor. "We are no longer betrothed. The fact that I will not marry when I have nothing to offer a woman does not strike me as untrustworthy, especially when I know she's the wrong woman."

Heather felt a shock go through her as if a rare fit of glee wanted to erupt, a glee totally out of place. She struggled to control it. It was cruel to feel pleasure over Arabella's loss, nor could Heather hope she was about to take her place. After all, he had just said he could not marry. She became aware Rigo was studying her face.

"Does this please you?" he asked, his voice low and husky.

"I have no right," Heather said, glancing away from his probing blue eyes.

"I asked if it pleased you, not if it was right. I have a great interest in the answer."

Heather abruptly got up and said in an agitated voice, "I'll get you a cool cloth for your head." As she walked to the pitcher on the table under the window, she could hear his chuckle following her. When she returned, Rigo seemed to be resting, which relieved her. Gently, she placed the cool cloth over his brow as she bent low over him. Opening his eyes, he took hold of her wrists and pulled her down on the settee. A manly smell, mixed with rum and tobacco, filled her nostrils. She had been foolish to get close to him, she knew. He always had the power to make her aware of him as a lover.

"Why haven't you the courage to admit how you feel about me?" he asked in a low voice.

As she felt the power of his gaze, Heather fought to remember how foolish it would be to give in. "You're so sure of yourself, Rigo," she said quietly, holding herself stiffly on the settee near him, aware of his hot thigh against her hip. "But I have grave doubts about the wisdom of my . . . feelings, and . . . you frighten me."

"Have I ever betrayed you in any way?" he asked softly, releasing her wrists. Heather could feel herself flushing as she thought of the merry widow and of Rigo's still unexplained pirating. She arose from the settee and distractedly went to open the drapes to let some fresh air into the stuffy room. Finally, she answered him.

"People say you spend nights away visiting a woman," she began softly. "But even if that's not true, your disappearances are still frightening, as is your being a pirate. I fear what I don't understand."

Rigo swung his legs off the settee and stood up, irritably shoving his white shirt into his breeches. He leaned down and picked up his suit jacket and scarf and flung them back on the settee. Then he looked at Heather with surprising gravity.

"My father is upset because I told him that I have been working for the Colonies, for the rebels, as a privateer and . . . as a spy."

Heather's hand came instinctively to her throat in a gesture of shock. "You jest!" she gasped.

"I do not. This country is at war with England. I serve the rebel side. My disappearances had nothing to do with any woman, but with . . . the war."

Heather knew immediately that what he said was true, but her relief at knowing her jealousy and distrust were misplaced was immediately destroyed by other thoughts. "But you may be killed! And your family! What will happen to them if . . ."

"Exactly," Rigo said. "You can see why I blame myself for my father's collapse."

"And the pirating," Heather asked, "That, too, was . . . the war?"

"Yes."

She was trying to absorb all these revelations and stood still, the green of her eyes seeming to Rigo even deeper with her concentration.

"But if they catch you . . . you'll be jailed!" she finally said.

"And if Crawley catches up with you, then perhaps we'll be neighbors," Rigo said, his eyes sparkling for the first time that afternoon. "You in one cell and me in the other—though I had hoped for a closer association." His mouth pulled up in a smile.

"You make light of it, but it's serious," Heather said.

"Yes, it is," he said, now with a furrow in his brow. "Very serious. And other than my father, you are the only one to know." He crossed the room to stand close to her, looking down with intense seriousness. "I've given you a powerful weapon against me," he added softly. He reached out to caress a stray lock of hair falling on her shoulder, his eyes sweeping over her creamy neck and partially exposed shoulders. They came back up to her widened green eyes.

"May I trust you to keep the secret? My life may depend on it." His voice was intimately low, his blue eyes asking more than the single question.

Heather nodded gravely. "You may," she whispered, putting a hand on his arm.

He was silent a moment, then a slow smile transformed his face. "I feel a fire inside my chest that a sun would envy, and I thank you for it." Rigo reached for her free hand and kissed the palm tenderly.

"As for the widow lady who worries you," he went on with a mischievous smile. "I've doffed my hat in her presence once or twice but nothing more, and I regret you've been led to believe otherwise." He reached out with one arm to encircle Heather's waist and drew her against him. "My taste in women runs to impostors engaged to another man." As he smiled at her, Heather tilted her head up to him. At the look in his eyes, she took in a breath, feeling his glance as a caress. He slowly brought his lips to hers, drawing her forward deeper into his arms. She surrendered, melting softly with him.

His mouth plundered the sweetness opened to him, stopping only to whisper softly, "I'm yours, my darling girl. . . . If you've doubted before, doubt no more. . . ." Rigo ran his tongue over the delicate curve of Heather's ear and down her neck, letting the fragrance of her hair intoxicate him. A wild fluttering began inside her, and leaping fires raced through her body until she felt engulfed in the flame. Even in the tight fierceness of his embrace, Heather trembled with the power of her feelings.

When Rigo finally released her mouth and was caressing her hair and face with a tender hand, Heather felt her senses stop reeling long enough to utter her first words.

"Oh, Rigo . . ." she whispered. "Your touch confuses me. I want it, but . . ." There was a gentle knocking at the study door, and they could hear Amy call in a concerned voice.

Heather took in a sharp breath, and Rigo gently and reluctantly let her go. In a dazed state, Heather moved slowly to the door, turning as she reached it to see Rigo going to the settee and gathering up his boots.

"We haven't finished our conversation," he said to her quietly.

Heather opened the door slowly to admit Amy, who was reluctant to enter lest her brother again become the bear who growled his displeasure.

"Are you all right, Elizabeth?" Amy inquired cautiously, peering into the dark study as if afraid an army of angry Rigos might come charging out at her.

"Yes, I'm fine, Amy," Heather said shakily. "Your brother is . . . coming out of the study and will join us tonight for supper."

Both Amy and Heather looked around at Rigo, who was seated and pulling on his boots. He nodded his agreement. Amy felt calmer and, emboldened by his nod, bustled into the room to throw open the last of the drapes and tidy up, chatting to Rigo as she did so of his father.

When Heather glanced briefly at Rigo, the message in his gaze was so direct that a blush rose to her cheeks and she turned to escape.

Chapter Twenty-two

HEATHER'S ENCOUNTER WITH RIGO LEFT HER IN SUCH A STATE of excitement and confusion that she was barely able to function. She tried to spend all her time in her room, her mind going over every word, every touch, every look of their last meeting and many of those that had taken place earlier. Feelings warred within her—her love for the man versus her fierce desire not to be taken in or taken advantage of. But for the first time, Heather was beginning to trust Rigo, and as she did, her feelings for him began to explode. Simply watching him walk across the courtyard beneath her window—the broad muscled back, the lean, long strides, the black hair ruffled in the wind—made her long to rush after him and throw herself in his arms and hang the consequences. So wrapped up in her thoughts of Rigo was she that when Bruce came up to her room the next afternoon and asked to speak to her, she feigned an indisposition and insisted on her privacy.

But Heather's dreamworld was shattered an hour later when, as she paced her room trying to see how her relationship with Rigo was going to end, Maggie abruptly burst in.

"Miss Southey, your trunks have come!" she announced with a cheeky smile.

"No!" Heather said, stopping cold.

"Oh, they be here all right. Come over this morning from Manhattan with one o' Mr. Somerset's men. They're unloadin' now."

"Close the door, Maggie, quickly!" Heather said, afraid they might be overheard.

Maggie shut the door, her small mouth open like a fish. "I thought you'd be glad of it. Yer fortune's made, there bein' no sign of the blackhearted Duncan Crawley with the loot. Mayhap the Somerset men did 'im in."

"Crawley was my main fear. You're sure he's not come?" When Maggie nodded yes, Heather sank on the small plush stool before her dressing table, her hands clasped in her lap.

"You do know what this means," Heather said, her throat parched.

"It means yer rich," Maggie answered readily.

"Or if they've found out that the real Miss Southey is dead, I'm exposed as an impostor and soon to be exiled."

"Whoops! I hadna' thought of that." Maggie nervously fluffed the little white apron she wore.

"I suppose I ought to go down."

"Her Ladyship is atwitter with excitement," Maggie acknowledged.

"Are either of her sons about?" Heather asked quietly, giving voice to another of her fears. For she wasn't ready to face either man on top of seeing the dreaded trunks again.

"Neither one."

"A small reprieve," Heather said. "Well, what are we waiting for? Let's get on to the noose or the nest. 'Tis remaining on the cliff edge that makes me most nervous."

Heather's concern was short, though, for Mrs. Somerset beamed approval on Heather when she appeared and was simply eager to see the contents. Heather obliged, but as she began to go through the contents of the first of the two trunks, she realized that the trunk with the silver had lightened considerably. After a brief hesitation, Heather told Mrs. Somerset that some things appeared to be missing. That lady then threatened to call the constable but eventually settled for asking her husband to look into the matter once he had recovered. With Heather worrying about how some of the clothing was going to fit her, the trunks were finally taken up to her room.

She was late coming down to supper. Amy had come in and informed her the men knew of the dowry's arrival and that Bruce was full of high spirits while Richard's mood had become subdued. Heather knew then that she had to leave Somerset Manor as quickly as possible. She could not wait for John Somerset to find her a suitable place. Having made that decision, she drew some courage to face both men and slowly entered the dining hall. She avoided looking at Rigo, who stood behind his chair while Bruce came to seat her next to him. Margaret preferred to have her own children on either side of her, and so Heather was opposite Rigo.

Heather made a long, slow job of seating herself and adjusting her dress but, finally, she couldn't avoid looking up. Rigo's eyes burned into hers. Heather flushed and quickly looked away with the feeling he knew all she thought—and why. It unsettled her.

Margaret said a simple grace and told them to begin. "This is the first evening we have all sat together since John's illness. He has asked me to receive visitors once more, but there is no doubt in my mind that he needs considerable rest and quiet. If you young people need your more boisterous friends, I suggest you meet them at their home, or tent, as the case may be." She looked at each of the men in turn.

"You needn't fear the disturbance of the household again, Mother," Bruce said. "I know you refer to my card games, but there's been a move afoot among the soldiers that I'm sure means their departure soon."

"Do they mean to leave us then?" Margaret asked.

"I am certain of it, Mother."

"It can only mean they plan an attack on the rebels. I must say, I will be glad when it's done with. Now, we'll have no more talk of soldiering, for I'm weary of the topic."

Rigo said nothing yet listened with apparent indifference, waiting to see if Bruce was going to say more. When he didn't, Rigo turned to Margaret, his clean profile drawing Heather's attention.

"I want to apologize to you, madam, for my recent behavior. In the light of your troubles, it was inexcusable."

Heather had never heard Rigo address his stepmother in those tones. They were not exactly humble but were sincere and mixed with regret. She looked across at him, unaware that her face was showing her interest and appreciation.

"And you," Rigo caught Heather's emerald eyes. "I thank you for reviving me."

Heather felt her composure nearly destroyed and carefully put her fork down on her plate.

Bruce looked over at Heather and, seeing her discomfort, asked, "How did she do that?"

"In a manner that only women seem to know the secret of," Rigo replied and asked to have the bread passed, as if what he had said would not goad his brother on or distress the already disturbed Heather.

"But I'm curious, Elizabeth. What is this sure remedy for drunkenness?"

"He was not drunk but . . . sick with a malady that only men seem to have—ill-timed boorishness," Heather finally said, her anger raised by Rigo's baiting sarcasm.

Bruce laughed, and Rigo himself smiled broadly. Amy giggled her approval, since the men seemed happy with the answer.

Margaret interrupted by asking after everyone's day, and the conversation became general. But at the conclusion of this, Bruce, who seemed tense, tapped his glass to get everyone's attention.

"This may not be the most appropriate moment to make this announcement, but I've decided to wait no longer," he said, firmly looking first at his mother and then, with a tense smile, at Heather. "With Elizabeth's permission, I would like to declare our intention to wed. It has been our secret, but now I'd like to share it with all of you." Bruce was still looking at Heather, who had gone pale and stiff. "My dear, I see no reason to wait any longer, as we agreed, for with the arrival of your trunks, there is no reason to do so."

Rigo sat still, a bare smile frozen on his face, his eyes on Heather. "I think her wit has deserted her," he said, "so I will answer for her on one score. Your announcement is not well timed. I don't think you've discussed this with our father, and it might upset him. That I object to. Strongly. I wouldn't carry this any further, if I were you." Rigo gave his brother a fixed stare, his hard body poised and waiting.

"Bruce, dear," Mrs. Somerset began, recovering her senses and touching her hand to her cap, as was her habit when disturbed. "I quite agree with Richard that it's not appropriate, what with the war and the way things are."

"Elizabeth," Bruce appealed to her. "I will assent to a lengthy betrothal. Will you?"

Heather couldn't speak. Her throat seemed constricted, so she nodded mutely.

"Then I am content, and I will do or say no more on the subject in deference to my parents' wishes."

The only thought that kept Heather from leaping up from the table was that she had made the decision to leave as soon as she could. Knowing that, she contained herself and tried to give Bruce a smile, but her eyes were glazed with her disbelief that he could have made such a speech without her consent. It penetrated her frozen brain that part of his reason for doing so was Rigo's goading. When she made this discovery, she looked over at Rigo's unreadable face.

"Shall I offer my felicitations, my lady?" he asked. "Or does that grim visage bode poorly for my hapless brother?" Rigo's voice was laced with only slightly concealed sarcasm. "Timing is everything, Bruce. You should have learned that lesson well from our many contests . . . on horses."

"I've not noticed your timing is any better lately,

if Arabella's mood is any indication," Bruce said, anger knotting his brow.

"Please!" Heather said, her lips finally unsealed. "I will abide by Aunt Margaret's wise decision, and I want no more said on this subject!" She got up, nearly knocking over the chair, but quickly stopped it from toppling over. "If you will all excuse me, it's been a long day." With that, she hurriedly left, not caring that Bruce had gotten up and come after her. She raced to the safety of her room and closed the door firmly in Bruce's face, knowing she would have to apologize later but not being able to stop herself now because of his foolishness.

Maggie fretted aloud as she gave Heather's long chestnut locks a good brushing till they shone like liquid brown earth and fire. Her mistress sat limply, staring at her reflection in the looking glass, her loose fitting white cotton shift draping her rounded but firm shape. Miss Southey's dark trunks sat in one corner of the room like coffins of her immediate past, and memories in devil's forms emerged when she saw them—Elizabeth's untimely death; Duncan Crawley's greedy hands; Barrett's perfidy; and the loss of all she had or had hoped for—events that had culminated in her being here falsely betrothed to one brother yet loving the other. And denied both. One was a royalist and the other a colonial rebel. One was willing to marry the lady she wasn't, and the other, a rake who had already shattered one lady's heart, was unwilling to marry anyone. One was a lord of this splendid manor while the other's fortune seemed bound to a New World where all was uncertain and crumbling, possibly a world he would never live to see. Heather shivered when that icy thought fingered its way down her spine. She took the brush from Maggie. Rising, she swept in long, graceful strides to her bed.

"Leave me, Maggie. My head is awhirl and I need to end this day." Sliding into her soft bed, she drew the coverlets up to her chin.

"You ain't touched yer tea," Maggie complained, unwilling to leave just yet.

"Leave it. Perhaps I'll try later."

"'Twill be cold," Maggie persisted, fussing in the room with clothing and adjusting the curtains. "Why, 'tisn't even dark yet. I hear the birds still acooin' in the trees."

"Tell Bruce I'll see him tomorrow if he asks for me. Tell him I've . . . a terrible headache. He won't believe it, but he'll have no choice."

"An' what will I be tellin' Richard? If he's a mind to see ye, no ache will keep him at bay!"

"I've nothing to expect from him. He's already told me what he wants, and it's unacceptable."

"Don't be crossin' 'im off so quick. For I'm thinkin' he'll not be a slacker in bed nor tossin' ye out when he's done."

"Maggie! Good night!"

"'Tis for yer own good I'm tellin' ye. It's not the first time yer in a pickle since I met ye. If yer runnin', ye better have a place to go."

Heather put her pillow over her head to signal the end of the conversation. With a last grumble, Maggie finally left.

Leaning over the night table to blow out the one candle still lit, Heather let her eyes roam the room, tracing its shadows. A large chipped moon began to rise, mingling its eerie light with the last of twilight. The house subsided into quiet. She doubted if Bruce was at home or in bed and wondered if Rigo had slipped off somewhere. It occurred to her he might come walking in, and it was this thought, as well as having no plan for the future, that kept her awake. Heather tossed and turned for awhile and then threw back the covers in disgust. She simply was not ready to sleep.

Drawing on a light, billowy robe, she carefully eased herself out her door, pausing to listen. Although she saw a light beneath the study door, the house was still. Heather hesitated, half wanting to find out if it were Rigo, but if it wasn't, she had no desire to see Bruce and decided against chancing it. Besides, Rigo would only want to press her into a questionable relationship, and her power to resist him was becoming weaker with each meeting.

Once out the front door, she felt a surge of relief and freedom. The house had become a prison. In that moment, Heather longed to be on a ship sailing to a warm home where friends and loved ones longed to see her, where she would be embraced once more and there was no doubt about her worth. She ran to the garden toward a favorite oak tree and leaned against it. An unbidden tear ran down her face, and she angrily wiped it away with a long finger. A broken sigh escaped, and she chided herself aloud for her foolish longings.

Heather was so wrapped up in her musings that she didn't hear the approaching footsteps until she saw a dark figure approaching.

"How did you know I was here?" she asked, recognizing the tall, dark form as Rigo. He stopped a foot from her and ran his gaze over her lightly clad body.

"I went looking for you, and Maggie spied you rushing outdoors, 'as if the devil was after her,' as she put it," Rigo replied in a soft, measured tone.

"She's not often mistaken in her identifications, is she?" Heather asked, a note of angry frustration in her voice.

"She has your interests at heart, as do I. Please don't make these moments together full of a mistaken lashing out at each other. There's no need for it. If you knew how often I've nearly made a fool of myself for you, you might show a little more mercy."

"Pretty words, full of flattery and wooing, and you do it so well!" Heather let out a breath.

Rigo stood quietly a moment, assessing her mood before answering. "It seems the more I ask for your trust, the less you're willing to give it, and the closer I come to tell you of my longing for you, the further you retreat. When you met me, you knew less about me than you do now and yet you were more trusting. What are you afraid of?"

Heather made a move to leave, but Rigo put out a hand and stopped her.

Heather sucked in her breath as she felt the warm hand on her bare arm. Shards of desire broke free from the fragile vessel that tried to contain them as her resistance withered. Her other hand came up to rest lightly on his chest, half to hold him back, half in an unintended caress.

"Shall I tell you why, since you seem unwilling to admit it?" Rigo slipped his other arm around her waist and drew her into the circle of his arms. On the instant of their meeting, a rush of heat flamed through Heather.

"Don't say more now. I . . ." Heather murmured, putting her other hand up between them.

"Even if I had the patience to wait, I haven't the time. Nor do you. I leave here tomorrow, never to return until this war is over." Rigo's eyes sought hers. Heather brought her eyes up to meet his, startled.

"Why?" Heather managed to ask after a pause. She leaned closer, as if to gather his warmth into her before coldness came. He put a hand up to her face, and Heather impulsively turned her lips and kissed it.

"I don't want you to go. . . ." she whispered.

"Oh, Heather, I don't want to go, but every moment I stay here is a danger to my family and myself, and I am needed elsewhere now. I can't stay."

Heather felt a shock go through her. "But where are you going?" She searched his face in the pale moonlight.

"For your own safety, I can't tell you. The English army has begun invading Brooklyn this very day, and I must leave." With both his hands at her waist, he pulled her closer to him. "But it's you I want to talk about. We've got to get you away from here."

"But where can I go?" Heather asked, distraught, a catch in her voice.

"When I'm able to get back to New York, I'll send a trusted friend here to pretend he is a distant Southey relative come to fetch you back to London. You will leave with him and remain in New York until I am free from . . . free to come to you." He was speaking in a husky whisper, his face close to hers, his hands hot on the small of her back. "Will you do that?" he asked softly. "I promise you my protection—from me as well, if that's what you think you need," he added with a teasing smile.

Heather nodded her head yes, realizing that she was

now accepting the possibly compromising offer she had rejected only two days before. But she could no longer resist Rigo. "I will say yes to coming to your house but not to your bed."

"Madam, you make me happy with just the one. Imagine my joy when you say yes to the other." He bent to brush his lips against hers, this time lingering to pass his heated tongue deliciously along her top lip. Heather let out a little gasp of pleasure and closed her eyes.

Rigo's muscles tightened momentarily as he gave up resisting for even one minute more. He took her mouth to satisfy his hunger.

"My darling," he went on in that soft, husky voice that sent tremors through her. "One thing more you must promise me for my sanity and that is to fend off my brother's advances."

"He is very insistent," Heather whispered a little teasingly, surprised and pleased at Rigo's jealousy, "and difficult when he wants to be."

"Just use your considerable powers of resistance," Rigo countered with a half smile, bringing a hand to her chin to raise her face closer to his. "If you resist him with but a tenth of the wiles and persistence you do me, I shall be quite content."

"If I didn't resist you every second, I would have been stripped of all pride and honor long ago," Heather said defensively.

"It's not your honor that would have been stripped. . . ." Rigo said with a mischievous smile, and then added more seriously, "But where you're concerned, I've developed a patience I didn't know I had."

The mention of patience sent a chill through Heather for it reminded her that he was to leave the very next day. "But you . . ." she began, lifting a hand in the darkness to touch his face. "You're going . . . to the war. I fear . . . When will I see you again?"

"You promise me you'll be waiting for me at my townhouse?" he asked, bringing his face down so close to hers that their lips were almost touching as they whispered to each other.

"Oh, yes, Rigo! I will!" she answered, beginning to cover his face with light kisses, her arms now up around his neck.

"Then I will fight my way through General Howe's entire army to get back to you, I promise," he answered, his lips seeming to caress her cheek as he spoke.

"I will be there waiting for you," Heather whispered.

Rigo bent further to press kisses into the hollow of her neck, his warm breath stirring her senses until she felt her arms tighten around his back. She arched her body into his. Rigo took her mouth then in a savage kiss, his tongue diving deeply into the sweet moistness, where he was received eagerly. When he finally released her mouth, he planted burning kisses on her soft neck, removing the silken tresses as he did so. His arms wove a tight net around her. Finally, both of them breathless, he cupped her head in his hand and sought her eyes with his.

"I love you, sweet lady," he said huskily against her lips. "I love you more than I thought any man could love any woman. You are my perfection . . . sweet, beloved one. . . ."

Heather felt such a dazzling rush of love that her arms went limp around his neck as her eyes swam in the glowing warmth of his. "Rigo," she moaned as she pulled herself tight against him. "I have known of my love for you for some time," she whispered back, "but feared to confess it."

"And you have bewitched me since I first burst into your room on the *Prospect*," he whispered, smiling now.

"Oh, yes," she said. "'Twas then, too, that you pirated my heart."

Again Rigo took her in a long kiss during which Heather could no longer tell where Rigo left off and she began. When they finally broke it, she sighed. "'Tis truly our last night?" she questioned softly, not wanting it to end, yet torn with the need to end it for her own protection.

Rigo nodded, still enfolding her tenderly in his arms.

"I would give anything to share your bed," Rigo whispered against her kiss-swollen lips. "I long to show you the ways of love." He felt her trembling slightly in his arms. "I'm not expecting you to yield to my desires, but I want you to know they are there. For the moment, I'll take your love with me and your promise for the future."

"I give it. I do love you. . . ." Heather murmured. "I will wait for your message to me and will come with all speed." She hesitated, and then added, "And I consent."

Rigo was at first stunned, then he leaned over and gently placed a kiss on Heather's mouth, now pliant and swollen from their kisses.

"Oh, lady . . ." he said huskily, the sound coming from deep within. "Then come with me." He took her hand and rushed back toward the dark house, stamping at the back door to check on the silence within.

Heather's heart beat frantically. She felt her legs ready to collapse at the enormity of her surrender to him and her still fearful knowledge of what was about to take place.

Rigo turned to her once they were inside, and saw her wide-eyed, dazed look. He reached down and picked her up, holding her close against his body. She rested her head on his shoulder, once crushing her face into his neck to give him a soft kiss as he carried her into his bedroom.

He put her on her feet and quietly locked the door, then went to light a candle on the mantle above his fireplace. Its dim light flickered on the wall.

Slowly Rigo turned and walked to her. His eyes filled with light and longing, he opened his arms to her. Heather felt no hesitancy now and fell into his embrace, raising her mouth to his.

He began planting light kisses on her cheeks, gently taking her lips for a brief moment, flicking his tongue across them to tantalize. Then he settled on them longer until he felt her yielding to him. He slowly pulled away, their breaths mingling. Rigo rose from his chair and offered Heather his open arms. She readily went into them, arching toward him, needing to have her body touch his. A soft expectancy in her eyes made Rigo take in his breath.

He brought his lips down on hers, creating an exquisite fire in each of them. When he ran his tongue lightly over her lower lip, she pressed against him, parting her lips. He drew her into his arms tightly, feeling a fresh urgency as their kiss deepened. Rigo ran his hand down over the soft curve of her back, pressing her in against his swollen manhood. Warmth rushed down Heather's legs, and a soft throb began to grow deep inside her. He released her, his lips still hovering close. She opened her eyes to see him looking down into hers, which were filled with a desire and a willingness that took his breath away.

Acting now on instinct, there was little left of the restraint he had placed upon himself. Rigo reached up to unfasten the buttons on her dressing gown to uncover the fullness of her taut, satiny breasts. Gently, he scooped their rounded fullness in his hands as he pushed her chemise aside and drank in the sight of their rosy, pink-tipped beauty. Lowering his mouth, he gently flicked his tongue over first one and then the other, his eyes glazed with passion. Rigo shuddered at hearing Heather's soft noises of pleasure, and he loosened his embrace to turn her around and unfasten the rest of her gown, his fingers sure in their flight to their goal. He stopped once to caress again her peaked, rosy globes and, with a groan, he pressed her into him, his lips trailing kisses across her shoulders. Heather leaned her head back against him, her eyes closed and lips parted, allowing him access to her nape, where he pressed his lips.

Gently, he turned her to him and let her chemise fall to the floor, his hands then falling to her hips. Gliding down her silken skin, Rigo's hands removed her last remaining garment. Heather stepped out of her slippered shoes and away from the heap on the floor, her eyes widening as she watched Rigo intently. His face flushed. Something undefined swept through her, a longing for something unknown, something he might be able to give to her.

Rigo slowly let his eyes drink in her beauty, studying the smooth, glorious shape of Heather's long, tapering limbs, the lush dark growth at the triangle of her body, the round curves, her perfectly formed breasts with pink nipples erect, her skin a pale rose gold, and the shining chestnut hair falling over her shoulders. He lifted his gaze to hers. His eyes were a dusky blue, and the look in them melted Heather.

"Oh, lady. I am lost. . . ."

Reaching out, Rigo scooped Heather into his arms, his eyes still on hers, and lowered her onto his bed. Then he stood beside the bed to remove his clothes. The dim glow from the lamps allowed Heather to see all. She watched and then shyly looked away.

Naked, Rigo knelt on the bed, looking down at her. A tanned finger turned her face to his. "Don't be shy with me," he whispered. "I offer you my body freely for your pleasure, and I won't be shy with yours." He let a hand glide over her smooth flesh and saw her breathe more deeply, her eyes darker. Softly, Rigo caressed her body, running his hands over every curve, then he bent to let his lips plant kisses from her stiffly nippled peaks down to the hollow of her belly on down to the sensitive junction of her thighs and down further to the moist valley between, where he nibbled and licked softly as Heather writhed and pushed on his shoulders in both pleasure and protest.

Rigo aroused her until her natural desire and the sweet chemistry exploding between them took over. Then her hands reached up to pull him down, and she arched toward him, her urgent whispering of his name igniting them both. Rigo shuddered and covered her body with his, still seeking her mouth. Heather parted her lips, tasting his mouth and drinking in his liquid as she used her own tongue to give him what he gave her. As Heather's fears were burned away in his hot embrace, Rigo gently brought her hips up and slowly entered her. This time she was ready and the hot stabbing brought only intense pleasure. Then, as he held her still, she felt a sweet opening within her and moved to meet him. When Rigo gasped in pleasure and began to rhythmically thrust, Heather surrendered herself to the unknown, overwhelming feelings riding her like a hurricane. Letting herself be his, an exquisite sweetness filled her body and ecstasy flamed in her heart, making all the world new with love.

They whispered in the night, waking after two brief hours to meet again, their bodies joining and exploring each other.

Heather let him do hitherto unimagined things with his mouth and hands to arouse her, his passion rising swiftly, fiercely. She, in turn, obeyed his instructions and listened to her own needs as he asked her to.

"I never thought love could be like this . . ." she murmured. "I didn't know a woman could need a man." She trailed soft kisses along his sensitive neck. She touched him boldly and he shuddered with exquisite desire.

"And I never imagined I would find a woman like you. My only one, my beloved. I love you. Come, give me yourself one last time before I go."

"Rigo, don't go. I'm afraid." she pleaded.

"I must leave. I've committed myself to this cause and I endanger all my family while I stay. Please understand. I'll return to you. Nothing can keep me away for long. I have no future without you."

She clung to him feeling a mixture of joy and fear.

He urged her to him, erasing her doubts with love.

Before dawn, Heather was ushered to her room. Rigo was not able to resist one last embrace inside her room, and then he left.

Chapter Twenty-three

Standing on a knoll overlooking the fields of central Brooklyn, Rigo watched the scene before him with mixed feelings. Three long columns of English troops were marching with bayonets set between a small herd of cows and a pond with a cluster of ducks. They were advancing, Rigo knew, on the American lines at Brooklyn Heights and soon a major battle—probably the biggest of the war—would take place. And he, the very day after he'd achieved more happiness than he'd dreamed of, was in the middle of it.

Already the distant thunder of cannon, which he had been hearing for half an hour, was now joined by the sharp crackle of rifle and musket fire. The most distant line of troops had formed into the horizontal double file which the English used for their advance into battle. The last of a Hessian battalion was disappearing off to his right into a copse and now rifle fire could be heard from that direction, too.

Listening to the rising noise of battle and seeing the immense masses of men advancing toward the American lines made Rigo suddenly feel that his spying mission was hopeless. If, by some miracle, he could now run through all those redcoats and get through to the American lines, what could he say? "You're being attacked by a large force"—hardly news to men who could probably not even hear him over the blasts of their weapons firing at the enemy.

A group of English officers appeared from off to the left and climbed the knoll to stand less than forty feet away. After a few minutes, a tall captain came over.

"What are you doing here?" the captain asked, his voice an interesting blend of authority, suspicion, and respect.

"I'm Richard Somerset," Rigo replied easily. "And I am here observing this great battle at the personal invitation of General Howe."

The officer stared at Rigo, his eyes narrowing. "You have a letter to that effect?" he asked.

"No, it was his personal oral invitation."

The captain's eyes narrowed further and, without a response, he wheeled and returned to the others. Rigo watched him reporting to the highest ranking officer, a colonel, then there was a brief discussion among the five. The captain strode back to Rigo.

"General Howe's express orders are that no civilians are to accompany His Majesty's troops," he said. "You will return to the beach and take the first available longboat back to Staten Island."

Rigo stiffened and scowled. "Where is General Howe?" he asked haughtily.

"You will retire, sir," the tall captain said coldly. "Or, if you are seen again among our troops, you will be shot as a spy. Those are our orders."

Rigo retired, but when he was out of sight in the woods, he exploded out loud with the expletives he had been mumbling to himself since turning away from the captain. Rigo knew he had now compromised his name—if the captain remembered it or had mentioned it to the others—and that his usefulness as a spy was ended. While he wished with his entire heart to see Heather, he knew that he couldn't remain on Staten Island a single second without implicating his whole family. His course was clear. He must try to get through to the American lines, gathering what information he could on the way. Finally, after two hours, he managed to get to the east of the battles that he could still hear raging. Abruptly Rigo came upon a sight that stunned him and quickened his pulse. There, half a mile away, marching silently and steadily in full battle gear was a huge column of English troops. They, like Rigo, were planning to come around behind the rebel lines to attack the unsuspecting Americans from the rear.

Trying to keep out of sight, he headed along the left flank of the English line of march and began running.

Fifteen minutes later, Rigo emerged from a copse to see a group of twenty or so men hauling an ancient ship's cannon toward the sounds of battle to the south.

"An English regiment is only five minutes march away to the east," he told the roughly dressed man who seemed to be in charge. "You should get that cannon turned around and positioned on the nearest knoll and try to slow them down. Where is the nearest concentration of our troops?"

The leader, a pudgy man wearing buckskin with a heavy leather hat and full black beard, chewed on his tobacco and then spit off to Rigo's right.

"Who you be?" he asked Rigo, as the other men, sweating and exhausted, stopped to listen to the exchange.

"I'm an American spy and I've just seen a battalion, perhaps even a regiment of English troops, coming this way from the east. I've got to warn the rebels."

"Yep," the man said after another pause and another spit. "You do that. And when you can get General Alexander to believe that and order me to turn this cannon around, I'll be happy to oblige. Meanwhile, you bloody bastards," he added, turning to his men, "haul away! That cannon ain't going nowhere with you leanin' on your asses."

Rigo hastened on alone. The sound of cannon and gun-fire was coming closer now and he soon came upon a cluster of wounded men being tended by a harried physician. When he asked for General Alexander they pointed him onward.

Two minutes later, Rigo at last came upon a splendidly dressed man reeking with authority and surrounded by a half dozen other men, several also dressed as gentlemen. They were standing on a slight rise and through a break in the tree line to the south Rigo could see the distant fields filled with redcoats crawling forward under the fire of the rebels. Rigo rushed uninvited into the midst of the rebel officers, to introduce himself to the bewigged, frock-coated man seated on a stool who was Lord Stirling. He quickly told him the story of his spying and his discovery of the flanking action of the approaching English forces. Lord Stirling stood up, squinting at Rigo while he asked if John Somerset was his father, then asked if he had any proof he was a rebel spy. Rigo pulled out his sketch-map of Brooklyn and, when it turned out to be identical to the one Lord Stirling had, the general nodded and paced off to the edge of the rise and stared down at the distant battle. Finally he turned to face Rigo.

"You are certain there is at least a battalion coming from the east?" he asked with calm dignity.

"At least," Rigo said. "I couldn't see whether there were others beyond it, but it was at least a battalion."

Lord Stirling nodded.

"General," Rigo went on spiritedly. "If the English appear behind our lines unexpectedly, there will be a rout."

Lord Stirling again nodded. Then he suddenly wheeled to his left.

"Major Higgens," he said calmly. "Get the Massachusetts and New Hampshire men to march immediately this way and continue east until they engage the enemy. Mr. Simpson," he continued, turning to another officer, "have Captain O'Malley's New Yorkers come with us right away. We've got to stop them." The officers who had been given orders moved off.

Soon a company of New York volunteers under Captain O'Malley appeared and, led by Lord Stirling, they all hurried back the way Rigo had come. They hadn't gone very far when, scrambling over a small rise, they saw less than a hundred yards away the head of the English column.

Even Lord Stirling lost his authoritarian calm at the abrupt closeness of the enemy, and he wheeled to order one of his officers to run back and inform the Massachusetts and New Hampshire men to hurry and inform General Greene that they were already engaged with the enemy.

Rigo managed to borrow a pistol from an officer who had two, but the sudden crack and spatter from the advancing English soldiers made him feel pitifully unarmed. Captain O'Malley got his company positioned along the rise and, with amazing coolness, waited until the advancing English were less than thirty yards away before ordering his men to fire. A dozen English soldiers fell at the first volley and, after a brief pause, another half dozen fell at the second round. When Rigo looked next toward the English, he saw that the initial rush had been broken but that a hundred yards away they were spreading out in a long line, preparing their second, more organized attack.

As he knelt behind the trunk of a fallen tree with two jerkin-clad New Yorkers, Rigo could see that the line of English redcoats stretched out of sight to the right. At two deep he could see more than two hundred men. The rebels numbered barely fifty. By this second attack, the rebels would be easily outflanked and certainly overwhelmed. As he reloaded his pistol and checked its prime, Rigo wondered how the general would handle the situation.

"Fall back, men!" Lord Stirling abruptly shouted, standing in his elegant dress with his sword drawn. "Fall back! Follow me! Fire that cannon there and then spike it. Fall back!"

The rebels retreated across a meadow and then began climbing a low hill. More reinforcements were arriving from the west, all dressed in a motley assortment of clothes and colors and armed mostly with rifles and muskets without bayonets.

"Form your line!" Lord Stirling ordered. "New Hampshire men to the east, Massachusetts men to the west! Spread out! Form your line! O'Malley! Form your men here at the center!"

Already the huge array of English could be seen spread out along the meadow advancing steadily in good order, their line so wide it disappeared off to the right. There were now perhaps two hundred Americans facing a force at least three times that size.

The next ten minutes were chaos. Rigo fired a musket he had taken from a fallen rebel, reprimed it, and fired again. As the English got closer he had no time to reload so he fired his pistol. Then the redcoats were among them, burying their glittering bayonets into the bodies of the desperately fighting rebels. Rigo drew his sword and sliced at the arms of the attacking British soldiers, then thrust his sword into them. For a moment, the rebel position was about to be overwhelmed, but then the English seemed to disappear, most of them dead or wounded, and a few retreating. Through eyes reddened by smoke and sweat, Rigo could just make out the center of the English line reforming just thirty yards away. To his right, shouts and screams made it clear the hand-to-hand combat was continuing, and soon a cluster of rebels appeared scrambling away, most of them weaponless, and trying to make it along the line to the rebel center.

It seemed the English were upon them almost before the rebels had gotten off a single volley. A huge Hessian soldier came barreling past the first line of trees at Rigo and, knowing he could not parry the powerful man's bayonet thrust, Rigo sidestepped him but still felt the blade slash through his side. As he grunted in surprise and pain, Rigo thrust his sword into the man's side, heard him scream, and pulled his sword out barely in time to slash the arm of the next advancing soldier. Screams, curses and shouts filled the air. Men fell all about him. The English appeared and disappeared like ghosts in the smoke and haze until finally Rigo realized that he, Lord Stirling, and two other officers were the only rebels left standing in their part of the line. They were surrounded by redcoats.

"Fall back!" Lord Stirling yelled again, but it was a command he himself was powerless to obey.

Many of the English soldiers rushed past the four rebels with their swords to pursue the more helpless men retreating who had no weapons left except their bare hands. At least a dozen English bodies lay around the four men who now found themselves surrounded by twenty English redcoats, most with blood-dripping bayonets at the ready and two with swords.

"I suggest, sir," one of the English officers suddenly said loudly even as he gasped for breath, "that you surrender."

Lord Stirling stood, as did Rigo, with his sword lowered at the ready and his knees bent slightly in a crouch. Slowly, he straightened. He looked to his right, where Rigo could see redcoats running after the retreating rebels, and to his left, where it appeared the same.

With a grimace of disgust, Lord Stirling reached forward and stuck his sword into the ground.

"Gentlemen," he said, turning to Rigo and the other two survivors. "I suggest you surrender. It appears we are, for the moment, beaten."

Rigo reached forward and stuck his sword into the ground, then removed his pistol and threw it there, too. The two other officers did the same. Just as Rigo was feeling an immense relief at somehow having survived the incredible carnage he had just been in the midst of, three other English officers appeared.

"My God," one of them said. "There's that man Somerset."

There, at the edge of the circle of soldiers surrounding them, stood the captain who had ordered him back to Staten Island only hours before. Beside him appeared the colonel.

"Then he *was* a spy!" said the colonel, his eyes beaming with pleasure as if he had predicted it. "Captain Stuart, arrest this man! I have the distinct feeling General Howe would like to meet this alleged friend of his."

As two soldiers advanced to take him into custody, Rigo's sense of relief vanished. The life of a captured spy was not likely to be a long one. The image of Heather abruptly filled his mind. With it came a sense of loss so deep that he had to suppress a groan. He had always felt he could face death, but losing Heather before they had had a chance to begin a life together would be too much. In a spontaneous burst, Rigo wrenched himself free of the two soldiers who had taken his arms and lunged through the ring of Englishmen toward freedom. But he hadn't taken more than a few strides when two men leaped upon him and wrestled him to the ground. Within seconds, Rigo was lying helpless, and the captain had the point of a sword at his throat.

"Do you wish to die as a man or as a stuck pig?" the officer sneered down at him, letting his sword point break the skin of Rigo's neck.

Rigo didn't reply. He had vowed to march through General Howe's whole army to rejoin Heather—and dying, no matter how bleak the moment, was not in his plans.

Chapter Twenty-four

THE REPORT THAT THE ENGLISH HAD ROUTED THE AMERICANS in Brooklyn and sent them retreating across the river to Manhattan in the dead of night had brought joy to most of those at Somerset Manor. Toasts were drunk. The few English officers remaining on Staten Island were feted and praised. The fact that a brilliant English flanking maneuver had been thwarted, was lamented, but the expected news of the surrender of General Washington, and, with it, the end of the rebellion was still hoped for momentarily.

Instead, a week after Rigo's departure, the Somersets received an unexpected shock. A subdued Captain Blair arrived one afternoon to announce that Richard Somerset had been captured and was going to be tried as a spy.

It was Amy's wailing that brought Heather down from her room and into the parlor. There she saw a tearful Amy kneeling on the rug, a white-faced Margaret Somerset standing rigidly near the door to the dining room, and a pacing and angry Bruce. When Heather entered the room,

Bruce wheeled on her as if she had committed some wrong.

"Richard has been captured by the English," he said in a cold voice devoid of any sympathy. "He was spying. He will probably be shot."

For Heather, it was as if the earth had been pulled out from under her. She swayed and barely steadied herself with a hand on the back of the settee.

"It can't be," she whispered, trying to deny what she had just heard.

"I suspected as much," Bruce went on, either not noticing or choosing to ignore her dismay. "He seems determined to ruin himself and our whole family. Only a scoundrel would act in this way."

"Oh, no!" Amy wailed from where she was kneeling on the rug. "He is a good man! They can't kill him!"

"They can and they will!" Bruce shot back at her angrily. "Don't you realize they may even suspect *us?* His joining the rebels may lead to our ruin!"

"Please, Bruce," Margaret Somerset said, still pale and shaken. "No one can blame us for Richard's . . . transgressions."

"Oh, poor papa!" Amy cried, holding her small hands fisted in front of her. "It will kill him to hear of this!"

Heather was leaning against the back of the settee, barely absorbing the exchanges as her heart pounded. Her mind tried to focus on what had happened, on what was happening.

"But where is he?" she finally gasped out to Bruce.

"We don't know," he answered, resuming his pacing and not looking at her. "Someplace with the English, obviously."

"But he is alive?" she whispered.

"As far as Captain Blair knows," Bruce replied, stopping and staring at her. "But he was captured four or five days ago and not until now has word reached us. They may already have shot him."

This last remark somehow galvanized Heather into a sudden fury—first at Bruce for his callousness and then at the English soldiers for wanting to kill her beloved.

"They have not and they will not!" she burst out. "We must save him!"

Bruce, who had stopped near his mother to comfort her, turned at Heather's outburst.

"What are you saying!" he almost shouted at her. "We must not get involved. Our fortunes . . ." Bruce stopped in mid-sentence, his angry face suddenly growing pale and almost frightened as he stared past Heather.

Turning around, Heather saw standing in the doorway leading to the stairs the thin, bent frame of John Somerset dressed only in a white cotton robe.

"What is happening?" he asked in a low, tentative voice. "I heard Amy scream."

All looked at John Somerset in silence, stricken with the knowledge of how he would respond to the news. Heather steadied herself, stood straighter, and hurried over to the older man, tears welling at the sight of his gaunt face.

"They have captured Rigo," she said to him gently, her eyes showing both her grief and her determination.

John Somerset's bloodshot eyes bored into hers, his face still expressionless. Then his eyes wavered, his face twitched, and he nodded almost imperceptibly, his eyes moistening.

"Aye, I feared it," he responded finally in a low voice, almost to himself.

"Richard is accused of spying, Father," Bruce announced from across the room. "Your fortune—and Mother's—may be in danger."

John looked up at Bruce briefly, nodded a second time, and then reached out a shaky hand and clutched Heather's arm.

"He still lives?" he asked, echoing the question Heather had asked only minutes earlier.

"Yes," she answered, seeing Rigo's only hope in John.

"Where do they hold him?"

"We don't know."

He straightened himself as his eyes, though still moist, now sparkled with anger. "I shall find out," he said loudly.

"Father, we shouldn't get involved," Bruce began.

"He is my son," John interrupted fiercely. "Spy or not,

he is my . . . son," he went on, almost choking on the word. "He shall not die if I can help it."

"Yes," Heather said eagerly. "If anyone can save him, you can! And please, let me help!"

John's eyes softened as he turned back to Heather. "I'm sure I couldn't stop you if I wanted to," he said, smiling slightly, then he turned to face the others. "Get me Hawkins!" he commanded with sudden energy. "Get my clothes! Send someone for Major Williams. I'm finished being sick. There's work to be done!"

Amy leaped up from the floor and ran into her father's arms, sobbing half with grief and half with joy. Heather wanted to do the same but remained standing nearby. After a moment, she became aware that across the room, Bruce's eyes were boring into her, his face suffused with anger. Her head high, Heather stared back at him coldly. To help Rigo, she would have to remain Elizabeth Southey for the moment and use every ounce of energy, but she could never forgive Bruce for abandoning Rigo, as he had just done.

The next week was agony for Heather. Despite all of John Somerset's contacts and efforts, they could not locate Rigo. Indeed, they weren't even certain he was alive until several days after they'd begun their search. They finally heard that he was being held by a Major Keilly someplace in Queens and that he was momentarily to be tried as a spy, with the outcome of the trial not in doubt. John managed to obtain a meeting with a Lord Mollifer, one of General Howe's aides-de-camp, to stop any execution, and the lord agreed to try to get a stay and to ask General Howe to intervene. He obtained the stay the evening before the morning Rigo was to be shot but was unable to speak to the general about treating Rigo as a mere prisoner of war, since the general was busy invading Manhattan and trying to crush General Washington's again retreating troops.

During the seemingly endless tension and despair of waiting for news and praying for Rigo's life, Heather also had to deal with the now unleashed jealousy of Bruce. She was making no real effort to hide her concern for Rigo and didn't hesitate to chastise Bruce for not showing greater concern for his half brother, but she did hide the depth of her love for the captured rebel. Because she thought that Bruce might in some way be crucial in saving Rigo, Heather again postponed breaking their engagement and was, most of the time, kinder to him than he deserved. But when he responded to her soft words with efforts to be alone with her or to touch her, she successfully resisted. "Only when Rigo is safe," she explained one time somewhat deviously, "will I be able to think again of kisses."

Finally came the first concrete news of Rigo's whereabouts. The Americans had retreated from lower Manhattan and the English had taken over. Rigo was now being held in the city jail with dozens of prisoners of war and two other spies. He had been condemned to be shot on the morning of September twenty-second. That was four days away.

This definite news, instead of increasing her despair, spurred Heather to renewed hope. He was alive. They knew where he was. She might see him. John Somerset, whose powerlessness had begun to depress him, was also galvanized. The very afternoon they received the news, he, Heather, Maggie, and John's manservant, Hawkins, were sailed across the bay to lower Manhattan to set up their "headquarters," as John called it, in the Somerset townhouse. Bruce indicated he would join them the next day but had business to attend to first.

John told Heather that he realized now that there was no longer any hope that they could get General Howe to commute the death sentence. Rigo's spying was too flagrant and had dealt too serious a blow to the English cause to permit him to escape the usual punishment. Their only hope lay in somehow arranging for Rigo's escape from jail before the twenty-second. John's plan was to contact some of the rebels from the *Contessa* crew, form an armed group, and hope to storm the jail at night and free Rigo. He would try to obtain a boat for Rigo so he could escape to sea.

As he explained all this to her as they sat side by side on

the wooden settee of the sailing launch, Heather was sickened to sense in John's tone that he had only small hope that his elaborate and dangerous plan to storm the jail could work. She sensed also that he was subtly trying to warn her that, despite all their efforts, perhaps Rigo would still die. Her youthful heart grew old and heavy at such an idea, and for the rest of the journey, Heather sat like a corpse, her unseeing eyes focused on nothing as she struggled with the thought that she might never again be able to see or touch or love the incomparable man Rigo, who was now her life.

In Manhattan, they went straight to the jail and there learned, to Heather's sorrow, that only members of Rigo's immediate family could see him—in this case, only John. So Heather was forced to sit on a dirty wooden bench in the large open reception hall of the jail while John visited Rigo. The English guards eyed her openly and a few made rude remarks as Maggie sassed them back in her usual fashion, but Heather was too filled with grief and hopelessness to notice or care.

When John returned after a half hour, her heart fell further. John looked as if he had aged another five years. He now walked slowly back to her, his head bent forward as if the dirty floor were his only interest. Heather stood up and ran to him.

"What's the matter?" she cried. "Did you see him?"

He looked slowly up, nodding.

"He asked for you," he said softly, continuing his slow walk toward the bench Heather had vacated. The man-servant Hawkins came forward now, too, and took John's other arm.

"But what's wrong?" Heather insisted. "Something has upset you. Please . . ."

John lowered himself to the bench with a groan, again nodding, and then looked up at her.

"He . . . was wounded in the battle," he said. "His side was pierced and is now bound up and painful."

Watching him, Heather sensed that this bad news was somehow not the worst.

"What else?" she asked in almost a whisper.

John's tired eyes flared in sudden anger.

"They beat him," he said. "They beat a helpless prisoner."

"Is he . . . Is he all right?" Heather asked, fearing there was yet more.

"He'll be all right," John answered forcefully and, with an unexpected scowl, "if he lives!"

Heather knelt in front of the old man and took his frail hands in hers, looking up at John as if he were a direct link with her Rigo.

"Does he have hope?" she asked shakily.

For the first time, a slight smile appeared on John's face. "Aye, that he does," he replied. "Three times already he's tried to escape. Guards searched me so thoroughly I thought they were hunting for diamonds." He squeezed Heather's hands with his. "He told me to apologize to you for not making it through the entire English army to meet you. He said the army was a little larger than he thought and he only got through half."

Hearing these words from Rigo was too much for Heather, and though her mouth broke into a smile, tears sprang into her eyes and soon streamed silently down her face. For half a minute, she and John were together, their hands clenched—tears on both their faces bespeaking the love they shared for Rigo. When they finally rose to leave, Heather held her head high and walked to the door like a queen. If Rigo had gotten through half the army to reach her, then she, by God, would get through the other half to reach him.

Still, the next two days produced no progress. John grew increasingly depressed at the number of troops and guards around the jail and despaired of being able to attack it with the half dozen men he had been able to raise. The *Contessa* had been sailed up the Hudson to Yonkers when the English took Manhattan, and he had managed to bring it back down the river and hide it in the wetlands on the Jersey side of the river across from New York. But he and Noah had still not been able to figure a way to get Rigo loose so he could even begin to get to the ship.

With an overwhelming sense of urgency, Heather determined she couldn't leave Rigo's fate to his father's plotting but for the first day or two, she was in despair as to how she could accomplish her aim. Then, on the third day, there appeared an opening.

Whenever John went to the prison, Heather accompanied him, usually sitting on that hard wooden bench in the crowded hallway of the jail. Often as not, the captain of the guards, a squarish man of middling years with a flaming red beard and thatches of darker red sticking out from under his hat, would come up to her, bow, and smile, engaging her in casually flirtatious small talk. He wasn't as coarse as some of the other soldiers had been on that first day, and he even chivalrously chastised one of his men for speaking to her rudely. When Heather petitioned him personally to permit her to visit Rigo, he smiled and shook his head no, saying it was against his orders. That he admired her, Heather had no doubt, for he would posture and boast of his exploits to his companions, if any were about, in order to attract her attention.

The first day or two, Heather would smile at him distractedly but offered him no further encouragement. His antics were even something of an embarrassment to her as he enjoyed striking poses that he thought showed off his fine legs and the breadth of his shoulders and muscled arms. Had she been less miserable, she might have laughed at his swaggering vanity.

Two days before Rigo's scheduled execution, however, John's gloom increased her desperation. With tears running down her face, she sat there waiting for him to return from another fruitless visit with her Rigo. After a while, she became aware that the big captain of the guards had come forward and was standing before her, shifting his large booted feet uncomfortably. When she glanced up at him, she could see that he was at a loss as to how to deal with her distress.

"Please, Captain," she burst out spontaneously. "I must see Mr. Somerset. Can't you possibly make an exception . . . just this once?" As she made her appeal, she sensed some hesitation on his part. "I can't bear it if I don't see him," she continued haltingly. "Have you never been in love . . . ?"

The man first looked startled and then his eyes narrowed as he pulled at his large, red mustache.

"You mean the man's your . . ." he began tentatively. "Why I thought . . . Well, I can see as how his being shot on the morrow could bring you to tears, milady. That's natural enough. But I've my orders, you see. I'd be taking a terrible risk to let you in, though it seems a shame you can't, just once."

"Do I look like I could overcome the guards and free him?" Heather pleaded, beginning to see some light in the darkness of the hour and the man's newly tentative refusal.

"Why, no," the captain answered, beginning to grin. "I doubt you'd overcome them with wrestling. But a pretty thing like yourself could sweet-talk a man into anything, I'd wager. You're a sight, miss, for these eyes and many another."

"Am I truly, Captain?" Heather asked, responding to the man's flattery intentionally.

"Yes, miss. Why, there's many a man would do a lot for a lass the likes of you."

"And you, Captain?" Heather tilted her chin slightly, giving a sidelong glance. "Would you do . . . much for me?"

The man straightened himself, thrusting his chest forward and his arms behind his back. "Depends . . . what you had in mind, miss."

"Elizabeth, Captain," she gently corrected him with a little smile.

He darted a glance around to see who was listening and, seeing no one, quickly brought his eyes back to Heather, revealing with a grin his imperfect teeth. The grin widened and his look said he was catching on to something that he liked and was willing to pursue.

In a move that startled Heather and almost had her jumping backward, the captain leaned forward and whispered that this conversation had better be continued in the pub across the street. He also requested that Maggie remain behind.

Heather agreed, and the man took himself across the street with great speed. Maggie, however, wasn't having any of it and insisted on accompanying her.

The pub was dark, full of locals and a handful of soldiers drinking beer. Maggie was right at home fending off drunken leers and roving hands, and she plowed their way through to the corner table occupied by the captain. When he scowled at the sight of her, Maggie stuck her tongue at him and then bustled off to wait at a table where an older man and woman sat eating and having a tankard or two.

The captain stood and gestured to the stool next to him and Heather sat down, wasting no time getting to the object of her visit.

"I had in mind a farewell visit to the prisoner that only you and I need know about—for which I would pay handsomely."

"Ahh . . ." He took a long draught of his beer. "Bribery's not my wont . . . Elizabeth," he said, stumbling slightly over her name but grinning meaningfully and winking. His eyes gleamed with pleasure as he set a trap for his pretty quarry.

Heather hesitated, not quite understanding him, but knew she still had his attention.

"The truth is, I don't have much coin, but I do have a locket worth much that I'd gladly part with."

"Now, if I was to let you in, not sayin' I will, now, but I'd be needin' more than your word and a pretty trinket." He again winked at her and, sidling closer, suddenly reached a hand behind her and gave her right hip a squeeze and a slap. "Heh, lass! You take my meaning?"

Heather was rocked by his quick movement, not expecting it, but she recovered and, inching her stool away, gave a trilling laugh. It was the only thing she could manage to cover her anger at the man's crudity.

"I do, Captain," she said, her eyes glittering, "but . . . I'm not worldly, sir, so if you would kindly tell me clearly what you require?"

"Why, yourself, sweeting—and not a word to a soul about your doings. A fair exchange, for your lover will soon be no good to you buried six feet under, and I'd be kissin' my captaincy good-bye were you to slip up."

Heather felt her stomach do a flop and squelched a sick feeling. He was serious, of that she had no doubt, but could she bluff? She quickly made a decision to try. This was no time to be squeamish. What was virtue if she lost the man she loved?

Heather lowered her chin and her eyes. "If you do this thing for me, in safety, I give you the word of Elizabeth Southey that you shall have the recompense you desire." Heather crossed her fingers a moment under the table for the lie and gave him a smile she hoped was winning. Her half-turned body, in itself a beautiful sight to behold, revealed the firm curves of her youth, and her eyes, bright with the need to win his favor, won her the man's approval.

His eyes darted over her lasciviously. He combed and pulled his beard as he contemplated the beauty before him. "After you see him," he whispered in a low, guttural voice, "you come here. I'll be watchin' and waitin'."

Heather nodded her agreement.

"Done!" he said as if he had just bargained for a piece of goods and gotten the price he wanted. He reached forward with his squat hands with nails that were not especially clean and stroked her arm much as one would a cat's back.

Heather had all she could do not to recoil from his touch. Keeping in mind her purpose, she firmly withdrew her arm and asked him to name a time and a cover to accomplish her goal. It was agreed upon for tomorrow night at nine, and Heather was to wear dark clothes and go to the side door of the jail. Her carriage was to wait in the next street. The arrangements done, she got up from the table to leave.

The captain rose to accompany her to the door. There, not caring who saw, he gave her bottom another pat, this time lingering longer until Heather pulled away to rush out the door, her cheeks aflame with embarrassment.

Maggie gave the captain a poke in his over-large middle, and he guffawed loudly and did the same to her. Maggie rewarded him with a kick to the shin and a door in his face.

Her ears still ringing with the laughter and coarse remarks of the soldiers in the pub, Heather let out an exasperated breath.

"May he be impaled on his own sword!" Heather blurted, and Maggie laughed at her unintended ribald humor that, when Maggie tried to explain, caused Heather's face to flame further.

Heather then dismissed the whole scene from her mind and concentrated on what she would do to set Rigo free. For she couldn't accept that it wasn't possible, and she was willing to risk herself to help him in any way she could.

John Somerset was already waiting inside the carriage and was wearily leaning against its interior. Heather felt as tense as a bowstring waiting for his report. He rapped for the driver to leave, then laid a hand on hers.

"How does he look?" Heather asked him fearfully.

"Better, better. His wound is healing," John said. "He is stronger."

Heather let out the breath she was unconsciously holding in. "Thank heaven. At least that is something in our favor."

John nodded stoically.

"I have convinced the captain of the guard to let me see Rigo tomorrow at nine," she said quickly in a low voice.

John's head swung sharply toward her. "A stroke of luck! How did you do it?"

"I offered the captain . . . Elizabeth's locket," Heather said, unable to tell John what she had really bargained with for fear he would refuse to let her go.

"She can hardly have use for it, and it finally serves a good purpose," John said in case Heather should feel any guilt over the trade.

"I want to take him a weapon, a knife or pistol. I can conceal it on my person. I'm sure I won't be searched." She leaned toward John hopefully.

"A pistol would do well. Are you quite sure you can manage it?"

"You of all people must know I can play any part well when 'tis thrust upon me in dire need," Heather countered.

John smiled warmly. "You have courage, Heather, and at the very heart of you, goodness. I have been more fond of you than you know."

"Sir, please!" Heather whispered, moved by his words to her, her heart quickening with pleasure and emotion. "This is no time for such compliments. I need every bit of hardness I can muster. There are moments when I am so frantic with worry that I think I will swoon from it. Don't weaken me with your kind words. For this is a soldier's work, and I would go to battle cold of heart and clear of mind."

"Then let's talk of our battle plan together," John said, smiling at her admiringly. "We are now fully allied."

Chapter Twenty-five

THERE WAS NO QUIVERING IN HEATHER AS SHE CAREFULLY donned her dress, so pointed was her direction. The dark blue frock of cambric was simple in cut and fitted her bosom and waist perfectly. The elbow-length sleeves and low-cut neck were trimmed with a creamy lace. A lace fichu covered her shoulders. She wanted to look her best yet show the guards that she had no place to conceal a weapon above the waist. She also wanted to wear a dark color to blend with the night. Maggie swept her hair back and let long ringlets fall in back from a topknot fastened with mother-of-pearl combs. Heather then slipped three garters to the calf of her left leg and carefully inserted one of John Somerset's pistols. It was cumbersome but fairly secure if she were careful. Next she pinned the pouches of powder and ball to the inside of her petticoat and walked around to get used to the feel of it as Maggie looked for any bulge that might give her away.

"There, Maggie. That does it," Heather said and let Maggie drape her long, black cape over her arm.

Maggie insisted on coming with her to the jail while

John was bent on getting his men ready to be at the prison just after the change of guard late at midnight, when Rigo was to attempt to break out. Heather had her fears that the captain would try to wrest his payment from her before it was due and then shut her out of the jail, so she was doubly glad of Maggie's presence.

"I'll handle that red beard. He'll not dare keep ye out," Maggie vowed. And she tut-tutted Heather when asked what she planned. "Never you mind. I'm an old salt when it comes to dealin' with these ships in the night."

The two women wrapped themselves in their dark capes, bidding the driver to stay awake and sharp in case they came running back. The man patted his musket and told them not to worry.

It was a hot, blustery night, dark and fetid with street smells. The horse dung was rank and a pack of five dogs prowled along in the shadows of the wooden buildings that lined the street, scattering several cats that were roaming free. The earth was sore from the many tramplings and dumpings, and the heavy air was enough to create a nervousness in man and beast. Heather and Maggie clung to the walls like silent shadows, speaking not a word as they made for the jail.

The captain accosted Heather outside the side door, stepping from the darkened doorway and grabbing her upper arm. She swung around, ready to give him a slap, before she recognized him and pulled back, anger on her face.

"Here, sweeting," the captain whispered in a hoarse voice, his breath stinking of wine. "No sense in yer rushin' into that pestilent hole. . . ." He stopped short when he spied Maggie just behind her shoulder. "You brought yer maid, I see, a wench who needs her manners shaped some. I told you to come alone." He looked back at Heather, not hiding his annoyance.

"Let me go, Captain!" Heather said, trying not to betray too much of her anger. "Speaking of manners, I've had gentler handling by my horse!" The man removed his hands reluctantly.

"Beggin' your pardon, milady," he said gruffly. "If

you'll be kind enough to take off your cloak. I need to be sure, you see, that you've nothing concealed."

Heather removed her cape and withstood the captain's eyes roving over her. She knew he was looking for more than just weapons.

"You see, Captain, I've nothing to hide. You can't believe I'd be so foolish. It would take many men, all well-armed, to storm this prison. I merely wish to make my farewell and respect any wishes he may have. It's what any man needs before he . . ." Heather couldn't admit, even in a ruse, to Rigo's death. It was too close to happening. She looked away.

"Aye. Well, then. If you can't be swayed from it, go to it. My men have their orders. But remember your bargain. I'll be waitin'." He stood solidly before her.

Maggie came forward, arms akimbo. The captain eyed her suspiciously. "A word with ye, Captain, while Miss Southey's in the dungeon."

Confident Maggie could handle the fellow, and with only the most sketchy of plans to escape his clutches later, Heather turned toward the only thing her mind registered any sense in or desire for—to see Rigo and effect his escape.

She was escorted by a tall, lean guard into a dark and stifling hallway then down some uneven wooden stairs into the basement, where most of the cells were. The guard unlocked a door at the foot of the stairs, made her pass, and then relocked it. In the dim light, Heather was aware of another guard sitting in a chair and a line of bars running along both sides of the dank hallway. The prisoners were kept here in these small, damp cubicles below street level.

As Heather followed the guard, she wrung her hands in anticipation. Her stomach tightened and her heart raced. Finally, at the last cell, the guard stopped, looked in, and, without a word, unlocked the cell door. He gestured for her to go in.

As she entered, Heather saw her Rigo lying on the single straw pallet on the floor. His clothes were torn and he was unshaven, his hair unwashed, his boots scuffed.

Rigo was thinner by several pounds. Upon seeing him, Heather stifled a cry.

"What have they done to you!" she managed, her voice quavering.

Rigo sat up quickly, blinking, and then his eyes fastened on Heather as if she alone were the food and drink that would stave off starvation. He leapt to his feet and Heather threw herself into his arms. They clung to each other, lost in the world that only they could share. Rigo rained kisses on her face.

"Forgive me. I'm foul. . . ." he rasped against her cheek.

"Oh, my love . . . This is the sweetest place to be on all the earth to me." She rubbed her cheek against his shirt, feeling the warmth of him beneath the heavy cotton, not able to get enough of him. When the guard who had admitted her made some scurrilous remark, she turned to him angrily.

"Can we have a moment alone, please?" Heather asked.

The guard, standing on the other side of the bars, seemed to mull it over a moment. "Not long, miss. Them's my orders."

"Have pity," Heather said, directing him a tearful glance. The man shrugged and sharpened his glance at Rigo.

"I'll be outside, just down the hall. There's no retreat and no way forward without running into a passel of guards. Ye'll be shot for attempting escape this time." He turned the key in the lock and disappeared down the hallway.

Heather turned to Rigo. The two tightened their embrace and drank in the sight of each other. Rigo let his lips touch hers gently.

"How humble I feel before you," Rigo said in a low voice. Heather searched his face with loving eyes.

"Tell me how you got in here?" he questioned her softly.

"I . . . bribed the captain," she said hesitantly.

"You did? But my father offered money to no avail."

"Shhh," Heather put her fingers up to his lips to silence him. "It doesn't matter," she whispered in as low a voice as she could. "I've a pistol concealed under my skirts. You must gather your strength and leave this place tonight."

"You have what?" Rigo asked, staring in amazement as she bent to lift her skirt and hand him the pistol and, after a struggle with the pins, the ball and powder. His brows knit tightly.

"You took a grave risk and probably for nothing," he said soberly. "If the escape fails, they'll know you were helping me. I won't have it."

"Rigo, please. You must take it," Heather insisted passionately. "Your father's men are waiting outside. John says he doesn't think they can fight their way all the way in to you. But at midnight, they will mount an attack, hoping you can use the distraction to break out from within."

"In his manner, he told me as much. We were guarded closely and never left alone. If it works . . . but I want you to promise me you'll go back to the townhouse and not linger here." His voice was low and insistent. Heather nodded her assent.

Rigo smiled for the first time since her entering. "There may be hope for us yet, if you're always this obedient."

"I try," she answered teasingly and raised her lips to him to deliver a soothing kiss. He pulled her to him to deepen it, unable to stem the impulse, and for a long moment, Heather lost herself in the kiss, so blissful was she to be in his arms once again. She was brought out of her happiness by feeling Rigo straighten and break the kiss.

"What's that?" he whispered.

Heather became aware now of a loud commotion on the floor above and shouts from the streets outside. From the basement, they couldn't make out the cries, and Heather wondered if John's men had started the attack.

"Is it John and his men?" she asked as Rigo released her and edged closer to the bars of his cell.

"There are no gunshots," he answered. "And it can't be midnight yet, is it?"

"It was dusk but an hour ago," Heather replied, clutching his arm and straining to see down the hall, but the angle prevented them from seeing the guards.

A loud banging on the door leading to the upper floor was followed by the sound of the key turning in the lock and the door creaking open.

"Fire!" a man's voice cried from down the hall. "Fire! The whole bloody street's on fire. Cap'n says to get up and lend a hand."

"What about the prisoners?" Heather heard one of the guards ask.

"Leave 'em locked down here!" the first voice replied. "Come on! We need ye to fight the bloody fire!"

"Guard!" Rigo shouted as he grasped the bars of his cell. "Guard! You must take this woman with you!"

There was an awful silence for several moments and then the sound of footsteps running up the hall toward them. Some of the other prisoners began crying and shouting, too, and several began banging on the cell doors. Heather's tall escort appeared and began fumbling with a key at the lock to Rigo's cell. As he did, Rigo maneuvered Heather in front of him and quickly loaded the pistol that was hidden by her body. The guard, fumbling with haste, finally unlocked the door and swung it open, drawing his pistol as he did so.

"Hurry, wench," he said, motioning with his weapon.

Heather took two steps forward and, acting on shrewd impulse, feigned a swoon, staggering into the surprised guard's arms.

In an instant, Rigo had leapt out of his cell and brought his own pistol crashing down on the guard's head, sending him to the floor. He then wheeled his pistol toward the end of the hall, where the two other guards stood staring at him in confusion. As Rigo strode toward them with his pistol leveled, they each slowly raised their arms above their heads. Heather, righting herself, hurried after Rigo, aware now that most of the other prisoners were at their cell doors shouting and clamoring.

"Release these other men from the cells!" Rigo commanded the guard who carried the large leaden circle of keys. At the same time, he pulled the weapons from the guards and kicked a musket off into a corner. But already Heather could smell smoke and hear the cries from up the stairwell of "Fire! Fire!"

Rigo handed her one of the large pistols he had taken from one of the guards and ordered her to watch at the stairwell while he helped free the other prisoners. Her heart racing, Heather peered up and saw men running across the head of the stairs and heard shouting. And now, for the first time, there were gunshots. Suddenly two soldiers carrying muskets came hurrying down the stairs toward her.

"Rigo!" she shouted, backing against the wall and holding her pistol in both hands, not even certain if it was loaded or if she knew how to fire it. "Soldiers!" As she looked back for Rigo, one of the freed prisoners rushed up to her, took the pistol, and immediately fired it at one of the approaching Englishmen. The gun misfired and the man screamed and began backing away. An explosion from the stairs sent him reeling back with a groan to collapse to the floor, a victim of an English musket blast.

As Heather pressed herself tighter against the wall, she saw Rigo kneeling and firing his pistol at the stairs. Seconds later, a redcoated body sprawled into view at her feet, his musket clattering to the floor near him.

Rigo dashed up, picked up the musket, checked the prime and loading, and then grasped Heather's wrist.

"We're going to have to try to make it up the stairs," he said to her, bringing his face close. "I want you to stay right behind me. Carry this pistol, and when I call for it, hand it to me. Are you all right?"

She nodded, aware that three or four other prisoners had gathered near them and were listening. Two of them were now armed. Rigo glanced at them, peered up the now-empty stairwell, and saw smoke beginning to slide lazily down from step to step. He released his tight grip on Heather's wrist and more gently took her hand.

"Come," he said urgently, and together they began to mount the stairs, the other prisoners following. Rigo was carrying the musket and, when they reached the top of the stairs, he let go of Heather and fired it, then swung the butt at an attacking soldier, felling him.

As Rigo again took her by the hand, Heather was aware only of the smoke, shouting, sound of shots, and screams. She stumbled, felt herself wrenched forward by Rigo's powerful grasp, and then, horribly, found herself gasping in smoke twice as thick as in the jail. She was dimly aware that her feet were now running over packed earth and that hot, smoky air was swirling at her from the left, blinding her, choking her. Heather stumbled again and fell. Rigo's arm around her waist lifted her and pressed her to his side. They were both crouched and running, eyes burning, not able to see more than a few feet in front of them. They knew only that the smoke and heat were coming primarily from off to their left. Occasionally other figures would stagger into or past them. How Rigo had any idea of where he was going, Heather did not know. She had her right arm around his waist and simply ran where he ran, fighting for each breath.

Exactly when they finally broke free from that awful fire Heather never knew. After what seemed like an eternity, she found herself lying beside Rigo against a wall, both of them coughing but free at last of the smoke. After a brief rest, Rigo gently urged Heather to her feet, and they pressed on. Although as far as she could tell they had never made contact with John or his men, Rigo seemed to know where he was going, and, after another half hour, they arrived at a wharf. There was no sign of a ship.

Behind her, Heather could see the incredible sight of a false dawn of fire blazing over lower Manhattan, flames licking the dark sky, illuminating ant-like creatures dashing to and fro. Then Rigo gathered her into his arms and held her as if he never intended to let her go. After pressing his lips to her forehead, he tilted her chin up to him.

"We seem destined to keep rescuing each other," he said lightly. "But I must complain that you cut this one rather close."

She smiled in return and brushed his lips with hers, her eyes still watering from the smoke and now from her relief.

"Then you must stop leaving me," she said.

"Aye, that sounds reasonable," Rigo countered, looking momentarily out across the darkened river, obviously expecting a ship. "I think you'd make a good . . . mate," he added, his lowered eyes glittering with the light of distant fire.

Before Heather could decide how he meant the word "mate," Rigo straightened up and, with his arm around her, hurried them both to the edge of the dock. Beyond him, barely visible as it emerged out of the darkness from across the river, Heather could just make out the ghostly outline of a sailing ship flowing gently toward them. Behind her, flames still leapt toward the sky. In front of her approached an unknown ship. But with Rigo's arm around her, for the first time in ages she felt at peace.

Chapter Twenty-six

THE *CONTESSA* HAD MADE IT SAFELY TO SEA. RIGO, NOAH, and a skeletal crew of only six additional men had sailed her that night of the great Manhattan fire from the lower Hudson out through the British fleet in New York harbor and into the Atlantic Ocean. By late the following afternoon, they were twenty miles off the New Jersey coast, sailing south and heading, Rigo told Heather, for the Delaware Bay. There he would turn northwest and head toward the still free center of the American cause, Philadelphia.

Only Noah and one other man had survived the attack on the jail and the fire to join Rigo and Heather at the wharf to meet the *Contessa*. Noah worried about John Somerset, who, although he had agreed not to carry a weapon, had insisted on being with his men before the attack. Noah and Rigo assumed that he had eventually gone back to the Somerset townhouse.

At sea, Heather slept. Rigo had directed her to his own cabin while he remained topside to command the escape through the English fleet, and though she had wanted to remain up simply to be with him, when she lay down "for a few minutes," she didn't awake again until almost noon. When she finally emerged up on deck, it was only in time to have Noah relieve an exhausted Rigo so that he could have his first real sleep in thirty hours. So it wasn't until twilight that afternoon that the two of them finally had moments alone together.

In Rigo's cabin, Heather admired the gleaming wood and shining brass oil lamps, one of which softly lit the room. A beautiful red-patterned carpet graced the floor, and the shelves, tables, and chairs were all made to fit perfectly in the corners, braced or fixed to withstand any storm. Heather lit a second lamp and moved to where Rigo lay sleeping. He hadn't had time to shave and had merely tumbled into bed, his clothes in a heap on the floor. When Heather put them away, she discovered others hanging in the narrow locker, clean and ready for him.

Heather bent low over the bed, loathe to wake Rigo, knowing how tired he was after the ordeal he had been through. It was a wonder to her where he found the stamina. It was as if these hardships were such a common occurrence for him that he accepted it all as routine. A smile came to her lips as her heart swelled with a sweet feeling of joy. Here was a man many a woman wished she had by her side, and fate had given her this privilege. Should I tell him and let him know how much I am his admiring woman? When her breath warmed his cheeks, Rigo opened his eyes.

Heather drew away slightly. "I didn't mean to wake you."

"I have never been wakened so happily, beautiful lady," he whispered, his blue eyes lighting with a tender flame.

"The cook has your supper waiting," she said and let herself be pulled down on the bed beside him. She felt a sharp thrill go through her at the warmth and intimacy of his gesture and blushed lightly. A great shyness came over Heather and lent a look of uncertainty to her ordinarily vibrant and confident face. The thought of his nakedness beneath the sheets made her confused with desire.

Rigo could feel the tentativeness in her tremulous

fingers, her unresisting yet tiptoeing touch of him. A smile spread over his face and he brought one of her hands to his chest.

"Don't tremble, my love," he said huskily. "I would never take by force what you're not ready to give freely." He let her hand feel the beating of his heart. Desire was in his eyes—he couldn't erase that—but he held himself in check in spite of her nearness and his readiness.

Heather's eyes fell and her acute embarrassment with herself was apparent. "I don't know why I'm still . . . shy . . . It's not as though I don't know . . ."

"What a great pleasure it will be for me, then, to . . . reacquaint you with myself," he said softly, smiling mischievously at her. "Don't be shy. I will . . . treasure every touch, every kiss." His voice caressed her taut nerves with its low timbre, his tenderness for her evident in his words and tone.

Heather raised her eyes to his, caught in their spell. She smiled gently, leaning toward him just a little.

"You weave a spell a hundred unsuspecting flies would be trapped into," she said, her green eyes brightening.

Rigo, laughing, restrained the impulse to sweep her into his arms, though he was hard put not to. "I've fallen under your spell, lady, and we'll leave it to others to decide who provided the honey. Now, I must rise and get dressed. You're welcome to watch. In fact, I invite you to, and then we'll sup together." His eyes teased hers, and he brought her hand to his lips and slowly kissed each of her fingertips.

Heather tugged her hand away, not wanting to, but her sudden intake of breath indicated a pulse had been touched that made her want to flee. "I'll await you outside. I'm sure you have need of some privacy."

"None, I assure you." He laughed wickedly.

"You are the very devil to tease me so!" As Rigo began to rise from his bed, Heather got up and flew toward the cabin door, knowing the man wouldn't hesitate to expose himself.

"You promised not to force me!" she said, half wanting to brave the unveiling.

"You promised you'd come to me willingly," he rejoined, his blue eyes compelling hers. The sheet barely covered his manhood.

"I never! 'Twas your own interpretation!" she threw at him, hand on the door handle. Then her eyes shone as she gave him a teasing sidelong glance. "But I give it now." With that and a girlish swirl of her petticoats, she left.

Heather went to tell the cook that Rigo was awake and then went on deck for a breath of air to steady her nerves. She was acutely aware that there was a vast difference this time in her being alone with Rigo. She chided herself for her undue modesty, wondering how to set aside her shyness. The air was heavy and the waters lazily rolling in giant swells that made the ship tip and rock with a loud rattling of lines and canvas. When Heather looked up, she saw that the light, puffy breeze barely filled the sails. The sun was setting to the west, but clouds hung down and a haziness made the reddish colors indistinct. When she looked over the side, the ship seemed to barely be moving at all.

"Sail ho!" a voice from aloft cried, and two sailors who had been splicing line amidships leapt up and ran to the rail to stare off where the lookout was pointing. When Heather followed, she could just make out the tiniest of matchsticks and cotton on the furthest horizon to the north. As she turned to question a sailor about what the ships were, she saw Rigo burst up out of the companionway wearing only his breeches and stride aft to where Noah stood with an eyeglass. Holding the rail against the rock and jerk of the *Contessa* in the swells, Heather moved aft to join them.

"Two ships, Cap'n," she heard Noah say to Rigo. "Three-masters they be." He handed the eyeglass to Rigo, who took it, swung it to the horizon and then, as the ship swayed beneath him, kept it locked on what he saw.

Heather found herself incongruously aware of his broad bare chest, the muscles rippling as he adjusted the level of the glass. She couldn't stop her eyes from sliding over him to where a fine line of black hair plunged below the lean waist into his black breeches, traveling lower to the rounded swell in between the powerful thighs. When Heather tore her eyes away, she saw him looking at her with a grin.

"I see you are deeply disturbed by the prospect of our being attacked by the British," he said to her, handing the glass back to Noah, who looked worried and apparently had noticed nothing of Heather's behavior. Rigo took her by the elbow and guided her to the rail. There he swung around once more to Noah.

"Take her on a broad reach, Mr. Wiggens," he said. "Although with this calm, we'll be lucky to outrun the seaweed."

"Aye, aye, Cap'n," Noah said, moving over beside the helmsman. "But the limeys won't be sailin' no faster."

As Noah began giving instructions to the helmsman, Rigo turned to Heather.

"Someone always seems to be chasing us," he said, smiling down at her. "It keeps interfering with our chasing each other."

Heather felt herself flush slightly.

"How do you know the ships are English?" she asked, grabbing the rail with both hands as the ship gave a powerful lurch.

"Because they control and patrol this coast," Rigo replied, squinting off to the north before returning his gaze to her. "American ships, like us, only sail singly. Come," he added, taking her again by the elbow and leading her back toward the companionway. "Our supper is waiting, and there'll be no danger in this calm."

"They won't catch us?" Heather asked, although she felt not the slightest fear.

"Not tonight. And by dawn, we hope to have disappeared."

Heather went first down the steps and led the way to Rigo's cabin. Once inside, Rigo pulled Heather to him, capturing her eyes with his.

"I'm glad you enjoy looking at me as much as I enjoy looking at you," he said, and her heart accelerated at the look he was giving her and the reminder of his having seen her admiring his body.

"You mock me, Rigo," she said softly, "while I'm in a constant state of excitement. 'Tis like I'm on a precipice, and I'm afraid of stepping off. . . ."

Rigo bent his head to hers, fingering a chestnut curl where it fell on her shoulders. The clean smell of soap rose from his skin.

"Don't doubt for a moment that I'll be there to catch you." He trailed his fingers to her chin and tilted it upward. "Look at me, Heather. I'm not teasing you. I'm trying to ease your way with me, to let you feel natural. Making light of it seemed . . . a step. I would not have predicted all these blushes from you—but then, you've always been full of surprises."

Heather lifted her eyes to his, a faint blush appearing on her cheeks as if to prove him correct.

"Why the hesitancy?" he went on, his voice a low, rough whisper. He leaned to brush his lips against hers, his eyes flowing into hers until it seemed all the world receded and fell away. "I'm in love with you. . . ."

As Heather caught her breath in pleasure, Rigo took her by the hand and led her into the room to seat her at the table prepared for them. She smiled up at him, though she was at a loss for words. He poured them both a glass of wine and, after putting on a silk shirt and pulling on his boots, set about to serve them both from the heavy pottery crock.

"Drink, please," he ordered quietly. "I'll join you in a moment." He placed a plate of steaming spicy stew in front of her and a crusted piece of bread alongside. When she looked down at the dish uncertainly, he added, "Very simple fare but tasty. Cook is good, but hasn't many recipes."

"It looks very good," Heather returned. "The salt air has me hungry."

Rigo then served himself, all the while conscious of his beautiful but uncertain companion who sat politely sipping her wine. He seated himself, picked up his fork, and then replaced it as he saw Heather tentatively pick up her fork to eat.

"I have something to give you," he said, rising from the

chair and going over to his locker. "It's not the most appropriate moment, but I think it best." He extracted a small package wrapped in a heavy square of purple velvet. Sitting down again, he put it in front of Heather and let the top fall open. A dazzling ring of sapphire surrounded by tiny diamonds winked in the lush velvet bed. He took Heather's left hand in his.

"I had to guess the size," he said gently, picking up the sparkling gem and slipping it onto her ring finger. Heather sat stunned, staring at her extended finger as Rigo still lightly held her hand. She raised her eyes slowly to his.

"I've not had much time to purchase you the jewels you deserve," Rigo went on. "In time, you'll have more. I don't have many family treasures to give you, but you shall have whatever I have. This was to be my wedding gift to you, and a matching necklace is being made. . . ." He paused, watching the emotions running across her face until he saw a tear escape to her cheek.

"I hope that is for happiness," he said gently and put a thumb up to wipe it away.

Heather closed her eyes tightly and squeezed his hand to control the bursting in her heart that threatened to erupt as tears rather than as the laughter of joy she wanted to share with him.

When she opened them, her eyes were shining, and her smile was as radiant as the sun. When she trusted herself to speak, she said, "You bring me so much joy, and I . . . bring you so much love. . . ."

A rush went through Rigo like a wild, warm wind. It was a few seconds before he could let go of the moment and, looking down, saw the steaming plates before them.

"I don't think any food will taste better, nor will I remember it less. Let's eat, my love, before I throw the whole thing out as a waste of time." The brightness of his smile matched hers, and Rigo pressed her hand one last time and then released it.

They ate, Heather's green eyes molten. Rigo talked of where they might go, where they could live, how the war might end. Heather listened, telling him she would live anywhere to be with him. Noah came briefly to the cabin to inform Rigo that a full moon showed that the two English ships were somewhat closer and that there was still almost no wind. A heavy cloud bank coming from the west was expected to obscure the moon in a few hours.

When Noah had left, Rigo frowned for a moment but then his face cleared and he began questioning Heather about her childhood and youth, getting her to recall her happy times with her parents. After the cook had cleared away the main dishes, he brought in a bread pudding and another bottle of wine. Then Rigo teased her about her playing the role of Miss Southey and wondered mischievously whether he was now engaged to Elizabeth or Heather or both.

"Whichever you choose," she said, her eyes flashing merrily. "I'll have you know, Captain Rigo, my heart belongs only to one Richard Somerset."

"I wish I had ten rings to give you, if they make you this giddy," he said lovingly. They leaned toward one another, their heads nearly touching. Dessert now finished, they lingered yet at the table drinking wine.

"It's not the ring," Heather answered. "It's the act, your manner, your promise to me . . ."

"Which I gave before . . ." he reminded her, his eyes a brilliant blue.

"I only remember this moment," she murmured.

Rigo gently placed feathery light kisses on her lips, her cheeks, her eyes. Heather returned them, her eyes molten with desire.

He rose from his chair and offered his open arms. She readily went into them.

Rigo took her into his arms gently, letting his lips fall to her, his tongue tracing the soft edges and when she parted hers, plunging inside to taste the sweetness, a thrill leapt into them, electrifying their bodies as they clung to each other.

Heather could feel the tension in Rigo as he restrained himself for her sake. His very gentleness, his willingness to sacrifice his own needs for her, unleashed her own longing and desire and she pressed against him willingly, her shyness gone.

"You are a wonder to me," Rigo said after a long, deep kiss during which Heather had molded her body to his.

She could feel his aroused manhood, and thought no more, all maidenly fears swept away in the desire to taste him, to return his gentle arousal of her, his tender regard for her fearful hesitancy. She slid her hand into his pants to caress the swollen hot flesh and he gasped with pleasure.

Rigo looked down at her eyes and saw all he needed to know there. She wanted him, her purest nature one of passion and love, free and unrestrained. He undid her dress with a purpose, exposing her body's curves, smooth and warm to his touch. Without a moment's wasted time, he stripped himself and then knelt before her and pressed his mouth and tongue into the lush triangle of dark curly hair, searching for the center of her pleasure, taking her buttocks in his hands. Heather moaned and tried to pull away, the excitement unnerving her, pitching her into frenzied movements, until she subsided, and leaned on him weakly. He released her, sliding himself up her surrendered body, to lift her to the bed, there he entered, thrusting deeply, arousing himself to a fevered state and took her once again with him on the journey they shared.

"You will learn to do the same for me . . . I would love it . . . if you would . . ." Rigo whispered against her gently, kissing her face, her sleepy eyes. His own satisfaction was complete, yet now aroused again and willing, as they lay in the aftermath of the loving.

"You won't go away?" she whispered.

"Not without you," he whispered back. "My sweet wife to be."

Heather sighed contentedly and nestled closer, planting kisses on his sensitive neck.

"Do you think you can now accustom yourself to my body, Madame Somerset . . . without shying away like a frightened rabbit?"

Heather put a finger up to his lips which he kissed softly and then nibbled sensuously.

"Your form is beautiful to me, but . . . I had not truly seen it before. The other times it was dark and I was too . . . intent."

Rigo chuckled in agreement. "Yes, your intentions were clear. I loved every minute."

"And I hadn't known a man before you . . . it's new . . ."

"And now? Do you know me?" he queried, teasing her hand with his lips.

"I will make a rash promise. I will never turn into a . . . a . . . weak-kneed spinster again. Next time, I shall seduce you!"

"If I let you escape my bed," he said smiling.

"There are certain needs . . ." Heather laughed gaily, her eyes sparkling.

"In due time, my love. Right now . . . the best use of you can be made without words."

"Plunderer! Thief!" she said teasingly.

"Pirate," he reminded her. "And no one dares take from the pirate his treasure!" With that he silenced her by offering her his mouth, which she took.

Chapter Twenty-seven

THEIR NIGHT WAS ONE OF LOVE, BUT THROUGHOUT, THEY were made aware of the approaching danger. Sometime after midnight, Rigo had to go on watch. They went up together, hands clasped, to see the full moon racing between the broken clouds that were arriving from the west. The two English ships were still barely visible two miles off, and the eerie calm indicated they might still be there by dawn. Although Heather could sense a rising concern in Rigo, she was too enraptured to feel any worry. Rigo said that the large swells that had been rolling in from the southeast for the last twelve hours meant a storm on the way along with wind, so the calm could not last much longer.

When the moon was blanketed by a cloud and the ship plunged into blackness, Rigo unexpectedly pulled Heather to him and again sent her senses reeling with a deep kiss that was broken only by an abrupt lurch of the ship that had them both laughing and whispering like children. Finally, Rigo announced that it was much too unbecoming a captain to frolic with a girl and lovingly ordered her below, warning that she could expect to have her sleep interrupted at the end of his two-hour watch.

Heather did sleep. And it was, indeed, interrupted. When Rigo finally left her near dawn, Heather lay on the disheveled bed feeling an awe that so many wondrous and amazing things could happen to her in so short a time. How incredible it was that every time she felt that now she could never feel more ecstatic, somehow their lovemaking would take her to a new point that would be equally or more miraculous. How could she be so fortunate? How could she possibly have earned the love of such a magnificent man? How could love be so ecstatic one moment and so gay and giggly the next? She fell asleep again with the serene and gentle smile of a woman who loves and has been thoroughly loved.

Although Rigo, too, was in awe at the depth of the love Heather stirred in him and the amazing delights of their lovemaking, he had less time to dwell on it. The dawn had brought wind but also the English ships, still only two miles away. In the moderate breezes of the morning, the swift *Contessa* began to pull away from her pursuers until, by one o'clock, they had been left almost five miles behind.

Rigo managed to get a few hours sleep in the early afternoon and had the pleasant experience of being awakened at the time he had ordered not by the gruff voice of Noah or a crew member but by the warm touch of Heather's mouth on his. Knowing the danger they were in, he this time resisted a renewal of their love play but permitted the eager Heather to join him on deck. There he found to his concern that the wind had risen to twenty-five knots and that the larger English ships were beginning to gain on them again. The sky to the southeast was an ugly black, and he knew they were in for a storm.

With the two English ships closing and less than two miles away, Rigo ordered the course changed to head toward the New Jersey coast. They were approaching Cape May and the mouth of Delaware Bay, and if he could get around that point, the shallower waters of the bay would give him places to escape and to hide. But an hour before dusk, with Cape May visible only five miles off their starboard quarter, a third English frigate emerged in front of them to the south. Rigo was trapped.

Now he ordered Heather to go below, tenderly telling her that he must be able to concentrate solely on the sailing. When she left, he was sorry to see that the joy that had been on her face all day was, for the first time, dimmed by her first awareness of the danger they were in.

Although there was less shoal water on this side of the cape, he was sure the deep-draft English frigates would be much less certain of these waters than he was. He now ordered the *Contessa* sailed directly landward, hoping at best that the English would be reluctant to follow into possibly shoal waters. At worst, he could abandon ship and escape to land. With a leadsman at the bow throwing the lead and calling out the depths, Rigo guided the *Contessa* closer and closer in, the wind now wailing through the rigging and sending long, white-capped combers rolling in from the sea to smash against the ship's aft quarter.

The frigate newly arrived from the south was closest to them now, and puffs of smoke sprouted from her sides as she sent a broadside across the roiling water at them. It fell short, and with the rough seas and gathering darkness, Rigo guessed he would have to endure only two more like that before the setting sun would free them into the total blackness of the night and the storm.

It was after the next two broadsides had been expended at him with no more damage than two holes in his reefed mainsail that Rigo began to realize that the greatest threat to the safety of his ship and crew now lay in the rising wind and seas and the nearness of the coast of Cape May. He doubted the English would dare sail after him with darkness falling, but even without that threat, the *Contessa* might have trouble beating back off.

A half hour later, it was pitch dark. Rain was pelting down. The wind had risen to gale force. Rigo ordered all the sails lowered except for a storm jib forward and a storm trisail amidships. The helmsman was having trouble getting the schooner's head up into the wind and waves so that she could claw her way offshore. Although the English had disappeared into the blackness of the night, the *Contessa* was being blown relentlessly sideways toward shore. The English, although probably waiting for him a mile or two out at sea, were no longer a worry. It would be all Rigo could do with his vastly undermanned crew to save his ship and Heather from the storm.

At midnight, the wind was now screeching through the rigging at hurricane force. With the storm jib torn to shreds and with only one of the two anchors Rigo had ordered set still holding, the *Contessa*, with a creak and groan, shuddered to a halt. She was aground in ten feet of water, probably a half mile from shore. As twelve-foot swells came hurling out of the darkness at her with a hissing roar to smash against her bow, Rigo ordered Noah to go fetch Heather and his crew to prepare to abandon ship. The *Contessa* had two skiffs, but the chances of either making it through the breakers to shore without being swamped or capsized seemed small. Yet to stay with the doomed schooner was equally dangerous. As the last anchor dragged further, the ship's bow was smashed sideways so that the seas began to crash into her port side, making her shudder from stem to stern and rolling her over forty-five degrees onto her side. The *Contessa*'s slanted starboard decks were now awash. Every six or seven seconds, a thunderous swell would pound into the helpless ship with a shattering crack, sending sea water and spray over the sides. The first such wave smashed the portside skiff into matchsticks, and the second swept a screaming crewman tumbling across the decking to disappear into the sea and the darkness.

Even before Noah returned with Heather, Rigo ordered the remaining crew to prepare to launch the only remaining skiff. With one of them holding the only source of light—a sputtering oil lamp—four men began struggling with the skiff's lashings ten feet in front of where Rigo clung to the useless helm. The skiff already had a foot of water in the bottom from the seas that swept across the schooner's deck, but it was their last hope.

Rigo was about to hurry below after Heather when at last he saw a second lamp and two figures struggling from the companionway aft. Soon they arrived, and Heather, almost invisible in a huge, dark cape of Rigo's that Noah had apparently insisted she wear, threw herself against him and held him in a fierce embrace. He had to shout to be heard over the roar of the wind and the smashing of the sea, but he got Noah and Heather to understand that he wanted them to get into the skiff. He knew that any moment now a wave might pull it away from the men who had undone the lashings but were trying to hold the skiff steady in the unpredictable rise and fall of the water along this starboard side of the schooner. He and Noah took Heather by the arms and, after yet another wave had crashed across the helpless ship, they staggered forward with her between them and lifted her unceremoniously into the skiff.

The crewman's lamp had been smashed by the previous wave and now there was only Noah's light. When the mate had followed Heather into the skiff, Rigo took the boat's bowline from a crewman and ordered him and the others to get aboard, too, and prepare to row. Each time the sea surged, the skiff would float. Each time it ebbed, it would bump back down onto the slanted deck, prevented from floating away only by the line that Rigo held.

"Get in! Get in!" Rigo shouted at the last crewman who seemed too tired or frightened to haul himself up over the skiff's coaming. As he was watching the man finally pull himself into the boat, Rigo became aware of a hissing roar so much louder than any previous approaching wave that he could barely believe his ears. Bracing himself and wrapping the line he was holding twice more around the cleat, he screamed, "Hold on!" The roar grew louder and louder, and he could see Noah's half-frightened, half-awestruck face staring past him at the approaching swell while Heather's face threw at him a last wordless appeal. Then there was an explosion of sound and spray, the cracks of splitting masts, and, finally, a tidal wave of water engulfing everything. The line to the skiff snapped like a mere thread, and Rigo was rolling over and over and over in the endless coldness of the sea.

Heather did not know how she still lived in utter blackness, always with water rolling over her, smashing at her tenuous grip on the skiff's coaming. Each second had seemed like her last, each breath a surprise gift of the gods. She knew someone else must be with her on the skiff only because she felt a painful clasp on her wrist or arm when an increasing roar warned them of another large breaker bearing down on them. When she had finally lost her grip on the boat, she assumed she would drown, but only seconds later, it seemed, she awoke to find herself gasping for breath, lying on the wet sand of a beach. The darkness was so total and the thunder of the surf and wail of the wind so loud that a man ten feet away could be shouting for her and she would not hear. When an extra high sweep of surf swept over her legs and then across her face, she crawled another thirty feet up the beach to escape its killing tongue. But the rain still lashed at her, and her body felt like it had been beaten by a dozen brutal men. At times, though knowing she was at last free of the sea, Heather had to struggle to draw breath. She wondered where Rigo was and once or twice called out his name, but the rage of the storm swallowed the pitiful sound before it had left her lips. Twice she raised herself to look for him—the first time to feel the rain slash into her face like a whip, the second to feel her wet hair blow around her eyes as she stared from darkness into darkness.

It was dawn before she could remember even this bit of her nightmare night. Heather must have slept for the sky was fully light when she again came to consciousness. The rain had stopped, and the wind, though still blowing hard, was now a mere gale. As soon as she remembered what had happened, her eyes leapt down the beach in search of Rigo, but there was no sign of life to the left or to the right.

Heather stood up and removed the soaked cape that weighed down on her like an anchor. Her shoes were gone and her linen dress was still soaked through. She began staggering down the beach in search of Rigo or Noah. Surely, it wasn't only she who had survived. She had walked more than a hundred yards, staying just above the surf line and about thirty feet from the sand dunes, when she suddenly realized that there in the sand were footprints. Although some had been swept away by the advancing surf, those she saw were obviously fresh and showed that someone had been walking the same way she was going this very morning.

This first hint of hope spurred Heather forward, her eyes always searching the beach far ahead of her, until her heart leapt at the sight of someone lying on the sand a few hundred yards ahead. She found she didn't have the strength to run, but she hurried on as best she could, once calling futilely for Rigo, while becoming aware that the figure on the beach was not moving. Still, she hurried on, and now she could see the form was definitely that of a man lying face down in the sand. As she approached, Heather's heart was heavy with dread, and she had to force herself to take the last ten paces. It was a big man with dark hair, dressed as Rigo had been dressed in black, but surely this wet, limp, sad form could not be her lover.

Heather fell to her knees beside the still body and fearfully touched the hair of the head that was turned away from her. With nothing but that touch, she knew for a certainty that the man was dead, and that he was not Rigo. Gently, she reached to feel the man's face, and its icy coldness told her of death. She did not have to look further. This could not be Rigo.

She arose numbed by this new evidence of their disaster, but as she walked slowly onward, Heather realized that this man could not have made those recent footprints. Someone else was still alive and still ahead of her.

A half hour later, she found him. Again, she knew before she could really see him clearly that the man was not Rigo. It was Noah, thank God, and it had been he who had been with her on the skiff, helping her, and whose footprints she had been following. He and a crewman, who had also managed to stay with the skiff, had left her at dawn to look for other survivors. They had found none—only one body here and another further down the beach. Both were dead crewmen. Rigo and four other crew members were missing.

All that morning, they searched. Noah tried to encourage Heather by reminding her that Rigo was an excellent swimmer, but the very forcefulness of his argument chilled her with an awareness of his own despair. If Rigo was alive, he would certainly be searching for them, and where was he? At noon, they discovered a third body in some marsh grass beyond the first dunes. Another member of the crew.

An hour later, Heather realized from the nervous glances being exchanged between the remaining crewman and Noah that they considered further looking senseless. If Rigo were alive, they would have found each other by now. His dead body was either out at sea or hidden in some marsh grass behind the dunes, where the highest waves had managed to reach.

"Go, Noah," she said to him. "But I must stay."

"No, miss. I cannot let you stay here by yourself," Noah said, shaking his head and trying to take her arm. "The Cap'n would want me to care for you 'til . . . care for you."

"He *must* be alive, Noah!" she appealed. "We can't give up yet!"

Noah nodded gravely while the crewman looked down at the sand.

They searched yet another three hours until they were all growing almost too weak to walk. Then Noah announced that they must find food and water. Still Heather might not have gone had not Noah also said that perhaps Rigo, too, had gone looking for food and shelter.

That evening, they found an empty fishing shack and the next morning a small village. They ate and drank and rested. They inquired. They waited. They returned to the beach and looked. They waited. When they finally left the village three days later, they had found not a single trace of Rigo.

Chapter Twenty-eight

THE PEOPLE OF PHILADELPHIA PANICKED AT THE RUMORS OF the seemingly unstoppable English advance through New Jersey. Every day, men arrived from General Washington's retreating army with more stories of desertions, hunger, and retreat. Pamphlets appeared rousing the citizens to fight for their liberty, for the right to govern themselves, for the right to the profits of their own labors. Criers shouted from the steps of the town hall of battles fought, of heroic deeds, of traitors to the cause, and always, at the end, of retreats.

But the turmoil barely touched Heather. For more than six weeks, she had been working as a seamstress for Noah Wiggens' cousin in a fashionable shop on High Street, six weeks during which every new knock on the door, every new stranger on the street would send her desperate eyes searching for her lost Rigo. Even now, with the autumn leaves strewing the streets and the air chilled with November winds, she would not give up hope that he would come for her. Heather could not admit to his death. Rigo was merely delayed. Lost for the moment. Each day, she hoped for his appearance or for the return of Noah from his dangerous journey through the battle lines to Staten Island to see if Rigo had returned there.

She was kept sane by her work for Anna Harris, a kind-hearted lady, graying and plump but vainly attached to fashion and fashionable people. Mrs. Harris flattered and fussed with her clients, determined to find the exact fit and the right detail for each dress. And Heather was a real find. Noah's recounting of the deliciously romantic love affair between the wealthy Richard Somerset and the persecuted orphan, with its tragic ending in the loss at sea of the gallant lover, appealed greatly to both Anna's fascination with the wellborn and her natural good-heartedness. That Heather turned out to be a tireless and creative worker, seeming to bury herself in her work ten and twelve hours a day, was the best bonus of all. The young girl could see at a glance whether champagne silk or plum velvet was right for a particular customer, whether square neck or high collar and lace were more pleasing, and, in addition, the number of well-dressed gentlemen who came to her shop to buy something for "their sisters" had increased measurably since Mrs. Harris had placed the grieving chestnut-haired beauty near the window to do her work. She suspected that more than one man had been ensnared by Heather's haunted eyes looking longingly out at the busy street from the shop window.

Heather worked hard for exactly the reason Mrs. Harris guessed—to prevent idle hours from bringing painful memories of Rigo crowding back. As she sat at the worktable of the small shop with the two other young women who worked for Mrs. Harris, she let her life be filled only with the mannequins, boxes of ribbons and lace, racks of thread, rolls of various cloths, and the endless task of sketching and cutting costumes, fitting and sewing, and smiling lifelessly at the clients who strutted and preened as if all of life revolved around the exact fall of a ribbon. Yet despite these distractions, Heather could feel a heaviness beginning to settle around her and knew that her glances out the window were now holding less and less hope.

The nights alone in the tiny attic room above the shop where she slept were the worst. At least, she no longer wept herself to sleep, as she had for most of the first month. Now Heather simply retreated into herself, quietly but not serenely. It was as if she had trained her mind to be empty. About once a week, a vision of some moment with Rigo in their all-too-brief life together would leap uninvited into her mind, and her heart would feel an almost unbearable ache.

Heather's only source of strength was the sapphire ring Rigo had given her the night before the storm. When alone, she would hold it near her candle, turn it in the flickering light, and sometimes see Rigo's blue eyes alight in its depths. This vision of Rigo never made her cry but seemed to hold out hope of his continuing life. The other working girls had been fascinated by and then envious of the ring, as if the death of the man who had given it were unimportant compared to her just having it. And some of the rich ladies cast her disapproving glances, as if she must have committed some terrible and disreputable act to be able to wear such a ring. In the privacy of her small office, Mrs. Harris loved to titillate these ladies with the sad story of Heather's love, and this mollified their disapproval and kept business booming.

With the few shillings she'd earned, Heather had made herself a simple frock of a silvery gray light wool for the coming winter. As the mornings became cold and the coals in the fire were kept low, she was glad she had finished the work and was wearing it. It and two other summer dresses she had made for herself were all the clothes she now owned.

And then, on the first day of December, a little incident discomfited her. As she was waiting on a lady to whom Mrs. Harris had just introduced her, the lady's companion, a tiny, bowlegged man with a white wig worn slightly askew, came quickly up to her.

"Heather Woode, did you say?" he asked excitedly. "My word, I believe I've heard the name."

"Oh, no, sir. You couldn't," Heather replied politely. "For I've not been in America long and have no relations here."

"No, no. I've heard it. I'm sure. . . ." he insisted, examining her with the rudeness of a rich man looking at an underling. "You say you've just recently arrived here. . . . Yes. Yes!" He said this last word with a sudden brightening of his tiny eyes and a knowing smile.

In a few more minutes, the man and his lady left, but the exchange left a bad taste in Heather's mouth. At the end of the day, Mrs. Harris told her that the man had made inquiries about her, wondering how she'd come to Philadelphia and whether she'd ever lived in New York.

"He was most unusual, I must say," Mrs. Harris rambled on as she and Heather neatened up the shop. "I mean, he didn't seem interested in your welfare or your figure, as most men are wont to do. Only your past. Imagine!" She raised an eyebrow at Heather to see if she would tell Mrs. Harris what the mystery was all about.

"I've never seen either of them before," Heather said, flushing at her employer's hinting at some secret past. "And you know I've come straight here with Mr. Wiggens."

"Yes, but you *did* land in New York, didn't you?" Mrs. Harris asked cheerfully.

"Yes," Heather agreed, then turned away to end the conversation. She suddenly felt that man's coming boded no good.

A week later, a carriage driven by a matched pair drew up outside the shop and three men alighted, one of whose abrupt movements looked to Heather's glance vaguely familiar, but, since he was not a tall man like Rigo, she looked no further. A minute later, the door opened and Heather's nimble fingers froze. Her face went white. Looking down at her with a crooked smile was Duncan Crawley.

"Did I not say we would meet again, my dear?" Crawley asked, his smile broadening and his figure becoming more erect, as if he were posing for her.

She stared at him mutely, the heaviness of her heart seeming to spread through her whole being. She could not speak and could not move.

"May I help you, sir?" Mrs. Harris asked, bustling up to serve him.

"You may, madam," Crawley said, seeming to crow with his expectations of triumph. "I would like the dress this young lady is wearing," he added, turning to indicate Heather. "And *everything* inside it."

"See here, sir," Mrs. Harris said with a perplexed pout. "This is one of my girls."

"*Was*, madam, was," Crawley replied confidently. "I fear I must inform you that this woman is my indentured servant recently run away."

"That cannot be," Mrs. Harris said, looking from the confident Crawley to the stricken Heather. "Why, she's been here for weeks and before that was shipwrecked, her lover lost at sea."

"And before that was indentured to a William Barrett, who sold her contract to me," Crawley returned quickly, no longer smiling. "I am afraid, madam, that she is illegally in your employ. I have a writ from the city magistrate notarized just yesterday certifying that she is legally contracted to serve me."

Again Mrs. Harris looked from the stiff, elegant figure of Crawley to the downcast Heather and knew that the man must have a case. Noah had hinted to her of some such possible trouble, she now remembered, but what could she do?

"Is this true, Heather?" Mrs. Harris finally asked gently.

Mutely, Heather gave a barely perceptible nod, her mind now as blank as on those nights when she despaired of ever seeing Rigo again. "But I will not go with him," she added listlessly.

"Oh, I think you will," Crawley countered, pulling from his vest a rolled-up scroll and again smiling confidently. "This woman here is not about to try to keep you if it means her going to jail. And I wouldn't try to escape. I've a man posted at the back door and a constable waiting on the street outside." Planting his walking cane pompously on the floor between his legs, Crawley tapped the legal-looking scroll coldly against his chest. "If you will be good enough, madam," he went on to Mrs. Harris, "to release her . . . and her worldly goods, we'll be on our way."

As Mrs. Harris fluttered about her hopelessly, Heather began to feel the first stirrings of revolt. It was as if it took the threat of a living death with Crawley to stir her back into life. She looked abruptly up at Crawley with sudden vigor and disdain.

"And where, Mr. Crawley," she demanded, her face flushing with anger, "do you intend to take me?" She wanted Mrs. Harris to know both Crawley's name and where he was taking her.

"Why, to New York, of course," Crawley answered easily. "The English have made it again a quite pleasant city to do business in."

"How did you know I was here?"

"Oh, news of your beauty travels far, I assure you," he answered with a sardonic smile, and Heather suddenly knew it was that little man who had recognized her a week before. "And, of course, fate intervened so that justice could, after a delay, triumph."

"If justice is to triumph," Heather replied, standing up, "then fate will have to intervene again and not allow this abomination."

"My, how erudite!" Crawley exclaimed with mock praise, stuffing his document back in his vest. "You challenge me, my dear. Indeed, you do. Otherwise, I would not be bothered with so troublesome a servant. Come. We waste time. We've a long drive ahead."

All that morning and afternoon, Heather, Duncan Crawley, and his valet rode in Crawley's private carriage northward toward New York. Heather was reminded of her other carriage journey with this hateful man, and now, like then, she plotted her escape. But this time, she was surprised to find Crawley highly nervous and agitated, always urging his driver to increase the pace, to keep a good lookout. Several times, they stopped while he sent his valet to ascertain if there were any American soldiers in the vicinity. They would have to pass through the American lines to get on to New York.

"It's an evil time to be traveling," he said to Heather in the early afternoon, one of the few times he had bothered to address her. He was wearing a green frock coat with large lapels and brass buttons, and he drew from it a large pistol, which he checked over before returning it to the inside of his coat.

"Do you expect robbery?" Heather asked, remembering she had seen a musket and a blunderbuss stored up near the driver. Crawley sat stiff and tense while they passed by an odd group of men gathered alongside the road, a few holding rifles.

"I expect this war with the colonial rabble to throw up anything," he answered, wiping his brow. "I'm prepared for the unexpected—both from outside and within," he added, giving her a chilling glance. "My travel to Philadelphia to claim you was not without event—I won't trouble you with the details—but I have learned that caution is necessary. I have already paid enough in time, trouble, and money for your precious services. I don't intend to pay more." He stuffed the scented handkerchief back in his cuff. "I trust not a single American."

"They fight for their freedom," Heather said quietly, and then realized that, for the first time, she understood the trouble in America. It was about domination, rule by an outsider who thought only of gain for himself or itself—her own situation enlarged.

"Are you mad?" Crawley said, turning to her with a flushed face. "Freedom! How do you think these adventurers and malcontents came here? By the grace of a sovereign to whom they still owe obedience and allegiance."

"No one owes allegiance to a cruel master," Heather returned, meeting Crawley's angry gaze with cold dislike.

"Look to yourself, Miss Woode," he said, narrowing his

eyes, "that I not take yet a greater dislike of you. Were we to fall prey to some of these barbarians, I might not lift a finger to protect you from their violence."

"Better the worst of these barbarians than you," she answered him, flushing with anger.

Crawley shook his head as his eyes narrowed. "Pretty packages sometimes contain nothing of worth inside," he said. "I fear I shall soon have to get rid of you."

"Then why did you take me from Mrs. Harris?" Heather asked, shaken by the meanness he was displaying.

"Revenge," Crawley replied, with a grimace, "against you and your captain. I will have my revenge!"

"You make my blood crawl!"

"We will see who crawls after all, won't we?" His mouth slanted cruelly, his eyes cold.

Heather leaned away into the corner of the carriage and closed her eyes, no longer able to look at him, frightened and revolted by his hatred. The carriage rolled on.

It was dark when they arrived in the village of Morristown, New Jersey, safe—from Crawley's point of view—within territory now controlled by the English. Though still fifty miles from New York City, Crawley had the carriage stop at The Bear's Head Inn. It was not the best but was the only inn with rooms still available.

As Heather was escorted in by Crawley and his ubiquitous valet, she was struck by how crowded and rowdy the main room was. Rough men in rough clothes were drinking ale side by side with equally rough-looking English soldiers. An ample number of crude women were serving them. Crawley was clearly made nervous by this crowd, especially as there was a hush when the strange threesome entered.

Crawley ordered two rooms and asked that three meals be brought up to them. The innkeeper replied he had but one room left, and Crawley impatiently said he'd take it.

"I will not sleep in the same room with this man," Heather said loudly.

"You will hold your tongue!" Crawley snapped at her, squeezing her elbow hard where he held her.

"I'll not have trouble in me house," the big-bellied

278

innkeeper said, squinting warily at the well-dressed Crawley and the defiant Heather. "I don't care how high ye be, not here. 'Tis bad for business."

"This woman is my contracted servant," Crawley answered waspishly, "and there'll be no trouble, I assure you." Releasing Heather to the firm grip of the valet, he took the innkeeper aside and, as Heather saw, slipped him a few additional pieces of sterling. The man nodded, scowling in Heather's direction, whispered a few words back to Crawley, and, when a few more coins changed hands, burst into a big grin.

"Why, certainly, sir," the innkeeper said with sudden boisterousness. "Glad to oblige you. Two extra mattresses for your servants and two bottles of Madeira for you. Coming right up. Haggerty!" he called loudly across the heads of the crowded room. "Take this good gentleman up to his room. Molly! Dinner and some wine! Let's step lively now!"

Only slightly reassured by the mention of two mattresses, Heather reluctantly let herself be escorted up the stairs to the rather large room that Crawley had taken. A maid was lighting a fire in the fireplace while a second servant brought up first the two mattresses and then Crawley's holdall and her small bag. Twenty minutes later, food was brought up and set out on a small table at the foot of the large bed. To her surprise, the valet left to eat down in the common room, and two places were set at the table. The valet locked the door after him as he left.

Equally to her surprise, Crawley began to treat her politely. Even when Heather protested the situation, he returned her insults with apologies and gentleness. Not for a moment did she trust this sudden change, but she did agree to sit and eat. She also drank the wine, although less than half what Crawley imbibed. All the time, she watched him, fearing what he planned, determined to fight and scream with all her strength if he tried to take advantage of the situation. But he spoke almost boringly of the successes he had had reselling the American ships he had bought at bargain prices to newly arrived Englishmen and of the new townhouse he had bought in Manhattan.

Crawley almost seemed to be indifferent to her as he boasted of his newly acquired wealth and hinted that she might even, in time, come to share in his success. At the very end of the meal, he casually drew from his coat a gold necklace and, with a polite and somehow meaningless smile, said, "For my beautiful Heather, I offer this humble gift."

As she looked at the lovely gold thread shimmering in the candlelight, Heather felt a cold chill. The necklace, she suddenly realized, had once belonged to Elizabeth Southey's dowry. She suppressed her anger and coldly accepted the gift, placing it indifferently and without a word of thanks in her small purse.

"You don't seem very appreciative," Crawley said, scowling as he lost some of his mellowness.

"I am not," Heather replied. "And you should know, sir, that no force or guile or stratagem will ever let you have a single ounce of my affection."

Crawley flushed as he pushed back his chair and stood up.

"In your affection, my dear, I have not the slightest interest," he said, sneering. "It's your body that interests me. I daresay that before I am finished, I shall have had such large and frequent helpings that I will have equally little interest in it." When Heather reddened, Crawley laughed aloud. "For the moment, good night," he added, moving to the door. "I feel like spending some time with more pleasant company."

As Heather watched suspiciously, he unlocked the door and left. The sound of his locking it again preceded his steps down the stairs.

Alone in the room, Heather went to the window but found the distance to the ground far too great to essay a jump. Restlessly, she moved one of the mattresses to the windowed corner of the room and prepared a bed for herself. When she was stoking the fire, a knock on the door was followed by the entry of Crawley's valet with some blankets and a large mug of hot milk.

"The milk is compliments of the innkeeper," the valet

said indifferently. "My master bids you sleep well. He has found another wench for the night." Without another glance at Heather, he left, locking the door behind him.

Furrows of puzzlement on her brow, Heather wondered at her reprieve. She held the warm mug in her hands, trying to decide what this newest example of Crawley's crude insults could mean. With a shrug of uncertain thankfulness, she finally drank the milk, happy for its warmth but finding the taste bitter. She left half of it undrunk.

After washing her face in the bowl on the washstand and relieving herself in the chamber pot, Heather crawled under the blankets. She wanted to concentrate on a plan of escape but found herself remarkably drowsy. She struggled to remain awake, and just before she lost that struggle, she had the sudden thought that the bitter taste in the milk might have been a drug. But the thought seemed unimportant, and the next moment she was asleep.

As Duncan Crawley looked down at the chestnut pool of a sleeping Heather's hair lying lush and soft on the coarse brown blanket, he felt vastly if somewhat tipsily pleased with himself. He knew that he could never have forced himself on a conscious Heather—her strength or screams would have undone him. But now she lay helpless and unsuspecting and unconscious in a locked room, and by the time the effects of the drug had worn off, she would have nothing left to protect.

He leaned over and pulled back the blanket, unhappy to see that Heather was sleeping fully clothed. Then, his eyes gleaming in anticipation, he knelt beside the mattress and took the material at her right shoulder and slid it down. Heather's breathing remained slow and steady, and he smiled at her deep sleep. Soon, of course, he would want the pleasure of having her submit wide awake to the humiliations he would force upon her, but for now, he was strongly aroused by the prospect of enjoying her voluptuous body without interference. When her weight prevented him from lowering her dress as he wanted, Crawley snarled in impatience and grabbed her dress at the bodice and yanked downward. Heather's body jerked with his pull but the wool and stitching held. His hands greedy, Crawley now put both of them on Heather and pulled her into a sitting position and, after undoing the buttons down her back, at last slid the dress off her arms and down to her waist. Seeing the outline of her bosom beneath the cotton chemise, he tore at the undergarment, ripping it down the middle and exposing, at last, her magnificently rounded breasts.

His whole body was quivering now, but Crawley stood up and went to the mantelpiece and took the heavy metal candelabra to bring it over to the windowsill near where Heather lay. He wanted to better see his treasure. Again, he fell to his knees and, upon seeing those gleaming, rosy mounds, he groaned and buried his face in them, his hands sliding up to squeeze and his mouth opening to kiss their warm flesh. When he felt her move and make a soft sound, he quickly raised himself to look at her face.

Heather's eyelids flickered but remained closed, and her breathing, though perhaps faster, remained steady. The thought that she might partially awaken but be too weak and confused to struggle effectively excited Crawley. With a tight-lipped smile, he reached forward, took a handful of her hair, and yanked on it gently, then harder, and harder yet until Heather's whole head bounced and her eyes flickered open.

"Awake, pretty bitch!" he said in a rasping voice. "It's time you served your master."

Heather's unseeing eyes closed as abruptly as they had opened, and she lay still. Crawley's lips again curled slightly in a tense smile as he began tearing at his own coat, removing it only after an awkward struggle. His eyes never leaving the rosy-skinned object of his desire, he stood up to pull off his silk shirt and then his boots and breeches. In a minute, he stood naked, staring down at Heather, his mouth hanging open almost in awe of what he was about to do. Then he fell a third time to his knees and, with a loud, half-angry groan, fell upon the helpless form of Heather.

In her dream, Heather felt herself drowning, being pulled down down down by hands in the sea. Then her dream began to merge with reality and the pulling was someone pulling at her dress. She opened her eyes and found herself looking at Duncan Crawley kneeling naked beside her, his hands on her dress, trying to get it past the roundness of her hips. On his face was a look of surprise that changed quickly into a cruel smile. "How nice of you to join me," he said hoarsely. "You can begin by lifting your arse."

For another moment, Heather just stared without comprehension, and then, with sudden and total clarity, she remembered where she was and what was happening. With a force and quickness that caught Crawley by surprise, she rolled away from him onto the floor and scrambled to her feet, pulling her dress up over her hips, though her breasts were still exposed.

His face creasing with annoyance and anger, Crawley got slowly to his feet. He saw Heather standing in a crouch with her back to the window, her fists clenched, and he hesitated to advance. Then he seemed to remember something, shrugged once, and stooped to pick up his brocaded coat. From it he removed a richly garnished and glittering knife. He held it now up in front of him.

"I grow tired of your resistance," he said in a low, threatening voice. He took a step toward her.

Heather inched herself along the wall away from him and, arriving at the windowsill, instinctively picked up the heavy candelabra. She said nothing but raised it above her head and braced herself to strike if he advanced further.

Crawley hesitated and then sneered.

"A servant who strikes a master can be hung in England," he said and took another step forward, stopping only five feet away. "Put that down before I am forced to bury my knife in you in self-defense."

Heather simply remained as she was, her every ounce of energy trained on keeping this man away from her.

Suddenly, Crawley's face exploded red in anger and frustration.

"You damn bitch!" he shouted and rushed at her, his knife pointed at her waist.

Heather swung the candelabra with all her strength, striking Crawley square in the forehead. The candles scattered onto the floor and the mattress, some sputtering and others still burning.

Dazedly, Heather could see Crawley sprawled naked at her feet, the side of his forehead red with his blood. Although she had felt only a pinprick of pain, she saw that her dress had been ripped more than six inches at her hip and blood showed there, too. With an instinctive modesty, Heather pulled up the two torn sides of her chemise to cover her naked breasts, and then she pulled up her dress. Only then did she kneel to examine the unmoving body of Duncan Crawley. She thought she saw his chest rising and falling slightly, but when she saw his half-open eyes looking glazed, she quickly stood up. Had she killed him?

Then she saw the fire. Her straw mattress and Crawley's silk shirt were both ablaze, and the fire had already spread to one of the curtains. Heather stooped to take hold of one of Crawley's limp arms, and she dragged him over toward the door. Breathlessly, she staggered back to search for the key in his waistcoat. When she found it, she quickly unlocked the door and dragged the limp body of Crawley out into the empty hall. The inn was amazingly quiet, and she realized the hour must be very late. Smoke had only half filled the room, but the flames were clearly spreading. Heather darted back inside to retrieve her small bag and then returned to the hall. Although worried about what would happen to her for what she'd done to Duncan Crawley, her desire to save everyone from the fire finally forced her to scream:

"Fire! Help! Fire!"

As doors swung open, she ran. Down the stairs, past the open-mouthed stare of a servant girl obviously only recently awakened, and past two bleary-eyed men who leered at her dishabille. As she heard shouts and screams from above, Heather paused in the vestibule just long enough to thrust her feet into a pair of oversized lady's boots and throw on a man's woolen cape to protect her from the winter night. Then she opened the inn door and dashed out into the cold night. Through the thin covering of fresh snow, she ran—running, Heather felt, no longer just for her honor, but for her very life.

Chapter Twenty-nine

WITH NO CLEAR IDEA OF THE DIRECTION OR DISTANCES involved, Heather decided to try to get back to Somerset Manor. There, she felt, was her last hope of finding word that Rigo was still alive. She was too frightened and desperate to care whether or not she would be welcome there.

For the first time in her life, she was forced to beg. After trudging through the snow and cold of that next day, Heather spent the last of the few shillings she had with her on a hot meal and a room in a small inn. The next morning, she begged at a stable for a ride as far as anyone would take her—toward New York or Staten Island, she said. Although thinking of herself as absolutely destitute, her youth, beauty, and obvious distress were assets she was unaware of, and a gentleman offered her a ride on the back of his horse. She next ate and slept at a local farmhouse, helping with the chores all the next morning as partial payment. They told her she was still forty miles from Staten Island.

After two days at the farm, Heather was given another ride with several people traveling to Staten Island. These were patriots who were suspicious of her English tones in spite of the farm family vouching for her. Had not the farmer given her a loaf of bread, cheese, and a few apples, she would have starved during the journey since the occupants of the carriage were untrusting.

Never far from her thoughts was the horror of her last encounter with Duncan Crawley. Heather prayed that he lived, unable to bear the thought of having caused a man's death. Yet she also feared his living, for she had no doubt he would now pursue her with more determination than ever. He might beat her this time, perhaps have her whipped or even kill her as he had seemed willing to do that night at the inn. Knowing nothing of colonial justice, Heather assumed it was like English law, and she would suffer as the poor and downtrodden always do in a case against a propertied gentleman. Crawley's money and influence would prevail upon the natural prejudice of those in power, she knew, and if he had died, his valet might even now be urging the authorities to pursue and apprehend his murderess.

A full week had passed and it was cold and lightly snowing when Heather finally alighted from the small boat that had ferried her across the river to Staten Island. A farmer who had met the boat offered her a ride near to Somerset Manor. Soon she was huddled in her long cloak, exhausted, and barely able to pay attention as the man chatted on until he mentioned that English officers were staying in the manor.

"And the Somerset menfolk?" she asked, shivering, her breath frosting the air. "Are they . . . all at home?"

"There be sad news, miss," the old farmer replied. "Fortune has not smiled on that family these past months. Mr. Somerset be banished for aidin' his son's escape, and Master Richard turns out a spy and then, they say, was drowned at sea. What's more, the English lass that was to marry Master Bruce was killed in the great fire, though there be others who say she took herself back to London."

The farmer spit off to the side and clucked to his horses before continuing. "It's bad, miss. Master Bruce has been hard put to keep the estate going, seein' as how his father and brother is gone, and the English general's a mite angry and suspicious."

"Are they . . . sure that Richard . . . Master Richard was lost at sea?" Heather asked, holding tightly to the buckboard. Her shoulders and hood were already covered with a light frosting of snow.

"Why, they held a memorial service in the chapel last month, they did," the man answered. "And put a stone up in the family plot. Buried him good and proper, though his body still be fish bait."

Even as part of her silently screamed, "It isn't true!" Heather winced and felt a heavy sinking feeling at the man's words. She had been struggling for a week through this bitter cold to hear just one word of hope about Rigo, and now, when almost there, she is told of his grave. She withdrew into the shelter of her cloak, her chin against her chest as the silent, hot tears froze on her cheeks.

So it was with leaden steps that Heather made her exhausted way the last hundred yards up to the door of Somerset Manor. The grounds and buildings looked stark and forlorn compared with their appearance in the summer, the only signs now of life being the dogs barking in the pen outside and smoke from four or five of the manor chimneys. She knocked at the door, but so lightly that she had to knock again. Since she was expecting a servant, when the door finally opened and Bruce himself was standing there, Heather was so glad she fell forward into his arms. Her only feeling was one of relief to be someplace familiar and to see a welcoming face.

"My dear God!" Bruce gasped. "We thought you lost!" He quickly closed the door and, agitated, released her. Then he held her again, pausing only to remove her hood. Finally, he stepped back and mutely stared at her.

"Oh, Bruce, it's so good to be back here," Heather managed to say, shivering still.

"Dear girl, I thought you gone forever," Bruce said,

taking her by the elbow. "But come, you're cold. Let's go in where it's warm." He led her into the main drawing room and then held a chair for her close to the large stone fireplace. Heather sank gratefully into it, reaching out her hands to warm them before the crackling fire.

"Amy will be so pleased to see you and know you're safe," Bruce went on, standing near and watching her. "As am I, though still stunned. But it's so bloody good to know you're all right."

Looking up at Bruce, Heather felt he looked older to her now, his boyish face taking on a more serious look—as if the events of the past months had pushed him toward maturity.

"You've changed," she said kindly.

Bruce drew up a chair and took her hands in his. "You can't begin to know what's happened here," he began, a serious look on his face. "First, my father's illness and then his headlong rush to save Richard from the firing squad. Then his being banished by the British. Your maid, Maggie, was kind enough to stay with Father, and is with him now. Finally, receiving letters from him from Boston telling of . . . you and Rigo escaping to sea, followed that very week by word from the English fleet that the *Contessa* had been wrecked and all hands lost. . . . You and Richard both drowned. . . ." He paused, and she realized that he must know of her feelings for Rigo. "I felt keenly for you both," Bruce went on somberly. "I was pained and jealous at first and then full of sorrow."

Heather paled, her hands clenching his. "Oh, Bruce!" she exclaimed. "Please don't give up hope. If I survived, surely there's a chance that he has, too."

Bruce searched her face, his brows knit in troubled thought. "But Richard, even more than you, would certainly have gotten word to us here," he said tentatively, then released her hand and sat back, watching the flames consume a log in the fireplace. His mouth was set grimly. "My brother and I have had many differences over the years," he went on, "but I recall many happy hours as a boy spent with him. It was he who taught me to swim and to ride. We explored this land together. In spite of these last few years, and in spite of losing you to him—a fact no brother can easily forgive another—I would wish him alive." He turned to face her. "Can you believe that?"

Heather's shoulders sagged as she raised her eyes to his. Seeing his sincerity, she folded her arms across her chest in a brief agony of grief—her heart aching at hearing him speak of Rigo as of the dead. Then she looked away, fighting to control the pain and tears she felt threatening to erupt. Heather wanted to refuse to give in and yet was tired of her fruitless hoping, a hoping that still had not yielded her a shred of evidence to support Rigo's being alive.

"I don't want to cause you more pain," Bruce went on quietly, "yet I think it best you move into the future." He raised his head and got up from the chair. "I hear Mother and Amy arriving. They've been visiting the Moncriefs, who are planning a visit to England."

Heather looked up at him blankly as he continued.

"They worry about this war. As for myself, the steady victories of General Howe make me hope that the rebellion will collapse this spring." He paused. "Although even an English victory is costing us dearly. Until last month, we were forced to billet a dozen English officers here, and most of them would think I'd foundered in my allegiance were I not to cry 'victory to the King' around the clock. Yet I know I must keep my eyes open and ears sharp, for my future is here no matter which side wins. It's not in England."

"English officers are here now?" Heather asked, her heart pounding as she remembered that she had helped Rigo escape and had possibly killed Duncan Crawley.

"There are only five now. The others have left to chase General Washington in southern New Jersey."

"Bruce?" Margaret Somerset called from the door of the sitting room, having been let in by a servant. "The Moncriefs wanted me to tell you . . ." She stopped a few steps into the room, catching sight of Heather. "Dear

Lord! Elizabeth! My dear child!" She rushed forward, her arms outstretched in a greater show of affection than any Heather had ever received from her before. And then Amy, with a cry, followed, showering her with embraces and questions. Unable to master the confusion of emotions this unexpected outpouring stirred in her, Heather found herself sobbing. A half hour later, she was in bed, drained, as yet a second time she found herself thrown up on the shores of Somerset Manor, penniless, pursued, and an impostor—and seemingly separated forever from the man she loved.

Although Heather recovered quickly from her fatigue over the next few days, she remained unusually subdued. Rarely would she speak except when directly addressed, and she showed little interest in the spinning or sewing or winter walking in which Amy tried to interest her. Christmas day passed quietly. After chapel, the family exchanged gifts and then had a lovely but almost melancholy dinner, there being little to celebrate. Heather had nothing to give and was embarrassed by the white fur hat and muff Bruce gave her and the mittens Amy had knitted for her even since her arrival. Although Captain Blair was clearly courting Amy, two other English officers began to pay a great deal of attention to Heather until Bruce coldly intervened. At least, she thought, they apparently were not planning to arrest her for aiding in Rigo's escape—and still no one had come to take her on behalf of Duncan Crawley.

Then shortly after Christmas came confused reports, first of some great English victory at Trenton followed the next day by a report that it had actually been a disastrous defeat. It soon became clear that the English, indeed, had been surprised and thoroughly beaten at Trenton, their first clear setback since June 1775 in the battle of Bunker Hill. The English officers began drinking heavily, and two of them were ordered to Princeton to join a force hurrying to avenge the defeat. When two sons of one of the Somerset tenant farmers ran off to join the American militia, Bruce, already agitated, was at first furious and then philosophical. He knew it would do nothing but hurt himself further if he threw the farmer and his remaining family out into the cold for their disloyalty. The next day, he went into New York City to try to get more news about the course of the war and when he returned that evening, he asked to speak to Heather alone in the drawing room.

As Heather again sat in the chair before the blazing fire, Bruce, handsomely attired in a well-fitting brown waist-coat and breeches and standing with his hands clasped behind his back, confided that things were suddenly not going well for the English. The forces sent to avenge the defeat at Trenton had themselves been surprised by a flanking movement and routed someplace near Princeton. It wasn't clear if the English were in full retreat or holding their ground in central New Jersey. Mrs. Somerset, fearful of the coming changes, was now planning to join the Moncriefs and go to England. Bruce himself was surprised at his reluctance to leave, realizing he loved the place of his birth and didn't want to lose the estate, although an American victory might mean its seizure. He had recently been monitoring and coddling his tenant farmers, trying to keep their loyalty—at least to the Somersets if not the Crown. He had repaired fences and sheds and roofs for them, but, unfortunately, the English soldiers had stolen much produce and paid unfairly low prices for what they bought, thus severely hurting both the Somersets and their tenants.

Throughout his long monologue, Bruce had been drinking slowly from a glass of port and, at last pausing, he put the glass down on the mantelpiece and turned to look down at Heather. Again Heather noticed a new weightiness and vigor to Bruce, undoubtedly brought on by his accepting new responsibilities. She herself had been staring into the fire as she listened, a pearl-white shawl over her shoulders and her toes pointed toward the hearth. She had bunched her chestnut curls on her neck and secured them with combs in a demure and restrained style. She had lost several pounds, and the simple gray wool frock she wore was loose at the waist.

"You are quiet these days," Bruce said softly. "You are not happy here?"

Heather shifted her shoulders uncomfortably, her features awakening from their repose to register a restlessness over the question.

"I . . ." she began but halted, sighing. She could find no way to go on, no purpose to her life. She existed in a state of waiting. Heather passed a hand lightly over her brow and then let it fall to her lap.

Bruce looked down at her compassionately, his tone even softer. "I don't like to see you this way. It's not good for you. You who should have all of life before you act as if . . . your life was over." He paused and added quietly, "I know you grieve . . . for Richard . . ." Heather looked up, not able to protest but wanting to lessen his pain if she could. Bruce made a sweeping motion with his arm to stop her.

"No, don't tell me you don't," he said firmly. "And don't speak with feminine politeness trying to lessen the sting. I accept your grief, but I want you to stop—for yourself. I want you to take hold of life again as I know you can." He hesitated then came forward to stand next to her. "I've asked you before, and now I ask you again. Marry me, Elizabeth. Let me take care of you. Time will heal your wound, and you will learn to love me."

Heather made a tiny noise of distress and closed her eyes. After a long silence, she looked up at him, her head resting back on the chair.

"Bruce," she began hesitantly. "I must tell you . . . that I'm not Elizabeth Southey. I tried to tell you once but you . . . wouldn't listen. But it's the truth . . . I am not she. My name is Heather Woode. I'm a penniless orphan, indentured. I may even stand accused of murdering the man who owns my contract—or at least of running away from assaulting him. You have been deceived in me, Bruce, and I am so sorry. . . ."

To her surprise, Bruce dropped to his knees in front of her and took her hands in his, a look of hope on his face.

"I know all this," he said in a low voice. When

Heather's eyes widened and she stared at him in complete surprise, he nodded and smiled.

"Yes, I know, and have known since before you arrived," he went on carefully. "My father wrote to me from Boston with an explanation of all that transpired in New York and all that he had learned about you earlier. As for your murdering the man you ran from, my dear, you could murder no one, of that I'm absolutely certain."

"You knew these past few days?" Heather asked, struggling to absorb all he'd said.

Bruce nodded.

"But how was I to tell you without frightening you?" he explained. "There never seemed to be a right moment. And now I thank you for telling me yourself." He kissed her hand tenderly while she reflected on his changed nature.

"I would have expected you to . . . cast me out," she said in a low voice. "Does your mother know?"

"No, my mother is not informed. My father prefers to do that himself—in person. My mother, as you know, is at times . . . excitable. As for my casting you out, I'm sorry you have such a low opinion of me." When Heather flushed, Bruce went on in the gentlest of voices, "I am still asking for your hand in marriage."

"But . . . but you were so keen on the dowry. . . ."

He shrugged. "I am still. It would be of great use to me after all the reverses I've suffered lately. And, with your troubles, it may be useful for you to remain Elizabeth Southey—at least temporarily."

"Bruce, the dowry must be returned to its rightful owner."

"To whom, then, should it go?" Bruce asked with a touch of impatience. "Her uncle? A distant uncle who, from all I can learn, was happy to be rid of her? Don't you see? It doesn't matter now."

"To me it matters," Heather insisted. "It seems now so much has happened. I need to order my life, live it more naturally, honestly. I . . ." Heather was at a loss for words to articulate how tender she felt about hurting or cheating anyone.

Still on his knees, Bruce reached his arms across her lap to put his hands on her waist.

"You would not be you if these questions of honor didn't affect you deeply," he said ardently. "I'll respect your wishes, of course, but I want to point out to you that Elizabeth herself might want you to have it. Please, say you'll be my bride."

"But Rigo, if he is alive . . ."

"If Richard returns before we marry, then, of course, I release you. I promise, Heather," he went on passionately, bringing his face closer to hers. "I beg you to accept fate's decree. I will protect you and love you as my brother did."

At the mention of Rigo's love, Heather's eyes filled with tears, and she remained frozen, her whole soul fighting the idea that he could be dead while the surface part of her felt grateful for Bruce's offer, knowing it to be the best solution to the myriad of dangers that still threatened her.

"Do you have an alternative, a better course?" Bruce asked gently.

"Bruce, you are good . . . to ask," she finally managed to answer. "But it's too soon. I love your brother. Please understand." Her voice was hushed, appealing.

Bruce brought a hand tenderly to her face.

"I will respect that," he said softly. "But I ask you again to think about my offer. We can arrange a quiet wedding, a simple ceremony in our private chapel. And I must remind you that it may be necessary for all of us to leave here for a time. Mother has already asked me to make the arrangements on the *Prospect*. And Heather, I won't be taking Richard's place. I will be my own man—and I swear you won't regret it."

Gently, with tears still filling her eyes, Heather pushed Bruce's arms off of her lap. She was still distraught by all he had said and was torn between her strong feelings of loss and yet gratitude for Bruce's graceful offer.

"I thank you," she said in a whisper, looking past Bruce at the fire. "And I promise you I'll think about it."

Bruce slowly got off his knees and stood up. For a long

moment, he looked down, watching the conflicting emotions transforming Heather's lovely features, then he quietly left the room.

But Heather couldn't think. It was as if her life had come to a standstill, and over the next two days, she threw herself into knitting a winter scarf for Amy, only answering Bruce's questioning looks by lowering her eyes. Then Bruce brought her a letter that made delay no longer possible.

He showed it to her when she was working alone in the keeping room, handing it to her without expression. For a brief moment, Heather's heart stuttered in fear and hope that it might concern Rigo, but when her eyes raced to the bottom of the page, she saw the flowery scrawled name of Duncan Crawley. The letter, addressed to Bruce, was short and to the point:

> "My dear Mr. Somerset,
>   It is my painful duty to inform you that the woman who presents herself as Miss Elizabeth Southey is, in fact, Heather Woode, a woman who is legally my indentured servant. Moreover, this woman, who had previously fled from her legal obligations, did recently attempt to murder me, severely injuring my head.
>   I have reason to believe that she may return to your manor, in which case I inform you it is your duty to hold her until the proper authorities can take her into custody. Should you fail to do this, I assure you my friends among the English officials, already properly suspicious of your family, will take vigorous action against you.
>   I myself will come to Somerset Manor as soon as my health permits.
>   Your servant, Duncan Crawley."

Heather let the letter drift down in her lap, then her shadowed green eyes lifted up to Bruce.

"The *Prospect* is anchored in the narrows," Bruce said

to her. "The Somersets and Moncriefs board her tomorrow afternoon for England. In the morning, we will be married."

For a long moment, Heather remained with her eyes directed at Bruce but unseeing. Then, mutely, she nodded yes and folded her hands in her lap.

Chapter Thirty

THE MORNING OF THE WEDDING WAS ONE OF CHAOS IN Somerset Manor. Margaret Somerset frantically organized her household to leave, packing trunks and valuables while lecturing the housekeeper on the management of the remaining food stores and furniture. Her visage was grim with determination to get through this horrible time. Her son's sudden plans to marry had upset her, but the possibility of their having to flee America made the connection with the Southeys tolerable. She herself was torn between going to join her husband in Boston or returning to her own family in England. That John could not attend his son's wedding was a painful reminder of the world falling apart about them.

Amidst all this, Heather's mood matched the mist-shrouded winter sky of pale white and the stark landscape of cold and snow. She had slept badly the night before, awakened twice by the high, shrill, piercing whinny of a horse in the stables. When she had recognized the sound as coming from Triumph, her heart had seemed to skip a beat, remembering Rigo's black stallion and the horse's attachment to his master. The second whinny left her fingering the sapphire ring Rigo had given her, looking into its brilliant beauty as if for an answer to her current dilemma, although for many weeks, Rigo's eyes had not appeared in its shimmering blue. As she turned it idly near the single bedside candle, dimly aware of the whine and sweep of the winter wind, she was suddenly jolted when she became aware of Rigo's blue eyes glittering out at her from the stone as if in laughter. Unexpected and intense was the vision, but when she strove to bring his whole face before her, the laughing eyes disappeared, and Heather found herself beholding only a lovely ring. The man who had given it to her was gone. Again. She finally slept and, when she awoke at dawn, guessed that the whole thing had been only a figment of a dream—a wish rather than a portent.

Now, only an hour before noon, she was all packed for the *Prospect's* return to England, and Amy was just finishing the final alterations on an exquisite creamy satin gown from Miss Southey's trunk. Amy had taken it out and handled the major alterations the night before. Tiny seed pearls were sewn on the square-cut, low bodice, and French lace spilled from the elbow-length sleeves in a long train and was repeated in an overskirt. The gown was beautiful, Heather knew, but it only increased the chill in her heart.

Amy quietly worked around her, taking in a tuck here and there, checking the fall of the train in back. She hadn't said a word to Heather about this abrupt wedding, but Heather was aware this morning that Amy wanted to speak. Finally, biting her lips and, with a flushed face, she did.

"Bruce is a good man. . . ." Amy said thoughtfully, wishing somehow to stir Heather out of her trance-like state.

"Yes," said Heather, idly touching her gown over her heart.

Amy's eyes clouded at the dull reply.

"But you . . . don't love him. . . ." she said.

Heather sought the dark eyes of Amy and saw there

the girl's love and concern for both her brother and herself.

"I will do all in my power to be a good wife," Heather answered after a pause.

"I fear for you both," Amy said, twisting her hands nervously in front of her. "'Tis such a step in life . . . to marry. I want to, myself, and yet . . . I don't think I could bed with a man I didn't love. I . . ." She flushed red at her own words and rushed to the sewing table to finger aimlessly at the material there.

Heather spun and paced to the window looking toward the stables.

"The horses were restless last night," she said, not wishing to think of bedding with Bruce or of her wedding.

"It was Triumph," Amy said.

Heather absently turned toward her vanity. "I think it's time to arrange my hair."

"I'll fetch Mary," Amy said, going to the door.

"I still love Richard, Amy," Heather said softly, capturing her eyes. "I will always love him. Nothing can ever change that. But I will honor Bruce as he deserves to be. Please don't feel ill of me. . . ."

"Oh, no! I do not!" Amy replied at once. "We share, in different ways, our feelings toward both. I . . ." But again she was overcome with embarrassment and hurried from the room.

Left alone Heather remained seated at her vanity, not moving, listening, inexplicably, for the sound of Triumph, but not hearing it. When there was a knock on the door she called "enter" without thinking and the serving girl Susan entered with a small package in her hand.

"'Tis a present for you, miss," Susan said, hurrying up to Heather with a smile, and curtsying. "One of the farmer's sons gave it to me. Said 'twas a wedding present for Miss Southey, that I was to give it straight to her hands."

Puzzled, Heather took the brown-wrapped package from Susan who, with another smile and curtsy, left. How could any of the tenant farmers know of her wedding— only planned the afternoon before? There was no name on the package and, without thinking, Heather tore the paper away. Revealed was a long black velvet box with a large scrolled "S" in the corner in gold. "Somerset," Heather surmised. Feeling a sudden spreading of gooseflesh run down her back and a pricking of the hairs on her arms, she slowly opened the case.

She gasped, and her hands began shaking so that she had to move back to her vanity table and drop the box there, gaping down at the magnificent sapphire and diamond necklace lying before her. Pale and breathless she stared at the brilliant circlet of stones. Then she ran across the room to her small silk purse and tore at the strings, finally removing from it her sapphire ring. Rushing back to the vanity she placed the ring beside the necklace and compared the two sapphire stones. They matched. A blush rushed into her cheeks and her heart thudded wildly. Rigo's promised wedding gift to his bride. But how? How and why had it come now?

She picked up the ring that she hadn't worn since leaving Philadelphia with Crawley. She slipped it on. Then she placed the necklace around her neck, set its clasp, and felt the stone nestling just beneath the hollow of her throat.

"Oh, I do love you so. . . ." Heather whispered to the man who was not there, her eyes now radiant and her complexion taking on a color it hadn't had in months.

But then she suddenly realized that the necklace might have been found among Rigo's effects after his apparent death. Perhaps it was a gift from Bruce? Or perhaps Rigo had left it with some trusted farmer and had left instructions with him to get it to her should he . . . die. Realizing these other explanations, Heather felt her heart deaden. Her shoulders slumped as the blood left her cheeks. There was no note with the gift, nothing to indicate that Rigo was still alive. Surely . . .

Her thoughts were interrupted by the arrival of Mary. The girl came quickly to Heather, smiling and excited at the prospect of a wedding, and began brushing and arranging Heather's thick chestnut hair in stylish high curls. Heather watched in a daze as Mary combed ringlets

301

to drop in back. The door opened and closed, and she turned to see that Amy had returned. But Amy seemed disoriented and stood just inside the room. Pale, her eyes were opened wide and her lips parted as a look of awe and puzzlement swept over her face.

"Leave," she whispered.

"What's the matter?" Heather asked, wondering what had happened. Mary looked up, brush in hand.

"Mary . . . please leave," Amy repeated again in a voice so soft it could barely be heard.

"Surely, miss," Mary answered promptly, putting the brush down and walking to the door. "Will you be needing me again, Miss Southey?" she asked as Amy remained standing like a statue facing Heather.

"No," said Heather, her eyes fixed on Amy, her heart inexplicably beginning to race. Mary left.

"Amy, what is it?" Heather asked, standing up and bracing herself.

Amy's young face, so pale and shaken since entering, for a brief moment brightened as at the sight of a lover. Then she again paled.

"Richard . . ." she finally answered in a barely audible voice. "Richard is alive."

Heather felt her whole being soar, experiencing such a tingling rush of emotion throughout her body that she felt as if she were suspended in space.

"He's alive! He's here!" Amy went on, her face showing awe at the unexpected miracle while Heather's face showed only rapture. For a few seconds, the two young women stood rooted where they had been since Amy's entrance, until Amy broke the trance and ran to Heather.

"Oh, Heather," she cried. "Richard's alive! He's come for you!" The two women embraced, as if each were a surrogate for the absent Rigo.

"How do you know?" Heather asked breathlessly, searching her face as if there could be found the answer.

"Peter Mitchell, one of the Moncrief tenants, came to me just now," Amy explained excitedly. "He gave me a note for you and said that Richard was alive and well but had to be careful. Oh, here! Here's the note!"

She pulled the note from her pocket and handed it to Heather, who tore open the seal and drank in the words:

Most Beloved Heather,

It has taken a damnably long time to find you, but I live again at last, knowing that you are alive. It is cruel of you to continually engage yourself to Bruce, but I suppose it's a just punishment for my almost drowning us both and my spending two months with Washington fighting the English. If you love me, as I love you, and trust me, as I trust you, then I ask you to have faith in me and go ahead with the wedding as planned. Don't fail me.

Your loving Pirate

Heather was astonished, not knowing which way to turn. She read the note again and looked up at Amy, her pretty mouth open, her eyes wide with confusion.

"What does he say?" Amy asked in hushed, urgent tones.

"He tells me to wed as planned!" Heather looked at Amy as if to confirm that she had not read correctly or that her lover had gone mad. Amy looked as stunned as Heather.

"Will you do as he says?" Amy asked.

Heather folded the note and tucked it deep within her cleavage. Her cheeks flushed and her flesh felt warm. Animation returned to her eyes as they flashed a warning for her absent and hiding lover.

"I would not do otherwise and 'fail him,' as he asks. Washington, indeed! He might truly have been killed, and all the while I was dying for want of a word from him. He is due for yet another battle, dearest little sister," Heather said excitedly, but her singing voice and brilliant eyes betrayed her great emotion. He, as she, was alive, and love made her go to the chapel with no other thought or wish than to glimpse the man who had made her his.

Chapter Thirty-one

STANDING WITH PETER MITCHELL, NOAH WIGGENS, AND three local patriots near the beach overlooking the *Prospect* at anchor in the narrows, Rigo felt exhilarated. He had known for two full days that Heather was alive, but only now was he close to being able to see her. His incredible plan to get away from Staten Island without being apprehended looked now like it might work. Even Noah, whose unexpected appearance as mate of the *Prospect* made the plan more feasible, was beginning to lose his skepticism. But it demanded perfect timing and luck—something he felt he hadn't been getting his fair share of lately.

Of course, that Heather had survived that terrible storm was enough luck to last him a lifetime. With that exception, fate seemed to be working against him, though. He attributed his own survival to his being a strong swimmer. That he had clung to a mostly submerged spar for two hours and had finally been washed up on the beach more than two miles further south than Heather and Noah, he had blamed on bad luck. That he had decided to hike north along the coast to the town of Cape May in search of Heather rather than going directly inland where, according to Noah, Heather had actually gone was also the evil touch of chance. And finally, when he had volunteered to join General Washington's exhausted and retreating army south of Trenton, he'd sent a letter and messenger to Somerset Manor informing his family of his survival and inquiring after Heather, but neither had ever arrived. While he waited for a reply from Staten Island, he had become a major of a battalion of New Jersey regulars and had crossed the Delaware with General Washington on Christmas Eve to fight in the American victories at Trenton and Princeton. With the fighting apparently over for the winter and still no knowledge of whether or not Heather was alive, Rigo had asked for permission to visit his family.

Even knowing that his life was in danger by returning to English-controlled northern New Jersey and New York, Rigo went and only then discovered, to his joy, that Heather had arrived a mere ten days before.

Rigo was transformed. He realized that he had only been going through the motions of living for the past three months. When he had learned, too, that the Somersets and the Moncriefs were sailing for England on the *Prospect* in a few days time, he began to plan to pirate the ship and carry Heather off that way, but the sudden news of her proposed marriage to Bruce had forced him to hurry his plans.

"Have you told your brother," Noah asked him now, "and let him know what ye be plannin'?"

"I have," Rigo said. "And I think he knows it will be for the best."

"And the English officers?"

"They will not go heavily armed to a wedding."

"And your lass?" asked Noah, squinting up at Rigo. "Ye be sure she will go along with your plan?"

Rigo smiled.

"General Howe, my stepmother, an English frigate—those I am sure I can handle," he said, smiling and looking back up the hill at Somerset Manor. "I make no claims about being able to handle this young English lass, though."

"Aye," said Noah, grinning. "She does more to confound you with a glance than them others with a full broadside."

Rigo returned the grin, nodded, and then started up the hillside. It was time to attend a wedding.

The small wood-frame chapel was tucked in a copse several hundred yards from Somerset Manor. A somberly dressed and powerfully built young man stood at the door, opening it as Heather and Amy approached with Mary and Susan.

Heather stood in the narrow vestibule and bade the young women go in and be seated. She needed this moment alone to collect herself. Having half expected Rigo to be within the door, she felt a pang of disappointment. Why was he asking her to go through with the wedding? She peered indiscreetly into the chapel, her eyes looking everywhere for him in the gloom. Gathered on the ornate wooden benches, she saw, were Amy and Margaret Somerset, two or three English officers—looking stiffly discomfited—a dozen household servants, and the waiting minister who, when he noticed her, beckoned to her to approach. When she came tentatively to the beginning of the aisle, the heads of all those present turned to watch her progress.

Heather was in a state of near panic, wanting to delay. First she went back and took off her cloak and hung it on a peg. Then, returning to the head of the aisle, she slowly lowered her veil over her face. Where was he? On the other hand, Bruce was not here, either. The restless shifting of feet and the minister's hand again beckoning her into the chilly, darkened chapel propelled her forward at last, one slow step at a time. A few candles flickered as a curtained alcove moved and a tall man in a dark navy suit and black boots appeared. When he doffed his hat and walked into view, Heather nearly toppled before the small assembly. She didn't hear the gasp that came from Margaret, who was even less prepared for this unexpected appearance. Nor did she notice Amy whispering to her mother. Heather's senses were only on the man.

He turned to her, holding out his hand as a smile lit his handsome face like a beacon.

"Rigo!" Heather's breath lightly floated his name to all, her eyes pinned to his dark features.

He took a step toward her, and she flew forward to take his hand. Rigo brought her close to his side then deftly lifted the veil and devoured her with his eyes, his soul joining hers.

"You are so beautiful, my love," he whispered, so softly it was like a rustle of silk in the wind.

Heather reached out to touch him, confirming his reality, and he took her hand and drew it tightly through his arm, bringing her against his body in a gesture of intimacy and possession. His eyes never left hers, and a tremor went through him that echoed in Heather.

"Never leave me. . . ." she whispered close to his ear.

"I never will again. . . ." her pirate promised.

As the minister read the vows, Heather leaned into Rigo, so suffused with happiness that twice the minister had to prod her to give the appropriate reply. At some point, she became aware of Noah Wiggens handing Rigo a ring and Rigo struggling to slip a gold band over her wedding finger. The only words of the entire ceremony that she remembered hearing were the last—"I now pronounce you man and wife."

As Rigo claimed his bride, Heather's face was radiant, her lips sweet and open to him. He gave of himself totally as she did to him. Rigo lifted his head slowly.

"I will cherish you and protect you all of my days and be only yours to love. . . ." he said, his lips a breath away from hers.

Heather clung to him, her body tingling with a warmth as from a heavenly fire. "I am yours and ever have been. I will show you how much I love thee each day," she uttered softly, her heart reaching out to him through her voice.

Amy and Margaret Somerset came forward, pressed by the household servants to wish the couple well. Amy kissed them both. Margaret was still in a state of shock until Rigo clasped her in an unaccustomed embrace and whispered something soothing in her ear.

"Take care of Bruce. . . ." Heather asked of Amy, her love for Rigo extending to all.

"I shall, and we will all meet again soon," Amy said reassuringly. "Don't fret. Bruce is strong, like his brother." The two women embraced.

"Captain Rigo!" came a deep voice from the back of the chapel. "We must away, sir!"

"So we must," Rigo said to his bride, whisking Heather to the door and stopping only a moment to wrap her tightly in her cloak. He then swept her off her feet and carried her out the chapel door.

It was then that Heather saw how many men he had with him and the muskets they carried discreetly. A fear crossed her face, easily readable by her new husband.

"Don't fear," Rigo said as he placed her down on her feet and bade her run with him through the woods toward the beach.

"Where are we going?" Heather asked between hard breaths as she hurried with him, her hand in his.

"To Boston," Rigo replied, signaling his men to pass them and take the lead. "I want my father to meet my new bride." He slowed them to a walk.

"And may I ask where you have been dallying these many weeks?" Heather asked, flashing him a smile.

"General Washington keeps trying to get me killed," Rigo explained, smiling back. "But in a worthy cause, I assure you, and I will tell you all soon."

"And what of Duncan Crawley?" Heather asked, a vague fear of the man in her voice.

"Once we Americans win, he will be deported back to England," Rigo said, his tone firm. "And as my wife, you are formally exempt from the contract with him. Have no fear, my love." There was a finality to his words that reassured Heather of their truth.

Heather could now see the *Prospect,* that big ship that so many months before she had come across on to this country and to this man.

"And now?" she asked next. "How does my husband expect to support his wife?"

"I thought I'd take up piracy again," Rigo answered, pressing her against him as they passed between two trees. "One meets such interesting women that way."

"I think you've met enough interesting women for a while," Heather protested as they arrived at the beach. Noah and two other sailors stood in two feet of water holding a ship's boat in readiness.

"You're right," Rigo said. "Another woman like you and I'd be ruined in a year or two."

"What!"

"You *do* plan to remain with me awhile this time, I hope," Rigo persisted, smiling roguishly, "and not disappear some morning chased by constables or go floating off to sea somewhere in the dark?"

"I promise," said Heather, drinking in the loving look in his eyes. "If you promise to avoid prisons, firing squads, fires, and shipwrecks to spend all your time in bed with me."

"If you insist, my love," Rigo said with an exaggerated sigh. He then lifted her into his arms and carried her out through the shallow water to the waiting boat. "But I'm not certain my heart will be able to take . . ." he lowered his voice and whispered huskily in her ear, ". . . so much excitement. . . ."

"I will be gentle. Trust me," said Heather, flushing with pleasure, and together they laughed.

Tapestry

HISTORICAL ROMANCES

Next Month From Tapestry Romances

FRENCH ROSE
by Jacqueline Marten
PROMISE OF PARADISE
by Cynthia Sinclair

POCKET BOOKS.

Home delivery from Pocket Books

Here's your opportunity to have fabulous bestsellers delivered right to you. Our free catalog is filled to the brim with the newest titles plus the finest in mysteries, science fiction, westerns, cookbooks, romances, biographies, health, psychology, humor—every subject under the sun. Order this today and a world of pleasure will arrive at your door.

POCKET BOOKS, Department ORD
1230 Avenue of the Americas, New York, N.Y. 10020

Please send me a free Pocket Books catalog for home delivery

NAME _____

ADDRESS _____

CITY _____ STATE/ZIP _____

If you have friends who would like to order books at home, we'll send them a catalog too—

NAME _____

ADDRESS _____

CITY _____ STATE/ZIP _____

NAME _____

ADDRESS _____

CITY _____ STATE/ZIP _____

368